...orld

'...the bloody battlefields of the Spanish Civil ... a huge and powerful novel' *Evening Standard*

'A magnificent international historical saga' *Bookseller*

'A sizzling read . . . exciting to the end'
Woman's Realm

'[The] setting is sheer glamour' *Evening Telegraph*

Last Year's Nightingale

'Matchless storytelling . . . a fine historical saga'
Yorkshire Post

'Unashamedly romantic' *Evening Telegraph*

'Gripping, vivid . . . a stirring tale' *Bookseller*

The Silver Link

'Lovers of romantic fiction will love this book'
Bookseller

'Yet another successful historical family saga – perfect holi...' *Yorkshire Post*

Claire Lorrimer wrote her first book at the age of twelve, encouraged by her mother, the bestselling author Denise Robins. After the Second World War, during which Claire served on secret duties, she started her career as a romantic novelist under her maiden name, Patricia Robins. In 1970 she began writing her magnificent family sagas and thrillers under the name Claire Lorrimer. She is currently at work on her seventy-first book. Claire lives in Kent.

Find out more about Claire: www.clairelorrimer.co.uk

Also by Claire Lorrimer and available from Hodder

CLAIRE LORRIMER

GEORGIA

HODDER

First published in Great Britain in 2013
by AudioGO Ltd, Bath

This edition published in 2015
by Hodder & Stoughton
An Hachette UK company

1

A CIP catalogue record for this title is available from the British Library

Paperback ISBN 978 1 473 61607 3
eBook ISBN 978 1 473 61606 6

Typeset by Sabon LT Std by Palimpsest Book Production Ltd,
Falkirk, Stirlingshire

Printed and bound by Clays Ltd, St Ives plc

Hodder & Stoughton policy is to use papers that are natural, renewable
and recyclable products and made from wood grown in sustainable
forests. The logging and manufacturing processes are expected to conform to
the environmental regulations of the country of origin.

Hodder & Stoughton Ltd
Carmelite House
50 Victoria Embankment
London EC4Y 0DZ

www.hodder.co.uk

For Lotte Clark
With many thanks and much love

PROLOGUE

1920

As he got out of his car, Gerald Driffield pulled the collar of his raincoat tighter round his neck. The driving rain, which had all but obscured the windshield, now beat against his face as he started towards the front door of the large, Elizabethan house. Rivulets poured from his bare head down his face like tears. In his hand he held his big, black umbrella, which had been turned inside out by the wild gusts of rain, giving him no protection.

Lights were shining from the upstairs window. The front door was unlocked and, removing his wet overcoat, he went into the hall. He put the ruined umbrella in the hatstand and, hanging up his coat, he turned reluctantly to go upstairs. The weekly visits to his bedridden friend had long since ceased to be cheerful occasions but he never failed to make them, knowing as he did how important they were to the invalid.

He reached the upstairs landing and, knocking twice as was his custom, opened one of the bedroom doors. A uniformed nurse was propping her patient more comfortably against the pillows. The young man in the bed lifted a welcoming hand and smiled weakly at his visitor as the nurse left the room.

Gerald tried to keep the note of anxiety out of his voice as he asked:

'How are you, old chap? No worse, I trust?'

Even as he spoke, he realised the absurdity of his remark. Just about everything that could be, was wrong with the man lying in the high hospital bed and they both knew he was not going to get any better. He and the invalid, Charles de Valle, had been friends since childhood when they'd first met as new boys at their prep school in Surrey. The same age with the same interests, they'd quickly become as close as brothers, and their friendship had happily continued at the same public school. At the age of seventeen, they decided simultaneously to join the school CCF with a view to enjoying full-time army careers when they finished their education. That plan had suddenly been negated on the outbreak of the war against Germany. Along with thousands of other patriotic nationals, at the age of eighteen they had both immediately volunteered to join the army and after a brief period of training, were packed off to France confident that they would be able to stop the German advance.

For the thousandth time, as Gerald stared at the gaunt face of his friend, he asked himself what unknown hand of Fate had brought him through the appalling hell of the trenches unscathed while virtually destroying Charles's life. More and more often he thought that it might have been better for Charles to have been killed outright. A shell had shattered his body, fragments mutilating his once handsome young face. He'd been only twenty years old.

There'd been three years of endless operations undertaken, leaving Charles alive but with only one lung, one arm, a horribly scarred face and a leg amputated below the knee. After a further year in a convalescent home Charles, by now twenty-four years old, had finally been allowed to go back to his own home with day and night nurses to care for him. Both his parents had perished eight years previously along with one and a half thousand other passengers on the ill-fated liner, *Titanic*. An only child, he had then inherited a sizeable family fortune. It covered the maintenance of his beautiful old Elizabethan house, the wages of the staff and nurses; but the present post-war financial depression the country was undergoing had affected his income. Gerald now supposed that it was his advice about Charles's investments that had prompted his request for this additional visit for what he'd termed '*a very urgent matter*'.

Gerald himself was feeling the financial pinch but with a desk job in the War Office, which he had acquired on his demobilisation, he was able to keep solvent and continue to support Isobel, the VAD he had married during the war, and his little daughter, Margaret. The birth had not been an easy one and the gynaecologist who had been overseeing Isobel's pregnancy had forbidden Gerald's young wife to have more children.

At the time, Gerald had been desperately disappointed knowing he would never now have the son he'd wanted, but the dreadful deprivations Charles suffered made him ashamed of his self-pity. He was always consumed with distress every time he paid one of his regular visits to his friend who, poor fellow, never left his room. Nearly all Charles's other friends had perished in the recent ghastly conflict along with hundreds of thousands of others. His one remaining relative, a middle-aged cousin, had emigrated to Canada before the war where he had been killed in a hunting accident. So Gerald knew himself to be Charles's only visitor. His general health was slowly deteriorating: his amputations refused to heal entirely, and he suffered painful abscesses. So weak was he now that he had to be lifted into a chair to sit by the window and gaze out at a world he could never again enjoy. Small wonder, Gerald thought, that Charles was so depressed.

'Gerry!' Charles's voice, surprisingly sharp, interrupted his thoughts. 'Gerry! I need your help!'

Staring at the haggard face of his friend, Gerald could see the look of desperation in his eyes. Hurrying to the bedside, he covered the thin hand that was lying palm upward on the sheet in an unconscious gesture of appeal with his own.

'Anything, old chap. You know that. Anything at all. As you know, I am no financial expert but . . .'

Charles's face softened into a wry smile as he interrupted:

'No, it's not money, Gerry: I wish it was. You might not be so free with your offer when you know why I needed to see you. I couldn't think of any other way of dealing with the problem. I think I may be about to ask you to do something illegal!'

He pointed to the chair beside his bed, saying:

'You'd better sit down, old chum: this may be a bit of a shock!'

There was no smile on his face as, once Gerald was seated, he said urgently:

'Swear on your word of honour, Gerry, that you won't just say yes because . . . because of the way I am and . . . oh, God, I wish . . . I've really no right to ask you . . . unfair, really. Damn it, Gerry, I wouldn't ask this if there was anyone else.' He broke off, and deliberately postponing the question he was finding so hard to ask, he continued: 'I wish my problem was something as simple as LSD. It's personal . . . it's . . . damn it, Gerry, I'm not finding it easy to say this.'

'For heaven's sake, who do you think you are talking to, Charles? No two chaps could be better friends than we are. How many years since we were eight years old? You should know very well I'll do anything within my power – anything at all.'

The invalid looked down at their hands and drew a deep breath before the words came out in a rush:

'I won't hold you to that! Look, Gerry, I won't beat about the bush any more. You probably won't believe this but . . . I've fathered a child – and don't look like that – the bloody Germans may have grounded me but it wasn't all that long after I came out of hospital before I found myself desperately wanting a woman. Never had one, y'know. We both left school as virgins and they didn't supply pretty girls in the trenches, did they? Nor was I in France long enough to get some leave and get one of the French mademoiselles to show me what's what!' He gave a brief smile before, having started his confession it seemed as if he could not stop talking.

'After I left hospital, I knew I hadn't a hope in hell of ever meeting a girl, let alone finding one who'd look twice at me – and don't deny it, Gerry, I'm not a pretty sight. I'd resigned myself to the fact that I'd die without ever knowing what it was like to make love to a woman. Then one night, Nita, she's one of my night nurses, came into my room when I was having one of my hellish nightmares. She . . . she's Spanish . . . much older than me . . . married with three children and I suppose she felt sorry for me or something! Anyway, she held my hand and started to sing something, could have been a lullaby. Like a stupid kid, I started blubbing so she put her arms round me and then . . . then . . . well, it just happened.'

Hiding his astonishment as best he could, Gerald said:

'Good for you, old chap! So what's the problem?'

Charles was now biting his lip, his expression one of acute anxiety.

'She . . . Nita . . . she's very happily married. Her husband . . . he's Spanish too . . . would never forgive her if he knew . . . she's pregnant, you see, with my child.' He broke off, his eyes filling suddenly with tears.

Gerald was momentarily speechless as he tried to digest this information. In one way, he was glad for Charles that despite his dreadful handicaps and disfigurement, someone had cared enough to allow him to make love to her. But that the kind-hearted, married woman was pregnant was indeed a problem. Charles was talking again, the words now pouring from him.

'Nita can't possibly confess it to her husband and she's too honourable a person to let him think the child is his. The only thing I could think of was asking you to find a doctor in London who would terminate the pregnancy, but that's not possible either even if you did manage to find someone. She's a Roman Catholic, you see, and it would be a mortal sin if she destroyed a life.'

Gerald now recalled the night nurse to whom Charles had referred. He had met her one evening when he'd been delayed after work and was very late making his weekly visit. Charles had told him how much he preferred her to his previous nurse who, while good at her tasks, was somewhat coldly efficient.

The Spanish woman, who he'd judged to be in her mid-thirties, had been far more lenient, allowing him to have his pillows as he wished or his eiderdown up to his shoulders, contrary to her predecessor who applied a hospital matron's ruling to the letter. She talked to him, too, holding his hand when he had one of his bad dreams. Where once Charles had dreaded the onset of night, he had confessed, he'd begun to look forward to the gentle, less clinical care she gave him.

He was now lifting his hand and grasping Gerald's arm, saying huskily:

'I thought we might be able to have the baby adopted but that's impossible, too. The mother has to be the one to sign the adoption papers in the area where she lives and she's terri-fied her husband would find out as they might ask for the father's name if they discovered she's married.'

Without knowing it, his grasp had tightened and it was as if he was a drowning man gripping his rescuer.

'You're my only hope, Gerry. I never thought I'd have a woman, let alone a child when I left hospital looking . . . well, like I do. I've thought and thought about it and it's asking one hell of a lot even of a best friend like you but . . . but I'm hoping you will adopt it.'

He was now stumbling over his words as he continued:

'Gerry, would you? Could you . . .? I mean, if you don't . . . Nita wanted *me* to have it . . . get nurses, nannies, what-ever: give me something to live for, but I can't. My doctor told me last week when I insisted upon an answer that I might have only six months left, a year at most. I wouldn't care about dying if I thought part of me was . . . well, living, I suppose. And I know you'd look after it . . .'

'Enough, Charles!' Gerald broke in now feeling Charles's desperation as if it was his own. Unsure if surprise or dismay was uppermost in his mind, he said truthfully: 'You and I couldn't be closer if we were brothers, and if as you say, I am going to lose you, your child would be part of you.' He paused a moment as he tried to consider what consequences there might be. 'I think Isobel . . . well, I told you, she can't have any more children, so your child would be the brother or sister my daughter would not otherwise have. If I explain things to Isobel, I can't believe she would raise any objections to our adopting your infant.'

Seeing the tears of relief on the dying man's cheeks he turned away, his resolve hardening as he realised that Isobel was most unlikely to welcome another woman's child. She had never really understood the incredibly close bond between himself and Charles; had resented his frequent visits at first to the hospital in Brighton, then to the convalescent hospital and recently to Audley Court, Charles's lovely old family home near Tonbridge. His visits often conflicted with something Isobel wanted him to do or to do with him. Moreover, she was perfectly happy to have an only child, doting on Margaret, their pretty little three-year-old daughter. She had not shared his disappointment that there would be no more children, saying she had never wanted a large family. Would he, he now asked himself, be able to get her to agree to adopting Charles's child? Quite apart from any other objections, Isobel had been extremely strictly brought up and she would be very shocked by its illegitimacy.

As it was, he found himself to be shocked by the thought that had entered his mind – that in this instance he would put his lifelong friend's peace of mind before that of Isobel's concerns, devoted as he was to his wife.

Charles was now saying:

'Nita told me she would have loved to keep the baby had she been able, but her husband would most certainly throw her out of the house if he knew she'd been unfaithful no matter what the reason, and he would refuse to let her see their children. She's confident he won't notice her pregnancy or if he does, when the baby is born, she will tell him she has had a miscarriage. We've talked and talked about it, Gerry, and Nita was so . . . so good to me; it horrifies me to think of the consequences for her if . . . if you can't . . .'

He broke off, his expression desperate as he regarded Gerald's face. It reminded Gerald suddenly of that self-same expression when he and Charles as eight-year-olds had been waiting for their first ever caning outside the headmaster's study. As it happened, the chastisement was not unduly severe but the shared experience had formed the first real link in their friendship.

'Stop worrying, old chap! I'll tell Isobel tonight. If the baby is not due for some time, it will give her a chance to prepare for it – tell her friends we've decided to adopt a brother or sister for Migs – that sort of thing.' Seeing the look of relief transforming the man's face, he forced himself to smile. 'I can bring the child to see you, so now you'll have something to live for, Charles, so don't talk to me again about dying! D'you hear me?'

But Charles de Valle lived only long enough to learn of the birth of his child and to see the baby once when he signed the document registering her as his daughter before he died.

CHAPTER ONE

1936

'We will always be friends, won't we?' Georgia said, linking her arms through those of the two girls who were walking up the mountainside behind their school. It was the start of the summer term, and despite the previous three-week Easter holiday in their own countries, they slipped back effortlessly into the French language common to all the pupils at their international Swiss boarding school.

They settled themselves comfortably amongst a carpet of wild narcissi, and Inge, the tall, fair-haired German girl, said eagerly to Georgia:

'You didn't forget to bring the letters, did you, *Liebchen*?'

'They are in my bedside cupboard,' Georgia replied, thinking gratefully that they all had keys to their cupboards – the only place that was not communal in the delightful mini *Schloss* situated close to the vineyards above the lakeside town of Vevey. It was a place where she was wonderfully happy, her adventurous spirit having fretted at the restrictions of her English boarding school. Here she could go skiing in the winter, with exciting walks down through the vineyards at four in the morning to catch the little train taking the party of keen skiers to the foot of the surrounding mountains to spend a weekend in the care of the easygoing discipline of their professor. Lessons were in the garden whenever the weather permitted. There were visits to the nearby town of Lausanne for shopping or to the theatre, and fascinating trips in the steamers that which plied along the picturesque shores of Lake Geneva. Most important of all the pleasures, Georgia thought but did not relay to her friends, was being far away from home, where she had found it impossible to be really happy for the past year.

Now, at the age of nearly seventeen she had made up her mind that she was never going to be a debutante and stay at home after her coming-out Season like her much-loved sister, Migs. She was going to become a journalist, preferably a war reporter – if she could find a war to go to.

Sitting beside the tall, broad-shouldered figure of her friend, Inge, with the brilliant blue eyes and long golden pigtail, Georgia could not have looked more opposite. Her dark brown, almost black hair, was, according to her mother, a hopelessly unruly mop despite the kirby grips and frequent trips to the hairdresser to have it cut into a neat bob. Her eyes were also dark, and her complexion, which tanned easily to a golden brown in summer, lacked the extreme pallor of Inge's face, against which her bright, rosy cheeks gave her a Nordic look that Inge herself called Aryan.

Georgia's other close friend, Hannah, resembled neither of them. She was short, thin and her face with its high cheekbones was angular, her features aquiline. Her large, thoughtful eyes and serious expression somehow tended to reject offers of friendship from the less discerning who did not see the deeply sensitive, caring nature that had been quickly recognised by Georgia.

'I'll read the letters to you this evening after supper!' she said now.

She was in no doubt that Hannah would find them every bit as intriguing as she did, but she was not quite so certain about Inge's reaction. Inge was a hugely practical, self-assured girl who knew exactly what she wanted to do with her life just as soon as she left school. She would live perfectly happily in her precious Fatherland, as she called her country. She was forever talking about her beloved Führer, Herr Hitler, and had full-size posters of him on the walls of her bedroom. She belonged to the Hitler Youth movement, which, for Georgia's benefit, she likened to the English Girl Guides – only better, with picnics and rallies and gatherings of both boys and girls round campfires singing patriotic Lieder.

By all accounts, although Hannah was also German, she did not enjoy a similar joyful home. For the past two years, she had always spent her holidays with an uncle and aunt who ran a guest chalet in the ski resort of Garmisch. Only occasionally did her mother and father join her there. Her father, who she adored, she had explained, was a doctor with a huge number of patients, mostly of Jewish faith like himself, but with numerous non-Jewish patients who had been treated by him for many years. He never talked about the changes that were taking place under the new chancellor, so often praised by Inge. Politics as a topic of conversation was not permitted at the school, whose pupils came from countries all over the world, but Inge often regaled them with the wonderful things her adored leader was doing for Germany and its people.

The three girls were all but inseparable. They skied, swam, played tennis, threw javelins, spent all their free time together, and trusted one another implicitly. Such was the closeness of their friendship, Georgia had confessed her deeply guarded secret to them on the last day of the previous term. Sitting on one side of Hannah's bed, Inge on the other, she had said:

'I'm not who you think I am. I mean, I'm not Georgia Driffield.' Seeing the look of astonishment on their faces, she'd added quickly: 'Well I am in one way but . . . well, I'm adopted. I was born to two other parents, only they weren't really parents, I mean they weren't married, and then the man died and Daddy, I mean he's my father now, adopted me so I've got his surname. My real father's name was Charles de Valle. I'm illegitimate! I looked it up in the dictionary and it means unlawful.'

She had expected them to see her henceforth as a different sort of person – someone not quite equal to themselves – but their reactions were totally opposite. Inge thought it fascinating and wanted to know more. Hannah was sympathetic and tried at once to reassure Georgia that whatever happened before she was born was not her fault and her parents must love her to have brought her up as their own child.

Georgia explained that she did not resemble her darling sister, Migs, who she believed her mother loved far more than herself. Not only was Migs prettier, she was far less trouble, happy to remain quietly at home playing with her dolls or, in recent years, shopping with her mother for pretty clothes. Georgia, on the other hand, had always preferred to join in her best friend Sebastian's boyish escapades, when he permitted, and was inclined to argue with her mother who disapproved of most of her activities. As for her father, she had once adored him when she was little and they'd had wonderful times together telling stories and playing games, and she'd half believed she was the favourite of his two daughters. Then last summer she had suddenly come into a very large sum of money left to her by her former father and thus discovered that he had withheld this truth from her for all those years – that she was not really his child. Neither then nor subsequently had she felt able to forgive him, the father who had always insisted that she should never tell lies or be dishonest, for pretending she was his daughter.

Had it not been for the way Sebastian had treated the news, she would not ever have told them, these two close new friends, about her adoption.

Sebastian was the only son of their next door neighbours. He was the same age as Migs and had entrusted Georgia with the secret that he had been in love with her sister since their early teens; that when the time came for him to leave university and get a job, he was going to propose to Migs. An only child, ever since his family had moved into the house next door he had had to make do with young Georgia's company if there were none of his own friends visiting. He openly called her his 'slave' because she always fell in with whatever activity he chose to enjoy, allowing him to confiscate her sweets or her toys for whatever game he had in mind with no more than a muttered apology if they were ruined in the process. Even though Georgia knew he only tolerated her company because she complied so readily with his demands and enabled him to see Migs so often, it was Sebastian's indifference to her adoption she valued, and she'd never yet taken offence at any of the derogatory names by which he often called her.

Far from being as shocked by the news as she had expected, he had merely grinned and said: 'How absolutely fascinating! Always thought there was something odd about you, Pugface. Tell me more!'

He'd been even more excited than she when they had discovered the letters and her ancestors' family tree. On her sixteenth birthday, having passed his driving test, he'd driven her and Migs down to Tonbridge to see Audley Court, the old house her original father had left her in his will. While Migs unpacked the picnic lunch on the grass in the overgrown garden, she and Seb had explored the house and discovered in the cellar a dusty, woodworm-ridden old desk with a secret drawer.

He had been as intrigued as she was to discover, in the first letter Georgia had read aloud, that it was from a pirate – by the sound of it a real one, professing his love for who must be one of Georgia's ancestors.

As a consequence Georgia had soared in his estimation and he had even agreed that when he was married to Migs he would permit her to live with them. As well as the house, according to her father Gerald Driffield, Georgia had also been left a huge financial legacy that, Sebastian told her, would make her rich enough when she was twenty-one to support him and Migs and her, too, if she lived with them, and at least half a dozen children. 'You can tell them stories about your piratical forebears!' he'd teased.

Sebastian was the only other person in the world, apart from Migs, with whom she'd been willing to share the letters. Now, because these two school friends had come to mean so much to her, she was about to share them with them as well.

That evening, sitting on the end of her bed, she unlocked her bedside cupboard and withdrew the dog-eared bundle, untied the blue ribbon and first read aloud the label attached to it. In Gothic handwriting it was addressed to '*CHANTAL DE VALLE, PRIVATE*'. She began reading out the first of the letters . . .

'18th Day of July, 1841

Meu querida Chantal,

How shall I begin to tell you of the joy Captain McRae's arrival on Coetivy has given me. It is two years almost to the day since you sailed away to your homeland, not a single one of which has passed without my wondering how you are. If you are well? If you married your titled English nobleman? If you are happy? If you have quite forgotten the happy times we shared here on my island?

Oh, Chantal, can you imagine what happiness is mine to learn from Captain McRae that it was you who persuaded him to divert his voyage to China so that you could have news of my well being here on Coetivy! So you have not forgotten me as I feared might be the case.'

Georgia stopped reading for a moment to explain that she had not brought the family tree with the letters but that she and Sebastian had worked out that Chantal was her great-great-grandmother and that she had married the 'titled nobleman', John de Valle, in 1840. As the pirate's letter was dated 1841, she must have been married after she left the island of Coetivy. Sebastian had looked it up in an atlas and found it was one of a group of uninhabited islands in the West Indies known as the Seychelles.

Their faces glowing with excitement, the girls urged Georgia to continue reading, words which by now she almost knew by heart.

'The Captain has given me paper, quill and ink with which to write this letter to you and has promised to deliver it to you in person on his return to England early next year. He has assured me that you have forgiven me for failing to signal either of the two ships who sailed so close to us and would have taken you from me; that time has allowed you to reach an understanding that my love for you was too great for me to facilitate your leaving me. I thought I would be unable to bear it, yet I have had to do so.

There are times, Koosh Koosh, when I think I hear your voice when the wind is stirring the leaves of the palm trees; or at twilight when the shadows fall and I think I see you running towards me from the rocks where you loved to fish, your long dark hair dancing round your shoulders. Your devoted servant, Zambi, swears she has seen your ghost in the moonlight slipping between the trees surrounding our clearing. We miss you! Sometimes I think I must leave here; go back to the sea and the life I led before you stole my heart. I make the decision to go but then I cannot bring myself to leave so many memories of you. Do you think of me, Koosh Koosh? Sometimes? Do you dream sometimes that you are back here on Coetivy with me and Zambi? When you read this letter, you will know that I cannot forget you and that EU AMÁ-LO-EI SEMPRE.

Dinez da Gama. Coetivy. July 1841.'

Hannah drew a deep sigh:

'But he is so sad!' she commented. Inge shook her head.

'Georgia said this man was a pirate,' she reminded Hannah, 'and that he had taken her prisoner after boarding her ship at sea: so we should not feel sorry for him.'

'That's what Seb said!' Georgia told her, 'but when I read you the next letters, you will agree that he really did love her.'

And he'd done so in a very poetic way, she'd thought each

time she had read them. She could not imagine Sebastian ever writing to Migs in such a vein although he was in love with her. But this was 1936 and as Seb had said, everyone had become far more down to earth since the war and people just weren't like that any more.

Urged by both girls, Georgia began to read the second letter. It was dated 1844.

'Meu querida Chantal.

How have I managed to wait three long years for your letter which Captain McRae brought to me today? I knew it would take him many months to return to England after his last voyage here, and still more to return to Coetivy and I could not be certain he would deliver my last letter to you, still less that you would reply.

I thank you from my heart for it. For your happiness, I will make myself pleased that you are now married to de Valle although I cannot but remember that magical day when my faithful Zambi witnessed the marriage you and I made here before God when I truly believed you would be my wife for ever.

It may surprise you, Chantal, to hear that two years ago at Zambi's request, she and I performed the same marriage ceremony as ours. She was carrying my child. Because you had wished our union to be as legal as possible without a Priest or ship's Captain to officiate, she wished it, too, and I did not have the heart to refuse her.

I have a little daughter who I have named Poquita Cantora because it is the closest I can come to your name in my own language. She is white skinned like me with green eyes which Zambi tells me would be just like mine if I only smiled as often as my little Cantora; but she understands my sadness and tells our Daughter loving stories of her Papa's captive white Princess!

Ah, Chantal, was it wrong of me not to open your cage door and set you free before you came to love me just a little bit? I will never know that truth but I will never regret those nine months we shared.

I congratulate you most sincerely on the birth of your Son. McRae tells me that by now you will have had a second child but that many children in England have succumbed to diphtheria this past winter and that you fear for your son's survival. I shall pray for him. As you know, we do not have such illnesses here on Coetivy. Zambi believes you will return to visit us one day but sadly I do not share her hope.

McRae tells me you are as beautiful as ever but he comforts me by telling me there were tears in your eyes when you read my last letter to you. I must confess, however, that he added that you were most happily married and that your Husband was most loving towards you.

Please Koosh Koosh, write to me again. I live now for my sweet Poquita Cantora and my memories of you.

Munca seu amor

Dinez da Gama'

'If you like, I'll read the last letters Dinez wrote to Chantal,' she said to the two girls, whose faces showed how intrigued they were. 'The writing is more faded but I know them almost by heart.'

She started to read the first page.

'Meu querida Chantal,

I truly believed my Heart was broken when you first left the island. Now I know a Heart can break a second time.

Last winter, a huge wave swept in from the sea without warning and engulfed my beloved little Daughter and poor faithful Zambi. When I discovered their poor lifeless bodies, I wished I, too, had perished.

Today our good friend Hamish McRae has arrived and I told him how I was high up one of the big palm trees by chance gathering coconuts when the sea swamped Coetivy.

He said it was more probably the hand of God than mere chance.

As you knew, Chantal, I was born into a Catholic family but relinquished my Faith when I led a life of piracy. I told myself God would approve my desire to rob the rich merchants in order to improve the miserable lives of the poor. Hamish has made me see that this terrible tragedy which has robbed me of my Daughter, may be God's way of showing me that I cannot remain here on this lonely Island with that great wealth of merchant gold buried in the sand.

This God-fearing man has offered to break his journey to China and take me and my treasure trove to the capital Island of Mahé some two hundred miles hence; there to have a new boat built to my liking in which I shall return to my homeland . . .'

Georgia paused to take up the second sheet of paper. She could see by the two girls' faces they were fascinated by this story nearly one hundred years old. The second sheet was dated two days later than the first. She continued to read:

'After much reflection, I have decided to follow McRae's advice if for no other reason than that I cannot bear to go on living here without my Daughter and Zambi and only my memories of you. I shall be going back to my homeland in Portugal, Chantal, and if McRae is right and it is God's will that my Life has been spared for a Purpose, I will journey safely these next two years with my treasure chests, and will use this wealth to set up an Orphanage for Destitute Children in my Daughter's name. Linked as it is with your name, my one true Love, I cannot think of one without the other.

McRae tells me you are well and content with your Life although you, too, have suffered the sad loss of three of

your Dear Children. Remember me if you will in your
Prayers as I remember you, always and always.
    Dinez'

All three were silent for a moment and then Hannah wiped
her eyes, saying:

'That's so sad, Georgia! He did get back to Portugal safely,
didn't he? Does he say?'

Georgia shook her head.

'I'm afraid not. I shan't read the last one if it's going to
upset you, Hannah.'

But Inge insisted she should do so.

'It is dated August, 1856,' Georgia said, 'and written from
an island called Madeira.' Handing soft-hearted Hannah her
handkerchief, she started once more to read:

'Meu amor um verdadeiro
    I and my three surviving crew have now been on this
beautiful island for six months. I have very little money left
after weeks of payments to the divers I hired to search for
the *Cantara* which was blown by a northerly gale towards
to the island where she hit rocks and sank to the bottom
of the ocean together with my sea chests containing my
treasure. I and my Mate had only a few gold coins left
when the dinghy in which our lives were saved reached the
shore. Two men have lost their lives in the attempt to salvage
my fortune, and I have now abandoned all hope of retrieving
it although I had hoped to do so having noted its distance
and direction from land.'

'This letter doesn't have an ending, but there's another page
dated over two weeks later that explains why not. It's very
sad, so don't start crying again, Hannah!'

'If this news ever reaches you, Chantal,' Georgia read, 'you
will know that I am no longer on this Earth. An horrific

Pestilence is sweeping this Island and Person after Person around me has died. My Mate and all the divers are dead and I myself have been unwell these last three days. There is no cure for this Epidemic which they call Cholera, and I do not deceive myself that I shall survive it.

Dearest Chantal, I do not fear Death, and I no longer grieve for my lost fortune lying for ever on the bottom of the sea. My only regret at leaving this Life is that I shall never see you again. It is a comfort to me that, God willing, I will be reunited with my sweet Daughter, Cantara.

Remember me in your Prayers, Koosh-Koosh. I shall love you unto Death and beyond.

Your devoted Dinez'

There was a brief moment of silence as Georgia stopped reading, then Inge voiced her opinion that the pirate's end was well deserved seeing that he had kidnapped Chantal in the first place! Both girls were intrigued by Georgia's relationship to the recipient of the letters.

That night, when her two friends were asleep in their beds, Georgia lay awake, her mind restless with unanswered questions. Had Chantal returned the pirate's love? If so, why had she not stayed on the island with him? Was the island still unpopulated? One day when she was twenty-one and could do what she wanted she would like to visit it. Even more urgently, she would like to visit Madeira, the place where the pirate had died, which she had found on the large globe her father kept in his study, to search for his grave and to discover if his boat had ever been raised.

On the point of sleep, her eyes closed but her mouth curved in a smile as the thought struck her – if she did fly round the world with Sebastian, as he intended when he left Cambridge University, they could visit Madeira and look for Dinez's boat. They might even land on the mysterious island in the Indian ocean and see where the pirate had fallen in love so tragically with her mysterious great-great-grandmother, Chantal.

CHAPTER TWO

1936

Dona Resita Reviezky lay on one of the lounge chairs on the balcony outside her sitting room looking down across the beautiful gardens of Reid's Palace Hotel. The large suite in which she had chosen to make her home was tastefully and luxuriously furnished; the service and food provided by the hotel was excellent and the moderate, all-year-round sunny Madeiran climate was exactly to her choosing.

Money was of little consequence to the elderly lady. When her husband, a wealthy Romanian, had died, she sold their house in New York and the beautiful furniture and furnishings, retaining only her jewellery and János's yacht. She had then sailed to the island of Madeira having fallen in love with the place when she and János had once holidayed there.

The yacht, which she seldom used, was an absurd extravagance but as she was a widow, childless and approaching seventy years of age, she could think of no better way to spend her money.

Many years ago, she had lost touch with her only relative, a brother called Nikolai Anyos. Despite the fact that her husband had left her a very wealthy woman, she was often lonely, and she decided to go back to his last known address in Europe and try to find him.

When finally she reached the street where he had been living, it was to be told by a neighbour that her brother had started to drink when his wife died and a year later he, too, had died, leaving a small son who was put in an orphanage run by nuns.

Now, as Resita waited for her adored nephew to return, she drew a deep sigh as she asked herself where those years had gone since she had begun her search for him. It had been no easy task, for by the time she began, the boy, aged fifteen, had left the orphanage and had found employment as a kitchen boy.

With no more to go on, Resita had spent a week searching the many local restaurants without success. She was on the point of giving up the search when she was contacted by a restaurant owner named Stefan who told her that he knew of a young waiter who answered the description of the lad she was looking for and would tell him to present himself to her at her hotel next day. Resita at once saw the strong resemblance of the youth to her dark-haired, brown-eyed brother, who even had the same name, Fedrik.

When she called to thank Stefan for finding him, the boy's first employer went to great lengths to inform her that he had spent many hours training the inexperienced boy, and reminded her quite unnecessarily how she might never have found her nephew but for him. Finally, aided by a handsome sum of money, he volunteered to square matters with the boy's present employer and allowed Resita to take him then and there back to her hotel.

It was, however, several further weeks before Resita and her nephew were able to leave the country while she went about the task of obtaining a passport for him.

Within a year, Fedrik had grown into a charming companion, filling the gap left by her late husband. He was an exceedingly good-looking young man, now six foot tall with jet black hair, dark brown eyes and amazingly long black lashes. He had only to give one of his charming smiles for women to respond to him and the young girls to blush. His manners were impeccable and he had a near perfect command of the English language, which he'd quickly picked up from the British guests in the hotel. He was not only charming, but always attentive to her well-being, and Resita developed a deep fondness for him, delighting in the knowledge that he seemed perfectly content to take care of her and be a companion to her in her old age.

Now, fifteen years almost to the day since she had found him, she stared out from her balcony at the hotel's beautiful tropical garden watching for his return. Seeing no sign of his tall figure approaching, she told herself he was doubtless down by the swimming pool in the rocks at the base of the cliff on which the hotel had been built. Although nearly seventy, she was still an elegant and attractive woman, but now an unsightly frown creased her forehead at this deviation from their habit always to take tea together at four o'clock after her siesta. She glanced once more at her watch as a waiter came on to her balcony carrying a large tea tray, including Fedrik's favourite cherry cake the chef had baked especially for him. Throughout luncheon he had been flirting with an American girl sitting alone at an adjoining table. Without embarrassment the young woman, called Christobel, had approached Fedrik in the foyer and enquired if he would be interested in a game of tennis or a swim after lunch. With his usual consideration, Fedrik had promised to be back in time for tea.

Although Resita never tired of her nephew's company, she realised that it could not be much fun for a young man always to be dancing attendance upon an old woman like herself, and she made a point of not sounding upset or resentful when he enjoyed other company than hers. She never implied that he was indebted to her not just for 'rescuing' him from his former life, but for the generous allowance she paid regularly into his bank so that he was never embarrassed by having to ask her for money. He adored the speedboat Resita had given him one Christmas, and although he did not own a car, she allowed him to drive her Bugatti for his own use as well as hers.

Resita now occupied herself reading the letter she had received that morning from her close friend, Priscilla Wiscote. Priscilla lived in London with her husband, Sir Archibald

Wiscote, and her letters were always full of amusing society gossip, the latest concerning the King's association with the American woman, Mrs Simpson.

'He should know better than to parade his paramour so publicly,' she had written. 'It's not common knowledge yet – press repression no doubt – but the establishment are hardly likely to approve of his increasing obsession with a twice divorced woman. A bit of discretion absent, I fear.'

She had gone on to say that she was giving a ball for her granddaughter, Margaret Driffield, a pretty girl who was currently enjoying her Season.

'It would be a lovely chance to see you, darling. Do try and come, and bring that handsome young nephew of yours.'

Resita put down the letter as at last she saw Fedrik's tall, athletic figure approaching from the beautiful, subtropical garden her terrace overlooked. By then, the waiter had long since removed the tea tray and put a bottle of wine in an ice bucket in her apartment. Fedrik came out onto the balcony and flopped down on a chair beside her, his white, open-necked tennis shirt contrasting sharply with his sun-tanned neck and chest.

'You're very late, my darling,' she said, a hint of reproach in her voice. 'It's almost five o'clock. I hope it wasn't anything unpleasant that detained you?'

The expression on Fedrik's face was one of resignation as he went over to the table and poured himself a glass of wine. There were times, he thought, when he resented his aunt's dependence upon him, and in particular during these last few days when he wished to spend far more of his time with Christobel, the pretty American girl who seemed every bit as interested in him as he was in her.

'So sorry, Tia Sita!' he said as he went to sit on the chair beside her. 'Our last set of tennis lasted far longer than usual.' He paused momentarily before adding casually: 'I hope you don't mind, I've arranged to play with Christobel again tomorrow.'

Resita felt a renewed frisson of anxiety. She wanted always to please him, but not to forgo his company too often in order that he could spend their precious time together with someone else.

She was being stupidly jealous, she chided herself. Fedrik was like any other young man of his age – interested in the opposite sex and enjoying their complimentary interest in him. As a rule, she took pride in the way her female friends and women guests were attracted to him. They were unable to ignore his good looks, particularly so when he smiled so delightfully and charmed them without seeming to realise the effect he was having on them. This new friendship with the American girl was, however, different. For a start, she was young, exceedingly attractive, very well, if a trifle showily, dressed, curvaceous and quite clearly more than a little interested in Fedrik. Not only that, but from Fedrik's enthusiastic description, she was not only independent but exceedingly rich. Looks and wealth had always been important to Fedrik and she had no wish for this budding friendship to develop into something serious. However, she was wise enough not to reveal such thoughts. With her customary tact, she now curbed any further complaint about his tardiness and smiled as she said:

'I'm so pleased you have found such a good tennis partner, Freddie, dear! We must invite her to join us for dinner one evening.'

Fedrik's face broke into a delighted smile. He put down his glass and stood up, helping Resita out of her chair.

'You are always so kind to everyone, Tia Sita!' he exclaimed. 'I'm sure Christobel will be very happy to accept your invitation. I think you will find her interesting if you ask her about her family. Her father has a hugely successful real estate business with outlets all over America. He gives Christobel – she's his only child – whatever she wants – just as you do me!' he added, bending once more to kiss her cheek. 'Christobel thinks it is why she and I get on so well – both of us spoilt!'

Resita relaxed. If the girl was rich, she would not necessarily be wanting a wealthy husband, which she might well presume Freddie to be. Resita smiled at him as he left her to go to bathe and change for dinner. Deciding to wear her favourite Molyneux gown, she too changed, and after fixing a diamond clasp in her hair she joined Fedrik in her salon. He, as always, was looking extremely attractive in his evening clothes, and as they prepared to go in to dinner, she decided that Priscilla's invitation would now be very acceptable for more than one reason. She linked her arm in his and said:

'I quite forgot to tell you, dear, that we have been invited by Lady Wiscote to a ball she is giving in London for her granddaughter. She telephoned me this afternoon to say she would be devastated if we didn't attend, so I said we would take the yacht over to England in ten days' time. We'll stay as usual at Grosvenor House, and her daughter, Muriel, is booking our usual suite for us.'

She glanced at Fedrik's face as they walked into the foyer and noticed his unmistakeable expression of aversion to the plan.

'But Tia Sita, it means I'll miss the tennis tournament the hotel is arranging for the fifteenth,' he protested anxiously as they walked towards the bar. 'Christobel and I were going to enter the doubles together and . . .'

He broke off, the thought suddenly striking him that his aunt might not be as ignorant as he'd supposed about how unconventionally close he and the American girl had become in the last few days. Living with his elderly aunt might be luxurious but for some time now, at the age of thirty-five, he no longer enjoyed to the same degree the transient flirtations with the daughters of passing hotel guests. What he now wanted was an on going relationship, and Christobel had made it clear she was in no hurry to move to another resort: that she was quite independent, could do whatever she pleased and that he pleased her very much indeed.

'You remember my friend, Lady Wiscote, don't you dear,' Resita was saying smoothly, avoiding Fedrik's scowl. 'The ball is to follow the week after Margaret's presentation at Court. It is to be held at her grandmother's London home in Mayfair. I read the other day that Ambrose's dance band is all the rage, and I don't doubt he has been engaged for the occasion, so you will be certain to enjoy it, won't you, dear boy?'

Fedrik now suspected his aunt was aware how upsetting these plans were for himself and Christobel.

'I don't expect you to remember Margaret, Freddie,' she continued. 'She's a very pretty girl, who, for some reason, they call Migs – such an unattractive name! Her mother is Lady Wiscotte's daughter, Isobel Driffield. They do have another child who someone told me they had adopted. Anyway, as I was saying, I expect you will enjoy yourself, dear boy.'

Later, when Christobel, although uninvited, approached them in the bar where they were enjoying a liqueur with their after-dinner coffee, Resita said ruefully to her:

'I'm afraid you are going to miss your tennis partner, my dear, but a girl as pretty as you will soon find someone else to play tennis with you. We are taking a little holiday in London in ten days' time. We're really looking forward to it, aren't we, Freddie?' she added turning to smile at him. 'That reminds me, dear, you must ask the porter to bring up our cabin trunks. We will need them to take all our glad rags to London, won't we?'

Christobel was now staring at Fedrik, a question in her eyes revealing her shock.

'How long are you going for?' she asked sharply. 'Can't you get back in time for the tournament?'

Before Fedrik could reply, Resita said:

'I'm afraid not! We may stay in London for several weeks. Freddie so enjoys London life, don't you, dear boy?' She turned back to Christobel, adding confidentially: 'He's so good-looking, isn't he? And so charming! I expect all the debutantes will be inviting him to their dances.'

Fedrik now turned anxiously to face Christobel.

'I'll see you when we get back,' he faltered. 'You plan to stay here for the rest of the summer, don't you?'

'I very much doubt it. It so happens, I am also planning to leave quite soon,' the American girl improvised furiously. Accustomed as she was to having what she wanted, she was angry enough to say: 'Frankly, I'm finding this place too staid for my liking; too many old people sitting around doing nothing . . .' She looked directly into Fedrik's face, her eyes narrowed in anger as the thought struck her that the man she had earmarked to be her lover was too weak to stand up to his aunt. She said coldly:

'Too bad I won't be here when you return from London, honey. By the way, I forgot to tell you, I won't be able to take that trip you mentioned to Porto Santo tomorrow. I quite forgot I have a lunch date with some friends in Funchal.'

Fedrik's face clearly revealed the shock of her announcement. As far as he knew, Christobel had no friends in Funchal and her decision to leave Madeira had been made on the spur of the moment in order to let him know that she wasn't going to hang around waiting for him.

Resita was certain of it, but took care to hide her pleasure in the success of her little ruse to scotch the American girl's plan to seduce Fedrik. She was reasonably confident that he would soon forget Christobel when he found himself the centre of an admiring group of pretty young debutantes enjoying their first taste of freedom at young Margaret Driffield's ball.

Declining Resita's invitation to take coffee with them, Christobel announced that she thought she'd had too much sun, which had given her a severe headache. If Mrs Reviezky and Fedrik would excuse her, she said coldly, she was going to have an early night.

As Fedrik escorted a stony-faced, silent Christobel to the

lift, he attempted to explain that he had been as surprised and upset as she was by his aunt's sudden decision to go to England, a decision she had only spoken about that evening.

'I will try and persuade my aunt not to stay in London for long,' he told her. 'I'll be back before you know it. Please don't leave, Christobel! You know how I feel about you. You've become . . .'

He broke off as Christobel interrupted him. Her face was distorted by anger as she turned to look at him.

'I'm not in the habit of being second best to anyone, Fedrik, and as a matter of fact, I've had enough of playing second fiddle to your aunt. As you seem to prefer her company to mine, I've no wish to continue our association, and I shall certainly not be waiting for you on your return!'

The doors of the lift opened and as a guest emerged Christobel stepped in. Without a word, she pressed one of the buttons and the doors closed, leaving Fedrik in no doubt that the American girl had decided he was not, after all, the lover she – and indeed he – had hoped he might be.

Resita, waiting patiently for Fedrik's return, was in no doubt either.

CHAPTER THREE

1936

It was three o'clock on a sunny April day when Georgia, alone with the maid, Polly, heard the telephone bell. She and Polly were closing down the house, Deerswood, for the Season. Migs had gone up to London with her mother to the Eaton Terrace house their father had rented for the Season, and was having a final fitting at the dressmaker for her Court presentation dress. Finding such events boring to a degree, Georgia had opted to stay and assist Polly to put dust sheets over all the furniture and pack away the ornaments. Cook had returned to her little sitting room beside the kitchen for her afternoon nap, so it was Georgia who answered the telephone. To her total surprise, it was Sebastian's voice she heard.

'That you, Jo-Jo? Thank goodness you're still there!' he said. 'I thought you might have left for London with Migs and your ma. Are you listening? I have to see you. It's frightfully urgent. Can you get away?'

For a moment Georgia was too astonished to reply. Sebastian had been rusticated at the end of the Lent term, and Deerswood had been put out of bounds to him until the summer vac. He had been forbidden to tell Migs or herself the reason for the ban and no amount of pleading by Georgia with her mother, or arguing that it was unfair to punish them as well as Sebastian, had altered Isobel's implacable stance. All they knew was that his crime had something to do with having girls in their rooms at the college, an event which, neither to Migs or herself, seemed heinous enough for Sebastian to be sent down: still less that his punishment was to continue for three whole months. It meant that he would not be allowed to accompany them all on their customary seaside holiday.

Despite the embargo Georgia had still managed to meet up with him briefly at the tennis club, although she had been forbidden to talk to him if she did so. She had taken the opportunity to ask him what exactly was his crime, but he had told her quite crossly to mind her own business. He did, however, admit that he was as gutted by the ban as she was as he could not see Migs, and that he had been hoping to see Georgia at the club because it meant he could write a note for her to take to Migs, who he was hopelessly in love with.

'I'm not being allowed to go to Migs's coming-out ball,' he'd told her, swinging his tennis racquet aimlessly at his feet. 'It simply isn't fair. The Pater has stopped my allowance as well, so I can't even buy petrol for my motorbike let alone a train fare to London.'

Now, not waiting for Georgia to speak, he said urgently:

'I need your help, Jo-Jo! Can you leave the house and meet me in the village in the teashop in half an hour's time? It's frightfully important.'

It was about the first time she could remember that Sebastian had actually asked her to do anything, Georgia reflected. As a rule he simply ordered her to carry out his wishes – a habit from their shared childhood. Three years younger than Sebastian, who lived next door, she'd always been happy to obey his commands! She now agreed at once to meet him, and, replacing the telephone receiver, she went to tell Polly she was going out for a walk.

Half an hour later, she was seated opposite Sebastian in the teashop he had assigned for their rendezvous. He had removed the helmet and goggles he wore on his motorbike, and his fair hair, ruffled into untidy curls, enhanced his somewhat poetical good looks. With sky blue eyes, generous mouth and tall athletic body, at the age of nineteen he was accustomed to admiring glances from the opposite sex, and now the young waitress hovering by their table waiting for their order was puzzled by his companion. It did not seem likely, she thought, that Georgia, in her crumpled cotton frock, white ankle socks and black plimsolls was his lady-friend; she must be his sister.

Georgia had been only four years old when Sebastian and his parents had moved into the house next door, their mothers becoming close friends. She had soon become the young boy's shadow, fishing for tiddlers in the stream at the bottom of his large garden, climbing trees, lighting bonfires, stealing straw-berries. Tolerated only when Sebastian, as an only child, had no friends of his own age from the village or a school friend visiting, Georgia was permitted to tag along behind him so long as she always did what he wanted. This was often dangerous or unpleasant and it was she who was ordered to get the half dead mouse out of the trap or the bloated corpse of a dead frog out of his fishing net – in fact any task Sebastian did not want to do himself. His willing slave, she was un-perturbed when he frequently referred to her as such. She had feared that when he went off to public school he would no longer desire her more juvenile company, but then at the age of fifteen he discovered he was in love with Migs, and Georgia was detailed to speak of him to her sister in the most favour-able terms, and to invite him to their house as often as possible so that he might see her. He had confided in Georgia that one day he intended to marry her sister when they were old enough; if, of course, she would have him. Now, having asked the waitress to bring two glasses of ginger beer and some cakes, he told Georgia:

'It's like this, Jo-Jo.' Leaning across the table as he looked at her intently, he said: 'The Pater has refused to let me go to Migs's coming-out dance. Of course I argued and pleaded – told him it was dashed unfair on top of all the other restrictions – but he simply said it was my own fault for disobeying the college rules, and he hoped it would teach me a lesson.'

Not waiting for Georgia's comments, he added with a scowl: 'Well, I'm determined to go. I know Migs wants me to be there because she wrote in that note you gave me saying how disappointed she would be if I wasn't allowed to do so.' While helping himself to a cake, he continued unhappily: 'I was hoping that maybe at the dance I could tell Migs how I feel about her and find out if she's as fond of me. I just have to go, and I have a plan. That's why I had to see you. I need your help.'

Nearly knocking over the ginger beer glasses as he leant even further forward to grasp Georgia's hands, he added:

'I'm absolutely determined to go, Jo-Jo, and I've thought how I can do it. You've always been such a jolly good sport, I know you'll help me. You will, won't you?'

Thrilled as she always was when an opportunity occurred to do something for him, Georgia rose instantly to the challenge.

'Of course I will, Seb, but how? I'll do anything you want but I don't see what I can do.'

Untypically, Sebastian left his slice of chocolate cake untouched. His voice deepening, he repeated:

'I've made up my mind. I *am* going to Migs's ball. Monty, my best friend, has come up with an idea. I'll go in disguise – you know, a false moustache and maybe a beard and I'll wear glasses.'

Instantly intrigued, Georgia drew in her breath excitedly as he added:

'I want you to warn Migs so she won't think I'm a stranger and refuse to dance when I ask her.'

Georgia nodded, but saw at once a possible danger.

'Even if you are in disguise,' she said frowning, 'I bet your parents will know who you are if they happen to hear your voice, and anyway, what about when the master of ceremonies announces your arrival?'

'I've thought it all out!' Sebastian told her. 'Monty said I can stay the night with him at his house and get changed there: and he'll find an excuse not to go to the dinner beforehand to which he and his parents have been invited. He'll help me into the disguise and then we'll go to the ball together later.' Sebastian's eyes were shining with excitement as he continued: 'He's going to say I'm a foreign friend he knew at school who's staying with him for a holiday. What makes it such a spiffing idea is that I can pretend I don't speak English if my parents, or anyone else who I know, sees me.'

He paused momentarily for breath and then, his expression changing to one of concern, he continued: 'It's all quite perfect, Jo-Jo, except for one thing . . .' His voice deepened as he said awkwardly: 'The parents stopped my allowance, so I'm stony broke and I'm going to need money for the train fare to London. I'd go on the old motorbike but I haven't enough cash to buy the petrol I'd need for a return journey . . .' he drew a deep breath, '. . . well, I absolutely HATE asking you, but could you possibly lend me a quid?'

Georgia was breathless with excitement, not only because Sebastian was including her in the daring plan, but because he had asked for her help to effect it. Then her spirits plunged.

'I've only got about two shillings left of my Christmas money,' she told him. 'I bought Migs a bracelet she wanted for her birthday and it cost quite a lot, and I won't get my next pocket money until June.'

'Damn and blast!' Sebastian exploded. 'I hoped you might have something left from the ten bob your grandmother gave you for that jolly good report you got from school.'

'Granny Driffield did give me ten shillings,' Georgia said, 'but I've spent all but half-a-crown.'

Sebastian's frown deepened as he said miserably:

'Well I've only got ten bob. Even with your half crown, I won't have enough to pay for my train fare to London and for my disguise when I get up there.'

For a moment neither of them spoke, then Georgia's face broke into a smile:

'I've not asked Granny for anything for ages and I'm sure she'd give me some money if I ask her.' Her face fell. 'I promised Polly I'd be home for high tea, and I don't see how we

can get to Ditchling and back by six. I daren't be late as Polly
would get into awful trouble if Mummy telephoned for some
reason and I'm not there. She's supposed to be looking after
me.'

'We'll go on my motorbike, silly!' Sebastian replied, ignoring
the fact that Georgia's parents had forbidden her to ride in
his sidecar. 'Nobody's going to see you – well, only your
grandmother.'

'Granny won't tell anyone I've ridden on the bike,' Georgia
said standing up. 'I'll pay the bill,' she added quickly.

As they walked out of the tearoom into the soft spring
sunshine, Sebastian was scowling.

'I hate you having to ask your grandmother for money,
Jo-Jo,' he muttered, as he put on his helmet and goggles and
opened the door of the sidecar for Georgia.

By five o'clock, they were seated in her grandmother's oak-
beamed kitchen drinking large glasses of her home-made ginger
beer.

'Well, my dears,' she said, smiling at the two youngsters,
'as you are riding in Sebastian's noisy motorbike, which I
believe is contrary to your mother's rules, Georgia, I presume
this visit is to be kept secret. Out with it, Sebastian, what are
you both up to?'

Looking somewhat sheepish, Sebastian said:

'I think Georgia might want to talk to you on her own. I'll
go and do a bit of weeding for you if you'd like me to, Mrs
Driffield.'

'That would be very helpful, dear. You'll find a hand fork
in the shed,' she replied. When Sebastian disappeared into the
garden, she turned to her granddaughter.

'Whatever it is, my darling, I will do what I can to help
you. You know that. Is it . . .?' She paused uncertainly, not
wanting to raise a subject she knew her favourite grandchild
found very distressing.

'No, Granny, it has nothing to do with my being adopted,'
Georgia replied. 'I haven't changed my mind about that, but

I'm teaching myself not to care if some silly old man was my real father or not. I just want to forget it.'

Clarissa Driffield decided this was not the moment to pursue the subject of Georgia's reaction when she'd found out the truth. Not without curiosity she asked:

'So what is the reason for you and Sebastian to come here unannounced at five o'clock on a Friday afternoon?'

'It's a bit of a problem me and Seb have got!' Taking a deep breath, Georgia spoke without pausing.

'I need to borrow some money, Granny, not a lot and I'll pay it back but I don't think I should tell you what I want it for because if Daddy or Mummy found out, they'd be sure to ask you why you lent it to me and they wouldn't approve of the reason, so it's best if you don't know what it's for, then they couldn't be cross with you, could they?'

This was by no means the only one of the child's confidences that Clarissa had received throughout her granddaughter's childhood. She had often felt that Isobel was not entirely fair to her adopted daughter: that while dear sweet Migs could do no wrong, bless her, Georgia always seemed to manage to get on the wrong side of her mother. She had therefore always tried to comply with Georgia's needs. This request for the loan of a pound however, was the first time Georgia had asked for money, and a trifle uneasy, Clarissa wondered what it could be for. Sensing her grandmother's anxiety, Georgia now said:

'It's awfully important, Granny, and I'll pay the money back, and I promise it isn't for anything nasty you'd not approve of.'

Which it wasn't, she thought as Clarissa went over to the dresser to get her purse. Of course, it was naughty, Sebastian breaking the rule about not going to Migs's dance, but it would not surprise her if her grandmother didn't give one of her frequent chuckles if she knew what Sebastian was up to.

It was only as she rode home with him that the thought struck Georgia that her granny wasn't really her grandmother at all; that like her parents, she wasn't even a true relation!

Fortunately, Sebastian's grateful hug when he deposited her at the end of her drive drove such uneasy thoughts from her mind. Thanks to her beloved granny he was happy again knowing, like Cinderella, he could go to the ball after all. Smiling, she opened the front door and went inside to confront the poor worried maid.

CHAPTER FOUR

1936

Georgia's Aunt Muriel and Uncle Vivian's identical twin daughters, her cousins Lily and Rose, were now twenty-one years old and despite being much closer in age to Migs and Sebastian than to herself, Georgia had always got on with them very well; their jolly, humorous natures and friendly, happy personalities ensured they were welcome everywhere.

Now of an age to do as they pleased they had decided to leave home and open a flower shop so they were self-supporting. They had subsequently found a little mews cottage in Chelsea to live in.

'Ma and Pa don't approve of us going into business,' Rose had told Georgia, 'but we've got our savings and Pa says he won't stop our dress allowance—'

'So we think . . .' Lily said, completing the sentence, '. . . we've got enough saved to begin and we just know we'll be able to make lots and lots of money.'

'People don't care what they have to pay if they are getting something really pretty . . .' Rose said confidently.

'. . . and Rose is frightfully good at arranging flowers . . .' Lily told the ever-attentive, fifteen-year-old Georgia.

'. . . and Lily is top hole at maths so she will see to the money side of things like buying the flowers . . .'

'. . . and deciding what to charge people!' Lily continued.

When she had plucked up courage to tell them that she had been adopted, instead of commiserating with her as Georgia had expected, they'd sounded as if it was all very exciting.

'That's perfectly fascinating, sweetie!' Lily had said. 'Whatever are you upset about? Nothing exciting like that has ever happened to us, has it, Rose?'

'You are a silly goose to have kept it a secret, Jo-Jo,' Rose said, hugging her. 'For all you know, you could be a millionairess.'

'And then you would be bound to find a husband. Pa said lots of men look for rich wives, especially if they themselves are poor!'

Greatly comforted by the fact that neither of the twins seemed to be considering her adoption a disaster, Georgia curtailed their speculation about her future.

'I'm never going to get married,' she told them. 'I'm going to live with Seb and Migs once they're married. Seb says I can!'

'We're not going to get married either!' Rose said. 'We don't need husbands, do we, Lily?'

'We're perfectly happy with each other!' Lily finished her twin's comment as usual.

Encouraged by their reactions, Georgia had tried to describe her horror at having been lied to by her parents for so many years.

'Well, not exactly lied!' Lily said. 'I mean no one told you an untruth.'

'They just let you grow up thinking they were your parents!' Rose said.

'I think you should stop minding so much!' Lily advised. 'You're a sort of interesting mystery person now.'

But despite both her father's and her mother's attempts to restore their former relationship, she had not been able to take down the barrier she had put between them. The long cosy chats she'd once enjoyed with her father were something long past, and she was indifferent to her father's distress.

Now, to her delight, her mother had given permission for Migs and herself to assist their cousins in their last-minute preparations for the opening of their Rose and Lily florist shop in Beauchamp Place.

On the day before the official opening, she and Migs were helping the twins trying to sort out the mêlée of flowers, wrapping paper, vases, gift cards and replies to their invitations to the cocktail party due to take place next day. There were to be canapés and champagne – paid for by their father who, they recounted, found their activities amusing. They had also planned for a buttonhole to be given to every guest on their arrival.

'Rose and I thought you might hand them out, Georgia, as people arrive. We've put that little table by the door where you can sit,' Lily said. 'There'll be time to make them up tomorrow morning as people aren't invited until twelve.'

'But we hope you two will be able to get here by eight o'clock,' Rose added, 'if it's not too early for you?'

By late afternoon the shop was beginning to look quite lovely, with vases of cut flowers fresh from Jersey, which they had bought that morning, and pretty pots of plants of all kinds. Blue, white and pink hyacinths in full bloom filled the room, their beautiful scent vying with a big silver bucket of sweet-smelling lilac.

'We're not going to charge as much for our flowers as Moyses Stevens,' Lily explained, 'so people will come to us instead!'

Rose laughed.

'Pa says he can't think where we got our business acumen from! We have invited all his rich friends to come to the opening party. And Ma has invited Granny's friend, Mrs Reviesky, who we know is frantically rich and mad about flowers, which is why she lives on an island called Madeira where flowers grow all the year round.'

'She's one of the refusals,' Lily said, 'but she promised her nephew will come in her place.'

'We know him!' Rose told Georgia. 'His aunt is Granny's ancient school friend from way back. Actually she's quite nice!'

'And so is the nephew – Frederick, I think he's called,' Lily volunteered. 'He's jolly good-looking – sort of foreign-looking. Ma said he would be quite a catch for one of the debs because he's his aunt's only relative, and one day he'll come into a fortune.'

'Better make a fuss of him tomorrow, Migs!' Rose laughed. 'I bet he's more interesting to talk to than all those juvenile ex-public school boys doing the rounds of debs' dances!'

Migs blushed.

'I'm not looking for a husband!' she said, 'I'm going to domestic college at the end of the Season. Anyway, I don't want to get married for ages. The very last thing I'd like is marrying a foreigner and having to go to some foreign country to live, not even if the flowers are as beautiful as they are in Madeira.'

'Madeira!' Georgia repeated, interested suddenly in the girls' conversation. 'That's where . . .' She broke off, unwilling to reveal the bolt of excitement that had coursed through her when she heard the name of the island where Dinez da Gama had been shipwrecked and died: where she intended to go one day. The foreign man who was coming would be able to tell her all about the island. He might even know about cholera, the disease that had decimated the population in the 1800s, and if there were records of pirates visiting the island, and if a record of ships that had been wrecked off its coast existed.

'It's getting awfully late!' Rose interrupted Georgia's thoughts. 'Your parents will be wondering where you are. You're staying the night with Pamela, aren't you, Migs? I'm afraid our telephone hasn't been connected yet so you can't ring her.'

'I'll go and get a taxi!' Georgia offered as Migs and the twins removed their aprons.

'You'd better get two taxis!' Rose told Georgia. 'Eaton Terrace is the opposite direction to us, and your friend lives north of Hyde Park doesn't she, Migs?'

'But our house in Eaton Terrace is on the way to Pamela's,

Jo-Jo!' Migs said. 'I can drop you off first and go on afterwards to Hyde Park Gardens. I'll be perfectly all right on my own.'

Georgia grinned.

'Better telephone Mummy when you get there. You know what she's like! She's probably having kittens right now!'

The girls laughed and, kissing the twins goodbye, Georgia went out into the street where she had no difficulty in flagging down an empty taxi that had been delivering homegoers to Beauchamp Place. Congratulating themselves on what their hard work had achieved, the twins and Migs saw Georgia safely home and five minutes later they arrived at their own front door. As Rose was paying the driver, a tall man wearing a dinner jacket and a white silk scarf round his neck and carrying a coat over one arm came hurrying down Prince's Gate Mews towards them. Not realising Migs was still inside the taxi, he waved his hand to stop it moving away and started to climb into it.

Lily's warning that the taxi was not free came too late and he was halfway inside before he saw Migs on the back seat.

'I say, I'm frightfully sorry . . . thought the cab was empty . . . dashed silly of me! I do beg your pardon!' he said apologetically.

Migs had been about to protest but the stranger's apology, delivered in a deep cultured voice, reassured her. There was a moment of confusion while he got out of the taxi to see the twins trying to hide smiles at his obvious discomfiture.

'So sorry!' he said for the second time. 'I'm terribly late . . . for the opera, you see . . . I mean that's why I was hurrying . . . well, I saw your taxi pulling up and when you all got out . . . that's to say when I thought it was all of you, I thought . . .'

'Please don't upset yourself!' Lily broke in kindly. 'We quite understand.'

'We could ask her if she would mind sharing,' Rose proffered. 'Is the opera you're going to at the Albert Hall?'

He nodded, protesting that he could get another taxi.

'But by then you'd be later still,' Lily broke in cheerfully. 'We'll ask Migs if she minds, shall we?'

Without waiting for an answer, she opened the taxi door wider and leant inside where, in a whisper, she explained the stranger's predicament.

'He does seem very nice,' she said. 'Well, what Ma would call "a gentleman"! You should be quite safe! Do say yes, you'll share!'

When, with Migs's agreement, the stranger got back into the taxi, he apologised once more and introduced himself as Captain Douglas McPherson. Before Migs could give her name, the taxi driver opened the dividing window and asked in none too polite a tone if he was to continue waiting or did the lady and gentleman actually wish to go somewhere.

The captain started to apologise again when Migs, now more amused than apprehensive, asked her fellow traveller if he wished to be deposited at the Albert Hall, at that point he insisted upon seeing her safely home first.

'Then you will be even later than ever!' Migs said laughing. 'You've probably missed the start anyway. Do please tell the driver to drop you off first. Then he can take me on to number fifty-three, Queens Gate.'

When, with even further apologies, he did as she asked and the taxi started up again, Migs thought it might put her companion a little more at ease if she introduced herself.

'I'm Margaret Driffield,' she said. 'My cousins, that is to say the two older girls you were speaking to earlier, are identical twins: I don't know if you noticed. The younger girl is my sister. We've been helping the twins prepare for the opening tomorrow of their flower shop in Beauchamp Place.'

As the taxi now turned into Prince Consort Road, her fellow passenger suddenly smiled.

'How very enterprising of them!' he said. 'I shall have to stop and buy some flowers when I'm in Knightsbridge. May I ask you, Miss Driffield, are you similarly employed?'

Migs laughed.

'I'm afraid not,' she said. 'I'm one of those rather useless debutantes who is about to come out. I'm going to a domestic science college at the end of the Season to learn how to cook and run a house and fold table napkins nicely – that sort of thing. And you? I suppose you must be in the army as you're a captain?'

The man beside her nodded.

'I'm in the Punjab Regiment, normally stationed in northern India, but I'm back here at Staff College for a course and some leave. Last year . . .'

He got no further, as the taxi pulled up outside the Albert Hall. Alighting from it, he told the driver to take the young lady to the address Migs had given him. Then he paid the fare to that destination and, putting his head through the open door, he said to Migs:

'I'm most awfully glad I met you, Miss Driffield. I do hope your party goes well at the flower shop tomorrow. I really am most grateful to you and your friends.'

Possibly from habit, although he was not in uniform, he saluted Migs and, closing the door, stood back waving to her as the taxi drew away.

He was really quite charming, Migs thought as she sat back in her seat. She sensed that beneath the man-of-the-world veneer, the captain was actually quite shy. When later she told the friend with whom she was staying about the encounter, she was unable to describe him fully. The best she could come up with was: 'sort of tall and sort of darkish with a military kind of moustache'.

She gave him no further thought until the following morning, when her friend came into her bedroom, her face beaming over the top of a huge bunch of roses.

'These just came for you, Migs,' she said, 'from Moyses Stevens. There's a card inside and I'm dying of curiosity. I can't think of anyone I know who might receive flowers at half past eight in the morning!'

The roses were beautiful, a dozen delicate primrose yellow buds just opening. Taking out the flower-edged card tucked amongst the blooms, Migs read:

'MISS MARGARET DRIFFIELD. Because of your kindness
I was just in time for the start of La Bohème. Please will
you have tea with me tomorrow afternoon so I may thank
you in person? Would four o'clock at Harrods be possible?
I will be at your friends' flower shop at 12.30 today when I
do hope you will say yes.

Yours very sincerely, Douglas McPherson.'

It was the first time Migs had ever been on the receiving end
of such a romantic gesture, and her immediate inclination was
to accept the invitation. As her admirer was an Indian army
officer, she thought her parents would surely not complain
about her having tea with a complete stranger.

'You will have a chance to take a good look at him: see
how old he is and if he's attractive,' Pamela said excitedly.
'You've only seen him in the dark.'

When later that morning Douglas McPherson walked into
the shop the moment the doors opened, Migs realised immediately who he was, partly because of his military bearing but
also because of his voice as he thanked Georgia for the buttonhole she had given him.

Migs was standing by the window holding a tray of glasses
when he approached her.

'Miss Driffield. May I carry that for you?' he said, his voice
instantly familiar.

'I'm all right, honestly!' Migs replied, blushing as she realised
he was staring intently at her. He was both younger and a lot
better-looking than she had expected.

'If I may dare be so personal, Miss Driffield, I would venture
to say you are even prettier than I had thought when I saw
you in the taxi,' he was saying. 'You ARE coming to tea with
me, I hope?'

More people were arriving and, aware that she was still
holding the tray of glasses, Migs said quickly:

'I'm not sure if I will be needed here to help tidy up.' She
prevaricated. 'Could we talk later? I'm supposed to be handing

these glasses around . . . that is, if you are not in a hurry to leave? Forgive me for not having yet thanked you for those perfectly beautiful flowers. They are quite lovely.'

He gave a sudden charming smile:

'I'm so glad you liked them, Miss Driffield . . .'

'Please do call me Margaret,' Migs broke in shyly, aware she was blushing again. 'Miss Driffield sounds so formal.'

'Of course, and you must call me Douglas,' he replied, 'and I will be pleased to stay until you are not so busy,' he added with a smile.

Relaxing now, Migs returned his smile, saying:

'I hope you won't have to wait too long!' and she hurried away.

Georgia was so busy looking at her sister and her mysterious admirer that she nearly omitted to give the newest arrival his buttonhole. When he told her that he really did not need it, she smiled at him, saying ingenuously:

'Well I'm afraid you've got to have it because I've been told everyone must be given one and I'm to explain that they are "on the house", which Rose said means you don't have to pay for it.'

Fedrik looked down at the young girl, an amused smile on his face as he held out his hand and introduced himself. His voice, she noticed, was slightly accented but his English was almost perfect.

'My aunt is a very old friend of the twins' grandmother, who I believe is your grandmother too,' he told her. 'As my aunt couldn't come today, I am here on her behalf as well as my own. I'm anxious to meet your sister Margaret. I believe I am invited to her coming out ball next week.'

Georgia smiled.

'We all call her Migs, not Margaret. She is really nice as well as awfully pretty. The twins said she is the most popular debutante of the Season. That's her over there by the window.'

'Then I must go and introduce myself,' Fedrik said, adding with a smile: 'and join the list of her admirers.'

As he made his way towards Migs, he realised that this duty attendance at the launch was turning out to be quite interesting. He had been missing Christobel and the prospect of a new conquest was always exciting. His aunt proposed staying in England for a month, so there was plenty of time to pay court to the young girl's sister, Margaret.

She was indeed exceedingly pretty, he thought as he reached her side and introduced himself.

'My name is Fedrik Anyos and my aunt and your grand-mother are very old friends, which is why I have been invited to your ball. I've met the twins several times in the past when they were children.'

Migs looked up into the face of the second tall, good-looking man she had seen in the past twenty minutes, but unlike the somewhat shy manner of the army officer, this man sounded very self-assured.

'I understand you are in London for the Season, and . . .' he improvised, 'my aunt has asked me to invite you and your sister to lunch with us tomorrow. We are staying at the Grosvenor House Hotel.'

Migs thanked him for the invitation but said she would almost certainly be needed by her cousins to help in the shop the following day.

Whereupon Fedrik said quickly:

'Then may I suggest tea tomorrow instead of lunch? We could make it half past four to give you more time to lend your assistance here. My aunt and I live in Madeira and we only come to London occasionally. She would so much like to have this opportunity to get to know you and your sister, and . . .' he smiled '. . . I could enjoy a little more of your company, too?'

Migs was now frowning slightly as she tried to remember why the name Madeira sounded familiar. Then the memory returned. It was off the coast of the island of Madeira where Georgia's pirate's ship had foundered and where he had died of some epidemic or other. Recalling her sister's obsession with her ancestor's old letters, she knew how much it would interest Georgia to be able to add a little more background to them.

Seeing Migs's hesitation, Fedrik added with mock seriousness:

'I will strike a bargain with you. If you say "yes", I will speak to the hotel manager with whom my aunt has an excellent relationship, she being such a frequent guest in the establishment. She can request that in future, he buys all the hotel's flower arrangements from the Rose and Lily Florist!'

Forgetting her shyness, Migs laughed.

'I very much doubt that the twins could handle such a big order!' Agreeably flattered by Fedrik's persistence, she thanked him and said that she and her sister would be happy to have tea with him and his aunt the next day.

'I shall look forward to tomorrow,' Fedrik said, and he gave a small bow, which struck Migs as very Continental, before she moved away, leaving him to mingle with the other guests.

By three o'clock, nearly all of them had departed, having voiced compliments and promising their patronage in future. The shop was now empty enough for Migs to see her admirer, Douglas McPherson, across the room. She had been too busy even to think about him or his invitation, but as he stood patiently looking at her with an expression that was part quizzical, part hopeful, she recalled he was waiting to discuss their meeting for tea. It would, she thought, be very nice to see him again in less crowded conditions. She was tired of the eligible young men who attended the parties given by the parents of her fellow debutantes. They were still boys, she thought now, whereas this good-looking army officer was older – in his late twenties, she supposed, and very much a man. His roses had been a very romantic gesture and would, she thought, please her young sister who was so absorbed in the romance of the discovered letters.

To Douglas's obvious delight, she thanked him again for the flowers, saying she would be happy to have afternoon tea with him the next day, and arranged to meet him at Harrods.

It was only after he had departed that Migs remembered the other invitation to tea she'd accepted from the dark-haired, good-looking foreigner called Fedrik with the funny surname. She hurried over to Georgia, who was still sitting behind the counter with a tray now empty of buttonholes, and told her about the embarrassing mistake she had made.

'I was about to explain we were unable to accept and then I remembered he said he lived in Madeira, so I agreed to go, Jo-Jo, because I thought you'd be interested! And now the awful thing is, I have arranged to have tea tomorrow with Douglas McPherson, the army officer who shared my taxi last night, and I'd much rather have tea with him!'

Georgia's face lit up with excitement.

'Please don't cancel the Grosvenor House man,' she begged. 'As I'm invited too, can't we just say you're not well but that I can go on my own? We don't have to tell Mummy. If he's all that keen to see you I can tell him you'll meet him another day.'

Migs's hesitation did not last long. The alternative to Georgia's plan must be to cancel the captain's invitation and she had no wish to do that. She would let Georgia tell Fedrik Anyos and his aunt the lie she had suggested – that at the last minute she had been unwell so there'd been no time to let them know – because she'd already made up her mind who she most wanted to see.

Back at the In and Out Club where he was staying, Douglas was dining with a fellow officer that evening and, before the end of the meal, was telling him he had met the girl he wanted to marry.

'Sounds a bit beyond-the-bounds to me, old chap!' his companion said. 'Thought you said you've only spent a few minutes with her and you don't really know her from Adam.'

'That may be true,' Douglas replied, 'but one thing I do know is that I'm head over heels in love, and I'm going to marry her and take her out to India with me when my posting comes through.'

His friend sighed.

'Have another drink, old boy! Tomorrow, God willing, you'll have sobered up and have changed your mind.'

But as the tea next day with Migs came to an end, Douglas was even more certain that crazy as it might seem, and however precipitate, he was determined to propose to her Migs just as soon as there was a suitable opportunity to do so.

CHAPTER FIVE

1936

'You can come out now, Taylor!' Monty said as he opened his bathroom door where Sebastian had been hiding ever since he'd arrived undetected at the house. 'It's all clear!'

David Montgomery's parents had finally departed in a taxi to Sir Archibald and Lady Wiscote's house in Park Lane where they were dining with twelve other guests before Migs's dance began.

'Let's have a look at your disguise,' Monty said as Sebastian entered his bedroom, 'see if I think it's any good. Can't risk anyone recognising you,' he added, his freckled face, topped by a head of ginger hair, creased with laughter lines. Both young men were now thoroughly enjoying the escapade, and Monty's laughter filled the room as Sebastian posed, stroking the moustache and a small goatee beard he had stuck on his face.

Monty stopped laughing and surveyed him critically then commented: 'Good thing you got so tanned last week as you're supposed to be an Arab. Come to that, your fair hair will give the game away. We've got to do something about that.'

His hair was something Sebastian had overlooked but Monty had already thought of a solution.

'Turban! That should do the trick. We'll tear up one of the old dust sheets. There's bound to be one in the linen cupboard. You will be this Arabian student who came for a term to learn English but was never any good at it which is why you, Seb, don't understand what anyone says to you! I'll do the talking.'

'Sounds as if you've thought of everything,' Sebastian said. 'Well, except a name. I'll need one when we're announced.'

Monty was still grinning.

'Thought of that, too. You're the heir apparent of a wealthy Arab prince called Turik who sent his eldest son to Eton – we had a maharaja's son when I was there. The Pater's such a racist and positively virulent when it comes to the Boches, but he actually quite liked the chap when I invited him home one holiday.'

'Jolly decent of you to be doing this,' Sebastian said gratefully. 'I owe you for these . . .' He pointed to his beard and moustache.

'Forget it! Just hope it works out okay with Migs,' Monty replied as they went along the landing in search of the sheet.

Two hours later a nervous Sebastian led by a confident Monty descended the stairs where Doreen, the parlourmaid, was polishing the handle of the drawing room door. She stood trying not to gape at the turbaned gentleman beside Monty as he asked her to flag down a taxi for them. Clearly she had not recognised Sebastian, and therefore, greatly reassured, the two young men arrived at the Wiscotes' house and joined other guests climbing the steps to the open front door. For a moment, Sebastian felt a wave of unease. He smoothed his moustache and pressed his turban more firmly on his head as Monty, grasping his elbow, drew him inside.

The ballroom was brightly lit with glittering crystal chandeliers, and huge arrangements of flowers stood on plinths at each corner of the room. Gilt chairs lined the walls and a band, its musicians identically attired in white tie and tails, sat on a dais at one end of the room; a table laden with sparkling glasses and jugs of punch and fruit juices was at the other. Double doors were open into the dining room, where a long table covered by a crisp white tablecloth stood ready waiting to be laden with the exciting dishes of food that would be served later.

Just inside the open double doors, Sir Archibald and Lady Wiscote were busy shaking the hands of newcomers as the master of ceremonies announced them. Joining the queue,

Sebastian felt yet another wave of unease as he caught sight of his parents chatting animatedly to another couple. Then he glimpsed Migs hurrying across the hall into the ballroom and, forgetful of his anxiety, his determination to go through with his plan was renewed. He could hear Monty's voice beside him giving both his own and Sebastian's foreign name. As they were announced they moved forward to be received by their host and hostess and Monty said to Sir Archibald:

'It's very kind of you to permit me to bring my friend but as I explained to Lady Wiscote, I felt I could not leave him at home on his own.'

'But of course, Monty, dear boy,' Sir Archibald replied, 'but I did not catch his name.'

'I think if you just call him Turik it will suffice,' Monty replied glibly. 'I'm afraid his command of English is far from good although he was at Eton with me for a whole term.'

By now a number of other guests were waiting to be introduced and, with a pleasant smile at Sebastian, their host turned to welcome the next arrivals.

'See, old chap, I told you it would be all right!' Monty declared as they made their way into the ballroom past the dancers and the orchestra to the refreshment table. A waiter poured them each a large glass of punch, which, having been supervised in the making by Sir Archibald, was a lot stronger than was noticeable.

The music came to a stop and as the dancing ended, Monty gave Sebastian a nudge.

'Better go and get your name down on Migs's dance card!' he urged in an undertone. 'Judging by the number of chaps milling round her, it will be filled up before long.'

Gazing across at the girl he adored, Sebastian's heart missed several beats. She was looking quite beautiful in a flowing cream-coloured dress, her fair hair held back in a sparkling band, and a white camellia was pinned to one of the straps of her dress. She was smiling up at a tall, slightly Italian-looking man who was spelling out his surname as she wrote it on her dance card. Sebastian felt a surge of jealousy that over ruled his nervousness. Pushing past the group around Migs, he finally gained her attention. Clicking his heels and bowing, as Monty had suggested he do, he muttered his fictitious name and pointed to her dance card.

Migs regarded him anxiously. She had been warned by Georgia that Sebastian was planning to turn up in some kind of fancy dress, but for a moment she did not realise the turbaned gentleman was he. Then she recognised him and said with genuine regret:

'I'm so sorry, but my card is full,' adding for the sake of the young men and girls surrounding her: 'You're a friend of Monty's, I believe. I'm so pleased you could come. If I can, I will try to persuade the band to add one more dance to their schedule. Meanwhile, let me introduce you to a friend of mine.'

Taking his arm, she led him over to the row of chairs where the proverbial wallflower, a plump, plain-looking girl, was sitting.

'Do let me introduce you to my friend, Miss Susan Sherman,' she said. 'I'm afraid I don't recall your name?' she added wickedly to Sebastian.

Desperately disappointed that he and Monty had arrived too late for him to sign his name for several dances with Migs as he had hoped, Sebastian had now to force himself to play the part Monty had invented for him. Bowing, he muttered incomprehensibly and as the band struck up a foxtrot, he held out his arm. As it happened, the girl was quite a good dancer, but he had no intention of spending the evening with her. All he wanted was a chance to talk to Migs and now he could not wait for an opportunity to do so.

Leading his dance partner back to her chair at the end of the dance, he escaped to the adjoining anteroom where those who were not dancing could sit comfortably in peace and quiet. A lot of elderly people and parents occupied most of the sofas and chairs, but seeing a window seat at the far end of the room, Sebastian made his way quickly to it. Before he reached this temporary haven, he was joined by a tall, dark-haired, exceptionally good-looking man in immaculate white tie and tails. He sat down beside Sebastian, looking at him curiously.

'If you will forgive me saying so,' he said, 'I see you are a foreigner like myself. May I introduce myself to you? My name is Fedrik Anyos. I come from the island of Madeira where I live. May I know your name?'

Although recognising the man who he'd seen Migs dancing with when they arrived, Sebastian had no wish to get into conversation with anyone. But he felt obliged to return the introduction.

'My name is Turik . . .' At which point his memory completely deserted him. Frantically he tried to recall the title Monty had found for him, but he was unable to do so. He resorted to his escape route. 'I no speak English!'

The look on his neighbour's face gave way suddenly to a quizzical smile.

'May I suggest that perhaps you do!' he said. 'Not only did you understand my request for your name, but I think you might be in a little bit of trouble.'

Seeing Sebastian's look of anxiety, he continued in a near inaudible tone:

'It is your beard . . . it has become detached from the side of your face, and your moustache . . .' Fedrik continued: 'It's not . . . well, not quite as it should be. I trust you will forgive such personal observations?'

Automatically, Sebastian's hands went to his face as he said desperately in his own voice:

'Great Scott! Are you sure? I mean is it very obvious? I mean could I get to the cloakroom without . . . without . . .'

Fedrik's smile widened.

'Without detection? I think not! But if it would be of any help, I will walk to the cloakroom with you which will at least hide the side of your face where your beard has slipped a trifle.'

Sebastian let out his breath.

'I say, that's jolly decent of you,' he said. 'It's fearfully important no one here knows who I am. You see . . .'

'Forgive my interruption but it is quite hot in here and I think we should proceed before any more of your disguise detaches itself,' Fedrik said, having noted the beads of perspiration on Sebastian's forehead. 'If you wish to tell me later why you are here incognito, I shall be happy to learn your secret. Frankly, I was finding this party a little tedious . . . the girls a little too young for my liking and the elderly too boring. Come along! We'll attract less attention if we walk quite casually. We will pretend to be talking to each other so that no one feels obliged to address us.'

With a huge surge of gratitude, Sebastian walked out of the room beside his saviour. Once in the cloakroom, there were further hazards as young men were coming in and out almost without pause. Eventually they were left alone for a few minutes and Fedrik tried unsuccessfully to stick back Sebastian's beard and moustache. Finally he said:

'I fear the heat of the room has dried the adhesive. Can you not remove both your disguises and rejoin the party as your natural self?'

More than a little grateful to this stranger for his attempt to rectify things, Sebastian now related his story.

'It's just that I'm really crazy about Migs, and I suppose it was silly of me to think an occasion like this a romantic sort of place to tell her, and to ask her how she felt about me,' he confided. 'As it's her dance, I should have realised how preoccupied she would be, but I wanted so much to see her and . . .' He broke off, looking at Fedrik gratefully: 'It's really very decent of you to try to help me, but I can't stay here without a disguise because my parents are here, too, and would recognise me. I wish there was a way I could thank you for rescuing me but I'm only in London for tonight, and I've got to get home first thing tomorrow before I'm missed!'

Fedrik regarded his disconsolate young companion with an amused smile.

'Don't concern yourself – I'm quite enjoying the adventure. I wasn't exactly looking forward to this evening. I'm only here because my aunt, who is a close friend of our hostess, insisted I do so. As a matter of fact I do understand your feelings. I myself am keen on an American girl in our hotel in Madeira. As to thanking me, please don't give it another thought.'

'Maybe one day if ever you are in trouble and I could do you a good turn, you have my word I'll do it. That's a promise!' Sebastian said warmly, 'I can't thank you enough. Now, I suppose I've got to get out of here somehow.'

'The slipped beard isn't too noticeable,' Fedrik said. 'If we can think of a way . . . yes, I know the very thing. Here, take this, and hold it to your face.' He handed Sebastian an initialled white silk handkerchief. 'I'll escort you to the front door and if we meet anyone, I'll explain you have serious toothache so are obliged to leave the party early.'

'What about your handkerchief?' Sebastian asked as they reached the front door without mishap. 'How shall I return it?'

'No need, I've got plenty more!' Fedrik told him as the butler called a taxi. 'But if you insist, my aunt and I are staying at Grosvenor House. You can post it to me there. Good luck!'

'There is one last favour you could do me,' Sebastian said hesitantly. 'It's my friend, Monty Montgomery. He'll start looking for me if he can't see me around. Nearly everybody knows him so if you asked . . .'

'Not another word!' Fedrik broke in, smiling. 'I'll make sure he gets the message.'

With a sigh of relief Sebastian climbed into the dark haven of the taxicab, where he sat back considering how tremendously lucky he had been meeting the dark-haired stranger. Not only would he have been the laughing stock of the evening if he had returned to the ballroom only half disguised, but his parents would have been horrified and very, very angry. Monty,

too, would have been in dire trouble and, not least of all the
possible repercussions, Migs would think him a complete idiot
and quite probably would never want to speak to him again.

He would return the handkerchief to his saviour, he thought,
with a note thanking him and insisting once again that if ever
in the future he could help him out of a difficulty, Mr Anyos
could count absolutely on his help.

It would be three long years before Sebastian was called
upon to keep the promise he had just made.

CHAPTER SIX

1936

That Christmas was an especially happy one for Georgia, mainly because Sebastian was spending the week with his parents and he came to their house nearly every day to spend time with her and Migs. He drove them into Brighton to do their last-minute Christmas shopping; helped Gerald erect the big Christmas tree in the drawing room and stood precariously on a stepladder to tie decorations to its topmost branches. Afterwards, the two girls sat in front of the nursery fire toasting the crumpets they had bought in the village on the way home.

As usual, Sebastian was lounging in one of the nursery chairs, his long legs in grey flannels hanging over one arm, his Harris tweed jacket discarded on the floor beside him. He had on his favourite, long-sleeved V-necked pullover, chosen by his mother for his nineteenth birthday because it was blue and exactly matched the colour of his eyes. He was feeling intensely happy. Now, with the ban lifted, he would often be seeing Migs during the Christmas vacation. His escapade in London last summer had remained undetected. Migs had even said how disappointed she had been because he'd had to leave early on account of his 'toothache'.

She was looking as pretty as ever, he thought, her cheeks flushed by the warmth of the nursery fire, a soft woollen frock with matching buttons in the same pale green colour from her neck to her slim waist. She was the epitome of daintiness in comparison with her untidy younger sister. As usual, he reflected with a smile, Georgia, back from her Swiss school, looked the very reverse of dainty. The hem of her skirt had come down in two places; there was a button missing at the neck of her blouse and one of her stockings looked as if it might come down altogether if she didn't tighten it.

He was not, however, in a position to criticise her untidy hair, because his mother had done nothing since he had returned from Cambridge but berate him about his own hair. Along with a number of other undergraduates, he had allowed it to grow and, being naturally curly, it crowned his head so the centre parting was no longer visible and it was anything but the normal short back and sides. Only Georgia approved, saying the tousled curls made him look like the actor, John Gielgud, whose picture she had seen on the cover of one of her parents' theatre programmes. It was for this reason he and his friends had decided to defy convention to make themselves more attractive to girls.

Life could not be happier, he reflected, remembering the surprise Christmas present he would soon be giving Migs.

The following day, after the morning service at church, they enjoyed the Taylors' traditional luncheon and, after the remains of the brandy-topped Christmas pudding had been removed by the parlourmaid, he announced they would repair to the drawing room to open the presents piled under the tree.

It seemed Sebastian had not got a present for Migs, or, Georgia thought, he was going to give it to her in private. The very last one to be handed out was a small square parcel for Sebastian from his parents. Mystified, he opened it and found a miniature balsa wood model of a Gipsy Moth, a present far more appropriate for a young boy than a young man. Sebastian's father was looking at him, his eyes twinkling over the rim of his glasses.

'Well, read the note inside, boy!' he commanded.

Sebastian took out the note and as he read it, gave a loud gasp. 'This is just . . . just matchless! A real aeroplane! A Gipsy Moth! I can't believe it!' He turned to his parents, his eyes shining. 'Thank you, THANK YOU!' he repeated.

Michael Taylor laughed, delighted by his son's reaction to his little joke and to his generous gift.

'Couldn't wrap it up and put it under the tree, now could we?' he chortled. 'It's parked down at Shoreham airfield. Won't take long to drive down there when the weather's a bit better.'

Joan Taylor now spoke.

'Your father and I had an excellent report from your tutor, Sebastian, so your father thought you deserved a little reward.'

'Little!' Seb gasped. 'It's absolutely top hole!' He turned to Migs and Georgia. 'I'll be able to give you a flip round the airfield,' he said, his eyes shining. 'There's nothing in the world to touch being up there in the sky. I just can't wait!'

'Well, I'm afraid you will have to.' His mother was pointing to her wristwatch as she went across the room to turn on the wireless to listen to the King's Christmas broadcast. To everyone's surprise there was, alas, no speech by the new King George, who had only just succeeded Edward VIII after his recent abdication. Michael Taylor said with a sigh that he doubted whether the King would ever be able to make a Christmas broadcast like his father had done, so severe was his stutter.

'A chap at the War Office who met His Majesty when he was Duke of York said the poor fellow managed to talk sense but with dozens of pauses and hesitations,' Gerald Driffield commented.

'That whippersnapper, Edward, should never have abdicated!' Michael Taylor said gruffly as his wife turned off the wireless. 'Load of poppycock that parting speech of his – "can't do his job as king without the woman he loves". Never heard such rubbish! Of course he could – he just didn't want to.'

'It's a great pity all the same,' Joan Taylor declared, although she agreed no one would have wanted the divorced American woman on the throne. 'Nearly everyone loved him and he even won over the miners' hearts, so he did do some good before he departed. Such a good-looking young man!'

'Duty is what counts, my dear, not good looks,' her husband

said gruffly. 'And who is going to succeed King George when he dies, I ask you? He's only got those two little girls. Can't see one of them on the throne, now can you?'

'Why not, Michael?' Joan Taylor argued. 'Queen Victoria was a female and she managed remarkably well, did she not?'

Sebastian, knowing from experience that such debates could continue for a long time, suggested he and the girls went for a short walk before it grew dark. When they went into the hall to collect their outdoor clothes, he turned to Georgia, saying:

'You don't have to come with us, Jo-Jo. Didn't you want a chance to write in your new diary?'

Georgia was about to point out that she could not very well start writing in her diary until the first of January, when she felt his elbow nudging her side. In a flash of understanding, she realised he was anxious to be alone with Migs.

'I don't much want to walk,' she said tactfully. 'I think I'll go and collect the trinkets from the crackers that I promised I would save for Cook for her little granddaughter.'

Migs now had a surprised look on her face, which Georgia pretended not to see. Sebastian gave her shoulder a quick squeeze and said to Migs: 'Better get our overcoats on, it's quite nippy. Wish we could have had snow. Christmas isn't quite the same without it.'

Migs's reluctance now gave way to enthusiasm as the outing would enable her to wear the Christmas presents her parents had given her – a warm camel hair coat with a soft sable fur collar and a fashionable cloche hat made of the same sable fur.

As soon as they were outside, Sebastian tucked his arm through hers and said:

'I thought we might walk down to the cricket club. It will be closed of course but I'm pretty sure I can get into the pavilion if it starts to rain. I've got a Christmas present for you and . . .' he hesitated, not entirely certain how he was going to proceed, '. . . well, I'd rather you opened it without all the family looking on. It's . . . well, sort of private.'

It crossed Migs's mind that Sebastian had arranged to get her on her own so that he could kiss her, something he had done several times in the past, although only on the cheek, but she said nothing as they walked the half mile down to the club. Sebastian did not speak again until they arrived at the pavilion. As he anticipated, it was deserted. He drew her towards the comparative shelter of the doorway and without speaking, pulled her towards him.

Migs was now shivering, not from the cold, but because she was almost certain what he was about to say. Sebastian, too, was nervous, realising that he had completely forgotten the words of the speech he had prepared to make. In his coat pocket was the silver engagement ring with a tiny diamond in the centre – all he had been able to afford from the tray of beautiful engagement rings the jeweller had shown him. He had hoped when he bought it that Migs would wear it on a chain round her neck where her parents would not see it until they might be considered old enough to become officially engaged.

Half of him wanted to abandon the whole idea of proposing to Migs this Christmas Day; put it off until he could find a more suitable venue. Girls, he thought, might not think a cricket pavilion a very romantic setting for a proposal. The other half desperately wanted to know that Migs was committed to him as he would not see much of her for the next three months as he was going to Switzerland after the holiday to augment his language studies and perfect his accents before returning to Cambridge for the Easter term.

In one way, he was looking forward to going to the Swiss college, having been told by Monty, who had just returned from there, that there were plenty of activities in Lausanne and, more importantly, that it was within easy reach of many of the ski slopes where he could learn the most exciting sport in the whole world!

He had promised himself he would propose when he was

home for Christmas, and he now knew that it would be cowardly to put it off any longer. The words came out in a rush, at the end of which he produced the little jewel box with the ring inside and closed her fingers around it.

'Please say you'll wear it, darling Migs! I've loved you ever since . . . ever since you were fifteen, I think; perhaps longer. I want us to be engaged. I won't be able to see you for three months while I'm abroad, and before I go, I must know if you love me . . . enough to get engaged, I mean . . .'

Seeing the expression of dismay on Migs's face, he broke off.

Migs was indeed dismayed. She had been expecting Sebastian might intend to kiss her, which she wouldn't have minded, but a proposal? A ring? She was very, very fond of Sebastian. He had so many good qualities and one of the nicest things about him was that he never boasted about his athleticism in most sports, still less about his rugged good looks and charming smile. But . . .?

Was finding someone so likeable the same as being in love? she asked herself silently. Would she want to spend the rest of her life with him? Fond as she was of him, she was aware they didn't seem to share a lot of interests such as cars, aeroplanes and motorbikes; taking things to bits and putting them together again. Was it necessary to like the same things if you were married to them?

Besides, she reminded herself, what about Douglas? She had seen very little of him since those few days in London in the spring. He had had to go to Edinburgh when his father died suddenly and see to his somewhat complicated financial affairs for his mother. He had written to her two or three times a week – not exactly love letters but stressing how much he longed to see her: how he couldn't wait to return to London when she must agree to see him. He hadn't actually said he had fallen in love with her, but he never failed to end his letters: '*from your devoted admirer, Douglas*'.

Would she, she wondered, still find him so attractive, so

likeable when she saw him again? She wished she could be more certain. It was so different with Sebastian, who she'd known all her life, and with whom she was never shy or self-conscious as she was with Douglas.

Now for the first time in her life she was feeling very ill at ease with Sebastian. Gently, she pushed the unopened box back into his hands and drew a deep, trembling breath before saying:

'Darling Seb, I do love you. I always have but . . . but I don't think it's a getting-married-or-engaged kind of love.' Seeing the look on his face, she added quickly: 'I don't think I'm old enough yet to know my own mind, and it wouldn't be fair to promise . . . to make any promises . . . well, not now . . . not yet.'

After the initial moment of despair, Sebastian now regained a little hope. Although Migs had said she was not sure if she returned his love, at least she had indicated that it could possibly happen in the future.

'You do believe I love you, don't you?' he said urgently. 'I think I always will. Promise me you will think about me . . . us . . . when I'm away?'

He sounded so unhappy Migs said quickly:

'But of course I will, darling Seb, and I'll write to you, and really, three months is not so very long.'

'It will seem so to me if I have to go that long without seeing you,' was Sebastian's reply.

They walked back to the house in silence, each wrapped in their own thoughts, the little box burning a hole in Sebastian's pocket. The memory of the wonderful Christmas gift from his parents did restore a little of his earlier happiness, but he only really felt better when Georgia, on being told the reason for the failure of his mission, reminded him cheerfully:

'Absence makes the heart grow fonder, Seb. Everyone says so! Maybe Migs will miss you so much when you go away next month, she will be really keen to get engaged to you when you come home.'

On Boxing Day, Sebastian drove Georgia down to Shoreham to look at his Christmas present. To his great disappointment, Migs had declined to go with them, saying she was afraid to fly in an aeroplane.

Georgia had done her best to reassure her.

'You really don't need to be scared,' she had volunteered. 'Just think of that woman, Jean Batten, who flew all by herself almost two thousand miles to Brazil. So you see, you'd hardly be in any danger just flying round the airfield: and what about Amy Johnson? I read all about her in a newspaper last summer when she broke a record for flying to South Africa.'

Miraculously, the dull cloudy weather that had pervaded throughout the month had given way to a cold but beautiful sunny day. There on the grass airfield stood the little two-seater Gipsy Moth with its standard silver wings sparkling in the sunlight, and enhancing its bright red fuselage. As Georgia started to walk towards it a similar little aeroplane with a blue fuselage took off and soared up into the sky. Her face was radiant with excitement.

'Are we going now? Can I get in?' she asked eagerly.

'I have to report my arrival and then give her a pre-flight check,' Sebastian told her as he patted the side of the fuselage. 'I expect the works will be the same as in the Moth I trained on. I'll be able to start teaching you to fly now, Jo-Jo. Maybe we can even get in a lesson or two before I leave.'

'I must give her a name!' he said excitedly as they walked to the control tower to report his arrival. It was not long before he was helping Georgia to put on the helmet and goggles she would need and then assisting her into the seat behind the cockpit.

He started the engine, gave it a quick run-up and checked the magnetos. Having had a green light from the tower, he bumped away across the grass. As the aircraft gathered speed, he applied gentle pressure to the control column and took off, climbing slowly into the sky. He was by now a competent pilot and Georgia had complete trust in him as he circled above the airfield. Occasionally he would talk to her through the Gosport tube attached to her helmet.

Half an hour later, he guided the Gipsy Moth down onto the airstrip where they bumped over the grass once more and came to a halt a short distance from the building.

Georgia was breathless with excitement as Sebastian helped her out of her seat, and asked him how soon he could take her up again? How soon could she have a lesson? How long would it take for her to fly solo? Would she be allowed to do so as she was only sixteen? She was still chattering about the experience as Sebastian drove her back to Deerswood. He stayed only long enough for tea before going home to start sorting out what he might need when he went to Switzerland. Although he was not actually leaving the country until the beginning of January, he was leaving home in the morning to stay with Monty, whose family were hosting a New Year's Eve ball.

He was particularly looking forward to it knowing that Migs would be there. He would, he planned, have a chance to monopolise her, and in the romantic setting of the festive ballroom, she might decide that she did love him enough to get secretly engaged.

CHAPTER SEVEN

1936–1937

Although traditionally Douglas would have – if at all possible – spent New Year's Eve in Scotland for the Hogmanay celebrations, his family were in no mood for festivities, so he was able at last to return to London.

Having learned in Migs's last letter that she had been invited to the Montgomerys' New Year's Eve ball, immediately on reaching London he paid a visit to his godfather, the elderly Brigadier Montgomery, who had been in the same regiment as his father. Meeting Migs for lunch the day before the party, Douglas said:

'I told him I was back in London on leave and desperately wanted an invitation because you would be there.'

Ignoring Migs's blushes, he continued:

'My godfather said he would be only too happy if I went along, as his wife was having trouble finding enough eligible young men to partner the girls!' Douglas' voice deepened as he added urgently: 'You will save lots of dances for me, Margaret, won't you? And I shall insist upon holding your hand as we sing "Auld Lang Syne" at midnight.'

Migs felt a thrill of anticipation. Not only was this her first grown-up New Year's Eve party, but now quite unexpectedly Douglas was going to be there. Moreover she was flattered by his determination to be so.

The next evening, she was torn between nervousness and excitement as one of the maids helped her into her pale blue silk evening dress. It had diamond-shaped net inserts in the full skirt, revealing a cream under dress that swirled round her ankles as she twisted in front of the mirror.

'You look absolutely gorgeous,' her friend Pamela said, as she came into Migs's bedroom. She then added with a smile: 'See what has just arrived for you? Not roses this time but a lovely corsage – an orchid, darling, which will look divine on your dress.' Migs blushed, well aware that she was trying to make herself look beautiful to attract Douglas.

Half an hour later, the taxi deposited her at the Montgomerys' house and a maid showed her to a bedroom where she could leave her velvet cloak. Not knowing any of the other guests who were titivating their hair or adding rouge to their cheeks, she took a last anxious look in the mirror and left the room to go downstairs.

Descending the wide staircase she saw a tall figure in the hall below, and believing it to be Douglas, her heart missed a beat. Then, as he turned round and she could see his face, she realised it was not Douglas but Sebastian. He was looking older, more sophisticated than usual as, immaculate in white tie and tails, he stepped towards her with his arms outstretched. The familiar, affectionate smile was on his face and she felt herself relaxing. She had no need to feel shy or nervous with Sebastian, who was like a very dear brother to her; but then, as he stood staring at her intently, his expression totally serious, and told her how beautiful she looked, she remembered the Christmas afternoon in the cricket pavilion when he'd told her he wanted far more than to be loved like a brother.

'The dancing has started,' he said, 'and I'm determined to have the first dance with you – and the last if I can.'

With growing unease, Migs refrained from saying she was hoping to have the last dance before the arrival of the New Year with Douglas, who she now saw approaching from the ballroom. He was in his scarlet regimental dress uniform. He glanced briefly at Sebastian and, excusing his interruption, asked Migs if he could have the next dance. She only just had time to hand him her dance card to mark before Sebastian dragged her away into the ballroom.

'So who was the fancy-dressed soldier boy?' he asked

dismissively as he guided her onto the dance floor. 'Don't think I know him, do I?'

'He's . . . he's a friend I met at Rose and Lily's launch party, well before it, actually,' she replied, conscious of a blush rising to her cheeks as she spoke. 'It's a bit complicated.' Aware she was now stammering, she broke off before explaining any further.

Sebastian stopped dancing and drew her to the side of the room away from the sound of the band.

'Not that chap Jo-Jo told me about who tried to nab your taxi?' he asked, his tone harshened by jealousy.

'He didn't try to steal the taxi,' Migs said weakly. 'Please, Seb, let's finish our dance. It'll be over soon if we stay here!'

Sebastian's scowl deepened.

'So you can get it over and dance with that . . . that popinjay, I suppose!' he said childishly. 'I saw the way he was looking at you, and you . . . you were blushing as if . . . as if . . .' He ceased talking, aware suddenly that he was behaving not only badly but stupidly. Of course the wretched fellow was going to look at Migs as if she was the most beautiful girl he'd ever seen! Of course Migs was blushing, which he knew perfectly well she did whenever she was embarrassed. His own behaviour was hardly likely to endear himself to her.

With a muttered apology he led her back onto the dance floor where the band was playing one of the new popular songs – 'Thanks for the Memory' – and drawing her close to him, he asked her to forgive him for being so stupid.

But he hadn't been stupid, Migs thought. His behaviour had quite suddenly clarified her feelings – nor for him, but for Douglas. She would always love Sebastian, but it was not the way that she now knew she was falling in love with Douglas. As Douglas had remarked in one of his letters, they enjoyed doing the same things; were never at odds with one another, and he wanted nothing more than to enjoy her company. He was the one person in the room with whom she wanted to be on this special evening.

No sooner had the music stopped and the dance ended than she saw Douglas coming towards her. In the brief moment while the two men stood side by side, she noted that Sebastian was quite a lot taller, even more handsome than Douglas, more vibrant, but it did not alter her new-found certainty that it was Douglas who had somehow found his way to her heart.

With a poise he had not known he possessed, Sebastian talked pleasantries to the man he sensed was his rival, and excusing himself, left the ballroom as the band struck up a slow foxtrot.

'Shall we?' Douglas said to Migs. 'As you know, I'm not the best dancer in the world, but I'll try not to tread on your toes.'

Holding her close to him as they danced, his tone of voice deepened as he told her that she looked stunningly pretty and that there was no one in the whole world with whom he would rather be celebrating this New Year's Eve.

'I couldn't stop thinking about you all the time I was in Scotland. I love you, dearest Margaret!' he whispered in her ear as the dance came to an end. He drew her into the comparative privacy of the conservatory where, without preamble, he went down on one knee and proposed to her, his voice husky with a mixture of anxiety, passion and hope as he ended by saying:

'I know it's terribly soon to be talking like this, but my posting has come through and I'll be going to India in twelve weeks' time. I don't want to go without you, Margaret. I couldn't bear to spend the next two years without even a chance to see you. Say you will marry me. I swear I'll do everything within my power to make you happy. I love you so very much.'

Feeling his arms enfolding her, hearing his voice vibrant with sincerity, Migs felt a curious emotion – in part anxiety, in part euphoria. She had no doubt that Douglas loved her, and she was more or less certain that she had fallen in love with him: but the anxiety was there, too, when after having been kissed passionately by Douglas a second time, he said that he would be leaving by boat for India at the beginning of March and that they must get married just as soon as it was possible to arrange it.

Encouraged by her silence, he continued to outline his hopes for their future together. She would, he told her, need time to buy clothes suitable for the very hot weather. They would live in comfortable married quarters and they would have as many servants as she wished, as well as his batman to look after them.

'There'll be garden parties and dances, tattoos, polo matches to watch and because you're so beautiful, my darling, you'll always be the most welcome of visitors to the Officers Club . . .' He broke off and stared down at her anxiously:

'You will come with me, dearest Margaret? I haven't said anything to put you off, have I?'

Remembering the dull routine of home life and the domestic science college, and comparing it with the life Douglas was describing, Migs thought it sounded tremendously exciting but at the same time she felt more than a little anxious at the thought of living so far from the security and devotion of her parents. Despite reminding herself that Douglas was a man of thirty who would know how to take care of her, she remained uncertain, not whether she loved him but whether she loved him enough to be his wife.

Only then did her customary common sense prevail.

'Douglas, I'm very honoured that you have asked me to marry you,' she said, 'but you haven't even met my parents, nor have I come of age. They're bound to say I'm much too young to think of marrying someone they don't know!'

Douglas was undeterred.

'I had thought of that, dearest Margaret,' he said. 'So don't you think that the sooner I meet them, the better?'

As he kissed her once more in the privacy of the conservatory, Migs began to feel more certain of herself. Douglas was right – she must take him home to meet her parents as soon as possible.

'I know it's very short notice,' she told him shyly, 'but would you be able to come home with me next weekend? I know Mummy and Daddy won't agree to me getting married, but I'm nineteen now so they may allow us to get engaged, and if you still wanted to, we could get married when you came home on your next leave.'

Douglas forbore to say that a long engagement was very far from what he intended, and moreover, that he had perforce pursued his courtship far too quickly.

It was with considerable anxiety that on the following Saturday morning, he borrowed a fellow officer's Alvis and drove down to Deerswood. He hoped very much that Migs had carried out her promise to explain the necessity for his untimely proposal. He had little doubt that without her parents' consent, his darling girl would not agree to marry him at such short notice.

At his first meeting with the family, he and Gerald hit it off at once, both being keen golfers and rugby enthusiasts. Mrs Driffield remained quite distant, saying no more to him than was required of a hostess. He was also uncomfortably aware that Margaret's young sister, Georgia, was doing her best not to make things easier for him. She seemed to argue with every point of view he expressed but he could see no direct cause for her antipathy.

Migs was also aware of it, but it was not until later that evening that she learned the reason for her sister's hostility.

'You can't possibly marry that man, he's a POM!' Georgia declared violently when she went to Migs's bedroom to say goodnight. Migs frowned at Georgia's use of their childish abbreviation, invented – needless to say – by Sebastian for use when they thought one or other of the grown-ups' male friends was a 'Pompous Old Man!' 'You can't possibly want to marry him!' she repeated. 'What about Seb? You know how much he loves you and you said you thought you might be in love with him.'

'Well, I didn't say that – only that I loved him as . . . as a brother,' Migs replied with unusual sharpness. 'What I feel for Douglas is quite, quite different.'

Georgia scowled.

'Well, you can't possibly want to marry an ordinary soldier rather than Seb,' she said. 'You promised . . .'

'No, I didn't and Douglas is not ordinary!' Migs defended Douglas, although deep down she thought that quite possibly in a way he was, and Georgia's antipathy to Douglas only served to strengthen her own certainty that she was in love with him, and that she would be quite devastated if he went off to India without her.

Although Gerald had taken a genuine liking to Douglas, he'd not been prepared to allow him to marry Migs and take her out to India in March.

'That's quite out of the question, my boy!' he'd said as they had driven back to the house from the golf club. 'An engagement, yes! But you have only known each other a few months. I'm afraid we could never agree to it.'

Isobel was both shocked and appalled.

'How dare he presume such a thing?' she said that evening as she followed Gerald into his study. 'He's a complete stranger. I simply don't understand it. Migs has always been so sensible, such a gentle, compliant child.'

She gave way to completely unaccustomed tears.

'We've always been so close!' she wept. 'I can't understand why she didn't confide in me when she first met this man.'

'Well, she invited him down this weekend,' Gerald broke in in an attempt to calm her. 'To be fair, I think he's a very nice chap, and he seems genuine enough.'

Isobel blew her nose and snorted angrily:

'She's far too young, Gerald! How can she possibly know her own mind? And anyway, we always thought she would end up marrying Sebastian. You know how fond of each other they've always been, and he has always adored her.'

'Yes, my dear, I know both the girls adore him, as you put it, but that is not to say Migs was ever in love with him, is it?' He put his arm round her shoulders, adding: 'Have you forgotten that you were only nineteen when you married me? Migs will be twenty in February, and if *you* knew your own mind at that age, Migs might well be capable of deciding whether or not she does wish to marry this man.'

'So you're going to allow her to get married, go off to India of all places, thousands of miles away where we'll never see her?' Isobel cried.

Seeing the look of horror on his wife's face, Gerald said: 'What I think we have to bear in mind, my dear, is if we were to forbid the pair of them getting married before McPherson returns to his regiment, which, I might say, is what I would want if I were in his shoes, Migs might elope with the fellow without our blessing.'

Hearing his wife's gasp, he said gently:

'Migs is not as hare-brained as our Georgia. She is a sensible girl, and I am prepared to believe her if she tells me she has no doubt that she loves this man and is certain that she would be happy married to him.'

Knowing his wife as well as he did and her passion for organising things, he now suggested she stopped wondering what might happen and set about making contingency plans in case there was to be a last-minute wedding, something he knew she would enjoy doing.

He did not add, although he nearly did, that his wife would have Georgia to comfort her if Migs departed. The poor child had always been a thorn in her flesh although she did her best to hide it.

Before Douglas returned to London, Migs asked if she could speak to her father alone in his study. He was seated at his desk and she went round behind him and placed her hands on his shoulders.

'I realise it's frightfully sudden, Daddy, and I almost don't believe it myself. But whenever I think of Douglas going to India without me, I know I couldn't bear it. Please, please, let me marry him. Please, Daddy!'

Reaching up behind his head, Gerald put his hands over hers. He loved this child as deeply as Isobel did. He was suddenly reminded of his own feelings twenty-one years ago in the war. His mind made up, he decided then and there that in spite of his own and Isobel's misgivings, he should give his consent if it was what his darling girl really wanted.

As for Georgia, aware as he was of her conviction that Migs would marry Sebastian, he hoped she would not take her sister's engagement too unhappily, and blame him for allowing the marriage. That would indeed jeopardise his hope to re-establish their former close rapport.

It was no surprise to him, therefore, when after Douglas had departed, Georgia came storming into his study.

Her eyes narrowed, her cheeks flushed, Georgia said:

'Migs says she is going to marry that man and she might go to India with him, and you've said she can if it's what she wants!'

Before Gerald could reply, she said angrily 'If Seb was here, he wouldn't allow it. That man can't possibly love her as much as Seb does. He's loved her for years and anyway, you don't know anything about that man, do you, and he might be a . . . a . . .' she sought desperately for a suitable derogatory adjective but failed to find one, '. . . well, a bounder,' she said, uncomfortably aware that a captain in the army was highly unlikely to be a reprobate, 'and she'll wish she never got married and be terribly unhappy, and it will be your fault!'

Almost out of breath, she finally stopped talking. Gerald was now uncomfortably aware that it would indeed be his fault if the marriage did turn out to be an unhappy one. He sighed, realising suddenly that parents could not always safeguard their children throughout their lives. Hoping to comfort Georgia he said:

'I don't think you need worry about Sebastian, darling, he's young enough to get over his disappointment if your fears are justified, and I'll wager it won't be long before a good-looking chap like he is will find himself another girl who cares even more about him than Migs!'

He knew at once that he had, with whatever good intention, only made matters worse. His daughter's eyes flashing, she turned towards the study door, saying in a cold, accusing voice:

'You don't understand about anyone's feelings, do you? You always said you really liked Seb but you just don't care how much you let him be hurt. You probably don't really care what happens to Migs either or you'd never, ever, let her go and marry that man.' Her voice now rose to a higher pitch as her feelings got the better of her. With one hand on the now open door, she stared directly at her father and said:

'You don't really understand anything, do you? You didn't understand about me either. And I just wonder why Mummy ever wanted to marry you!'

The remark was so unexpected, so irrelevant, that Gerald leant back in his chair, and, staring at Georgia's defiant back as she left the room, he didn't know whether to laugh or cry.

CHAPTER EIGHT

1937

Clarissa Driffield was filling the little bird feeder outside her kitchen window when, to her astonishment, she saw Georgia hurrying up the path to the front door. Her misgivings intensified as she saw her granddaughter's woeful expression.

'Darling, how lovely to see you!' She gave her usual greeting. 'You look frozen. Come into the kitchen; it's beautifully warm in there. Then you can tell me what has brought you here.'

Georgia followed her grandmother into the small kitchen where an old-fashioned range was winning the battle with the bitterly cold January day. A casserole on the top gave out a delicious smell. Despite the urgency of her visit, she was suddenly ravenous.

Seeing her gaze, Clarissa said smiling:

'Sit down, my darling, and tell me what has upset you.'

Georgia felt some of the tension leave her body as she removed her overcoat and gloves and sat down on the milking stool in front of her grandmother's rocker.

'It's Migs!' she blurted out. 'She's going to get married to a silly old army captain who she has only just met, and she's sort of half engaged to Seb – well, not exactly but I know he wants to marry her . . .' She paused for breath before adding: 'I've got to warn him, Granny, so he can come home and stop her marrying this stranger!'

Clarissa was more than a little surprised by the news that Gerald and Isobel had given their permission for Migs to marry a man who she had only met recently. An old proverb now came into her mind: 'Marry in haste and repent at leisure.' She could now well understand Georgia's anxiety.

Clarissa looked at her granddaughter's flushed cheeks and trusting expression, and wondered how she should deal with this situation. In principle, she should support Gerald's and Isobel's discipline, and they would most definitely NOT condone Georgia sending a telegram to Sebastian in Lausanne telling him to come home! Gerald had not as yet seen fit to advise her, his mother, of his elder daughter's impending marriage. As far as she knew, Migs was not even engaged.

Could the child possibly be pregnant? she asked herself, but rejected the suspicion immediately. Migs was not a hot-headed passionate young thing who would ever contemplate such unorthodox behaviour as to allow for such a possibility.

'We've got to let Seb know so he can come home and stop it all happening,' Georgia repeated. 'Don't you see, Granny, Migs can't possibly want to marry this Douglas man. She only met him a few months ago. Anyway, Seb is going to marry her – well, when he's a bit older. He bought her a ring before he went off to Switzerland. So you see, we've just got to tell him Migs is about to make a terrible mistake so he can come back and stop it before it's too late.'

Clarissa drew a deep breath as Georgia's indignant tone of voice gradually ground to a halt. How was she to explain to this passionate, impulsive granddaughter that it was not for her to try to control other people's emotions? She knew very well how fond Georgia was of Sebastian and that he'd developed a crush on Migs.

With a deep sigh she looked at the unhappy girl opposite her.

'Georgia, I will allow you to send Sebastian a telegram if you really think it wise to do so. I don't doubt that he loves Migs but clearly she is not in love with him or she wouldn't be wanting to marry someone else.'

Georgia looked at her grandmother, her face stormy.

'You don't understand, Granny. Seb told me all about him

and Migs. She didn't actually say she would never marry him and I know he felt there was a good chance that she would agree to get engaged when he gets back from Switzerland. That's why he bought her that ring. He does love her, I know he does! Please, Granny, please, please let me send him a telegram. Even if you're right and him coming home won't alter anything, at least he'll have had a chance to talk to Migs before . . . before she gets married to someone else.'

Clarissa now took a moment of time to consider Georgia's request. Maybe, she thought, the telegram Georgia wished to send Sebastian could do no harm. However hurtful the poor boy might find the news, the sooner he came to terms with the facts, the better it would be for his future happiness. In any event, unlike Georgia, she did not believe for one moment that he would come racing back to England in the hope of changing Migs's mind.

'Let's have lunch, Georgia dear, and talk more about this after we have eaten,' she said. 'Another hour or two won't make any difference, will it?'

As Georgia sat down to enjoy the meal with her grandmother, she began to feel a little calmer. She realised how devastated Sebastian would be when he received her telegram, and she had no doubt he would immediately come home. Maybe then, when Migs saw him, she would suddenly realise that she didn't love the army captain after all. Maybe . . .

Before Clarissa drove Georgia home in her little green Austin Seven, she allowed her to dictate a telegram to the telephone operator, wondering what effect it would have upon him. He was nineteen years old, which was surely old enough to know that with the wedding only two months away, it would be better for him to stay where he was and lick his wounds in private.

She would have been even more anxious had she known Sebastian's nature as well as Georgia. Forty-eight hours after receiving Georgia's telegram he arrived at Deerswood and asked their parlourmaid, Polly, who opened the door to him, where he would find Migs.

Gerald had been in his study when he heard Sebastian's voice in the hall. He got out of his armchair and went out to greet him.

'Thought you were in Switzerland, old chap!' he said, taking Sebastian's arm and leading him into the drawing room. As he turned to face him, he decided that it would not be tactful to point out to the young man that he was very much in need of a haircut, and his Harris tweed jacket and trousers looked as if he had slept in them!

'Heard you telling Polly you wanted to talk to Migs,' he said, 'but she's upstairs having a fitting for her wedding dress. You heard about the wedding, did you?'

Sebastian nodded, and Gerald went across to the table by the window and took the top off the decanter of sherry.

'Expect you'd rather have this than tea!' he said, handing a filled glass to Sebastian. 'Georgia's having her bridesmaid's dress fitted. Place has been in an uproar ever since Migs dropped the bombshell on us that she was off to India in a few weeks' time! Nice fellow, though, McPherson. Regular army, so he'll be able to support her all right. You haven't met him, have you?'

Sebastian shook his head.

'No, sir! I've been up at Cambridge . . .'

Their conversation was now interrupted by the entrance of Polly, who looked apologetically at Gerald.

'Beg pardon, sir, but Miss Margaret's dressmaker is just leaving and Miss Margaret says as how she'll be down directly.'

Sebastian rose clumsily to his feet and nearly spilled his sherry in the process. Gerald, guessing that the two young people might wish to be alone, muttered about having work to do in his study, and left the room.

This is my last chance, Sebastian told himself as the girl he adored came in. It was inconceivable that she should marry anyone else. A captain in the army could afford to get married, whereas he still had two more years of study before he could get his degree. Was there a possibility, as Georgia seemed to think, that he could persuade Migs to cancel her wedding and wait for him?

Such hopes as Sebastian might have were dashed by the very first words Migs spoke when she came into the room, looking radiantly pretty. She was wearing a heather-coloured frock with a cross-over top, which fitted tightly over her slim figure. Her silky fair hair was sleek on top of her head, with curls framing her face in a way that made her look different from the girl he'd left behind a short while ago.

'I'm so sorry, Seb!' she was saying as they sat down side by side on the sofa. 'I should have written and told you about my engagement to Douglas, but somehow so much has happened in such a short time. Mummy tells everyone I was swept off my feet! I suppose I was.'

Sebastian cleared the lump in his throat as he reached out and imprisoned her two hands in his.

'Are you absolutely sure, Migs? I mean that you really do love the chap? I thought . . . I hoped . . . well, that one day you and I . . .' He broke off before saying urgently: 'I suppose it's too late for you to change your mind?' The words now started to come out in a rush. 'I love you, Migs. I always have and I always will. Please, please say it isn't too late? People do break engagements just before a wedding . . . when they suddenly realise they don't want to get married, and . . .'

Migs' voice was quiet but forceful as she broke in.

'Please don't go on, Seb. I do love Douglas! I think I fell in love with him the day we met. It may sound crazy to you and maybe to everyone else, but I'm absolutely certain I do want to marry him. I'm so sorry, Seb!' she added, drawing her hands gently out of his grasp. 'I'm sorry if I let you think that one day you and I . . . I've always been so very fond of you. I sometimes thought what I felt *was* love, but this is different. I didn't know the difference until I fell in love with Douglas. You'll find someone else, Seb, I know you will!

Someone who you'll probably love much more than you ever loved me.'

'Never!' Sebastian declared. 'Never! I shall never marry anyone else.' His voice husky with emotion, he added: 'I hope you'll be happy Migs – and I mean that.'

Tears threatening behind her eyes, Migs pleaded:

'You will come to my wedding? I so much want you to meet Douglas. You'll like him, I know you will, and you'll understand why I'm in love with him. You'll come, won't you, Seb? Promise?'

She was digging the knife even deeper into his heart by her request, Sebastian thought bitterly. How could he bear to sit in the church and hear her voice promising to love and cherish another man?

'I'll have to go now.' He spoke the lie as calmly as he could. Glancing unnecessarily at his watch he added: 'Sorry to rush like this, Migs, but it's time I was off. I'm staying with old Monty in town and he's expecting me for lunch. We're doing a show with a couple of girls he knows. Should be fun!'

Whether or not Migs guessed he was lying did not seem to matter. Deep down in his heart, ever since he had received Georgia's desperate telegram, he had known that there was hardly even a glimmer of hope.

Suddenly she leant forward and kissed him, her eyes sad.

'I'll always love you, Seb. Always! And I'm so sorry it's just not the way you wanted.'

Knowing as he drew away from her that his misery was so intense he might all too easily weep, he hurried out of the room into the hall, and without turning to look at her again, grabbed his overcoat and all but ran out of the house.

Standing in the road outside his own home, he realised that he would have to stay somewhere as Monty was at college. Certain now that he would not go home, he decided to return to London and visit the twins. He could have supper with them before catching the night train. When he reached Victoria

Station he would book himself on an overnight sleeper to Geneva.

When Rose and Lily had got over their surprise at seeing him walk into their shop, they noted his crumpled clothing and unhappy face and realised something was obviously very wrong. If Sebastian wanted them to know about it, they supposed he would tell them when the shop closed later that day.

Giving Sebastian the key to their mews cottage, they told him to make himself at home. When he explained that he had been travelling the previous night, Rose suggested he should have a nap and a bath and a shave if he wished. That evening they would go round to a French restaurant they knew in High Street Kensington.

'We go there regularly,' Lily said.

'. . . because we don't like cooking!' Rose explained, 'and we're usually too tired to be bothered at the end of a busy day to feed ourselves.'

Leading him to the little kitchenette behind the showroom, she made him a cup of coffee. As he was still unusually silent, she continued to chat as he drank it.

'Our shop is doing frightfully well!' she said. 'We've already had advance bookings for some of the Coronation parties, although it isn't until May!'

In the cheerful, optimistic company of the twins, Sebastian felt a little less forlorn. He took their advice and, much to his surprise, actually managed to have a sleep, and they had no difficulty persuading him to accompany them that evening. He was uncomfortably aware that he was starving. Too filled with anxiety and trepidation, he'd had no breakfast on the train journey to London, although it had a Pullman dining car. All he had thought about was getting to see Migs as quickly as possible.

Before leaving their cottage, he explained the reason for his sudden appearance from Switzerland. They understood completely his distress but were nevertheless obliged to give him a reply when he asked what they thought of his rival. Their honesty forbade anything but the truth – that he seemed a very pleasant fellow, and it was obvious Migs was really smitten. Sebastian did his utmost to hide his misery, knowing as he now did that there was absolutely no reason why Migs might change her mind at the eleventh hour.

Now, as the three of them sat down at the table in the restaurant that, Rose said, was always reserved for them, the charming French owner arrived and, with a theatrical flourish, placed a carafe of red wine on their table along with the menus.

'Pierre always does that!' Rose whispered to Sebastian. 'They spoil us terribly here!'

'Because we're such jolly good customers,' Lily added.

They were trying to decide on their meals when Sebastian heard a deep-throated laugh from a neighbouring table. It was a laugh he would have recognised anywhere and he turned to see one of his university friends sitting nearby with another undergraduate who was unknown to him.

'It's a chap I know called Jumbo!' he told the twins. 'Will you excuse me for a moment while I go and have a word with him?'

Many years later, Sebastian was to remember that evening and how a chance meeting, in an unknown restaurant on an unscheduled day, had been instrumental in changing his life. Jumbo's and his friend's political leanings were, like many other undergraduates, strongly anti-Fascist. They had all been watching, with growing unease, the Fascists' progress in Spain where a civil war was raging. Ever since last summer the Fascist army, led by General Franco and his generals, had been fighting the Spanish Republican government troops. With their superior armaments and experience, they were steadily overcoming the Republican resistance.

The previous autumn, Jumbo and many other undergraduates had joined the hundred thousand protesters who had gathered in London to build barricades to prevent the seven thousand black-shirted Fascists led by Oswald Mosley, from marching through the working-class districts. Jumbo had described the furious and violent battle that had taken place in Cable Street, and how he had been badly bruised by a thrown brick.

He now explained that when he and his friend, who he now introduced as Fergus, read the news of the Republican militia being overwhelmed by the Fascists in their defence of Madrid, they had decided it was time to postpone getting their degrees and offer such assistance as they were able to give to the Republicans. Despite the embargo the government had imposed on the many British volunteers going to help the Republicans, a large number of young men like themselves had nevertheless done so, and had made their way from France over the Pyrenees into Spain. There they had joined the International Brigade.

'It's why we're here in town,' Jumbo explained. 'We know that a number of English chaps have been captured and imprisoned, and a hell of a lot of them have died, so we feel it's our duty to go and offer what help we can. We're catching the train to Paris later this evening and then we're going to travel south across France and into Spain – do what we can to help oust the invaders. If you've nothing better to do, why don't you join us?'

It took less than a quarter of an hour for Sebastian to make up his mind to go with them. His passport was still in his pocket, and he already had his ticket to Paris. He could send a telegram to his college in Switzerland and tell them he wouldn't be returning. There was nothing – nothing whatever – to stop him going to Spain instead; nothing to keep him in England, and it had the added benefit of getting him out of attending Migs's wedding, which he knew his parents would expect him to do. Best of all, he would be gone before they could do anything to stop him. It would not only be an adventure, but above all it would be an escape, a way to help him forget the unbearable pain in his heart.

He told the twins that he intended joining Jumbo and his friend, and begged them not to inform his parents of his intentions for at least a week. Despite their protests, he then scribbled a quick note for them to give Georgia on the back of a menu, saying:

'Thanks for trying, Jo-Jo, but it was too late. I'll try and send you a postcard from Spain . . . Seb.'

Then he quickly forgot her and an hour later joined his friends in the waiting taxi and began the first, and what was to prove the only, safe leg of his journey to Spain.

CHAPTER NINE

1937

It was a chilly Saturday afternoon and other than Cook and Polly who were downstairs in the kitchen, Georgia was alone in the house. Isobel was not yet back from her bridge afternoon and Gerald was entertaining a friend at the golf club. Migs, too, was absent, having gone up to London to the Savoy where Douglas was hosting a lunch party for his mother, sister and grandparents who had all come down from Edinburgh in order to meet his fiancée.

Although she had been delighted when her mother had agreed that she should have a term away from her Swiss school, as she hoped that even at this last minute she might be able to get the wedding cancelled – or at least postponed – she was not enjoying the agreed holiday. Not only was she alone, she thought unhappily, but she hadn't received even one postcard from Sebastian who was fighting a war in Spain and might even be dead! The only way she could divest herself of such horrible thoughts was to lose herself in a book. She was therefore curled up on the sofa in the drawing room in front of a glowing fire, and so immersed in a wonderful new book called *Gone With the Wind* that she did not hear the front door bell ringing.

Polly's voice as she came hurrying into the room brought her back to reality. The young maid looked flustered, and sounded even more so as she spoke.

'It's Mr Peters, the taxi driver from the station, Miss Georgia! He's brought Miss Margaret home and he wants paying and something's wrong with her and will Madam please come, but Madam isn't here and he said to get whoever was at home and . . .'

Georgia scrambled to her feet and, interrupting Polly, she told her to calm down and go downstairs and ask Cook to lend her a shilling.

'The fare can't be more than that,' she said. 'Is Miss Margaret hurt?'

'I don't know, Miss,' the maid replied. 'She's still in the back of the taxi and she's crying and sobbing and . . .'

Georgia didn't wait to hear any more. Pushing past Polly, she hurried out to the hall where Mr Peters, the regular driver of the station taxi, stood twisting his peaked cap between his hands. He was looking both anxious and apologetic as Georgia approached, and he touched his forehead, saying:

'It's not the money, Miss; it's the young lady, her as is your sister. She were crying as she came out of the station and her hasn't stopped since. She wouldn't say as to what was wrong. All her said was for me to take her home and fetch her mother. She won't leave the taxi else.'

With growing concern, Georgia followed him out to the taxi. The passenger door was closed. When she opened it, it was to see Migs hunched up on the seat, her face buried in her hands, her body shaking.

'Migs, it's me, Jo-Jo!' she said, leaning in and touching Migs's shoulder. 'Mummy's not back yet but she will be soon. Are you feeling ill?'

Without replying, Migs turned and gasped between sobs:

'Yes! No! I want Mummy. Please get Mummy!'

She sounded like a very small child who had fallen over and hurt herself. Georgia decided that the quicker she got Migs indoors and up to her room the better. If needs be, she would telephone the doctor. Despite her anxiety, she turned to the open-eyed maid saying in as calm a voice as she could manage:

'Give Mr Peters the money and then help me get Miss

Margaret upstairs. Please keep the change, Mr Peters: you've been very kind.'

Her arms embracing Migs's shaking shoulders, she managed to pull her out of the taxi, only then noting how crumpled was the beautifully tailored coat and skirt she had worn up to London, how tangled her fair hair. There was no sign of her hat although the taxi driver followed them into the hall and gave Polly Migs's smart crocodile handbag and gloves before deciding his passenger was now in safe hands and he could depart.

Once in her bedroom, Migs refused quite emphatically to let Georgia or the maid undress her. Georgia sent Polly off to fill a hot-water bottle and managed to settle Migs in the bed beneath her pink eiderdown. She had stopped crying but was shivering violently.

'Have you been sick, Migs?' Georgia asked. 'Shall I call Doctor Mayhew?'

Migs grasped Georgia's hands, gripping them fiercely as she whispered:

'No, no! I don't want to see him. I don't want to see anyone. I want Mummy. Please get Mummy!'

Now even more deeply concerned, Georgia went downstairs to see if she could find in the address book the telephone number of the friends with whom her mother was playing bridge. It was some minutes before she succeeded and another few minutes more before her call was answered. While she waited, her mind was working furiously. What could have happened? Their mother had put Migs safely on the London train that morning and Douglas was meeting her at Victoria Station. If he had failed to find her, he would most certainly have telephoned them to say so. Migs had so been looking forward to meeting her new relatives and had shown no sign of nerves at the prospect. So what else could have happened to upset her so dreadfully? Had Douglas's family been nasty to her? Had he and Migs quarrelled? Worse still, was she seriously ill?

Greatly relieved when Isobel said she would come home at once, Georgia returned to Migs's room where she found her sister huddled under the eiderdown, her face turned to the wall. She seemed to have stopped crying but was still shivering violently.

As she sat quietly by the bedside waiting for her mother's return, a sudden thought struck her: had Douglas broken off their engagement? Was the wedding next month to be cancelled? Supposing his relatives had not liked Migs and said they wanted him to marry a nice Scottish girl and not a southerner? However unlikely that explanation was, it would account for Migs's distress. She'd been really soppy about Douglas ever since she'd met him and they were quite sickeningly lovey-dovey whenever she had seen them together, holding hands and gazing up into each other's eyes and spending hours discussing their wedding and the life they would share when they were married.

Her concerns were brought to a halt as she heard her mother's voice in the hall. Going out to the landing to greet her, Georgia whispered the few facts about Migs's extraordinary arrival home. Together they went into the bedroom, and hearing her mother's voice Migs turned round to look at her, her pretty face ravaged by tears.

When Isobel hurried to the bedside and gathered Migs in her arms, Georgia decided that it would be best if she absented herself since Migs had not wanted to tell her what was wrong.

Downstairs Polly was on her knees in the drawing room putting fresh coal on the fire.

'Is Miss Margaret all right, Miss?' she asked as she stood up, wiping her hands on her apron.

Georgia sank into the nearest armchair, frowning.

'I don't think so, Polly,' she said in a worried tone. 'She wouldn't talk to me so I don't know what has happened.'

Polly clasped her hands together, a faint colour staining her cheeks as she said:

''Afore Cook went off for her afternoon nap, she said as how she thought Miss Margaret might've been interfered with.'

Georgia's frown deepened.

'What do you mean, interfered with?' she asked.

Nearly as innocent as Georgia, Polly blurted out:

'Well, I asked Cook and she said . . .' she gave an embarrassed little shrug of her shoulders. 'She said it meant interfering with your privates.'

'With what?' Georgia asked.

Polly looked even more embarrassed.

'Well, Miss, Cook wouldn't say no more. She said as how I'd know all about such things when I was properly growed up.'

Georgia sighed sympathetically.

'That's exactly the answer I get whenever I ask Mummy questions.'

'I dare say it's something like our monthlies,' Polly said. 'No one told me afore it happened to me and I got ever such a fright.'

The conversation was halted as the back door bell rang and Polly hurried away to answer it. Georgia's thoughts returned to her sister once more. Her mother was still upstairs, so she sat down at the foot of the stairs to wait, wishing as always that Sebastian was home and she could ask his opinion as to what might be wrong.

Isobel was white-faced as she sat down by her daughter's bedside. She had so very rarely seen Migs even mildly upset that she was finding the sight of her daughter's distress quite shocking. She helped her gently into a sitting position and with growing concern, stroked the damp hair back from her beloved daughter's tear-streaked face.

'There now, darling, Mummy's here!' she said as if Migs was only five years old. 'You must tell me what has upset you so we can put it right.' As there was no reply, she added softly: 'Is it Douglas, darling? Have you had a little quarrel?

I thought he was going to bring you home after the lunch party.'

For a few moments, Migs appeared to be struggling to speak, then the words poured from her in a long, continuous stream.

'He couldn't come with me . . . he's been called back by his regiment . . . he put me in the train at Victoria . . .' Her voice now changed to a wail: 'He'll never marry me now! I can never marry him now!'

With the wedding only four weeks away, and over fifty acceptances already received, Isobel was shocked into momentary silence. Then, recovering her equilibrium, she said firmly:

'You know that's nonsense, darling. Of course you're going to marry Douglas. Now, if the pair of you have had a little tiff, that's not to be surprised at. Lots of brides – and bridegrooms – start panicking just before a wedding. As for Douglas not wanting to marry you, I never heard so much nonsense in my life. You know perfectly well he adores you and . . .'

Migs's anguished cry halted her attempt to be reassuring.

'You don't understand, Mummy. I *can't* marry him now. He wouldn't want me to be his wife if he knew . . . if he knew . . .'

With increasing unease, Isobel did her best to speak calmly.

'Knew what, my darling? Did you say something unkind, nasty to him? About his relatives, perhaps? Whatever has happened to cause this upset can't be this bad.'

Migs's voice was anguished as now in almost a whisper, she said:

'It is! It is! You don't understand . . .' And she burst into tears again.

Isobel decided that for whatever reason, Migs was having a nervous breakdown in which case, the sooner she telephoned their family doctor the better.

'I'm going downstairs to ask Dr Mayhew to come and see

you, darling,' she said soothingly. 'He'll give you something to make you feel better. Now you are going to have a lovely warm bath, pop into one of your pretty nighties and back into bed. I'll ask Polly to bring you up a nice glass of hot milk.'

Ignoring Migs's tearful protests, Isobel did as she had declared. Although Migs allowed her to run a bath for her, she refused to allow her mother to stay in the room and help to bathe her. By the time Isobel returned upstairs, after having located Gerald at the golf club and telling him he must come home immediately, Migs was out of the bath and in bed, the bedclothes pulled up tightly to her chin. She was clutching her favourite babyhood sleeping companion – an old rag doll her grandmother had made for her when she was a year old. The glass of hot milk on her bedside table was untouched.

With deepening concern, Isobel stared down at her daughter who was now lying with her face turned to the wall. It could not have been made clearer to her that Migs did not want to talk. She decided to go downstairs to wait for the doctor.

Georgia was waiting for her in the hall, and immediately plied her with questions.

'Your sister has a very delicate disposition, Georgia. She may well be having a nervous breakdown,' Isobel announced.

Never having had a nervous breakdown, Georgia was unsure how it might manifest itself but decided to wait for her father's return. He, or nice Dr Mayhew, might have something more concrete to suggest such as Migs's hair had started to fall out like one of the girls at school who had suddenly become bald. Maybe, she thought, Douglas wouldn't want to be married to a bald wife, and that was why . . .

Her imagination was curtailed by the simultaneous arrival of her father and the doctor. Both nodded to her and Dr Mayhew patted her on the head, and as he always did, said: 'Great Scott, child, you've grown!' as if it wasn't perfectly obvious that unless she was going to be a dwarf, she must have got taller.

He disappeared upstairs with her father and mother and Georgia was left alone once more.

'I don't understand why Margaret won't talk to me, Dr Mayhew,' Isobel was saying almost tearfully as she opened the bedroom door. 'We have always been so close and as a rule she tells me everything.'

Gerald took hold of her hand and said:

'I think we should let Dr Mayhew examine Migs before we waste more time speculating, my dear,' hiding his own anxiety from her. He turned to the doctor. 'My wife and I will wait for you downstairs.'

It was another half an hour before the doctor joined them in the drawing room. He was not smiling as he accepted the glass of sherry Gerald held out to him. Avoiding Isobel's face, he said:

'Your diagnosis was quite right, Mrs Driffield, Margaret is having a kind of breakdown although I would think a reaction from shock might be a better description. The fact is . . .' he looked anxiously at Gerald, '. . . the fact is, she has been molested, on the train. She is quite badly bruised and of course, it has been a truly horrible ordeal for her. It is not surprising she is reacting in this manner.'

Isobel had stopped listening after Dr Mayhew used the word 'molested'. What did he mean? Assaulted? Robbed? Not . . . not physically molested, surely? Douglas would have put her on the train at Victoria Station and seen her safely into a Ladies Only compartment, so how could Migs have been attacked? But despite these frantic speculations, she knew that it exactly explained Migs's extraordinary behaviour since the taxi driver had brought her home.

She turned to Gerald.

'If . . . if she has been molested . . .' she used the word with difficulty, '. . . we should notify the police at once.'

'My dear, we don't know for sure that . . .'

'I'm afraid we do,' Dr Mayhew broke in. 'I'm sorry if this shocks, Mrs Driffield, but we should face the facts if we are to help Margaret to recover. She has been sexually assaulted.'

Isobel turned very pale and grasped Gerald's hand.

'What can we do?' she begged him, and turning to the doctor, posed the same question.

Now sitting himself down in the chair that Gerald was indicating, the doctor looked up at the man's shocked face. There was anger there, too.

'It's up to you, Mr Driffield, whether you decide to inform the police. That would necessitate Margaret being questioned, which is very far from desirable. She tells me that she was on a stopping train from London to Hayward's Heath and although she was in a Ladies Only compartment, a man got in at Redhill just as the train was about to leave the station. Margaret says he had longish hair and was hatless, so it sounds as if no one would have realised at a quick glance that he wasn't a woman. His overcoat was so long, it covered what might just as easily have been a skirt as trousers. Margaret herself did not realise at first that it was a man.'

He stopped to allow Gerald to refill his glass before continuing:

'The man was strong and determined, and Margaret was unable to defend herself. Nor could she reach the communication cord. Understandably she did not wish to describe to me in detail what happened. When her ordeal was over, her assailant left the train at the next stop. She says she huddled in a corner of the carriage until it finally reached Hayward's Heath where she got out and found Peters waiting with his taxi. She climbed into the taxi and collapsed.'

'Oh, my poor darling!' Isobel whispered. 'That villain should be shot! Gerald, he can't be allowed to get away with this. We must tell the police.'

'No!' Gerald said firmly. 'Dr Mayhew is right – it would make things worse for Migs if she had to relive her ordeal.

Besides, we have to think how we are now going to help her.'
He turned to the doctor. 'Is it possible . . . I mean could . . .
could she conceive a child as a result of . . .?' He broke off,
too embarrassed to further express his fears.

For a moment, the doctor did not speak. Then he said
quietly:

'I'm afraid it is possible. It depends somewhat on her
monthly cycle. If it is now late in the month, it isn't so likely.'

'Oh, dear God!' Isobel gasped. 'The wedding! Douglas! No
wonder Migs said that they could never be married now.
Douglas will have to be told. No man, however much he loves
a girl, can be expected to marry her knowing she could
be carrying another man's child. The wedding will have to be
cancelled.'

She burst into tears. Gerald put his arms round her. He was
looking appealingly at the doctor.

'You're not obliged to inform the police, are you, Mayhew?
If we just pretend none of this dreadful business has happened,
Margaret may not be pregnant and the pair of them can still
be married. If McPherson does love her as much as he's always
saying, he'll know it was not her fault.'

Isobel's expression was now one of acute anxiety. 'How
long . . . how long before we'll find out?' she stammered.

'Depends, Mrs Driffield. One or more weeks if she keeps
to her monthly cycle. The important thing now is to try to
help her recover from her ordeal. It's probably best not to
talk about it unless she herself wishes to do so. Meanwhile,
may I suggest you tell her young man that she is ill and can't
see him for a while?'

He looked sympathetically at Isobel.

'If it makes things easier, Mrs Driffield, I'm more than
prepared to diagnose exhaustion and the necessity for complete
bed rest until Margaret has recovered: forbid any visitors.
That should give everyone time to decide what is in her best
interests.'

He stood up, promising to look in again next day. As Gerald

followed him into the hall, Isobel thanked him and hurried back upstairs to Migs.

Dr Mayhew took the opportunity to say to Gerald:

'Didn't want to upset your wife – no need for her to know, but there was quite a bit of bruising, internally as well as elsewhere. I've given Margaret a sedative. Nasty business! I'm really sorry.'

'Makes one ashamed of one's sex, doesn't it, Mayhew?' Gerald said as he handed the doctor his hat and overcoat.

They both nodded to Georgia who was still sitting at the foot of the stairs. Neither was aware that a few moments earlier she had had her ear to the study door and had partly heard what was said. She was now aware that whatever it was Migs had had done to her on the train, it was serious enough to mean that she and Douglas might not get married as planned.

It was not as if she disliked Douglas, she reflected, as the doctor departed and her father went back into his study, but she had never wanted him and Migs to get married. Now, she told herself a little guiltily, the wedding could be off, Douglas would go to India without Migs, and Seb would come home from Spain and be able to marry her after all.

It would be a happy-ever-after ending, she thought, as she tried her very best to feel more sorry about whatever it was that had upset Migs.

For seven long days, Migs was confined to her room and Georgia was not permitted to visit her. Only her mother went into the room, and Polly with her meals. She needed complete peace and quiet, Isobel had told Georgia, because she was having a nervous breakdown. Georgia insisted that she only wanted to see Migs for a few minutes, just to tell her she loved her, but her mother was adamant.

'But what about the wedding?' Georgia now asked. 'That's only twenty-one days away. Will she be better by then?'

'Enough questions, Georgia!' her mother replied sharply. 'Go and fetch your coat and hat. We're due at the dressmaker in half an hour for the final fitting of your bridesmaid's dress.'

Georgia's hopes plunged as she realised the wedding, by the sound of it, was not going to be cancelled after all. Quite apart from this major concern, she was far from keen on the long pink satin bridesmaid's dress, which had a big white sash tied round a full skirt in a huge bow at the back of the waist. It made her look like a Christmas tree fairy, she had complained, but Isobel had ignored her protest.

'What I will permit is for you to remove your tooth brace on the day!' she had conceded, ignorant of the fact that Georgia had already decided she would do so.

Two days later, Isobel opened Migs's bedroom door and found her sitting by the window in her dressing gown. For the first time, she was actually eating the breakfast on a tray on her lap. She greeted her mother with a tentative smile instead of the usual downcast look that invariably ended in tears.

Isobel went forward to kiss her before sitting down beside her on the window seat and saying hopefully:

'So you are feeling better, at last, my darling?'

Migs nodded before, after a slight pause, replying awkwardly:

'Sort of, Mummy! I mean when I woke up this morning, I found I had . . . well, started . . .' She broke off, overcome with embarrassment. After her mother's initial brief explanation the first time Migs had had a period, the subject had never been mentioned again. A supply of sanitary towels appeared regularly in Migs's bottom drawer so she was never obliged to go into a chemist and ask for them.

Understanding at once to what Migs was referring, Isobel drew a huge sigh of relief.

'I'm so pleased, my darling!' she said delightedly: 'That's truly wonderful news. Now we can ring Douglas, who has been so worried, poor man, and you can tell him you have quite recovered from your breakdown.'

Migs put down her breakfast tray beside her and turned to look at her mother, her face a deathly white as a horrible thought struck her.

'Mummy, you didn't tell him . . . about . . . about what happened?' she gasped. 'I know we can't be married now but I don't want him to know why . . .'

It was as far as she got before tears started pouring down her cheeks. For once Isobel did not hurry to comfort her and was now staring at her daughter with a look of shock.

'What do you mean?' she asked sharply. 'Of course you will get married. Your wedding is only three weeks away and we can't possibly cancel it. *Of course* you are going to be married!'

As the tears continued running down Migs's face, she struggled for words.

'You know I can't . . . everything's changed . . . I'm not . . . Douglas would be sure to find out and . . . Mummy, I *can't* marry him now . . . not . . . not unless I tell him and he forgives me, and I can't possibly do that.'

Isobel's expression was now one of grim determination. Placing a firm hand on Migs's shoulder, she looked at her daughter's tear-stained face, saying:

'Listen to me, Margaret!' She slipped into Migs's full name, which she only ever used on the few occasions she was stressed. 'You are being a very selfish girl. What do you think poor Douglas would feel if you told him you weren't going to marry him now, never mind the reason? He's very much in love with you. Is he to go back to India without you? That would be most unfair since none of this unfortunate business was his fault.'

It flashed across Migs's mind that it was only a few weeks ago that her mother had been totally opposed to the hasty marriage. Now she was proving equally adamant that it should take place. It was almost as if she wanted her far away before her disgrace was discovered.

Isobel had paused very briefly to draw breath and now continued:

'As for telling Douglas what that . . . that wicked man did to you, I see absolutely no need to do so, and the sooner you forget it the better. You don't have any wrongdoing to confess to Douglas. That old adage is all too true: "What you don't know can't hurt you". You don't want Douglas to be hurt, do you?'

Migs had remained silent during her mother's tirade. Now she said in a near whisper:

'Wouldn't it be cheating, Mummy? Not telling him I no longer have my . . . my virginity? When I asked Dr Mayhew what that . . . that horrible man had done to me – why it had hurt so much, he said I had been violated, and I asked what that meant and he said I'd lost my virginity: but he was sure Douglas would understand if I told him what had happened. So I must tell him, Mummy, in case when he knows, he doesn't . . . doesn't want to marry me.' She broke off, tears running down her pale cheeks.

Isobel fought to keep her voice calm as it came home to her how innocent her daughter was . . . an innocence she had striven to maintain. While telling the girls it was essential they should remain virgins, she had never explained what the word 'virginity' actually meant. Her daughters were not enlightened about the structure or the functioning of their bodies any more than she, herself, had been before she was married.

Her voice now more gentle, she reached out and stroked her daughter's hair.

'Trust me to know what is best, my darling. You can take my word for the fact that Douglas will at all costs want the wedding to proceed without any further upsets. When you feel ready to come downstairs, it will be as if nothing horrible had ever happened. Promise me, darling, that from now on, you are going to forget all about it. Everyone thinks you have had a nervous breakdown brought on by there being so much to do at the last minute for the sudden wedding, so no one will ask any awkward questions. We are going to forget it, aren't we, sweetheart?'

Migs looked into Isobel's implacable face and wondered if in this instance, she should carry out her mother's wishes.

CHAPTER TEN

1937

Sebastian was among the hundreds of casualties fighting with the Republican troops in an attempt to stem the Fascist advance towards Brunete, west of Madrid. The volunteers of the XVth International Brigade had been ordered to take Mosquito Ridge and halt the Fascists, who were well armed and had the advantage of their position on the high ground.

The number of casualties was vast. So ill-equipped were the volunteers, they had little with which to defend themselves. Even the canvas shoes many had been reduced to wearing were so worn that they had wrapped rags round them to hold them together.

Short of ammunition, food and cigarettes, he and his companions were under a continuous barrage of shells and grenades, and were also being attacked by air. Apart from these dangers, they were all suffering intensely from the over-powering heat of the sun from which there was no shade. Far worse still, was the lack of water.

Hardened although Sebastian now was to the constant threat to his life, what tormented him most was not the physical danger caused by the grenades the enemy were throwing down on them from their superior positions, but the all-consuming thirst. Every man was taking what cover he could behind the wall of rocks they'd built in front of themselves, the ground being baked too hard to dig trenches. Their thirst in the sweltering summer sun was a torment, some even dying from dehydration in the searing heat.

It was a relief, Sebastian told himself, when he received

a wound to his right arm, making it impossible for him to fire his rifle. Although there were many stretcher bearers taking the wounded down to the overflowing makeshift hospital at the foot of the hill, after a dressing had been put on his wound, Sebastian proclaimed himself better able to walk down to the hospital than some of the far worse casualties. What he had not taken into account as he stumbled down the hill was the effect of the intense heat and lack of water.

Dizzy and hopelessly disorientated, he obeyed an instinctive need to get away from the sights and sounds of the battle raging above him. Stopping every now and again to rest, he forced himself to stagger on downwards, unaware in his semi-conscious state that the direction he was taking was leading him ever further from those who could help him.

By evening, the loss of blood from his wound and the onset of dehydration took their effect, and he sank down barely conscious behind a stone wall, which, with nothing else in view, afforded him some shade.

He drifted in and out of consciousness as the hours passed. At last the sun disappeared behind the horizon and the air cooled a fraction. Realising he must have water at all costs, he pulled himself upright and stared around him through the dusk. At first, he could see no sign of habitation but he now realised that the rough stone wall against which he had been sheltering from the sun must border a farm or dwelling of some kind. With his last vestige of strength, he edged his way along the side of the wall looking for a gap that he hoped might lead to some kind of habitation. He had just reached his goal when a shot rang out, and a bullet missed his head only by inches.

Instinctively, ignoring the pain in his arm, he sank as close to the ground as he could, hoping the wall would give him cover from his unseen assailant. For several moments, he lay still, hearing nothing but the night sounds of the hillside. Then a low-pitched voice said sharply:

'*Manos para arriba! Rapidamente!*' Sebastian had no difficulty in interpreting his captor's demand, but weak as he was, he could barely lift one arm, let alone the injured one as well. '*Manos en el aire. Inmediatemente!*' his captor ordered again. The shadow Sebastian now saw standing over him pointing a gun at his head he presumed to be that of a soldier. As the figure moved closer, he felt the barrel of the gun pressed against his forehead, and realised he was about to be taken prisoner or, worse, about to die. Too exhausted to try to defend himself, he lay still, staring helplessly at the shadowy figure of the man he supposed to be his enemy.

Quite suddenly, the whole hillside was flooded with light as a brilliant moon slid slowly from behind the clouds. Irrelevantly, it crossed Sebastian's mind that if this was to be his last sight of the world he was about to leave, it could not have been more beautiful.

Turning his head towards his captor, who had lowered his rifle, he saw with a shock that the figure in front of him was not that of a man but of a woman. The strap of the rifle now slung over her shoulder was pressing her shirt between her breasts. She wore baggy trousers, in the waist of which was tucked a forage cap.

Sebastian lay still, too weak to move. He found himself thinking how ironic it was that in the last five months he had come through innumerable battles and dangerous defeats without serious harm, and now he was to die on a peaceful hillside at the hands of a woman. He closed his eyes, his last wish before he lost consciousness not for freedom but for water.

When he regained consciousness, he became aware of a wet piece of cloth being squeezed between his parched lips. He felt an earthen floor beneath him where he lay and a rough cotton jacket was rolled up beneath his head. The wound in his arm was throbbing mercilessly but he saw that his captor had bound it with a ragged piece of cloth so that it was no longer bleeding.

The woman's face appeared above him, and a heavily accented voice said:

'You *Inglés, no?* Fight for people army? *No enemigo! Usted habla espanol?*'

With an effort Sebastian shook his head, his knowledge of the language limited more or less to conversations with the Spanish fighters who had attached themselves to his company after losing touch with their own.

The woman, still only a shadow in the darkness of the room, shook her head. He could hear a smile in her voice as she said:

'*No importante!* Before the war, I teach English to *niños* in school. You have a hurt arm but I am helping *you. Attesa!* You wait!'

With little alternative but to do so, Sebastian turned his head to watch her shadowy figure cross the room. Minutes later, he saw the flicker of candlelight and his captor coming towards him. Despite his weakness and the throbbing of his head and arm, he noticed with surprise how young she was. Her long dark hair hung in ragged locks around a delicate face that reminded him inconsequentially of a Russell Flint watercolour depicting a Spanish *señora*, which hung in Monty's drawing room.

'Consuela!' she introduced herself, handing him a bottle of water. 'Drink now, *Inglés*!'

Sebastian needed no second bidding. It was only after he had gulped down half the bottle of brackish, lukewarm water that it occurred to him the woman might also need some. He held out the bottle but she shook her head.

'*Dos botellas!*' she said, holding up two fingers and indicating he should finish the bottle he was holding. He needed no second offer.

Sebastian wanted to ask her where she had obtained the precious liquid but his head was swimming and his eyes closed as he lay back against his makeshift pillow. Within minutes he was in a restorative sleep. When he next became conscious, it was to find himself in total darkness. There was a cool breeze touching his body from which, he realised, his sweat-stained clothing had been removed. He felt a water bottle against his lips again and drank greedily as he became aware that all the tension had left his body, leaving him almost back to normality.

He put the bottle down on the earthen floor of the hut, and saw a glimmer of light shining through the open doorway. As he watched, the light grew brighter until the room where he lay was flooded with moonlight. The sky around the moon was ablaze with stars. The silence was almost tangible in contrast to the horrifying sounds of battle he had left some-where far behind him. He was, he realised, alive, and slowly regaining his memory as well as his senses.

'*Sensación mejor?* You feel better, *si?*'

He turned his head and saw the young woman sitting beside him. She was smiling. Her name came into his mind.

'Consuela?' he asked. Her soft laugh followed her assent. Only then did Sebastian realise that like himself, she was without clothes.

Seeing his eyes on her body, she shrugged, the movement lifting her breasts, which were surprisingly full.

'*Muy caliente!*' she remarked, seemingly without embar-rassment at her nudity. Sebastian had heard the words 'hot' and 'heat' often enough to understand what the woman was saying. Despite his wound, despite his weakened state of health after five months of fighting what he realised was proving a hopeless defence against General Franco's army, his body was responding to the girl's naked beauty.

He felt her hands running gently over his body, reminding him suddenly of his sexual initiation at the hands of the Swedish under-matron at school. Her voice, a mixture now of Spanish and English, was almost a whisper as she murmured admiring compliments about his physique. Her fingertips were now outlining his lips and instinctively he kissed them. She drew quickly away from him, breathing deeply, and he felt her shadowy white body trembling. Was it possible, he thought, that she was afraid of him?

As if in answer to his thoughts, she said in a voice that was little more than a whisper:

'They came to our flat in Malaga. They were shouting, singing, very drunk, the *soldados*. Sylvester, *mi marido,* is closing the door and the shutters, but the animals knock the door down with their guns.'

Her voice became harsh, discordant, as she said almost matter-of-factly: 'No *manos para arriba* – just shoot the guns at my *marido* . . .' She paused briefly before continuing in an anguished tone: '*Mi pequeo hijo*, Carlos, he hear the noise from his room where he sleeps. He comes to see what is the big noise. He runs to his papa who is lying dead on the floor; but before he reach him, a *soldado* lift him and carry him to the window. With his feet he kicks open the shutter and . . .'

For the first time, the woman's voice faltered and it was a minute or two before almost inaudibly, she resumed her dreadful story.

'Another *soldade* lift my Carlos by his feet . . . My *bebé* . . . he cry very loud. I try to go to him, but *diferente soldado* hold me so not *posible*.' She paused once more and then spoke in little more than a whisper.

'They throw my Carlos from the window. I know he die when he fall down to the road.'

Her voice suddenly became harsh as she continued:

'I was raped then by a *soldado*, then next – *uno, dos, tres, cuatro, cinco* . . . then they go. I am on the floor beside my dead husband. As *uno soldado* shout they come back soon with *camaradas*.'

Sebastian listened to her story with horror. Hardly able to believe his ears, he was nevertheless in no doubt that it was factual. When she had spoken of the brutality, the shocking facts of the soldiers' behaviour, without emotion or tears, the only sign of her feelings could be gauged by the rigid stiffness of her body where she lay beside him.

She turned suddenly and gripped his uninjured arm with both hands as if clinging to a lifeline.

'Is why I am here!' she said simply. 'I run away and join the first group of our *soldados* I see. They not ask questions. Many *señoritas* leave homes to fight like me. Many do for *escapar* the *disciplina* of family and *maridos*; for me, it is *para tomar venganza* – for revenge. One day *posible* I see *mi Carlos asesino* and I kill him. This way I do not go *demente*. The much soldiers I kill, is more good I feel. I kill for *mi marido* and *mi* Carlos, and is good for me.'

She now leant over him with a half smile replacing the distortion of hate.

'If you were one of those *soldados, Inglés,* lying there by the wall, it is *no importante* you are wounded, I shoot you.'

Before Sebastian could speak, her voice now suddenly softened, her tone that of a young girl as she said quite matter-of-factly:

'After that day, I have not had love with a man again. Many of our *soldados* have ask me. But with you, *Inglés,* I think it possible for me because you do not make me think of those *bestias*. How old you are?'

Sebastian found his voice.

'Nearly twenty!' he told her, 'and you?'

'Twenty-eight. My Sylvester was older. Like me he was the teacher at school. Our *hijo* was just two. You are young, strong *hombre*: tonight perhaps you help me to forget. We think only of love, not death.'

Despite the previous day's exhaustion, despite the painful wound in his arm, despite the fact that the woman now straddling him was a stranger, Sebastian felt a compelling need to help dispel the horrors of Consuela's dreadful memories.

What had begun as pity, quickly turned to physical desire as Consuela's hands started to caress him. He drew her down to him, her breasts now close to his lips, her naked body clearly visible to him in the moonlight. Her eyes were closed but he could feel her body pressed against his own and he could hear her hurried breaths before his kisses silenced them.

For one brief moment, Sebastian found himself wondering whether the woman in his arms was imagining him to be her dead husband; then he forgot the thought, not caring for what reason she had come to him, a stranger, for love. He forgot, too, the pain from the wound in his arm, his earlier fatigue as she leant forward to kiss him.

He knew he must be very gentle, very tender with her if he was not to remind her of the brutal rapes she had endured and, curbing the sudden urgent desires of his body, he forced himself to be patient; to let her set the progress of their coupling.

He caressed her body, his hands lingering on her voluptuous breasts, which felt to him as if, like his own body, they were on fire. Although the night air had cooled the scorching temperature of the day, they were both bathed in sweat as his hands gripped her hips and she began to move above him. As he moved with her, for the first time she broke the silence with a low moan. Their bodies were now moving in unison and Sebastian tried to curb his own desires as she threw back her head and began to rise and fall ever more quickly. Suddenly, she gave a soft cry, and as the tension eased in her body, he knew that it was right for him then to give way to his own need.

For some moments they lay entwined, and then she lifted herself up and lay down beside him. Sebastian wanted desperately to talk to her again; to hear her talk to him; she was touching him, caressing his cheek. Not knowing what he could say to her, and knowing that he must not question her as to whether he had been able to dispel some of her dreadful memories, he remained silent, his hand stroking the dark hair away from her face. He felt both pity and love for her as well as gratitude for the pleasure she had given him, even if her reason for doing so was in order to dispel her nightmarish memories. Then exhaustion returned and without warning, sleep overcame him.

When next he awoke, it was a moment or two before he recalled the night's extraordinary events. When he did so, he turned at once on his side expecting to see Consuela there, but the space beside him was empty. He sat up, looking around him and, seeing a heap of empty potato sacks in one corner, he realised he was in a kind of barn. There was no sign of Consuela. Then he saw the bottle of water by his feet, a torn piece of paper wrapped round it.

Shocked by the realisation that he must have slept on while Consuela left, he opened the paper. It contained two simple words: '*Gracias, Inglés*'. There was also a rough drawing indicating where they had both sheltered and the path leading back down the hillside to the village below. He knew then that he would never see her again: never be able to ask her if he had made her a little happier, less bitter, ask where she was going; where she had obtained the precious bottles of water. If, as he now hoped, she had kept some for her own survival.

For a few moments, he was overcome by a great feeling of sadness. The fact that perhaps she had used him to assuage her grief for a little while did not matter to him. She would always remain in his memory as the epitome of the beauty, the sadness, the savagery of this country's bitter civil war. It was not, after all, his war, he told himself. He had come to Spain partly because at first he'd thought it would be an exciting adventure that would help him to forget the acute disappointment of Migs's marriage to another man, and then because he believed so strongly in the right of the Spanish people to resist the Fascists.

Now, he thought, it was time he went home. Perhaps one day he would come back. Perhaps Fate would bring him and the Spanish girl together again in happier circumstances. One thing he had no doubt about as he pulled on his clothes, picked up the water bottle and the map and stood in the doorway momentarily blinded by the already blazing sun, was that he would never forget her, her beauty, her sadness, her passion. He wished now to forget all the horror, the death, destruction and brutality of the war that he had once imagined to be such a noble one. Only the memory of this past night would never fade and was one he knew he would always cherish.

As he walked out into the fierce heat of the day, he could hear the gunfire in the distance, hear the scream of shells, the drone of an aeroplane engine; but as he set off down the hill, he no longer cared. He was going home.

CHAPTER ELEVEN

1938

'I do love having lessons in the garden,' Hannah said to Georgia as they walked the half mile down to the tiny village bakery to buy their favourite Japonais patisseries.

'I do, too,' Georgia replied, 'but I love it here in the spring when we go up the mountain to pick the wild narcissi! It's really nice of the school to give us boxes to pack them in to post them home.' Georgia looked less happy as she added: 'My sister had narcissi in her wedding bouquet.'

She sighed and quickly put the memory out of her mind as she recalled Sebastian's distress and the way he had rushed off to Spain. There had still not been a single letter or postcard from him.

Her best friend, Hannah, who was closer to her than the jolly, outgoing Inge, thought it best for Georgia not to think about it and volunteered:

'It's good too when we go skiing, it's a pity you missed so much last term.'

Inge, who had been unusually silent until now, was nodding her head vigorously as she said:

'I cannot think why the French girls think four o'clock is so early, but I suppose they do not learn to enjoy such outings as we do in my country.'

This sunny May afternoon, as they neared the village, Hannah started singing a German song unfamiliar to Georgia. It seemed to be exactly right for the mountainside, which was bathed in warm sunshine.

'Now I am eighteen, this term is my last here at the *Institut*,' she said, adding wistfully: 'Because I am an only child, my parents have become very protective of me, but if you could come and stay with me, Georgia, it would be so much happier for me. *Mutti* suggested I invite you when I told her how friendly we had become. I would so love it if you did, but I won't blame you if you don't want to.'

Georgia did want to go to Munich. She and Hannah seemed able to have fun wherever they went, and with Migs far away in India and Seb in Spain, there was no one to encourage her to go home for the summer holiday. Her mother hadn't yet forgiven her for refusing to be presented, and her relationship with her father had, albeit at her own instigation, remained distant.

He had written two days previously, to tell her that Mr Willoughby, the solicitor, wanted a meeting with her regarding her inheritance, and that he was arranging it for the week of half-term. She wrote back to say she had been chosen to play in the tennis tournament that week against a finishing school in Lausanne, and would not be able to go home. Her father's reply by return of post was the sternest she had ever received from him. The meeting was to do with her inheritance, he wrote, and the documents could not be signed by him.

I shall expect you home for half-term as arranged, and under no circumstances will I change the date of our meeting with Mr Willoughby.

Georgia was a little shaken by the tone of her father's letter. Now that Hannah had become her best friend, Georgia thought, as arm in arm they returned to the school, she could talk to her about being adopted.

Later that evening the two friends were sitting together doing the prep for the following day's lessons. A number of the girls had gone by coach to Lausanne to see a play by Molière, so they had the *petit salon* to themselves. The subject matter was about the Great War. Knowing her friend was intrigued rather than shocked by her adoption, Georgia now told her that she had been taken once to see her father.

'He was an invalid,' she told her, 'he was wounded in the war, and he died soon afterwards.'

'My father was also wounded,' Hannah commented. 'He was awarded the Iron Cross for bravery. Even so, the National Socialist Party who govern our country now don't like him or our family.'

Georgia was astonished by her friend's remark.

'Not like you! But why?'

Hannah almost whispered the words: 'Because we are Jews!'

'So what's that got to do with it?' Georgia asked. 'I thought that a Jew was a sort of religious thing like . . . like you might be a Roman Catholic. We had several Roman Catholic girls at my school in England. They were just the same as us except they had to eat fish on Fridays.'

Close to tears, Hannah whispered.

'You might not wish to be my friend any more now you know. In my country, nearly everybody hates the Jews.'

'But why?' Georgia asked. She thought Hannah must be exaggerating because it seemed to her inconceivable that anyone should hate Hannah, let alone 'everybody'.

'My father says it's because the Führer, Herr Hitler, hates us, and nearly everyone loves him because he has helped our country recover after the war when people were starving and had no jobs and no hope!' Hannah said, repeating the explanation she had been given by her parents.

'He invented the National Socialist Party and everyone has to belong to it, even children, who are in what is called the Hitler Youth Movement. That's like the Boy Scouts and Girl Guides you told me about in your country.'

'So are you in it, too?' Georgia enquired, intrigued by Hannah's description of life in her country.

'Jews aren't allowed to join! We have to wear yellow stars on our clothes all the time so people know who we are. That's

why my parents sent me here. Jewish girls like me aren't to
stay in their schools any more.'

'Just because you are a Jew!' Georgia exclaimed incredulously,
adding after a minute: 'Why don't you just pretend to be a
Catholic or a Protestant or something?'

'Because we all had to sign documents and produce our
birth certificates and things like that, so the Party officials
know all about us.'

'I wonder what they would have done about me if I lived
in your country,' Georgia mused. 'I mean, if my real father is
dead, he couldn't exactly register himself even if he was a Jew,
could he? Maybe he was, for all I know.'

Hannah felt a huge wave of relief sweep over her. Here
in the room beside her was someone who hadn't the slightest
wish to treat her as a lesser person. On one of her visits
home Oma, her grandmother, had told her that when *Herr*
Hitler and his Nazi Party had first seized power, things were
quite normal: but gradually over the past five years, the Party
had become more and more opposed to anyone of the Jewish
faith. She had even said that they were now sending Jewish
people to work in concentration camps where they didn't
get enough to eat and were so hard worked, they sometimes
died.

Hannah did not believe such tales for surely, she'd thought,
her father would have told her how dangerous things had
become. In the three years since he had sent her here to
school, she had only been allowed home for a few weeks in
the summer holidays. The rest of the time she spent with her
uncle and aunt in Garmisch. When she was at home, apart
from seeing some people in the streets hurrying along with
a yellow star on their clothes, the new heavy restrictions her
parents had put upon her movements were all that had given
her room for anxiety. There was, of course, the word *JUDE*
written on the front windows of empty shops that had once
been run by Jewish people. Sometimes the windows had been
broken, smashed, but her parents refused to discuss the

political situation. Hannah, her father had said, was not to bother herself about such things, adding:

'Go and learn how to be a fine, well-educated person in your Swiss school. You are still a child and should not worry about the future.'

'We never talk about politics at home,' Georgia now commented. 'Mummy says it's boring and Migs thought so, too, so Daddy gave up reading to us bits about what's going on in Parliament when he gets his morning paper at breakfast time.'

Suddenly Georgia smiled.

'Everyone was talking about our King Edward and the American woman. Mr Baldwin, who was our Prime Minister then, said Mrs Simpson couldn't ever be Queen because she had been divorced twice. When he abdicated, Daddy let us listen to the King's abdication speech on the wireless. It was terribly sad, and Mummy and Migs both cried. Of course at school we were mostly told about the good things in the newspapers like the new airport called Gatwick which is near where we live. Seb, my friend, is learning to fly an aeroplane but that is at a place on the south coast called Shoreham.'

Hannah had been listening intently, relief flooding through her at the knowledge that Georgia's parents sounded unlikely to refuse to let Georgia visit her that summer. Both girls were bound even closer than before by the evening's exchange of confidences and were equally delighted by the arrival a few days later of a comforting reply from Georgia's father, giving his permission for her to visit Hannah in the summer holiday if that was acceptable to her friend's parents.

However, much as she disliked the idea of travelling to London to see the solicitor, four weeks later she was sitting beside her father in Mr Willoughby's office in King's Bench Walk. The confrontation – if such it could be called – was far more serious than she had expected. The elderly solicitor was staring at her over the top of his gold-rimmed spectacles.

'Perhaps you have considered the possibility, young lady,

that when you are a great deal older, you might wish to live at Audley Court,' he was saying to her. 'On the other hand, there has been an extremely handsome offer for the estate of twenty thousand pounds.'

His expression became avuncular as he added: 'Your father, as one of your trustees, has consulted his bank manager, Mr John Saunders, who is your second trustee. That is to say, they are guardians of your inheritance. They are in agreement that the offer is an exceptionally good one and if you wish, they will agree the sale on your behalf.' He then added with a smile: 'You would then be able to afford to buy forty houses if you so wished, young lady!'

'But it's only an old house,' Georgia said, frowning. 'Seb and I explored it and it was all creaky and cobwebby.'

The solicitor nodded and went on to explain:

'As I understand it, the agents are aware that the offer for the house is a great deal higher than its true value but the developers' intention is to pull it down. They say that there is a very high demand for family homes, of which there has been a dearth since the war. There are fifteen acres of land that go with the Audley Court estate and this, they reckon, will allow the building of thirty houses on the site, each with half an acre of garden space, the houses to be priced at around seven hundred pounds each. Thus, when one has done the calculations, it explains why the developers are willing to pay so much for the property. Do you understand all that, Miss Driffield?'

He cleared his throat.

'The property was not up for sale but Parker and Collins were approached by the developers, who insisted that their offer should be put to you personally.'

Gerald, who had been silent until now, turned to Georgia.

'It is a quite exceptionally high offer, darling: a very great deal more than the house itself would be worth if it came on the open market. Were you twenty-one years of age, it would be a decision you could have made without my involvement, but as you are still a minor, it is my duty as one of your trustees to offer my advice.'

Georgia felt a mixture of emotions. Twenty thousand pounds was too huge a sum to be properly understood. At this precise moment, she would be very pleased if her father gave her two pounds with which to buy a new bicycle. Her existing one was old-fashioned and hard to pedal, and she had seen a new one with three-speed gears in the window of the bicycle shop adjoining their local garage. If she agreed to sell the house, would she be allowed to have some of her inheritance money now or would she have to wait until she came of age?

Georgia decided this was not the moment to discuss her bicycle in the austere presence of Mr Willoughby, who was now addressing her again.

'I should remind you, young lady, that you are not without other considerable means. What remained after Mr de Valle's death duties and, er . . . debts were paid, was valued for probate as eight thousand pounds. This, of course, has been held in trust for you, and your father has wisely invested it so that the sum has been earning considerable interest and will be even higher than before. You have no need, therefore, to accept the developers' offer if it is your wish to keep the house. You have until July 1st to make up your mind, and my suggestion is that you go home now and think about it before doing so.'

Georgia's thoughts winged back to the hot summer's day nearly three years ago when she and Sebastian had explored Audley Court together and found the letters. If she was really going to be so rich, maybe she would be able to afford to go to the island where the pirate's boat had foundered; and if it still lay undiscovered at the bottom of the sea, she could pay as many divers as she wished to search for it. To do so would be the most exciting thing in the world. The strange foreign man with whom she had had tea at his hotel lived in Madeira and had said he would be happy to help her arrange a search for the pirate's ship if ever she wanted one.

'Georgia!' Her father's voice brought her back to the present. 'I think Mr Willoughby's advice is right – we should go home now and talk about all this. Thanks to Mr Willoughby, the deadline for a decision has been extended to the end of the month and . . .'

'No, Daddy,' Georgia broke in, her cheeks flushed. 'I've made up my mind already. I wouldn't ever want to live in a great big house like that. It . . . it doesn't have any sentimental memories for me, and I absolutely know I'd hate living there.'

She did not add that the man who had lived there meant nothing to her, whereas the letters . . . Chantal . . . she was an ancestor with whom she felt a strong link.

'Are you quite certain, my darling?' Gerald asked anxiously. 'If you sell Audley Court now, you wouldn't have the opportunity to buy it back if you changed your mind when you were older. You do need to be absolutely sure.'

Georgia's eyes went directly to her father's.

'I am nearly eighteen years old, Daddy, and quite old enough to know my own mind. I will never want to live at Audley Court, and I want to sign those papers to agree the sale.'

An hour later, as she and her father sat side by side in the train taking them back to Hayward's Heath, Georgia's imagination winged forward to the far-off day three and a half years hence when she would be old enough to take control of her fortune: go to the island of Madeira and search for the sunken ship and the pirate's grave.

All-consuming though such thoughts had been, they were wiped from her mind the moment she walked through the front door of her house.

Isobel was waiting for them, a smile on her face as she greeted them.

'Joan has just been to see me,' she said, looking from her husband to Georgia. 'She has had news of Sebastian. He is alive but has been in hospital in France after escaping from a Fascist prison camp. It seems he was caught by the enemy soon after he had been wounded. The good news is that his wounds are healing and he has come home to convalesce. Joan is expecting him back tomorrow.'

Audley Court, the money, the island of Madeira, the letters, were all instantly forgotten. Nothing else mattered to Georgia at that moment but the news of Sebastian's safety, and that he was home.

CHAPTER TWELVE

1938

There was only one more day of half-term left, during which Georgia could visit the convalescent Sebastian, who was now home and being fussed over by his mother as he waited for his leg to heal. A piece of shrapnel had pierced his thigh and the subsequent lack of antiseptics had led to a serious infection. It had been a stroke of luck that a passing Republican soldier had taken him to a hospital where he'd been told he was lucky not to lose his leg.

He was bored to tears, he told Georgia when she hurried round to see him, although grateful for still being alive. Except for the fact that he'd been woken up at the crack of dawn in the hospital ward, he was almost less bored there than here at Medlars. Consequently, he was really pleased to see her.

'Good to see you, Jo-Jo!' he'd greeted her with unusual enthusiasm, 'and thanks for these!' he added as she handed him a packet of humbugs – his favourite sweet since childhood.

'The doc said I was to have complete rest and quiet and of course the Mater promptly forbade any visitors – not even you! Anyway, I told her yesterday morning that if she wouldn't tell you I was back, I'd get up and go round and tell you myself! After all that you had to have gone to London for the day!'

He drew a long, self-pitying sigh, adding: 'Who on earth would want to be stuck here for at least another two weeks, the doc says.'

It was a beautiful early summer day with the sun streaming through the windows of the conservatory where Sebastian lay with his leg propped up on a mound of cushions. Georgia sat down in one of the basket chairs near him.

'Just think!' he said wistfully, 'we could be down at Shoreham buzzing along the coast with a cloudless blue sky above and the good old English Channel below.'

'How long will it be before you can fly again?' Georgia asked sympathetically, noting at the same time how thin he was. His face was drawn, and his eyes, with dark shadows beneath them, seemed much deeper set than before. He had lost a great deal of weight, she thought anxiously, and there were hollows in his cheeks. His hands, still brown from the burning Spanish sun, trembled slightly as he lit a cigarette. Only his eyes were the same sky blue as they smiled a welcome.

'The medics won't say, but I can tell you one thing, Jo-Jo, I'm not going to waste the summer lying here one minute longer than I have to. What about you?'

Georgia's expression changed to a sudden smile.

'After Migs's wedding and you'd gone off to Spain, Mummy tried to get me to agree to be presented and have a Season next year and threw a fit when I refused. She only calmed down a bit when I said I would go to a secretarial college and learn how to type and do shorthand.' Seeing Sebastian's look of disbelief she added: 'I've made up my mind I'm going to be a journalist!'

'Sounds just like you, Jo-Jo!' For a moment he didn't speak, then, his eyes suddenly thoughtful, he said: 'I don't suppose you've heard from Migs, have you?'

Deciding that it was better not to prevaricate, and to get the news over as quickly as possible, Georgia told him:

'The parents have had lots of postcards from her saying how different everything is in India and how colourful and . . . well, what a good time she's having. She's sent me cards in Switzerland too. I suppose she didn't send you any knowing you were in Spain.'

To her surprise, Sebastian seemed to take the news quite calmly.

'So she hasn't regretted dashing off at a moment's notice with the army fellow!' he exclaimed.

It was a statement of fact rather than a question, and Georgia realised that her sister's impulsive marriage to someone other than himself was not quite so painful to Sebastian as before. Nevertheless, she changed the subject.

'Were you sorry to leave Spain when you got wounded? Did you have to kill a lot of people?'

Sebastian's expression was now one of bitterness and dejection.

'It's hard to describe the sheer awfulness of it, Jo-Jo: first the cold and then the heat, the hunger, the dreadful atrocities which were committed by both sides – our own, as well as theirs. To be truthful, we, the Republicans, were – and still are – fighting a lost cause; no proper weapons, no trained commanders, no proper support. The Fascist commander, General Franco, had a conventional, trained army, and they even had the German aeroplanes trying out their dive-bombing techniques and killing hundreds of civilians, women and children, and destroying their homes, even cities . . .'

He broke off momentarily as he reflected that it was as much a political civil war as a territorial one. It was no secret that even now members of the same family, the same village, were fighting each other; those whose proclivities were with the Republicans and Communists against those who endorsed the Fascists who had invaded their country. Even the English newspapers were reporting that many people now thought the German aerial involvement in the Spanish war was a prelude to their own country going to war.

He looked at Georgia's innocent, trusting face and, remembering the horror of the aeroplane bombardments, he said sadly:

'We aren't going to be able to ignore what the rest of the world is up to much longer. Pa thinks that if governments don't soon do something to stop Germany's rearmament programme, the Germans will simply get stronger and stronger: and what would be the point of that if they didn't intend going to war again! Their aeroplanes are devastating – whole formations of them killing women and children and old people and destroying historic buildings and irreplaceable works of art. It's frightening, Jo-Jo.'

Georgia was shocked by what Sebastian was saying.

'Well, my friend, Inge, is German and I'm sure she doesn't know anything about all that!' she said dismissively. 'She does get a bit boring the way she keeps talking about Adolf Hitler and all the good things he's doing like building new roads and getting all the unemployed people back to work. Most of the time she's really nice to be with. She and Hannah and I have agreed to stay friends after we leave school.'

Sebastian eased himself into a more comfortable position and said:

'I'm surprised to hear your parents are letting you go to Germany to visit your friend Hannah this summer. The Pater said everyone was horrified about the way Adolf Hitler is treating the Jews. I shouldn't think it will be much fun staying with her.'

'Well, Hannah is counting on me going,' Georgia replied defensively. 'We can't wait for the term to end, so we will be able to do things together. It's so boring here – Mummy wanting me to go shopping in Brighton or London which I hate and Daddy saying I can walk round the golf course with him. I've nothing else to do.' She drew a deep sigh, adding: 'I can't think why they imagine I want do to things with them. I've stopped feeling very close to either of them ever since I learned I wasn't their daughter.'

Sebastian frowned.

'That was two years ago, and you're really quite lucky to have such nice parents. I've told you before, Jo-Jo, you might easily have been adopted by some horrible people.'

Georgia sighed.

'Well I'm not arguing against that possibility, or that if I'd been someone else's daughter, I wouldn't have had Migs for my sister, or grown up in the next door house to you! But when I can't sleep sometimes and I'm lying awake wondering about things, I keep thinking about those letters – you know the ones I mean, Seb – about my great-great-grandmother and the pirate who loved her?'

'What about them, then?' Sebastian enquired.

'You may think I'm being silly, but suppose if Chantal and Dinez had been sort of married on the island and she was going to have his child but didn't know it until after she was rescued and married the John de Valle Englishman? Then I wouldn't be a real de Valle either. Maybe I've inherited the pirate's dark eyes and dark hair and I've got Portuguese blood which would explain why I look so different from the other English girls.'

Sebastian burst out laughing.

'You are an idiot, Jo-Jo!' he exclaimed. 'With your imagination, I reckon you should write books in preference to becoming a journalist. As a matter of fact as soon as I'm fit, I'm going to get down to some research and then I'm going to write a book about my experiences in Spain. The Mater has promised to buy me a typewriter.'

'What a topping idea!' Georgia commented, adding after a moment's thought: 'If you become a proper author, you could write another book about Chantal and Dinez and the Seychelles island.'

'Jo-Jo, I love you very much but there are times when you can become extremely boring,' Sebastian told her. 'Don't you think it would be a good idea to forget those soppy letters and get on with your life?'

'I am getting on with my life,' Georgia argued indignantly. 'And I don't want to forget them, and what's more, when I had tea with Fedrik what's-his-name – the man Migs and I met at Rose and Lily's launch party – and his aunt, he said that over the years there'd been dozens of wrecked ships round the coast of Madeira, and many are too deep for the divers to have found them last century, but they have better equipment now and may be able to find my pirate's boat.'

So lost was Georgia in her story that she was unaware of Sebastian's reaction when she mentioned Fedrik Anyos. He was remembering Migs's ball when his disguise slipped and the foreign chap had come to his rescue. Even now, he could feel the same embarrassment at his dilemma.

He forced his attention back to what Georgia who, still on the same subject, was now saying excitedly:

'Dinez, the pirate, noted the exact position his ship went down in a postscript to one of his letters, and he was hoping to recover the money.'

'Well, I hope you weren't stupid enough to tell all that to this Fedrik chap!' Sebastian said, adding half in earnest: 'He could hire some modern divers and get your pirate's gold and disappear to America or somewhere where you'd never find it or him!'

'Now you're being stupid!' Georgia retorted, her cheeks flushed. 'Of course I didn't tell him! I want to be the one to find Dinez's ship. And I'm going to see if I can just as soon as I get the money my . . . my other father left me. The solicitor said I am now a very rich person but I'm not allowed to have the money until I'm twenty-one. So that's where I'll be going when I come of age. You can come with me if you like!'

'Rich or not, you'd be wasting your time and your money, you silly chump!' Sebastian said fondly. 'Well, I'll say this for you, Jo-Jo, you had as many crazy ideas as I did when we were kids and I was the one who implemented them. Do you know, I thought about those days sometimes when my fellow soldiers and I were up in the hills in Spain trying to find shelter from the biting wind and snow. We built camps with whatever we could find, and stuffed the gaps with straw to keep out the wind, and then we'd make a fire if we could find enough wood and melt snow in an old tin can – the way you and I did! We were lucky not to have burned ourselves to death! I remember that you never once cried when our best building efforts blew down in the wind. You were a good sport, Jo-Jo!'

'And you were my hero!' Georgia said smiling. 'Still are, I

suppose, though why you wanted to go and fight someone else's war, Seb, I can't think!' Seeing the sudden pallor of his cheeks, she bent over and kissed him. 'Got to go now, Seb! I'll drop in again tomorrow morning if you like. Anything I can bring you?'

Aware now of the throbbing pain in his leg and growing fatigue, Sebastian reached for Georgia's hand and squeezed it.

'A few more humbugs, maybe!' he replied with a smile. 'And thanks for coming, Jo-Jo. Halfwit though you may be, I'm very fond of you, you know! As the Mater won't allow Monty or any of my other friends to visit me, at least you are better than nobody!'

As Georgia turned to go she was reminded happily of the way Sebastian spoke to her in their childhood, and felt a moment of real pleasure before reminding herself that life was pretty miserable for him at the moment and she should be feeling pity for him instead.

Fedrik had become increasingly bored as there had been no unattached young women staying at the hotel to keep him amused. It was, therefore, of interest to him when his aunt told him that she'd had a letter from her friend, Lady Priscilla Wiscote, saying that her granddaughters were going to have a fortnight's holiday in Madeira. They had chosen the island so that they could see all the many colourful wild and cultivated flowers for which it was renowned. Although they were somewhat plain in looks, their personalities were so delightfully ebullient and unconventional that Fedrik suspected it would be impossible not to enjoy their company.

Resita now said: 'Priscilla tells me in her letter that the girls' flower shop is flourishing, and she thinks they are planning to buy much bigger premises off Sloane Street. It would be a kindness, Freddie, if you would chauffeur them on trips into the hills and along the coast.'

'Willingly!' Fedrik said, lying back on one of the lounge chairs in their suite and easing his back, which ached after a particularly strenuous game of tennis with the pro.

'I shall have them here to dinner with us in the evenings!' Resita continued. 'It will be nice for us to have an alternative to each other's company, will it not?'

Resita was far more aware than Fedrik realised how tedious he had been finding life of late. Although they had been to Monte Carlo for two weeks the previous month, he had not had much luck at the tables, and although his aunt had willingly made good his losses, he was still disgruntled that his 'luck was out', as he had put it. Was she being selfish, she had asked herself when they'd returned to their hotel in Madeira, expecting him to go on living with her? At his age, ought he not to be married? With a family? Or at least have a lucrative career where the cut and thrust of the business world might occupy his mind?

The prospect of living the last few years of her life alone, without his companionship, his sharp, acerbic conversation, was not one she often cared to consider. It was true that the hotel staff, many of whom had been employed there long before her arrival, would take care of most of her daily comforts. There were, too, a number of elderly couples who were permanent residents like herself with whom she played bridge occasionally or, if Freddie were otherwise occupied, who invited her to their table at luncheon or dinner. If Fedrik did ever leave her, she would not be totally devoid of companionship.

However, the truth was she adored her tall, handsome nephew and often found herself wondering how the rather dull, predictable late brother she had known as a girl could have produced such an engaging son.

During the week following their arrival, Fedrik drove Rose and Lily round the island, where they exclaimed excitedly about the multitude of flowers: the wisteria, the bougainvillaea, the passion fruit vines tumbling over garden walls. They were fascinated by the wonderful view of the island from the summit of Pico Arieiro, and the fishing boats in the bay at Camara des Lobos. With somewhere different to visit every day, Rose and

Lily said sadly on the last night of their holiday that they had still only explored a quarter of the island and its treasures.

'You must visit us again,' Resita said with genuine warmth. 'And bring that nice young cousin with you,' Freddie added.

Rose, looking almost pretty in a long blue evening dress, the twin to Lily's except that hers was in a pretty shade of green, was laughing as she said:

'Georgia, I know, would love to come here.'

'She's forever talking about Madeira,' Lily added.

The next day Fedrik took the twins down to the harbour and with genuine regret saw them safely on to the launch that would take them out to the waiting liner and thence to England.

As he made his way back to the hotel, he recalled the twins' suggestion that Georgia should accompany them if they made a return visit. What now passed through his mind as he drove the Bugatti up the hill away from Funchal was not a pleasurable expectation of a visit from Georgia, but the prospect of retrieving the caskets of gold coins that were purported to have gone down with the pirate's ship.

Ever since Georgia had told him about the letters, the idea had grown at the back of his mind that were he somehow to get possession of such wealth, he would be able thereafter to cater for all his needs without having to be at his aunt's beck and call, at present necessary to earn the many financial indulgences he had grown to expect.

CHAPTER THIRTEEN

1938

The summer term at the *Institut* was as enjoyable as ever. Georgia decided to learn German so that when she went to stay with Hannah in Munich at the start of the summer holiday, she would at least be able to converse with Hannah's parents who, Hannah said, spoke very little English. She was greatly looking forward to the visit although as the term wore on, Hannah became more and more anxious about it.

'*Vater* writes to say my grandmother *Oma* has not been well, and as he doesn't like to leave her they seldom go out now,' she explained. 'I'm not sure if we will be allowed to go out on our own, Georgia. *Oma*, who has just come to live with us, has also written to me saying there is much danger for us now in the streets. Of course, she's very old now and maybe not quite right in the head.'

Her frown deepened as she added, 'I've never known my parents to be so anxious about anyone else coming to visit!' she said. '*Vater* asked me in his last letter if I could persuade you to promise you will not change your mind.'

'Of course I promise,' Georgia told her as they threw small sticks into the waterfall beside which they were sitting on the flower-covered mountainside behind the school. 'Inge was telling me about the wonderful torchlight parades you have when *Herr* Hitler goes to Munich and she said we must go and see one for ourselves. And I can't wait to go ice skating with you.'

Hannah looked doubtful.

'I don't think we'd be allowed to go to the parades!' she

said. 'My father would think we'd get hurt among the huge crowds which line the streets on such occasions.' She sighed. 'He always was very protective of me even though I am no longer small, but he's been far worse these last years since I came to school here. I suppose it's because he knows there are so many people in our country now who don't like the Jews.'

Georgia sighed.

'Sounds like those stupid political things again,' she said vaguely. 'Seb has just got back from Spain where one lot of Spanish people are fighting another lot. I think it's so silly, and poor Seb got quite badly wounded.'

'*Oma* says it's the National Socialist Party who don't like Jewish people and want to rob them of their houses and jobs, and take all their money for themselves. She told me they have made a lot of rules about not letting Jewish children go to schools or people work in shops, and things like that.'

'Did you notice things were different when you went home last holidays?' Georgia asked.

Hannah shook her head.

'I didn't go home. We all, even my grandmother, went to stay with my aunt and uncle who have a large chalet on the outskirts of Garmisch where they rent rooms to skiers who come for the weekend. It's really nice there, Georgia. *Mutti* said the people there didn't know we were Jewish as we weren't wearing yellow stars and *Vater* said we would all have been in a lot of trouble if anyone had found out.'

'So why don't you all go to live with your uncle and aunt?' Georgia enquired.

'I asked *Vater* that, but he says my uncle and aunt are very poor as they only make any money in the skiing season, and if we lived with them, they wouldn't have any rooms to let to other people.'

'Couldn't your father give them some money? My father said the school fees here are very expensive so your father must be quite rich, too.'

Hannah shook her head.

'I've been here for three years now and *Vater* paid for all my fees even before I started here when I was fifteen. He said something about not being allowed to send money to other countries at that time so it was best to safeguard my education while he could.'

'It all sounds very odd to me,' Georgia said as she threw another stick into the stream and watched the current carry it away on its journey to the valley far below. 'Anyway, my father says I'm going to be really rich and I can do what I like with my money when I'm twenty-one: so if you're still very poor, I can always give you some money then.'

Before Hannah could reply, they saw Inge coming towards them carrying a basket on one arm that proved to be full of freshly picked strawberries to be shared with them.

'I dare say I could have bought some cream from the *laiterie* in the village,' she said as she sat down beside them, 'but I realised we wouldn't have any bowls or spoons. Never mind, we eat and enjoy!'

The fruit was locally grown and sold in the greengrocer's shop next to the dairy. Inge further produced a letter from the pocket in her dirndl skirt that she handed to Georgia.

'Sorry it's a bit crumpled,' she apologised. 'I hope you don't mind!'

Georgia didn't mind in the least as she had recognised Sebastian's handwriting. After half-term, he'd written every week – short jokey letters saying he was getting better and had started to hobble around; or that Rose and Lily had been down from London to visit him and were full of stories about Madeira. Never more than two paragraphs long, the letters nevertheless managed always to be funny – the drawing of a leg in plaster on which he'd signed his name; an old snapshot of his mother with a paper bubble coming out of her mouth saying: 'Are you sure you're all right, dear!'; a sketch of a typewriter with a blank sheet of paper in the roller and a caption saying: 'As you can see, the book is going at full speed!'

Neither Hannah nor Inge believed Georgia when she insisted that the letters she received so eagerly were from a friend, not a boyfriend. It had proved pointless repeating that Sebastian had been her sister's boyfriend before she married someone else. She always wrote back to Sebastian with equally silly drawings – one of a moth with two tiny propellers on its antennae and the words: '*Tiger moth in flight*' written underneath; another of a tree house falling off the end of a branch; and once, in their secret code, which Sebastian had instigated when they were children.

At the time they had imagined it indecipherable but it was no more than a simple opposite to what they wanted to say. Thus: '"*Tell the grown-ups I am not hiding in the summerhouse*,"' would mean '"*Don't tell the grown-ups I am hiding in the greenhouse*."' Then they would sign their names backwards – *Bes* for Seb and *Aigroeg* for Georgia. Aged about six and nine, they had considered themselves very clever.

Both Inge and Hannah envied Georgia her regular male correspondent. Inge said she once had a kind of admirer – well, she corrected herself, he was a *Luftwaffe* cadet in *Kampfgeschwader 255,* and when she'd been to one of their dances, he had chosen her to be his partner at least six times. Then he had asked if she would be permitted to go to the opera with him if he got tickets, but before she could ask her parents for their consent, he'd been posted somewhere else and she never heard from him again.

The dances were very formal, she told them, and were arranged so the cadets could learn how to conduct themselves correctly on social occasions: how to approach their prospective dance partner, click heels, bow over her hand and ask if she would be so kind as to dance with him. When the dance was over, he was expected to return the girl to her seat, thank her, click his heels together once more and bow.

'I suppose the cadets weren't much older than me and my friends,' Inge said. 'Some were very shy and were sweating in their hot grey uniforms, but Rudolf, who was a lot taller even than me, was quite cheeky. You would have liked him, Georgia, because he was mad about aeroplanes like your friend! All he could really talk about was flying.'

'Sebastian's father gave him his own little two-seater plane for Christmas – a Gipsy Moth – and he's promised to teach me to fly when I go home this summer.'

When the three girls were not having academic lessons, they were out in the garden learning how to throw a javelin or play tennis or they walked down through the fields of ripening grapes to the lakeside to swim.

It was a time, Georgia decided, when she had never felt so carefree and happy until the arrival of a letter from her father saying:

> Your mother and I think it is best if you come straight home at the end of the term. Germany has now sent a whole army of troops to the Austrian border, and it is thought an invasion of Czechoslovakia is imminent.
>
> I know you planned to spend two weeks of your holiday with your friend in Munich, but your mother and I fear you might be trapped out there should hostilities commence as is now considered a very real possibility. I don't want to disappoint you but I'm sure you will agree it is sensible for you to return home at the end of term.

Georgia discussed her father's fears with Inge, who insisted that the *Führer* was far too busy trying to improve conditions in Germany to want a war with anyone. As a consequence Georgia decided her father had been given entirely the wrong impression, quite possibly by the War Office where he worked. She wrote back to him by return of post.

> Inge says the big gatherings you may have seen on the newsreels are nothing to do with war but are huge parades to welcome the *Führer* when he visits a city. She says her parents say no one wants another war.

Please don't worry about me! I am quite old enough now to take care of myself. Hannah is really looking forward to me going home with her, which in any case is only for a fortnight, and if there was any trouble, I'd simply catch the next train home.

She sent it airmail and promptly forgot about her father's letter. When she did get a reply from him a few days later, it was to acknowledge that possibly his anxiety was unwarranted, but he insisted he review the situation near the end of term before a final decision was made.

The trouble with her father, Georgia decided, was that he was prejudiced against the Germans because of his experiences in the last war. He had only talked about it once other than on that dreadful day when he told her about her real father's injuries. He had described their life in the trenches as 'a hell on earth', and declared he would never forgive the nation who had done such terrible things to his best friend.

Putting such thoughts from her mind, she saw that Inge and Hannah had like herself finished eating their strawberries. Inge suggested they walk down through the vineyards to the lake and swim as they would have plenty of time before the evening meal. Usually it was she who galvanised her two friends into physical activity, telling them they would feel much better if they were as physically fit as she was. Fitness was important. In her country, it was considered a duty as well as a pleasure. Since she was fourteen she had been a member of the '*Bund Deutscher Mädel der Hitler Jugend.*'"

Seeing the look of incomprehension on her friends' faces, she smiled, her pretty young face glowing with enthusiasm as she explained: 'It means, "League of German Girls of the Hitler Youth". We wear uniforms and have much more freedom than our parents permitted before the League started. We go to summer camps and sing songs and go on hikes with backpacks the same as we do here when we go up the mountains. Now

I am eighteen, I can belong to the "*Glaube und Shönheit*" section, which means "Belief and Beauty"'.

'Except for the "Belief and Beauty", it sounds just like our Girl Guides,' Georgia remarked. 'Do you belong to the Hitler Youth thing, Hannah?'

'I am not allowed,' Hannah said frowning.

'Everyone has to join the League, Hannah,' Inge protested, 'except of course the Jews.'

It was on the very tip of Georgia's tongue to say that Hannah was Jewish, but then she remembered that soon after they had first become friends, Hannah had asked her to keep her religion secret.

'*Oma* told me many of our shops and synagogues are being destroyed,' Hannah told Georgia later that evening. 'My parents have forbidden me to talk to anyone about the religious customs we have at home, and never to say we are Jews.'

Hannah herself had not believed her grandmother's frightening stories, which even included forecasts about the National Socialists wanting to kill them. Her grandmother was very old and, according to her father, her mind was beginning to wander. As Hannah had only been home for a few weeks in the last year, she'd not felt certain what to believe. On one of her rare visits, she had seen a shop belonging to a friend of her father with its windows smashed and the Star of David painted on the door, but her father said it was done by vandals. Sometimes, she confided in Georgia, she wondered if *Oma* could be right and her father was not telling her what was really happening. Whenever she did question him, he just said: "You go on enjoying your life in Switzerland, *meine Liebling*: be happy and don't worry your head about what is happening at home."'

Georgia sighed.

'My father is a worrier, too! Sebastian says the National Socialists are Fascists and they don't like the Jews. I think politics are utterly boring and we shouldn't bother talking about them.'

That night, as she climbed into bed, neither Hannah nor

Inge were in her thoughts. That evening she had received a surprisingly long letter from Sebastian that she'd only just had time to read. His news was a great deal more cheerful than the previous one. Although he was still living at home, he was now able to hobble around on crutches and was researching for his Spanish Civil War book. He had also written two short stories that had been accepted for publication, the payments for which were the first money he had ever earned!

The summer term had almost come to an end, when Sebastian's next letter arrived shortly before Georgia departed for Munich with Hannah. In it he announced that he had acquired a publisher who, on the strength of the first two chapters of his war book and a synopsis for the rest, had offered him an advance payment as well as future royalties. On the strength of this success, he was moving into a little house three doors away from that of Rose and Lily, where he would be independent. In future she was to write to him at his new address.

Georgia's delight at his news was soon forgotten as the day finally arrived when she and Hannah caught the train to Germany. The journey was uneventful but for a slight hold-up at the border when their passports were scrutinised in such a way as to cause Georgia to comment that they might be criminals trying to escape from prison! Their arrival in Munich was, however, an exciting experience for her. The whole place seemed to be in a festive mood. Flags were hung from top windows; everywhere people were laughing, singing and clearly enjoying the lovely sunny weather.

There were students to be seen all over the city, Hannah's father, *Doktor* Klein, told her in his halting English as he drove them home from the station. Many were English but others came from all over the world.

'As they do at our school!' Georgia remarked.

Hannah, who until now had been silent, enquired after her mother's health.

'She is much better,' her father replied, 'but what I have not told you in my letters, *Liebling*, is that your grandmother is not at all well: that is to say she has become even more confused in her mind since she had pneumonia last winter.'

Hannah looked distressed. As a little girl, she had often stayed, sometimes for days at a time, with her *Oma* at her beautiful house in Berlin. Although widowed in the war, she'd had a large retinue of servants to take care of her needs, and a great many friends, mostly talented musicians. She herself had played the violin and the piano and had possessed a delightful singing voice. Hannah now wanted to ask more questions but her father changed the subject and told Georgia of the outing he had planned, as the weather was so warm, for them to go swimming in a lake called Tegernsee as soon as Georgia had had time to settle in.

When the front door was opened on their arrival by a thin, gaunt old lady, Georgia assumed she was a servant, but to her surprise, Hannah introduced her as her mother. In the nick of time, relieved that she had not handed her her hat and gloves, Georgia managed to smile and shake her hand.

Frau Klein, Georgia decided, was like a nervous little hen, her head turning from side to side, her steps faltering as she reached up to her daughter and kissed her.

'So long since I saw you, *meine Liebling!*' she said. 'And so good of you to come with Hannah, Georgia. We were afraid . . . that is to say . . . we would have been very disappointed if you had changed the plan. Hannah, take your friend up to your room. Your father has put a second bed in there for Georgia as we thought you might wish to be together.'

For some reason Georgia could not entirely explain, some of the euphoria she had felt when she and Hannah had boarded the train in Switzerland disappeared as she began to unpack her clothes and hang them beside Hannah's in the large wardrobe.

Hannah must have felt it, too, because she linked her arm through Georgia's as they went back downstairs, saying in a whisper:

'I do so hope you will be happy here, Georgia. I think my parents are worrying about *Oma* which is why they don't smile much any more. They used always to be laughing. I will go back upstairs and visit *Oma* as soon as we have had tea. I expect *Mutti* will have made the *Apfelstrudel* she knows I love, and maybe a cinnamon or a ginger cake for you.'

Her expression became more thoughtful again as she added: '*Vater* wrote and told me our cook had left and *Mutti* had not replaced her. *Mutti* is not very experienced as she never had to cook anything in her life before!'

It was on the tip of Georgia's tongue to enquire why the cook had not been replaced, but they were now in the large dining room where tea had been laid for the four of them. The table was large enough to accommodate at the very least a dozen people. The heavy brocade curtains had been drawn for some reason, shutting out the sunlight so the room was sombre and filled with shadows. Conversation consisted for the most part of questions to Georgia about her own home life. She longed to ask why so many men in black and brown shirts were in the streets: if the black uniformed ones in the jackboots were Fascists, like the ones Sebastian had described.

After the meal was over, Hannah took her upstairs to introduce her to her grandmother. The frail, white-haired old lady sitting in a huge mahogany armchair by the curtained window, looked almost doll-like in the vast room. A big four-poster bed stood in one corner, a washstand and what Hannah later told her was a commode stood in another; but dominating the room was the beautiful rosewood piano with sheet music opened as if the pianist had not long since been playing.

Hannah hurried forward and, kneeling down by the chair, put her arms round the frail little person sitting there. Although they greet each other in their own language, Georgia neverthe-less guessed from the tone of their voices how poignant this moment of reunion was for them both. Loving her own darling granny as she did, she understood the fulsomeness of their greeting. Hannah now turned to Georgia and, with tears in her eyes, said huskily:

'*Oma* has lost so much weight since I last saw her!' She then introduced Georgia to her grandmother, who smiled as she said in broken English:

'You will be the guardian for my precious Hannah. No one will harm her when she is with a foreigner.' Seeing Georgia's incomprehension, she beckoned her to come closer. 'You are not a Jew, you see, and the government do not wish your country to know what the National Socialists are doing to us.'

'Oh, *Oma!*' Hannah protested. 'You must not say such things, they are like dreams – only in your mind.'

The old lady glanced up sharply, her voice suddenly stronger as she said:

'Yes, that is what your father wishes you and me to believe. Why do you think he moved me from my home and shut me up here in his house? It was to stop me speaking the truth, to stop me finding out more what these evil men are doing. Yes, Hannah, and also because when I went outside my house and met other people I refused to say: *Heil Hitler!* and would only use our old greeting: *Grüss Gott!* Your father tried to make me believe that nothing is wrong with our country; that I must try to believe *Herr* Hitler is a good man with no evil intention to rid Germany of our race.'

She paused, momentarily breathless. When she spoke again, there was a strange note of pity in her voice as she took Hannah's hand and held it between her own.

'It is best you should know the truth, child,' she said, 'then there is hope that you will be spared. Ask yourself, *Liebling*, why your papa, so good a *Doktor*, has so few patients now. It is because he is forbidden to treat anyone but Jewish people. Why do you think he has closed his beautiful surgery and moved what was possible into this house?'

She paused briefly, fighting once more to regain her breath. Then she said in a near whisper:

'Before I came here a month ago, my friend *Frau* Abraham told me that she has heard there is a plan for all Jewish people to have the letter "J" on their persons as well as the yellow star we must now wear. Last May, *Herr und Frau* Abraham were turned out of their beautiful home, and it was given to a non-Jewish family. Last month our precious synagogue was burned to the ground. Your father has hidden me up here because he is afraid I will protest about such atrocities and be sent to prison or to one of the labour camps *Frau* Abraham was talking about.'

Suddenly she shrugged her thin shoulders.

'Maybe he is right to silence me, for of a certainty he, your mother and you, too, *meine Liebling*, would be denounced. It was his hope early this year that our family could emigrate, but I cannot go. I have an illness which makes it impossible for me to walk and soon I shall not even be able to sit up. It is my wish that your parents should leave while there is still time but your father is a stubborn man, and he tells me he cannot desert his patients, but I know that is not the reason he stays here.'

Now clearly exhausted, she leant back against the cushions and beckoned Georgia to come closer.

'When I heard Hannah was bringing you home for a visit, my heart gladdened, for while you are here she will be safe. You will be able to enjoy yourselves like other young people, but you must stay always at her side. You will promise me, yes?'

Georgia promised. Filled with a mass of conflicting thoughts, when they reached their own bedroom, they sat down on the bed and she put her arm round Hannah's drooping shoulders.

'Maybe your father is right, Hannah, and your grandmother doesn't understand what she is talking about. Perhaps her mind is disturbed in the way your father said, and she just made up all those stories about what's happening here to Jewish people.'

It was several minutes before Hannah replied. Then she said in a choked voice:

'I think *Oma* knew exactly what she was saying; that it is *Vater* who is trying to pretend that nothing is wrong. Why are all the curtains drawn? Why did he close his beautiful old surgery where he used to have so many patients, some of them important men? Why did our cook leave? She was a Protestant and perhaps was forbidden to work for a Jewish family? Oh, Georgia, I should not have invited you here if I had known any of this!'

Georgia hugged the weeping girl.

'Your grandmother said you will be quite safe if you are with me: we can still enjoy our holiday!' she said. 'We can still go to the opera as you promised. As you know, I have never been to one before; and I have never been sailing on a lake. Besides, we shall be together, Hannah, and we always enjoy ourselves whatever we do. You can pretend not to be a Jew, can't you?'

A thought suddenly struck her. Inge was part of their happy threesome at school: had she after all known what was happening in her country? Had she been told that she mustn't be friends with a Jewish girl?

No, she decided, Inge was as ignorant as herself or, indeed, as Hannah, of what Inge's adored *Führer, Herr* Adolf Hitler, was allowing to happen. She'd spoken only of the good things, the new motorways, the factories, jobs and organisations for the young people like the *Hitler Jugend*. Surely the Austrians would not have welcomed the Germans taking over their country if Hitler was really discriminating in such a horrid way against half their population?

Hannah was now looking a little less unhappy.

'You know, Georgia, I wonder if perhaps my grandmother really is inventing some of these awful things after all. It could all be happening in her mind yet seem real to her. Sick people do have delusions, don't they?'

'Yes, they do!' Georgia replied, but as they went off arm

in arm to run the hot water into the big white bath they intended to share, it struck her as inconceivable that happy, friendly, nice girls like Inge could ever be made to do the awful things Hannah's grandmother had described. But at the same time, she was of the unhappy opinion that everything the old lady had said was not imaginary but all too true.

CHAPTER FOURTEEN

1938

Sebastian was sitting in the armchair in the twins' mews cottage. He had taken to dropping in in the evenings when he'd temporarily run out of ideas for the next chapter of his novel, and the girls always made him welcome. From time to time, he took them out for a drink at their local public house where the regulars no longer stared at the twins. The Dog & Deer had become almost a second home to the three of them.

The heat of the summer sun had cooled a little, and a soft breeze blew in from the windows as Sebastian took occasional draughts of beer from the glass he was holding. For the past half hour, he had been listening to the girls' excited chatter about their new premises in Cadogan Place. They had become so successful that they were unable to keep up with all the orders they were getting.

The girls were always interested in what Sebastian had to tell them and seemed genuinely so in his enthusiastic praise for the American tycoon, Howard Hughes, who had broken the record in July for flying round the world.

'He did it in three days, nineteen hours and seventeen minutes in his twin-engined Lockheed aeroplane,' Sebastian told them. 'He clocked up nearly fifteen thousand miles, would you believe?!'

He was gratified by their reactions when they suggested the day might come when he himself broke a flying record. He had grown very fond of them, he thought as he glanced from one to the other. They were sipping glasses of gin and tonic and were perched either side of the window.

Rose now enquired if he'd had any recent news from Georgia.

'I had a letter from her yesterday,' he told them. 'It was full of details about the fun she and her school friend were having in Germany. It seems her latest idea is to become a journalist with the long-term aim of becoming a war correspondent. She doesn't seem to know a female can't do things like that.'

'Why ever not?' Rose said. 'Look at those women aviators . . .'

'. . . and Freya Stark who trekked round Arabia on her own . . .' Lily added.

'. . . and what about all those Spanish women you saw fighting with their armies?' Rose said.

For a moment, Sebastian was once again reminded of the beautiful young female soldier who had saved his life and who, on their one unforgettable night on a mountainside, had seen him as a means to forget her dreadful memories. Then he turned his attention back to the twins as Rose continued:

'Did Georgia say when she was coming home?'

'She's been in Germany for absolutely ages!' added Lily.

Sebastian nodded, his expression now concerned.

'She was supposed to be there for three weeks,' he said, 'and it's now over a month if not six weeks. Your Uncle Gerald is quite cross as well as worried. He has sent her two telegrams telling her she must come home at once because of the political situation. She simply tells your aunt and uncle not to worry: that she's having a really good time, and promises to return home soon, whatever that may mean. So Mr Driffield telephoned her friend's parents again but all the father said was that everything was quite calm and that they were all so much enjoying Georgia's visit.'

The twins were now regarding Sebastian anxiously.

'You don't really think there will be a war, do you, Seb?'

'A lot of people obviously do think so,' he replied. 'Why else should the government order a thousand Spitfire fighters last month, and the Royal Air Force have a big recruitment programme going? My parents don't know it, but I volunteered for the air force because I am, after all, already a qualified pilot, but I got turned down on health grounds as I'm still receiving treatment for the damage done to my leg in Spain.' His mouth widened into a boyish grin. 'Mind you,' he added, 'that hasn't stopped me nipping down to Shoreham every other weekend to give my little Moth an airing! As soon as you can get away, I'm going to give you a spin in her as a thank you for getting my place ready for me to live in.'

'I think that's perfectly sweet of you!' they both cried and, jumping up, went over to his chair and kissed him, each one on either cheek.

'We didn't want a reward,' Rose said.

'We did it because we love you!' Lily explained.

After Sebastian had left, they looked at one another, each with the same thought.

'He's such a nice chap, it's really . . .'

'. . . a shame Migs married someone else.'

'Maybe he'll find another girlfriend soon . . .'

'. . . and forget all about Migs.'

They exchanged smiles.

'At least we don't have to worry about having our hearts broken.'

'We'd prefer a thousand times to be selling and arranging flowers to having to look after husbands!'

'Even someone as nice as Sebastian!'

'Did you ever see such a mess as the state of his place?'

'I suppose we'll have to go round there again next Sunday and do some more tidying up for him.'

Reminded of the next day's early morning visit to Covent Garden, they decided that it was time for bed.

Further up the road, Sebastian, too, had retired for the night, but he was not asleep. He lay awake wondering whether Georgia would be safe if, as the recent news indicated, it might well now happen that Germany would march into Czechoslovakia

as they did Austria: there and if so, would Great Britain decide
to intervene and would there be war?

As was Hannah's custom, she was upstairs talking to her
grandmother before the evening meal. She liked to spend at
least an hour a day with the old lady. For the present her
mother was busy in the kitchen where she was preparing their
dinner, and Georgia was in the drawing room writing in her
notebook details of the excursion she and Hannah and six
other students had made to Augsburg. One of the German
boys had an accordion and in the train they had all sung songs
to his accompaniment. There had been several interruptions
from two SS officials with questions, and many 'Heil Hitler's
and Nazi salutes, but as soon as they mentioned their nation-
alities and produced the identity cards with which they had
been issued, they'd been told to enjoy themselves and have a
pleasant day.

   She was now disturbed by Hannah's father, who came into
the room to ask if she would be so kind as to go with him
to the library that he now used as a surgery. Hiding her
surprise, as no one was permitted to enter it, Georgia followed
him into the room.

   The heavy brocade curtains were drawn so the room was
shadowed and the atmosphere musty. In the dim, murky light,
Georgia was only half aware of the locked medicine cupboards
and medical appliances. She watched as the doctor removed
the dust sheets from his desk and the chair opposite it. Despite
the heat of the summer's day, she had a strange feeling of
apprehension. It had once or twice previously occurred to her
that *Doktor* Klein's bright smiles and jolly tones were a little
forced, but he was always so gentle and loving to Hannah
and friendly towards herself that those moments of doubt had
been brief.

   Now as they both sat down, his face was grey and his voice
trembled slightly as he said in his heavily accented English:
   'I have a confession to make to you, Georgia, which I must

now correct. I do so because I have come to know and respect you these last weeks, and I have no choice but to turn to you, young as you are, for help.'

His face was now so drawn and pale, Georgia felt obliged to say that she would do anything she could do to help.

At her response the doctor looked as if he was struggling not to weep. His voice was husky with emotion as he said in a long torrent of words:

'I have tried to keep from my *liebe* daughter, and from you, too, details of all the frightening things which have been and are happening to Jewish people like ourselves. As you know, I told you and Hannah that her grandmother was suffering from a form of dementia. *Das ist nicht so!* Everything my mother may have said to you about the present dangers for us German Jews is true! We are in great danger, and there is nothing I can do to prevent whatever is to happen. Indeed, it is now questionable whether any of us will survive.'

He paused only to draw breath before continuing in a voice that, despite his efforts to remain calm, trembled from time to time with emotion.

'Because you are here, Georgia, it has been possible for Hannah to enjoy these past happy weeks because she is with you and with other young people from foreign countries who are not concerned whether or not Hannah is Jewish. But after you have gone home – and last night on the telephone your father insisted that you do so – Hannah will be subjected to the same treatment all the Jewish people are now suffering.'

Both shocked and puzzled by what *Doktor* Klein was telling her, Georgia waited for him to continue.

'Although until recently I was permitted to practise medicine, but only with Jewish patients, my medical certificate has now been withdrawn; and since last month, I may only act as a nurse. Furthermore I have had to surrender to the authorities nearly all my savings: but that is not why I have asked you to be here.' He broke off for a moment, looking close to tears, and a moment later he continued:

'Perhaps it was wrong of me to hide the truth from Hannah, but I wanted her to remain a carefree child a little longer. I lied to her when I told her we have to wear the yellow star of David on our overcoats just to show everyone we are proud of our religion.'

Doktor Klein now drew a trembling sigh.

'My wife and I so much wanted to see our daughter happy this one last time and I hoped to protect her from the truth.'

How was it possible that she herself had stayed in this country and not been aware of all the dreadful things that were going on behind the scenes, Georgia thought. Yes, she had seen men and women, even children, with yellow stars on their clothes; she had once seen a tailor's shop window shattered and been told a brick had been thrown through it, but the German student who was walking with her at the time merely shrugged his shoulders and told her the owner was a thief and a degenerate who they were well rid of. Georgia had given it little further thought, supposing as she did that the man had been a common criminal, but now, in retrospect, she remembered there had been the word JUDE written across one unbroken windowpane, and realised the owner had been a Jew.

Somehow she was finding it difficult to reconcile the charming, well-mannered German students who were hers and Hannah's friends with the Nazi oppressors *Doktor* Klein had been describing. She and Hannah had happily joined in the crowds who gathered in the streets to cheer Adolf Hitler when he was passing in his car. They had happily accompanied all the other students to torchlight parades and raised their arms in salute and shouted '*Heil Hitler*' as everyone did. It had all been great fun: no one had said or done anything unpleasant to Hannah. Granted she had not been wearing a yellow star on the pretty cardigan she had borrowed, so perhaps no one had realised she was Jewish. Even had they done so, she, Georgia, could not believe that their friendly companions would have behaved any differently towards Hannah. Was it possible, she asked herself, that Hannah and her family's lives were really in mortal danger?

Doktor Klein reached across the desk and took Georgia's hands in his. Steadying his voice, he said:

'It hurts me to burden you with knowledge of these dreadful things, but now I must. I have been warned by a medical colleague who is not Jewish, a friend since our student days, who lives in Berlin and has important patients in the government, that there exist labour camps where any number of Jews have been sent far from their homes to work. There are rumours that hundreds of inmates have died in these places.'

Appalled by what she was hearing, Georgia held her breath as *Doktor* Klein continued: 'I fear events have overtaken me,' he said. 'I had thought we were all safe for a little while longer, but . . .' His voice shook and he paused before saying: 'Last night, my neighbour, a friend for the past twenty-two years, called round to see me after you were all in bed. Although perforce he has become a member of the Nazi Party he came to warn me that contrary to my expectations, we are on a list of people for deportation.'

'Are you telling me your lives are in danger?' Georgia asked.

Seeing the look of disbelief on her face, *Doktor* Klein cleared his throat and, with an effort, tried not to shock her with the facts he was about to relate.

'As I think you are aware, we, the Jewish people, are no longer wanted in our country. Many of my friends and former patients have departed to other countries and I, too, would have left had it not been for my mother's health. There is no way she could undertake such an arduous step into the unknown. I do have a sister who lives in Australia but she is a widow and lives in a very small apartment on the tiny legacy her husband left her, so even were we able to emigrate, she could not accommodate us.' He looked down at his hands, which were clasped tightly together.

'I have made considerable savings over the years,' he

continued, 'but it is not permitted for Jews to take money –
our money – out of the country, so even were my mother able
to travel, it is doubtful if we could obtain visas to Australia,
being unable to support ourselves.'

For a long moment, the doctor did not speak. Then, with
an apologetic smile, he said:

'If I am digressing a little, it is because I wish you to understand the situation with which I am currently faced.'

He leant forward and peered over his spectacles at Georgia's
face, his eyes suddenly filling with tears.

'It is so sad . . .' he murmured '. . . so sad that you young
people should have to know these terrible things!'

In an attempt to comfort him, Georgia said:

'Hannah is my very best friend and if I can help in any
way at all, I will certainly do so.'

The doctor attempted a smile.

'You are very kind and my Hannah is most fortunate to
have you for her friend.' His expression now became grave
once more as he said emphatically: 'I have to find a way to
get her out of Germany before it is too late. My neighbour
tells me that it is only a matter of a week, two at the most,
before they will come to take us all away.'

'Away?' Georgia questioned, horrified. 'You don't mean to
one of those labour camps?'

The doctor nodded.

'It is quite probable that we would have been taken before
now, but they would not do this while you, a foreigner, are
here. My neighbour saw the list of Jews who are soon to be
deported, and he recognised my name and he came to warn
me of the danger I and my family are in.'

Georgia was beginning to understand his obvious desperation.

'Is there nowhere you could hide?' she asked. 'Your relations
in Garmisch . . .'

'I cannot allow such a thing!' he broke in. 'At present, they
have been able to conceal the fact that they are Jewish. It
would soon be reported that they were hiding us and then

they, too, would be deported. Also . . .' he drew a long sigh
'. . . there is my mother. Her mind is quite clear at times, but
at others, she cannot understand that she must not persist in
speaking of our religion and vilifying the regime. I must stay
with her. As for my wife, she will never be parted from me.
No, Georgia, I am resigned to whatever Fate has ready for
us, but if it is humanly possible, I must save my darling Hannah
who has all her life ahead of her.'

Shocked by the doctor's revelations, Georgia did not for a
moment consider them to be fabricated. In the short time she
had known him, it had become clear to her that he was every
bit as well informed as her father.

'What can I do to help?' she asked.

It was a moment before *Doktor* Klein spoke, then he said:

'It was not until yesterday I realised my need to be concerned
for Hannah. Suddenly, ten days ago, we were ordered to hand
in our passports and the authorities informed me we could
not have them back. I explained about Hannah's further education at college but they refused to return them as a Jewish
girl had no need of more education.'

Seeing the look on Georgia's face, he felt a moment's
compunction as to what he was about to request of her: but
his love for his only child was uppermost as he outlined his
plan.

'I am aware you have a ticket back to England,' he said,
'and, of course, a British passport. If you were to lend these
to Hannah, perhaps she would be able to travel in your place,
although I fear you are not very alike in looks. After she is
safe in England, you could report to the British Consul that
your passport has been lost. I believe that in such a case they
would provide a new one for you. If somehow it was discovered that Hannah had used it, you could say she must have
stolen it.'

Georgia's eyes were shining. This was just the kind of
adventure she and Sebastian might have invented as children.
Then a second thought occurred to her.

'With little resemblance to me, what would they do to Hannah if she was caught crossing the border?' she asked, frowning, adding: 'Her English is not nearly as good as her French, and when she does speak it, her accent is such that she sounds as if she is still speaking German!'

Doktor Klein drew a long, trembling breath.

'I, too, have thought of this, but it is the only chance left for her to reach safety. I can give you money for her – why should not an English girl on holiday have German marks? – and a letter to your father asking him if he would use the money I will give her to buy a ticket to Australia for Hannah so she can go to my sister.'

'Oh, I'm sure he would help!' Georgia said at once. The plan did seem feasible but dangerous, taking no account of the fact that both she and Hannah might be destined to have a horrid life in the camps were their subterfuge discovered by the German authorities. Moreover, would Hannah agree to leave her family?

'*Herr Doktor*!' she exclaimed. 'What will you do if Hannah refuses to leave you all? Australia is so very far away and . . .'

The man sitting opposite her looked stricken.

'I fear she will not go willingly. Last night I was unable to sleep while I tried to think of another way to get Hannah out of this country, but I cannot. It is so sad, is it not, that open the door of its cage, a bird can fly free; but there is no one to open the door for my beloved child but you, Georgia. Please believe me that I shall not hold you in any disregard if . . .'

He was interrupted as Georgia sprang out of her chair and leant across his desk, her eyes sparkling.

'I know what we can do,' she said breathlessly as an idea took hold. 'When you spoke just now of a bird, I was reminded of my friend's aeroplane. It flies just like a bird and . . . don't you see *Herr Doktor*, if Sebastian can fly out here and take Hannah back to England in his Moth, there would be none of the risks if she was going by train.' Her thoughts leapt forward. 'She could wear the helmet and goggles I wore when Seb took me flying, and then it wouldn't be noticed that she doesn't look like my passport photograph. And it's just the sort of thing Seb would love doing and . . .' As she finally ran out of breath, the face of the man sitting opposite her was lit with hope.

'Is it possible,' he asked, 'that your friend would do this? What if the impersonation were discovered? He would be in a great deal of trouble. And you, Georgia, how will you get home without a passport? And . . .'

Once again Georgia interrupted.

'When Seb returns to fetch me he can bring my passport back with him. He can drive here in his car so no one will remember that "I" flew home a week or so earlier!' She now elaborated her plan. 'You said no one will harm your family while I am staying here, and I will stay until Seb gets back. It will work, *Herr Doktor*, I know it will.'

For a moment, the doctor remained silent, hardly daring to believe that this young girl's plan might be the solution he so desperately wanted to save his daughter's life. If Georgia's friend was willing to play his part, he could think of only one thing that could stand in the way of its execution – Hannah's refusal to leave.

It was only a minute before Georgia came up with a solution for this, too.

'I have often told her how exciting it is to be flying in an aeroplane,' she said, 'so what is to stop me when Seb gets here, saying he has offered to take her up for a spin.'

'A spin?' the doctor queried.

Georgia laughed.

'What we call a joyride – flying just for fun. I'll say Seb has offered to give both of us a go and Hannah can go first. The aeroplane can only take one passenger at a time. Once they are in the air, there would be nothing Hannah could do to stop Seb flying out of Germany. I dare say she will feel betrayed because she hasn't been able to say goodbye to you all, but you could write a letter for Seb to give her once they are safe explaining why you had to send her away.'

Doktor Klein drew a deep breath, partly of enormous relief and partly of astonishment that so young a girl as Georgia had such a quick, inventive mind. She had courage, too, showing no regard for her own safety if the plan went wrong. Was she right in thinking her father would agree to it? The doctor was frowning as he said:

'If we are to accomplish this, we must arrange things quickly, but you cannot telephone your friend because almost certainly the operator can – and they often do – listen in to our calls. I am probably the only Jew in the country who still has a telephone, and then only because I am a doctor.' He sighed: 'I fear a letter may take too long.'

To his surprise, Georgia laughed.

'Seb and I have a secret language,' she told him excitedly. 'We say exactly the opposite of what we mean. "I am sad" means "I am happy!" I can say *"Don't even think about flying out in the Moth to see me as the last thing I want is to come home yet. No point coming for ages and ages as I might not be here!"'*

Seeing the man's bewildered expression, she translated happily:

'"*Do fly out in the Moth to see me as I want to come home now. Come as quickly as possible. Will definitely be here.*" And I'll sign it "*Aigroeg*" – that's "Georgia" spelt backwards – so he'll know the message is in our code.'

It was at that moment, *Doktor Herr* Klein realised with a mixture of sadness and hope, that he might well be able to send his daughter far away to safety even though it would mean he might never see her again.

CHAPTER FIFTEEN

1938

In the twins' shop, Sebastian replaced the telephone receiver and waited for the customer currently buying flowers to pay their bill and leave. Then with a deep frown furrowing his forehead, he said:

'I'm seriously worried about Georgia. According to that telephone call, things aren't too good out there. The family she's staying with are Jewish, and if the newspapers are to be believed, they're having a pretty bad time of it, and I think Jo-Jo may be in trouble as she used the silly nickname I gave her so I'd know she was talking in code'.

He took the glass of beer Lily was handing him and added:

'She wants me to go out there as soon as possible, in the Moth. It doesn't make much sense, as I know for a fact her father sent her with a return rail ticket. He has telephoned me from time to time to see if I'd heard any news as he's convinced that there's going to be a war. Poor chap's worried to death about her. He tried to telephone the father of the girl she is staying with but was told they were not receiving calls. Last time I spoke to Mr Driffield, he told me he was intending to go to Munich to fetch Georgia if she wasn't back by the end of the month. He was quite angry.'

'Suppose she really is in trouble, how can you help her?' Rose asked as she wound some pretty paper round the bouquet she was arranging.

'Will you really fly all the way to Germany in your aeroplane?' Lily asked.

'What about Uncle Gerald and Aunt Isobel? Shouldn't they be told if Georgia is in trouble?' Rose asked thoughtfully.

Sebastian's look of concern deepened.

'Part of me thinks I should tell them, but, silly as it might sound, Jo-Jo and I had this sort of unwritten rule that we never told "the grown-ups" what we were up to. It's one of the reasons we had the code. I think it drove both sets of parents wild when we refused to own up to each other's misdeeds.'

'That was all very well when you were little,' Lily protested.

'Didn't she say what was wrong?' Rose asked.

Sebastian shook his head.

'No, she didn't tell me anything specific on the telephone, so I'm assuming the operator might have been listening which is why she used our code. No, I think Jo-Jo is in some kind of danger. Maybe she broke a law or was rude to one of those jumped-up Fascist black-shirts who, if the newspapers are to be believed, are all over the streets and swarm round their precious *Führer* like flies!'

'I suppose you hate the Fascists because you were fighting them in Spain . . .'

'. . . and were shot by one of them!' Lily concluded.

Sebastian shrugged.

'Maybe I am prejudiced, but I can't *not* go to Munich. Flying there shouldn't be too difficult: six or seven hours' flying time if wind and weather permit. I'd have to refuel at least three or four times, so it will probably take me the best part of two days to get there. If I left tomorrow morning, I should be there Tuesday evening. Getting hold of the money for landing fees and fuel might hold things up a bit.'

'We've got plenty of money!' Lily volunteered.

'We haven't banked the week's takings yet,' Rose added; and Lily went at once to the till and extracted a large envelope filled with ten shilling and one pound notes.

Before Sebastian left to go and pack an overnight bag to take with him, he used the twins' telephone to send Georgia a telegram asking why she hadn't answered his letter, by which he hoped she would realise that he had received and understood her telephone call asking for his help.

Seeing no point in delaying his departure, Sebastian thanked the twins profusely, drove down to Shoreham where he booked into the Foresters' Inn and spent a restless night wondering what on earth had happened to Georgia that was serious enough to warrant her asking him to make an urgent aeroplane flight all the way to Munich. The environs of Shoreham airfield were the extent of his usual sorties, other than a flip across the Channel to France. Not that he'd had an opportunity as yet to make any long journeys, for the simple reason that he'd been in Spain for a year and was convalescent when he got home. As a rule he was more interested in the sports pages of newspapers than in day-to-day affairs, but now he recalled his father's comments when reading his *Times*, about the growing anti-Semitism in Germany. There had been rumours, too, about concentration camps to which some Jewish families had been deported for work; but all Georgia's postcards home had only mentioned the fun they were having. What, he now asked himself as he lay awake in bed, could have gone wrong? He was still pondering the question when finally he fell into an uneasy sleep.

When he was airborne next day, the sun was shining in a brilliant blue sky dotted here and there by little white cotton wool clouds, and his spirits lifted. He would never, ever tire of flying, he thought. He loved his little Gipsy Moth and would not have exchanged it for one of the new bigger Tiger Moths. Its hundredhorsepower engine enabled him to cruise between eighty and ninety miles an hour. Since his parents had given it to him, he had notched up fifty flying hours, and he felt totally at one with his little aeroplane.

Flying across the Channel at fifteen hundred feet, he could see the boats like toys beneath him, and when he crossed the coast into France, so good was the visibility that sometimes he saw a person waving to him and he would dip his wings to acknowledge their greeting.

After two hundred miles of flight, he was glad of a brief break when he stopped at the airbase north of Reims to refuel. After a quick cup of coffee, he departed once more to Stuttgart, his next refuelling stop. On his arrival there he was warned by the Met Officer that there could be heavy thunderstorms on the next leg of his journey, so he decided to remain where he was for the night.

When he booked into a small *Gasthof* near the airport, he became aware immediately of a different atmosphere from that to be found in guest houses in England. He was greeted by the owner with a raised hand salute and a loud '*Heil Hitler*'. Both dining room and bar were dominated by grey-blue, black-and brown-uniformed men who were clearly enjoying themselves. It sounded as noisy as an undergraduate end-of-term jolly, he thought, their loud voices and laughter totally obliterating the needs of other guests wishing to converse with one another.

Sebastian had barely finished the excellent plate of *Spaetzle mit Gulasch* put in front of him before he was approached by one of the young men who he guessed by his uniform was a member of the *Luftwaffe*. On hearing Sebastian was English and had flown to Stuttgart in a Gipsy Moth, the German air force pilot cadet was instantly interested. After introducing himself, he invited Sebastian to join his party at the bar where they were drinking large *Steins* of *Pils*. Seeing no reason for refusing this friendly gesture, Sebastian was soon the centre of attention, those of his new companions who were fellow aviators plying him with questions in excellent if guttural English. Their enquiries were not only about his aeroplane and his flying experience, but they also wanted to know if he had come to Germany for a holiday and where he was going.

He had been about to reply that he was going to Munich next day to visit a friend when some sixth instinct impelled him to make up a fictitious friend in Austria. He was instantly besieged with information about the country and how thrilled the Austrian population had been to be reunited with Germany, and to have Adolf Hitler as their *Führer*. Did Sebastian's friends in England know what a wonderful leader the *Führer* was? How greatly he was revered by every German man, woman and child?

'Excepting by the Jewish rabble!' one of the black-shirts commented, whereupon they set about outdoing each other vilifying the Jewish people. Only Sebastian's pilot friend, Rudolf, less inebriated than his friends, was not so virulent.

'They aren't all as bad as that!' he said. 'I had a Jewish history master at my school who was not only clever but a really good teacher.'

He was promptly shouted down.

'Of course they are clever, clever enough to get all the best jobs and make themselves loads of money!' one of the black-shirted men said scornfully. 'You should get rid of them in your country, my English friend! Do you have no idea how evil and grasping they are?'

'You should warn your people when you go home,' another said, 'before they take over your banks, your shops, and steal all the art treasures that should rightly belong to the real citizens of your country as they have done in ours.'

It struck Sebastian that he was listening to a recitation of political propaganda instilled by their leaders. What, he wondered, would happen were he suddenly to announce that he was visiting a Jewish family?

He explained that he was making an early start next day and must excuse himself. Thanking them for the beer they had insisted upon buying him, he retired to his room. As he climbed into bed it suddenly occurred to him that this anti-Semitic attitude was almost certainly reflected by people in Munich, and that Georgia's Jewish friends could be suffering from the same irrational prejudice as that trumpeted by the young men downstairs.

* * *

It was five o'clock in the evening when the taxi Sebastian had hired to take him from Oberwiesenfeld Airfield to the Kleins' home arrived. Although it was still daylight, he noticed that all the curtains in the windows had been drawn. Those of a house on the opposite side of the street were fluttering in the slight breeze, and with a shock, he saw that the glass had been broken as if by a brick or other heavy object. On the doors of both this and the Kleins' house was a large capital letter 'J'.

He paid the driver, who took his money with a strange look on his face as he said:

'*Englisch? Wissens' net, san Juden? Gehen lieber Hotel?*'

Sebastian shook his head and thanked the driver, who he guessed thought he had been doing him a kindness by warning him it was a Jewish household. Telling the man he had no wish to go to a hotel, he stepped up to the front door and rang the bell. He was obliged to ring it several times before it was opened tentatively by Georgia. Seeing who it was, she flung herself into his arms and burst into tears.

Sebastian was now seriously worried. Throughout their childhood, he had almost never seen Georgia cry – not even when she had fallen and cut one of her chubby little legs so badly, the doctor had to be called and, while she lay on the kitchen table, had put three stitches in the wound.

He picked up his overnight bag, which he had dropped on the doorstep in order to hug Georgia, and followed her into the dimly lit hall.

'Oh, Seb, I'm so pleased to see you!' she said, her tears drying rapidly as she opened the door into *Doktor* Klein's library and all but dragged Sebastian inside. 'I was afraid you had not understood my telephone call or weren't able to come!'

As he sat down on the edge of the chair by the doctor's desk and Georgia pulled up another chair close beside him, he was frowning.

'Didn't you get my telegram? I telegraphed you to say I would be with you by Tuesday, today.'

Georgia shook her head.

'No, I didn't get it. I suspect the telephone people wouldn't deliver a telegram to a Jewish household. Oh, Seb, you don't know how awful things are here!'

Sebastian looked confused.

'All those postcards you sent – you said you and your friend were having a wonderful time, and by the way, you've got a smudge on the end of your nose!'

Georgia rubbed it with the back of her hand and smiled shakily at him.

'I'm just so very glad you're here, Seb, even if you are rude to me!'

No longer smiling, she explained why she had brought him into the library rather than into the drawing room and proceeded to outline her plan.

'It's absolutely essential Hannah doesn't know about it. You will fly her home, won't you, Seb?' she ended.

Sebastian was silent as he digested Georgia's crazy scheme to rescue her friend.

'It's very risky, Jo-Jo,' he said eventually. 'Even if I get Hannah back to Shoreham safely, suppose I'm prevented for some reason from getting back to Munich to collect you? Or if the German authorities thought, rightly, that you were involved in Hannah's disappearance, things could turn very nasty for you. Or they might find you here and think you are part of *Doktor* Klein's household. You wouldn't have your passport to prove otherwise, you might even be arrested!'

Georgia's expression was deeply serious as she looked into Sebastian's eyes and whispered:

'*Doktor* Klein has discovered that his whole family are soon to be sent to one of the labour camps. I can't go home and just leave Hannah here, Seb. Either I stay with her or she goes home with you.'

'I'll have a word with her father: see what he has to say.

If he thinks no harm will come to you before I can return with your passport, I'm prepared to have a go.'

Georgia stood up and flung her arms round him once more.

'You always were my brave hero!' she said tremulously. 'I've thought it all out, Seb: this evening you will tell Hannah and me that tomorrow morning you will take us both for a spin round the countryside in your aeroplane. She will be thrilled. At the last minute, I'll call off, saying I'm feeling sick. By then I will have given you my passport and a letter from her father for you to give her after you have flown safely out of Germany and have stopped for refuelling.'

Sebastian drew a deep sigh.

'I can see you've thought of every contingency, Jo-Jo. Maybe, Mata Hari, we'd have had a better chance of winning the war in Spain if you'd been our commander!'

'So who's Mata Hari?' Georgia asked, happy now that she was almost certain Sebastian was going to fall in with her plan.

'A spy in the last war!' Seb told her. 'Now let me meet the rest of the family, and don't get too excited yet, Jo-Jo. I've promised nothing, and won't do so until the doctor can assure me you will be safe for the week I have to leave you here. I'm far too fond of you, believe it or not, to put Hannah's safety before yours. This isn't one of our silly childhood games, you know.'

Georgia nodded and, as so many hundred times in the long-ago past, she stood to attention and said with a grin:

'Agent Aigroeg at your service, sir. I'm yours to obey!'

But this time, Sebastian neither smiled nor made any response. He was far too worried, and if the worst happened, he would never, ever forgive himself.

For the night following Sebastian's departure next day with Hannah, her parents, as well as Georgia, were on tenterhooks. Despite their careful planning, they knew the hazards were many. Hannah had departed happily enough with Sebastian to enjoy what she believed was a joyride over the city. She did not see the look of concern on Georgia's face as she waved goodbye nor the tears of the parents she left behind, unaware as she was that she might never see them again.

Sebastian had promised to telephone the moment he and his passenger touched down at Reims and it came as an enormous relief when he did so, saying their flight had so far been uneventful. Neither Georgia nor Hannah's father were able to comfort *Frau* Klein, whose tears streamed from her eyes seemingly uncontrollably, at the thought of the sacrifice they had had to make to ensure their daughter's future.

Perhaps hardest of all was the need to find rational excuses when Hannah's grandmother kept asking why she had not paid her usual visit that evening. They dared not tell her the truth lest the authorities arrived unexpectedly making enquiries. Georgia invented a fictitious friend who had invited Hannah out to dinner, and the old lady did not question the excuse.

After Sebastian had telephoned Hannah's parents he telephoned his mother to tell her where he had been and that he was bringing Hannah home in Georgia's place. Joan promptly hurried next door to bring the Driffields up to date.

'I knew something must be wrong when Georgia refused to come home when I instructed her to do so,' Gerald expostulated. 'I don't doubt this is all Georgia's doing, aided and abetted by your son, Joan,' he added in none too friendly a tone. 'One would think that at his age Sebastian at least would act more responsibly.' He gave a deep sigh as he rang for Polly and asked her to bring in the sherry and whisky decanters. 'I suppose we should not be surprised by anything he does after the way he rushed off to Spain at a moment's notice. I dare say Georgia would have gone with him had he given her the chance!' he added sardonically.

Isobel now spoke up.

'That child has always had a will of her own!' she said.

Gerald frowned.

'Georgia may have an adventurous streak, Isobel, but criticising the child is no solution to the present situation,' he said sharply.

'It seems to me there isn't any point in worrying,' Joan broke in. 'Sebastian said he and the German girl should be here tonight.' She sighed: 'I suppose this Jewish girl is a refugee and we should do what we can to help her. Sebastian did say she was going to Australia to live with her aunt.'

'If she can get a visa!' Gerald said dourly. 'Frankly, Joan, I am more concerned about my daughter. It doesn't seem to have occurred to anyone that her passport will be stamped when the Hannah child comes into this country pretending it is hers. Yes, Sebastian can take it back out to Georgia, I suppose, if, as he told you, that is the intention, but what if the German authorities make a house check for some obscure reason and find the girl missing and Georgia without a passport and unable to prove she is British. It's all highly dangerous.'

Isobel stood up and, going across the room to the sofa table where Polly had placed the tray of drinks, filled a glass with sherry and took it over to Joan. For once, she had nothing more to say.

'All this speculation is getting us nowhere.' Gerald turned now to look at Sebastian's mother. 'We must just wait until they get here. We talk about Georgia being adventurous, but I ask myself who taught her to be that way? If any harm comes to Georgia, a great deal of the blame will lie very squarely on your son's shoulders, Joan,' he said flatly.

Although not entirely agreeing with Gerald, Joan was almost as worried as he was.

After she had returned home, a further consideration occurred to Gerald: that the notoriety such a case might receive from the tabloid newspapers if it became known what the young pair were doing, would be bound to reach the ear of his seniors at the War Office. However, this thought, worrying as it might be, was as nothing compared to his overriding fear that the child he loved so dearly could already have come to harm.

It was not, however, in Munich that Georgia was nearly killed. The plan for Sebastian to return by car to take her back to England was effected without interference from any of the German authorities. The danger to both their lives befell as they drove through France.

CHAPTER SIXTEEN

1938

'I think we'll have to stop if this rain gets much heavier!'

Sebastian sounded anxious as he peered through the water streaming off his windscreen at the blurred outline of the road ahead. Like so many of the French roads, it was as straight as a die, and visibility in good weather would have enabled him to push the speed of his car up to seventy miles an hour. This summer evening, however, the unseasonable thundery down-pour had slowed him almost to a crawl. Very occasionally, another car or lorry would come looming towards them through the spray, headlights glowing briefly as they passed by.

He and Georgia had crossed the border from Germany into France soon after dawn, and he had planned to catch a return boat ferry to Newhaven before dark. At the speed they were travelling it now looked as if that would be impossible unless by some miracle the rain eased up. Through a brief lull in the downpour he glimpsed the sky heavy with black clouds fore-telling worse to come. The euphoria he and Georgia had both felt when they had successfully passed through passport control into France, leaving Germany behind them, helped to lessen the distress they had felt when leaving Hannah's heartbroken parents to whatever unpleasant future their country had in store for them. However, not even this was foremost in their thoughts as Sebastian said in worried tones:

'It isn't safe to go on driving in this. We'll have to stop at the next hotel or inn that we see, so keep your eyes open, Jo-Jo. Give me as much warning as you can if you see lights ahead.'

Five minutes later as flashes of lightning lit up the sky, and even heavier rain made visibility worse, he said anxiously: 'If I pulled up suddenly, a car behind us might easily drive straight into the back of us. I keep looking for a safe place to stop, but there doesn't seem to be a farm or field entrance anywhere out here in the wilds!'

However, it was not from behind them that the danger came: it was from a car speeding towards them far too fast for the conditions. The driver must suddenly have glimpsed Sebastian's headlights and he braked violently. With his tyres finding no adhesion on the wet surface of the road, the car skidded across the highway towards Sebastian's M.G. out of the driver's control.

Watching this happening as if it were in slow motion, Sebastian realised he had only a split second to avoid a head-on collision. With the certainty that this would probably mean death for all of them, he swung the wheel sharply over to the left without any idea of what lay on the opposite side of the road.

The oncoming car clipped the back wheel of the M.G. so that it went over the verge sideways and fell into the field below, landing on its roof, which caved in. Both Sebastian and Georgia had been flung sideways, and for several minutes, they lay in the semi-darkness across the front seats. There was a shocking smell of petrol.

Sebastian was first to speak. His voice was shaky as he asked:

'Are you all right, Jo-Jo? For God's sake, say something, will you?'

Hearing the panic in Sebastian's voice, Georgia struggled to find her own to reassure him. She was slightly winded and her head throbbed, but as far as she could tell, she was not seriously hurt. It was a moment or two before she could ascertain where exactly they were: then she realised that not only was the car upside down but that the flattened roof would have struck both their heads, almost certainly killing them, had they not fallen sideways. There was only just enough headroom for them to sit upright.

Sebastian, too, was struggling to right himself. His voice was shaking as he said urgently:

'We're leaking petrol. We've got to get out – quickly! I can't get this ruddy door open. It's jammed! See if you can push with me . . .'

It was no easy task with the car upside down, but with both of their efforts it creaked ajar. Sebastian gave it a last shove and it opened sufficiently for him to push Georgia through the aperture. As she fell into the sodden field that mercifully had cushioned their fall, Sebastian scrambled out beside her. Within seconds, they were drenched by the heavy rain. It beat down on Georgia's head, and she became conscious of a dull throbbing in her temples beneath her dripping rain-soaked hair.

Sebastian now disappeared round to the other side of the upturned car, and reached through the smashed windscreen to turn off the ignition – something he had forgotten to do in his concern for their safety. Although the petrol seemed to have stopped leaking out, he remained concerned that despite the rain the fluid might ignite and he dared not light the cigarette he now badly needed.

Hair plastering his forehead, he reached once more inside and drew out a car rug, the only temporary shelter he could find for Georgia as he draped it over her head and round her shoulders.

'Sure you're all right?' he said again. 'We're damned lucky to be alive, Jo-Jo, if you'll pardon my language. Trouble is, what do we do now? Think we can climb back up that bank to the road?'

The water was streaming down it from the roadside looking like a mini waterfall, and the ground beneath their feet was a quagmire. Georgia's body was now beginning to ache all over but she said nothing as Sebastian tried to find a foothold and pull her up the slippery surface.

'If only this confounded rain would stop!' he gasped as they managed to scramble on to the tarmac. 'It'll be dark any moment and I don't imagine there'll be much passing traffic. Even if something does go by, I daren't step out into the centre of the road to flag them down else they might skid like that stupid fool who nearly killed us. You'd think he would have had the decency to stop and see if we were alive! He must have known he was driving far too fast for the conditions, and done a bunk!'

He put an arm round Georgia's shoulders and drew her against him.

'I wish you'd say something, Jo-Jo. It's not like you to be so quiet. Are you sure you're all right?'

Georgia felt as if at any moment she might burst into tears.

'Of course I'm all right!' she told him. 'Only we can't stay here all night in the pouring rain. I do wish it would stop!'

Sebastian was only half listening to her for he had heard the sound of an approaching car. He stepped out into the road as far as he dared, ready to flag the car down if he possibly could.

There was no need for him to do so. A police car pulled to a halt in front of him and two uniformed *gendarmes* climbed out. They fired a volume of questions too fast for Sebastian to fully comprehend what they were saying. Although he spoke some French, he quickly referred them to Georgia who he knew to be almost bilingual, having spoken the language so consistently in her Swiss school.

Georgia's account of what had happened brought forth a fresh torrent of words from one of the *gendarmes*. She turned to Sebastian.

'He says the car that hit us stopped at the next town and reported that we had fallen off the road into a field and were almost certainly dead! The driver gave them our exact location in kilometres, which explains how they've found us so quickly,' she ended.

She now translated the second *gendarme*'s instructions.

'He says we are to leave the car where it is; that they will arrange for a garage to collect it in the morning. Meanwhile we must permit him to conduct us to the hospital to ascertain our damage!' She managed a smile and Sebastian looked less worried.

'Thank goodness you can understand the lingo so easily!' he said. Mercifully, it finally stopped raining and he and the younger of the two *gendarmes* slithered back down into the field. With the aid of a torch, they managed to retrieve the suitcases from the back of the upturned car.

'They are a bit damp but otherwise intact,' he told Georgia as he joined her in the back seat of the police car. It was fractionally warmer inside but both of them were now shivering with the cold as well as from shock. Seeing this, the *gendarme* sitting next to the driver told Georgia she must not worry about anything: the hospital would ensure their good health, after which they would be conducted to an *auberge* where food and accommodation for the night would be provided for them.

'You have money?' he enquired. 'English notes will suffice if you do not have francs.'

'We have sufficient money to pay for an inexpensive hotel,' Georgia said, 'but not nearly enough to buy a new car if ours is so badly damaged it can't be repaired. It is almost certainly insured, but I imagine it would take time to reclaim the money.'

'*Ce n'est pas de quoi!*' they replied in unison. 'You are an English gentleman and lady, and so we trust you. The garage will lend you a car if necessary, or we will lend you the money to buy train tickets to your home.'

Georgia felt the unaccustomed tears threatening once more as Sebastian remarked on the kindness being proffered them. In his halting French he told the *gendarmes* that he did not think either he or Georgia needed hospital treatment, but they insisted it was obligatory after an accident such as theirs.

'He says that in the morning after we have had a good night's sleep and eaten our *petit déjeuner*, they will come to our hotel for us to assist them to complete the necessary documents for their reports,' Georgia told him.

An hour and a half later, after a thorough inspection by the hospital doctor to ensure they had no broken bones, the *gendarmes* once more acted as their taxi and conducted them to what was little more than a small *auberge*. They were immediately assigned the one vacant bedroom by the owner, which, he told them proudly, had a huge double bed, adding that they might make use of the gas boiler in the bathroom. Furthermore, having been told by the *gendarme* of their accident and observing the large, shapeless but warm dressing gowns the hospital had lent them, he took possession of their bags of wet clothes, saying he would put them to dry by the boiler in the cellar. An evening meal would be brought up to their room to enjoy in front of the fire that the *fille de chambre* had lit when the *gendarme* had telephoned to ensure their accommodation.

'Such hospitality! And not even a request to see our passports!' Sebastian said to Georgia after he had thanked their tubby, moustached host, and they had been shown to their room. 'Did I gather from what he was saying downstairs that this place sports only one bedroom?'

Georgia smiled as she went to the glowing fire to hold out her cold hands to its welcome warmth.

'They have three other rooms, one occupied by him and his wife, and two single rooms currently occupied by travellers. I think he believes we are married, or if not, that we are lovers! Rose and Lily once told me that the French love romantic intrigues.'

Sebastian laughed.

'Then we won't disappoint them. When our evening meal is brought to us, I shall call you *chérie*, hold out your chair for you to be seated and lovingly kiss the top of your head!'

'Then I'd better get my hair dry,' Georgia said, laughing for the first time that evening. 'They lent me a towel in the hospital but it's still damp. Bags I first bath!'

By the time she had fought the antiquated boiler until it finally provided steaming hot water and she was ready to get out, her skin was glowing and her circulation was fully restored. The dressing gowns the hospital had provided were made of warm flannel and were so large, Georgia's enveloped her head to toe. When she returned to the bedroom to tell Sebastian he might now use the bathroom, he burst out laughing.

'With your hair all messed up and in that thing you are wearing, Jo-Jo, you look like a cross between a polar bear and a clown!' Suddenly serious, he took a step towards her and put his arms round her.

'Don't ever again let me call you a silly goose. You've been absolutely splendid, and for what it's worth, I admire your courage. Lots of other girls might have had hysterics, burst into tears, complained about everything – and there has been plenty to complain about. Damn glad I have you for a passenger and not one of them, Jo-Jo. You're the tops!'

Georgia was too choked by his unaccustomed praise to speak, and was glad when he left for the bathroom so that she could give way to tears. They were partly from weakness caused by delayed shock, and in part a release of the tension that had built up that morning as they'd left Munich and driven to the German border. As it transpired, they had been waved through all the control points after no more than a cursory glance at their British passports.

The accident may have been the catalyst, she thought, but it was Sebastian's unexpected compliments that had undermined her. They had been unsolicited and sincere, and as she bent down in front of the fire to dry her hair, she thought how lucky she was, in her turn, to have him as a friend. Now, for the first time ever, he had told her he valued her friendship, and that was more important to her than anything else in the world.

Although the large tray of food sent up by the *aubergiste* looked delicious, Georgia was only able to eat a little as she had begun to feel slightly sick. Fortunately, Sebastian was hungry enough to manage two helpings. He did so, he declared, so that the kind innkeeper would not be upset if his offerings were sent back uneaten. Sebastian then persuaded Georgia to drink a small glass of brandy. It had the magical effect of bringing some warmth back to her body, after which he insisted she go straight to bed and he busied himself putting their dishes back on the tray.

Georgia was feeling a little better as she climbed into the high double bed. She noticed that while she had been in the bathroom, Sebastian had removed the heavy quilt that had covered the big feather duvet, and that it now lay over the back of one of the two shabby armchairs by the fireside. Likewise, one of the two pillows had also been taken from the bed and put on top of the quilt. Was it possible, she wondered, that Sebastian was intending to sleep there? Tall as he was, he would be extremely uncomfortable.

Snuggling down beneath the duvet, she shivered at the touch of the cold sheets, and when Sebastian came back from the bathroom, she said:

'Do hurry up, Seb! I'm absolutely frozen.' As he made no move, she added: 'You *are* going to get into bed with me, aren't you? I can't seem to get properly warm by myself. I can't stop shivering.'

Sebastian stood looking down at the small hunched figure in the bed and felt a wave of anxiety. Could Georgia be suffering delayed shock, or had she been more seriously injured than the hospital had thought?

Seeing his hesitation, Georgia said:

'Why have you moved the quilt and the pillow? You are going to sleep with me, aren't you, Seb?' she repeated.

Sebastian's hesitation was only brief as it struck him forcibly how totally innocent Georgia was. Had nobody – her mother, one of her friends – told her the facts of life? He pulled back the duvet and climbed in beside her. She was, indeed, shivering and he put his arms round her as she snuggled up against him.

'My head hurts!' she murmured. 'It was a horrible accident, wasn't it? If it had to happen at all, I'm glad it was with you.' She gave a sudden, unexpected giggle.

'So what's funny?' Sebastian asked, glad to see that her good humour had been restored.

'Not exactly funny,' Georgia replied, 'but it suddenly crossed my mind how absolutely horrified my parents would be if they knew I was in bed with a man! They'd have a fit, though I can't see why!' Her face became suddenly thoughtful. 'Have you ever been in a bed with a girl before, Seb?'

Sebastian swallowed as he sought for suitable words. Deciding to ignore her question, he said:

'It's only married grown-ups and children who are supposed to share a bed, Jo-Jo, and that's why I'm going to sleep over there in that chair.'

Georgia looked at him with dismay.

'But why on earth do that, Seb? It's absolutely stupid! Even if we aren't supposed to be in a bed together, who on earth would know if we don't tell anyone? You'd be horribly uncomfortable and . . .'

Sebastian's voice hardened as he interrupted her, repeating that only married people shared a bed, and that it would be wrong for them to do so.

For a moment, Georgia was silent. Then she said thoughtfully:

'My real mother pretended she was married to my real father. That's how I got born. I thought you had to be married to have a baby. When I asked Polly if she knew why you were sent down from university, she guessed it was because you were doing it, but none of the girls at school knew what that meant. So if you were, Seb, doing it, I mean, will you tell me what "it" is? I promise I won't tell anyone else.'

Touched once more by her innocence but knowing Georgia's persistence, he sought to find a suitable explanation for her. Putting an arm round her shoulders, he said:

'It's a matter of loving someone, Jo-Jo, and it isn't always married people who want to be as close as they can to each other. It's best if people are married because that can mean when they have babies there will be parents and a home for them. Otherwise they only belong to the mother.'

'Sounds jolly unfair to me!' Georgia said. 'But what do they do to make a baby, Seb? It isn't just kissing, is it? Hannah said her parents had told her it was the father planting a seed in the mother and the seed grew into a baby. But how did he plant it? And if the baby grew inside the mother, how did it get out?'

'Oh, Jo-Jo!' Seb exclaimed. 'You may be a silly goose but I do love you! Look, this is all something you'll find out when you get married. There's absolutely no need for you to bother about it now.'

Georgia frowned.

'But I do bother and I want to know, Seb. Why won't you tell me? Or better still, why don't you show me what they do? I love you very much and you just said you love me, so even if I did have a baby, I could get it adopted like Daddy and Mummy adopted me, so . . .'

Sebastian's hand across her lips silenced her.

'And it would be as unhappy as you were when you found out you were adopted. Have you forgotten how upset you were?'

Georgia paused, then she said:

'Well, maybe it is better to wait: but Seb, you haven't told me about doing it. You *have* done it yourself, haven't you? A girl at school said her brother said it was all men ever think about, but you think about your aeroplane and having adventures like going to fight in Spain and writing your book, and . . .'

'Jo-Jo, let's talk about this some other time!' Sebastian interrupted gently. 'Right now we both need some sleep.'

Georgia's continual references to sex had begun to unsettle him. He was uncomfortably aware of her warm, feminine body close to him and, far worse, his own body reacting to it. Her breasts were pressed against his chest and she had flung one arm across his waist.

There had been many occasions in the past when he, Monty and a group of their friends had discussed the fact that there were girls who 'did' and girls who 'didn't', the latter belonging to backgrounds such as their own. Only one of the graduates had a sister who had permitted the boyfriend she was in love with to make love to her and that only because her parents had refused to allow them to get married and the sister had known if she got pregnant, that her parents would whisk her very quickly up the altar!

Well, Jo-Jo was like a sister to him, and as his body was doing its best to betray his lascivious desires, the sooner he put some space between them, the easier it would be for him to stop wanting to make love to her. With an effort, he drew away from the temptation of her unconscious femininity and said:

'Look, Jo-Jo, it's been a pretty awful day and I think we both need some sleep.' As casually as he could, he turned on his side, managing to put a space between them as he did so.

He both heard and felt the huge sigh Georgia gave before saying:

'All right, but you will tell me some other time, won't you? I know somehow it's got to do with love, but I don't see how . . .' Her voice trailed away.

Aware that she was falling asleep and relieved by the fact that she had made no further mention of her aching head, he slipped out of the bed and walked across the cold floor to the armchair. As Georgia had said, he was going to be extremely uncomfortable trying to ease his long legs and body into the small space now available as he pushed the two armchairs together.

Tired as he was, as well as his discomfort, he felt curiously restless both physically and mentally. What he needed, he told himself ruefully, was the release a woman would give him: a woman like the passionate Spanish girl, for example. The fact that a short while ago he had been lying beside the warm, feminine body of a young girl was, he knew, responsible for the arousal of his senses. It was not that he had ever once in his life considered Georgia in a desirable female light: she was and always had been his kid sister, his companion, his friend, and she looked up to him as she would to a brother. Even now, she had been asking him to enlighten her as to sexual behaviour without the slightest idea of encouraging a different relationship with him.

Thinking about Georgia he realised that it would probably be only a year or so before some man found her attractive and wanted to kiss her. She could be quite pretty when she bothered to make herself so, but the Georgia he knew didn't care about such compliments, desiring only his approval, and his admiration for being the kind of companion he wanted. He had never once, since he had first met her, wished she was different in any way. It was only when she lay with her body so close to his that, just for a moment, he had wished she was not his 'obedient Aigroeg', his self-appointed slave, but a girl as hungry for love as himself.

Then without warning, exhaustion overcame his discomfort, and he fell into a dreamless sleep.

The following morning, having completed the formalities at the police station and been given money for the journey home, they caught a train to Paris. It was a slow journey as the train stopped at every station. Georgia drowsed against Sebastian's shoulder explaining that she had not slept very well because of his snoring. Laughing, Sebastian denied he snored and said she had woken him twice with nightmares relating to their accident. What Georgia did not tell him was that her headache had worsened, and when Sebastian settled her more comfortably with his arm round her, she slept on and off throughout the long journey.

In Paris, she was barely conscious when Sebastian bought tickets for the boat train to Newhaven. Certain now that Georgia was far from well, he telephoned Gerald, gave him a brief account of their car accident and asked him to meet them in his car at Newhaven.

When Gerald replaced the telephone, he was torn between varying strong emotions. First and foremost he was enormously relieved to hear that both the children, as he thought of them, had survived what sounded like a near fatal accident. He realised that Sebastian's cool head had probably saved their lives, but at the same time, he was still angry with him for not vetoing Georgia's dangerous plan to rescue her German friend.

Should he, he wondered after he had replaced the receiver, not greet them with hugs? Or, more appropriately, with criticisms of their fecklessness? Would he give Georgia a real telling-off for causing Isobel and himself so much worry; or would he praise her for her courage and enterprise? And what of Sebastian, who was old enough to know better, yet had been willing to face whatever unpleasant or dangerous outcome there might have been to assist Georgia, his errant daughter, in one of her mad schemes?

He forgot what retribution he might have employed when he went to the port to collect them. Georgia was so drowsy she was all but unconscious, and Sebastian was white-faced with anxiety.

'They said at the hospital in France that Jo-Jo was unharmed,' he told Gerald as they lifted her into the back of the car, 'but the doctor didn't ask for X-rays to be done. I'm worried that she may have hurt her head. When we got to Paris, she said she was feeling sick. I remember learning in Spain when I was in hospital out there that nausea could mean a head injury.'

Gerald suspected the same thing. He tried to hide his anxiety as he drove away from the coast towards home, and when Sebastian asked how long he thought it would be before they arrived, he realised the lad was just as worried as he was.

Georgia was confined to bed for two weeks with concussion. Even Isobel was seriously concerned when she heard Georgia saying such things as: 'Have you had Migs from a letter this week?' Or, 'Could I have tea for honey and toast?'

No matter how many times Georgia tried to put the words in the order she knew they should go, somehow they continued to come out of her mouth in the wrong sequence.

'Sounds like you are trying to talk to me in one of our codes, Agent Aigroeg!' Sebastian teased her gently when he called to see her. 'Better let me do the talking. Doc says you've got to rest.'

He informed her that his mother had taken it upon herself to look after Hannah until Georgia was better as Isobel was preoccupied with Georgia's care. He also told her that her father was now certain he could get a visa for Hannah, and that the insurance company had paid in full for a new M.G. as his old one had been a write-off.

Georgia slowly recovered and Hannah came every morning to see her. She was tearful as she thanked Georgia for helping her out of Germany, but confessed that she cried at night when she thought of her parents and grandmother. She had written several letters to her parents assuring them of her well-being but as yet had had no reply.

Most of all, Georgia enjoyed Sebastian's visits. He had elected to remain at home where, he told her, he could continue writing quite as well as he could in London. Knowing it would cheer her up, he reverted to their childhood relationship, telling her that she looked like a gargoyle with the big black bruise on her forehead that also encircled her eyes; but always with the fond smile she knew so well.

'Still lazing in bed, I see!' he said on his fifth visit. He was sitting by the window, his long legs stretched over one arm of the chair. The afternoon sun was streaming through the open window and a slight breeze had ruffled his fair hair into an untidy mop over his forehead. At the same time the familiar smell of smoke from his cigarette was wafting across the room. At Georgia's suggestion, he had moved his chair away from the bedside so that if her mother, who had forbidden smoking in the bedrooms or drawing room, came into the room without warning, he could throw his cigarette out of the window.

'Anybody would think you'd been in a car accident,' he added, which made her laugh.

He talked, too, about the night in France.

'I haven't dared tell your mother or mine that we shared a bedroom,' he told her, adding, 'when you were delirious I was worried you might talk about it. It's best if we keep quiet about it, Jo-Jo!' He smiled. 'If you'd been a bit older, who knows what I might have done to you,' he joked, 'and don't start asking me questions again which I am not going to answer!'

Best news of all, he told her, was that his publisher was delighted with the first draft of his new book, and had invited him to lunch the following week to discuss its future.

'And . . .' he said with pretended casualness, '. . . I asked him if among his many contacts, he knew of any newspaper publisher who might take on a junior reporter who, though young, was both able and tremendously keen. He sounded quite hopeful.'

Georgia was regarding him starry-eyed.

'You mean me? That I might be able to get a job when I'm better? Seb, don't be so mean! Tell me! Is it true?'

It was true, although Sebastian did not elaborate on the fact that he'd let it be known that Georgia was so keen to be a journalist that she would almost certainly be willing to work for a minuscule salary.

'Sebastian Taylor, I love you!' Georgia enthused. 'I really do!' she added, breathless with excitement. 'Why didn't you tell me you were going to try to get me a job?'

'Because, you silly goose, I didn't want you to be disappointed if I was unsuccessful,' Sebastian told her.

'You said you would stop calling me rude names!' Georgia reminded him, 'but I'll forgive you everything and anything for being so helpful, Seb.'

'For heaven's sake, calm down,' Sebastian said smiling, 'or your temperature will go sky high and I'll be blamed. Now I've something else to tell you – not about you this time, but about me. I've met someone who I'm really keen on. Her name is Nancy Saunders, and she's one of the up and coming editors my publisher employs.'

Seeing the bemused look on Georgia's face, he went on to explain that whilst his publisher made all the final decisions, authors were guided by an editor who might point out errors in the text, or suggest a new approach or a change of name, or even a different ending.

'In my case, this girl, Nancy, has been assigned to me. Well, she isn't exactly a girl: she must be getting on for thirty, I suppose, as she's been working there for ten years, she told me. I went up to London last week and she took me to lunch at the Ivy. She's frightfully modern and insisted upon paying the bill.'

His face was serious as he looked down at Georgia, who was now lying back against her pillows.

'I wouldn't say this to anyone but you, Jo-Jo – at least not for the moment, but I think I might easily fall in love with her. She is amazingly pretty – sort of dark hair and eyes a bit like yours – only she has her hair cut really short and wears dangly earrings. Everyone stared at her when we went into the Ivy for lunch, because she was wearing a terrifically smart black and white check jacket thing, with large round black shiny buttons down the front. She didn't mind in the least being noticed – said it was good for the firm if people thought it could afford to pay their staff to dress expensively and eat at smart restaurants. Apparently the jacket was made by someone called Schiaparelli, or something like that.'

Staring at Sebastian's flushed cheeks and hearing the excitement in his voice, Georgia was not entirely unprepared for what was to come.

'You know, Jo-Jo, I've never been really interested in any girl since . . . well, since I was in love with Migs,' he confided. 'I suppose I went on loving her even though she married that army bloke, sort of half hoping that maybe the marriage wouldn't last and she'd come home; or he'd get killed, or something!'

He gave a self-derisory laugh.

'Sounds stupid now, doesn't it? But since I met Nancy . . . well I'm really keen on her. What I used to feel for Migs – a kind of adoration, I suppose – was never like this. I just can't wait to see Nancy again. She rings me up quite often to see how the book is going.'

He paused briefly for breath and then added:

'Just as soon as you are on your feet again, Jo-Jo, I'm going back up to London so I'll be available when she's free. Of course, she's frightfully busy as she has a number of other authors besides me.'

He stood up and walked over to the bedside. Reaching for Georgia's hands, he grasped them in his own.

'I've told Nancy all about you, Jo-Jo and she says she'd love to meet you, so I'm going to organise a lunch for the three of us as soon as you're well enough to come up to London. You're going to love her, Jo-Jo and I know you're going to be great friends even if you are a lot younger.'

He bent over and kissed her lightly on the cheek.

'You're the only one I've told about Nancy, Jo-Jo. It's our secret and I just had to tell you because you are, and always have been, my very best friend.'

After he had gone, Georgia lay awake thinking about Sebastian's new love, Nancy. She wished he had not told her his secret, which had left her feeling both anxious and upset as she realised it might not be long before the Nancy woman took her place as Sebastian's best friend.

CHAPTER SEVENTEEN

1938

Three weeks before Christmas, Georgia went into her senior editor's office. She had been waiting for this interview for over a week, and at long last Bob Batten's personal assistant had informed her the boss would see her at eleven-thirty. He was very busy, she'd been told, and could only give her ten minutes at the most.

Despite the confidence she had acquired when finally she was allowed to dispense with her eyepatch and teeth-straightening plate, Georgia's heart was racing when she knocked on 'Mr B''s door, as the staff referred to him whenever he sailed through the big office where they worked. He was a tall, heavily built man with iron grey hair and moustache, piercing hazel eyes and a booming voice that instantly commanded the attention of reporters, secretaries and other minions such as herself.

His greeting, however, was civil enough as he told Georgia to sit down and asked what her problem was.

'Not a problem, Mr Batten,' Georgia told him, warming now to the project near to her heart. 'It's just that I've been working here for the past seven weeks, and all I have done so far is make the tea, go to the library, take instructions to the printers, or the cutting room, put stamps on letters and . . .'

'I get the message,' he interrupted. 'So how old are you, Miss . . .?'

'Driffield, Sir! Georgia Driffield. I'll be nineteen next birthday.'

Suddenly the man's face twisted into a half smile.

'So you want to edit this newspaper, do you, young lady?'

Georgia did not return his smile.

'What I want, Mr Batten, is a proper job,' she said. 'I want to be a journalist, not a "gofer".' She used the office jargon for the juniors who were at everyone's beck and call to go for this or that. 'I may not have had a university education but I am literate, and I may be young but I've had quite an adventurous life so far, and I don't want to waste the rest of my life handing round tea and biscuits!'

Bob Batten was barely able to conceal a smile. People who came to his office usually spoke deferentially, did not demand anything, and did not come to him to complain about the work they had to do. This girl, young as she was, clearly had spirit as well as ambition, and he could foresee a time when she might make an excellent reporter.

As if guessing his thoughts, Georgia said:

'I want to be a reporter, Mr Batten, and I know I can write well. I have here a brief account of the time a friend of mine and I rescued a Jewish girl from under the noses of the German authorities, and smuggled her out of the country. Please will you read it?'

He took the pages Georgia proffered him and skimmed through them with a practised eye. It was several minutes before he could find his voice. When he looked up, it was with genuine interest.

'Is this fact or fiction, Miss . . . er Driffield? At your age . . .'

'Fact, Mr Batten!' Georgia told him. 'I met my German girl friend at the Swiss international school which I left last summer. Whilst I was there, I had the chance to get to know other girls from practically every country in the world. Another of my friends was an ardent admirer of Adolf Hitler who your paper wrote so much about a month or so ago. I could have written an article for you about my friend, Ingeborg, who is one of his most ardent devotees. You reported that dreadful business last month when hundreds of Germans went quite mad, beating up the Jews, smashing the windows of their houses, their shops. *Kristallnacht,* it's been named, hasn't it? Well, I stayed in a house with a Jewish family who lived in fear of what next would happen to them, and I could have written an article for you about that.'

Bob Batten hid his growing interest and decided to test the girl further.

'Which is all very interesting, young lady, but what else can you write about? At your age and with your background, you cannot have had many other interesting experiences of life.'

Georgia flushed pink with indignation.

'I've been upside down in a ditch in France after a fearful car accident. I have a sister who married a captain in the army and has gone to India with him where she is having an incredible time because of the thousands of Indians who are demanding independence. I have letters written in the last century by a relative who was captured by a pirate and marooned on an island in the Seychelles . . .'

'Enough, Miss Driffield,' the editor interrupted her. 'Young as you are, you have convinced me that it is at least worth my while to give you a few months' trial. Bring me some decent articles and I may even put you on the permanent reporting staff roll. I shall ask for reports on your progress in three months' time, and understand this, young lady, if you are not up to scratch, you will return to your job as a "gofer". This newspaper is not a training ground for children, you know!'

He was amused to see the heightened expression of indignation on Georgia's face but decided not to comment lest she lost her cool and said something unpardonable. He was intrigued to find out if the pretty young girl, now on her feet looking as if she was about to protest at his description of her, was as promising as he suspected, and decided to maintain his authority.

'Out!' he said gruffly, pointing to the door. 'You've wasted enough of my time already and I have better things to do than designate staff. That's the job of my personnel manager. Now off you go and report to him, and by the way, there will be no increase in your pay packet until you have proved you've earned it.'

Later that day, when Georgia left the newspaper offices and returned on the underground to Rose and Lily's house where she was staying, the first thing she did was to telephone Sebastian.

'I've got it, Seb! I've got the job I wanted! Please thank your publisher or whoever gave me the introduction to the paper. You can't believe how excited I am!' She laughed happily.

'I think we should go out and celebrate. Rose and Lily aren't back yet and I'm much too excited to sit here waiting for them. Shall we meet at our usual pub in half an hour, and maybe go round to Le Faisan Noir for a meal afterwards? My treat, by the way, as I've still got two pounds left from last week's salary.'

She broke off, aware that she had been talking non-stop and Sebastian had not been able to get a word in.

'You still there, Seb?' she asked.

'Yes, yes I am!' Sebastian's voice sounded strange, hesitant. 'Of course, it's all wonderful news, Jo-Jo, and I'd love to celebrate with you, but . . . well, I'm frightfully sorry but I can't make it, not tonight anyway.'

Georgia's disappointment momentarily rendered her speechless. It had never occurred to her since she had left Mr Batten's office that Sebastian might not be there to share her pleasure. It was true that for the last few weeks since she had moved into the spare room in the twins' mews cottage, he had been so busy trying to finish his book he'd only once joined the three of them for one of their evening meals at Le Faisan Noir. They had all understood his preoccupation with his work but he'd put that aside when they were celebrating Rose and Lily's twenty-third birthday.

'. . . frightfully sorry, Jo-Jo, but I'm going to the theatre,' Sebastian was saying. 'You remember me telling you about

Nancy, my editor? Well, she's got tickets for *Dear Octopus* and I can't . . .'

Georgia was having difficulty in hiding her disappointment but she realised it would be churlish at the very least if Sebastian dropped out at the eleventh hour and upset his editor. Trying to hide her feelings, she said:

'Never mind, Seb. We can celebrate tomorrow. By then I'll have had my very first day as a real live reporter!'

There was no answering laugh from Sebastian.

'Jo-Jo, could it possibly wait? It's my book, you see . . . that's to say it's research for the middle where my hero has an accident at the steelworks in Sheffield. Nancy has made an appointment for me to meet the former manager of a steelworking factory. She's driving me up there as she says we'll need a car to tour the old mines in the surrounding neighbourhood.'

For several minutes, Georgia found it yet again difficult to speak. It wasn't simply that Sebastian would be unable to celebrate with her; it was the constant references to the editor, Nancy. It was beginning to sound as if she was taking over his life! She herself knew nothing about editors, but somehow it sounded strange that the Nancy woman was willing to drive all the way up to Yorkshire and perhaps even stay the night up there.

Georgia now told herself that it was none of her business what Sebastian chose to do, and that she had no right whatever to expect him to give her; first claim on his time. She attempted to sound nonchalant as she told him that it wasn't really important; and he was to telephone her when he had a spare moment.

'Have a safe journey, Seb!' she concluded. 'See you soon!' and rang off before she burst into tears.

When the twins arrived back from work, they noticed at once that Georgia was looking anything but happy and supposed she had failed to get the job she wanted, until Georgia confessed that she was being very silly: that having been right on top of the world, she had been brought down with a bump when Sebastian told her he wouldn't be available for her celebration.

The twins looked at one another and then turned to Georgia and took turns trying to console her.

'Darling Jo-Jo!' Rose said as she took one of Georgia's hands in hers, 'Sebastian is twenty-one years old . . .'

'. . . and it's high time he had a girlfriend,' Lily added.

'It took him years to get over Migs . . .'

'. . . so we should all be happy for him if this Nancy is keen on him.'

'The other day Seb told us she was quite a bit older so I dare say she is the one making the running.'

'Everyone thinks that awful American woman, Mrs Simpson, seduced King Edward, so it's not unusual for women these days to let the man they fancy know they are available.'

'Of course it's quite possible Sebastian's editor is only inter-ested in him as a writer . . .'

'You wouldn't mind if she seduced Sebastian, would you, Georgia?'

'Of course not!' Georgia replied. But later that night, she found herself wondering if she would mind. Ever since they'd travelled back from Germany and had the car accident, they'd seen a great deal of each other. When she had recovered from her concussion, and Sebastian had got her the job on the *Daily Chronicle*, she had moved up to London where the twins had let her have their tiny spare room as a base. Inevitably, with Sebastian living only a few doors away, they had spent a great many evenings together and were as close a foursome as it was possible for them to be. For Sebastian to drop out so suddenly brought home to her the fact that, good friends though they were, she was now only a very minor participant in his life.

On her way by underground to her new job the following morning, Sebastian and his possible love life were forgotten. Although her first few days as a reporter were spent accompanying an older girl to a somewhat dull court case where a man pleaded guilty to being drunk and disorderly, she had found the court itself and its procedure interesting. Slightly more so was her attendance at a minor celebrity's wedding. In both cases, she had been required to produce her version of events, which she did, reckoning she had made two rather uneventful events sound quite interesting.

To her mortification, her articles were returned to her with no less than half their content blue-pencilled with the word '*dull*' written in the margin, and a comment at the end saying: '*Try writing the same report minus the adjectives. Your job is to write news, not views!*'

However, the next article she submitted about a serious fire in a large exhibition hall, relating it to the devastating fire the previous year when the Crystal Palace had been similarly razed to the ground, had been sufficiently praised for her senior reporter to declare it better than her own. With a certain amount of cutting, Georgia's article appeared in print, and she returned to the twins with several copies of the newspaper, which she proudly showed them when they returned from work. It had been at the back of her mind that she might show Sebastian a copy of her first ever publication, but his car was not outside Number 32. She would send a copy to her parents, who were now reconciled to the fact that she wished to have a career rather than follow Migs's example and be a debutante.

She did wonder whether Sebastian was going home for Christmas. The festivity was only a week away and the offices were closing from Christmas Eve to the day after New Year's Day, but she was not greatly looking forward to the short holiday, mainly because it was not the same as it was before Migs left home and she couldn't be certain that Sebastian would go back. The thought of being there on her own with only her parents and Mr and Mrs Taylor for company was depressing, so much so that she declined to accompany the twins to their restaurant and opted to have a slice of cheese on toast in the kitchen while she was working.

As a consequence, Georgia was alone when the front door bell rang. She pushed the portable typewriter she now used to one side and, with a sigh at the interruption, went down to answer it. For a split second before she opened the door, it crossed her mind that it might be Sebastian, but it was not. The man standing outside in the rain was Fedrik Anyos. Behind him a taxi stood waiting, its meter ticking over.

'It's Miss Georgia Driffield, isn't it?' he said with a surprised smile. 'I was expecting the Misses Rose and Lily Murdoch. I lost their telephone number, you see, so I thought I'd drop by on the off-chance of finding them in.'

Rain was dripping off the brim of his black trilby onto his fur-collared overcoat, so Georgia quickly opened the door wider to allow him into the hall. 'They've gone out for a quick meal!' she told him. 'I don't think they will be more than an hour. Would you like to wait for them?'

Fedrik said he would be happy to do so. He paid off the taxi driver and on removing his wet hat and coat Georgia saw he was wearing an immaculately tailored dinner jacket. He was obviously dressed for the evening, she thought as he followed her into the sitting room. When he was seated by the gas fire in the chair she indicated, she apologised for the fact that there was only sherry to offer him.

Fedrik said it would be perfect although he never normally drank sherry, his aunt's favourite tipple. He now tried to conceal his astonishment at the appearance of the young girl who was pouring the drink for him. When he and his aunt had invited her to tea two years ago, she had been a slightly overweight schoolgirl with braces on her teeth, dark, uncoiffed hair and wearing thick lisle stockings and lace-up shoes.

The wire contraption on Georgia's teeth had now vanished, her hair was cut short and she had clearly lost most, if not all, of her puppy fat. The transformation from ugly duckling to swan could not have been a more appropriate description, he thought as she handed him the glass of sherry. She gave him a charming, friendly smile.

'Are you staying in London for Christmas?' she asked as she sat down opposite him. 'I seem to remember you telling me you and your aunt always come to London to do your Christmas shopping.'

Fedrik nodded.

'And to see friends!' he added, 'although not very many of them are in London now. My aunt has gone off to visit the Wiscotes, your grandparents, I believe? So finding myself at a loose end, I thought I would drop in on your charming cousins. However . . .' he gave her a delightful smile, '. . . it is a very pleasant surprise to find you here.'

Georgia felt herself blushing. It was not just Fedrik's compliment that had suddenly made her self-conscious, but the way he was looking at her. Her experience of flirtation was, to say the least, somewhat limited, she realised. Both she and Hannah had had their hands held by two similar-aged students they'd met on a pleasure steamer on Lake Geneva. Subsequently, they had been on picnics up on the mountain behind the school, but their flirtation had never progressed beyond hand-holding and once in a while an awkward kiss if they thought themselves unobserved.

Fedrik Anyos's searching gaze seemed very different from the boys' shy glances, and Georgia was by no means sure she liked it. Within minutes, however, he had put her at her ease.

'It must be nearly two years since you came to tea with me and my aunt,' he was saying. 'Would I be wrong in remembering you were interested in Madeira where we live?'

Forgetting her shyness, Georgia explained why the island held such a great interest for her and her determination to go there to find Dinez's ship.

Fedrik smiled.

'Am I right in remembering that he was a pirate who kidnapped one of your ancestors?'

Georgia's face turned pink with pleasure.

'How clever of you to remember,' she said. 'I was still at

school when I told you I'd found the letters he wrote to my great-great-grandmother.'

Fedrik's interest deepened still further. Seeing the typewriter on the table by the window, he asked if it belonged to her, whereupon she told him about her job.

'It is clear that you have talent,' he said, amused by her obvious enthusiasm for her work.

Georgia shook her head.

'I don't see myself as a "talented" writer. I'm merely a fledgling reporter with lots to learn. I'm hoping one day to become a war correspondent, that is if there is a war somewhere in the British Empire. Then they would have to pay me a much bigger salary than they do now. Anyway, it won't matter to me how much I earn in two years' time because of my inheritance.'

Fedrik looked at her with genuine interest.

'I seem to recall you telling me about a property left to you by a relative. You asked my aunt and me if we would send you postcards of Madeira. But it must be all of two years ago since then. Had you forgotten?'

Georgia drew up a chair closer to that of the visitor, her eyes shining as she told him how pleased she had been to receive them. She could now recall the several thank-you letters she had written to his aunt.

'I'm still intending to visit Madeira as soon as I'm twenty-one,' she informed him. 'The house I inherited has already been sold to some developers who are going to pull it down and build a large housing estate in its place. That's why it fetched such an amazing amount of money.' She grinned as she boasted: 'My father told me I was now rich enough to buy Buckingham Palace if the King decided to sell it!'

Fedrik joined in her laughter and, after congratulating her again on her articles, suggested that as the twins were already dining out, he should take her somewhere for dinner as he had no wish to eat on his own.

'I can always see Rose and Lily tomorrow or at the weekend,' he said. He looked at the gold watch on his wrist – a recent birthday present from his aunt – adding: 'It's only nine o'clock. We could dine at Quaglino's and then go on to a nightclub – or to the Savoy. I expect you know that Geraldo is currently playing there. I hear he's supposed to be really good.'

Georgia looked at her companion uncertainly.

'I'd love that,' she said truthfully, having never yet been to a nightclub. She decided she would not admit she had already eaten cheese on toast, and explained regretfully that she only had one evening dress in London, which was probably unsuitable.

Concealing a smile, Fedrik said: 'I am sure you will look delightful in whatever you are wearing.'

Georgia felt a quick thrill of anticipation. Although the visitor was so much older than herself – he might even be thirty! – he was very charming and well-mannered and, by the sound of it, great fun, too. The older girls at work had once talked about there always being celebrities at the best hotels and nightclubs. She might even see someone really famous to write about the following day. As for her dress, she decided her made-over bridesmaid's dress would not do despite what Fedrik said, but that neither Rose nor Lily would mind if she borrowed one of their far more grown-up styles.

Catching her lower lip with her teeth, she looked at Fedrik anxiously.

'It would take me at least twenty minutes to change,' she said, 'and I don't suppose I can do anything about my hair. I got caught in the rain on my way home and—'

'And it looks very chic the way it is!' Fedrik broke in smoothly. 'So have you any more excuses – Miss Georgiana, is it not?'

'No, just Georgia,' she said laughing. 'And I'll be very happy to join you. Will you have another glass of sherry while I'm changing? And please, do smoke if you wish. The twins don't mind and Seb – our friend – he even smokes his pipe when he's here.'

'Then I will have a cigarette,' Fedrik said, withdrawing a slim engine-turned silver cigarette case and lighter from his pocket, 'but no more to drink, thank you, and please don't hurry on my behalf, Georgia. I am more than happy to wait for you as long as it takes.'

As Georgia left the room, she reflected that it was not so much his words as the tone of voice he'd used to express them that was affecting her. It left her strangely anxious and yet excited, too, because it sounded as if he really wanted her company and she was not simply a substitute for the twins.

CHAPTER EIGHTEEN

1938

'Let's go to Paris, sweetie!' Nancy's voice was tinged with excitement. 'We could go over on the night ferry and spend the whole of Christmas and Boxing Day at a hotel I know near Montmartre – in bed if we wanted!' she added seductively as she reached out and touched Sebastian's cheek.

They were lying naked beneath a huge feather eiderdown in the Metropole Hotel in Brighton; the rest of the bedding lay in an untidy heap on the floor. They had arrived at the hotel the previous day – unintentionally as far as Sebastian was concerned. He and Nancy had spent the entire weekend in Sheffield where he'd planned to research the development of the steelworks as background for his book. Instead, they had dined out, had a great deal to drink, and ended up in bed where he'd made passionate love to her. Which was not quite true, he'd thought on the drive back to London – it was Nancy who had made very exciting love to him. She was insatiable, he'd discovered, wishing he had as much stamina as she had.

It was only after their solitary meeting with the former manager of the steelworks factory that it dawned on him Nancy had all the time been planning an affair. He was embarrassed by his naïvety, having genuinely supposed it was to have been a working trip: not that he'd objected to the change of plan – far from it. He found his female companion hugely attractive with immense sex appeal. She had told him candidly that from the moment they'd first met, she had intended them to become lovers.

Tiny, with brilliant aquamarine blue eyes in a perfectly oval face, Nancy was like a bird – a tropical bird, he'd told her as she darted round the room, naked as often as not, and covered not only his face but his body with tantalising little kisses. Only too willingly he had let himself be seduced, and Nancy had not been negligent in teaching him how to give a woman pleasure. He'd been shaken at first to discover how ignorant he was despite the strange night he'd spent in Spain with the unknown, sad, dark-eyed female soldier. He had often wondered since he'd returned home whether or not she survived the war. He'd remembered her for a single instant on the first night when Nancy had – without his invitation – climbed into bed beside him and pressed her warm naked body against his own just as the Spanish *señora* had done.

Now, after three days of continuous lovemaking, he was exhausted, and when Nancy suggested they return to London where she could move into his mews cottage, in which they could continue their affair, he rejected the idea.

Anxious as he was to please her, for she was not only his lover now but also was still his editor, he was nevertheless unwilling to fall in with her plan. Despite her annoyance, which she barely troubled to conceal, Sebastian remained adamant. His cottage was only a few doors down the mews from that of the twins, who would almost certainly disapprove, he explained. Moreover, his childhood friend, Georgia, had a key and was in the habit of dropping in at odd times for a chat. She was still very much an innocent child, he added, and he was not going to be responsible for shocking her by finding them naked in bed.

Nancy's resulting petulance wore off after two or three Martinis, which she liked to drink. Despite Sebastian's protest, she frequently picked up the bills that, they both knew, he could ill afford to pay and it had been her idea to continue their affair in Brighton. Sebastian was delighted by the thought that he could take her over to Shoreham and show her his precious aeroplane; perhaps could take her for a spin.

However, the weather since their arrival had not permitted

any flying during the whole weekend. It rained so hard they had been unable even to go out for a walk. The wind had been whipping up huge waves that crashed over the promenade, and the hotel barman warned them that one of his clients had said the pier itself was at risk. Nancy had not been in the least put out. She was not an outdoor person, she'd told him, adding: 'Why don't we go back to bed, sweetie?'

Sebastian was now ready to go home. Occasionally his injured leg throbbed quite painfully when he became overtired: besides which, he'd promised his parents he would be home for Christmas. An ugly scowl distorted Nancy's pretty face when he told her he couldn't disappoint them.

'Won't you have to put in an appearance at your office?' he asked her. 'Do you realise we have been away a whole week?'

Nancy reached up and ruffled his hair.

'I telephoned from the hotel in Sheffield and said I had caught influenza!' she told him, adding with a sigh: 'I suppose I shall have to spend Christmas in London without you!' She touched his cheek with her scarlet-painted fingertips. 'You're quite sure you don't want to take me home with you?'

How could he possibly do so even had he wanted to, Sebastian asked himself? Nancy was the epitome of a woman his mother would call 'fast': the kind of young woman she deplored, saying girls like her had no morals and no manners, and were little better than tarts. The fact that Nancy at thirty was not exactly a girl and surpassed him in age by eight or nine years would, he knew, heighten his parents' disapproval. Moreover, Nancy could not be less like his gentle Migs, his sweet first love, Migs, who his mother had adored and hoped one day would be her daughter-in-law.

'I'll be back in London the day after Boxing Day, Nancy,' he said. 'We can spend New Year's Eve together, so a few days apart now won't be so awful, will it?'

Nancy's scarlet lips pursed in a moue.

'I shall miss you quite terribly, sweetie! You will miss me, won't you?'

'Of course!' Sebastian said reassuringly. 'I can't think how I lived to the ripe old age of twenty-one without you.'

They made love for the last time before Sebastian drove her to Brighton railway station where he put her on a non-stop Pullman train to London.

It was only as the train drew out of the concourse and disappeared from view that he felt a confusing rush of emotions. He was going to miss her; miss their lovemaking; miss the way she made him feel so much a man, so important to her. Yet at the same time, as he returned to his car and started the drive home across the South Downs, there was just the slightest feeling of relief. At home, he would be able to relax, get into his old clothes and talk about sport or politics or books with his father; play the occasional game of backgammon with his mother, and perhaps see young Georgia, who would almost certainly be home for Christmas. She was a good kid: brave, too, he reflected when finally he drove past her house and into his driveway. Somehow he couldn't imagine his lovely Nancy risking her life to rescue a friend, or calmly surviving a horrid car crash without a single complaint. If the weather improved, he would take Georgia up in the Moth and give her another opportunity to handle the controls. She was quite fearless and a quick learner, and he was certain he could help her to get her private pilot's licence.

His thoughts returned to the way Nancy touched, kissed him, and not least the way she made him feel so special. He would make up for this Christmas separation as soon as he returned to London, and tomorrow he would send her flowers with a note saying how important she was to him.

Bob Batten looked at the young girl in front of him with interest. As a rule, it took a very junior addition to the reporting team the best part of a year before they could be said to have earned their pay. It had proved to be an entirely different kettle of fish with Miss Georgia Driffield. On her own initiative, she had interviewed one of the many hundreds of mothers whose children were being evacuated from London to places considered safe in the event of war. The article about their evacuation had been quite moving and had brought in a great many comments from readers saying how well the reporter had managed to express their own emotions.

His fledgling reporter had also produced a delightful account of the Christmas party the King and Queen had given for one hundred children at which the two little princesses, Elizabeth and Margaret, were present. The public were always avid for gossip about royalty and this, too, had brought in a number of comments from readers – not all favourable since unemployment was currently endemic and, as one reader had pointed out, their child was lucky to get a bowl of soup instead of jellies, ice cream and lemonade.

Georgia had on her own initiative followed that article up with a moving account of the two million unemployed and the effect this was having on the poorest families. Furthermore, she had interviewed a number of women for their comments about the new gas masks now being issued, and how, if war did break out, they would be obliged to wear the unsightly objects.

'I suppose you've come to ask me for a rise!' he now said to Georgia, looking at her over the top of his spectacles.

Georgia frowned as she said:

'No, sir, I haven't come here to ask for a rise. I don't need your money anyway as I have plenty of my own.' This was not strictly true as yet. Her father had insisted that her fortune remain intact until she was twenty-one, and she was still only eighteen. 'As I said before, I'm here to ask you if I can have a column of my own for articles I believe would be of particular interest to women. Nearly all your newspaper is aimed to please men.' Forgetting for the moment who she was addressing, she added:

'And can you call me Georgia instead of Miss Driffield? Everyone else does!'

'Miss Driffield – Georgia, if you prefer – I do not require

a lesson from the most junior member of my staff on how to run my newspaper,' Bob Batten broke in with mock reproach. Secretly, he admired her nerve as well as her aplomb.

'So what particular articles have you in mind? I take it you are not suggesting a *daily* column?'

His sarcasm was not lost on Georgia, and her flush deepened. In a quieter tone, she said:

'I didn't mean to sound rude or conceited or anything like that, Mr Batten. If you don't think I'm good enough . . .'

'As it happens, I do think you are "good enough",' he interrupted, 'at least for a trial. I have a feeling your fellow reporters may not be too pleased to hear you have been given an opportunity to excel and they have not. However . . .' he gave a wry smile '. . . however, it may ginger them up. So, young lady, is there anything else you wish to say to me?'

'Only thank you, sir! Thank you very much! I won't let you down, I promise. I'm planning . . .'

Once again, Bob Batten interrupted.

'I prefer to read the finished article rather than waste my time listening to you telling me what you hope to do. Off you go, young lady, and . . .' he added with a sudden unexpected softening of his tone, '. . . good luck!'

Georgia was ecstatic and brimming over with excitement as she sat in the taxi taking her to Grosvenor House that evening. Fedrik Anyos had telephoned her early that morning and invited her to drinks in his aunt's apartment and afterwards, to dine in the hotel restaurant. When his aunt retired, he said, he would take her on to a nightclub.

Resita greeted Georgia with a welcoming smile and a kiss on both cheeks. She had no doubt the girl was much too young to interest Fedrik, but she would provide him with some female company whilst they were in London. As far as Georgia was concerned, all she seemed interested in was hearing further detail about Madeira. It was obvious to her that Fedrik was deriving some amusement from initiating Georgia into the novelty and pleasures of London's nightlife.

This evening he was taking her for the second time to the nightclub Les Ambassadeurs.

'Don't keep the child up too late, my darling!' Resita told him when, after the three of them had dined together, they were ready to leave.

Georgia was wearing a long, creamy yellow crêpe-de-Chine evening dress that enhanced her dark colouring. It gave her a slightly Italianate look that was unusual as well as becoming. A diamanté clasp was shining in her hair, and she wore a single strand of pearls that one of the twins had lent her. Fedrik as usual looked immaculate in tails, a white silk scarf round his neck and a carnation in his buttonhole.

He helped Georgia into her fur-trimmed evening wrap, telling her that she looked 'utterly adorable', as they went down in the lift to the foyer.

Georgia thought this last compliment a bit over the top, comparing it as she did with the usual: 'You'll do!' from Sebastian when he took her out for a meal or to the cinema. She was nevertheless flattered by Fedrik's attentions, which had become even more effusive when he had kissed her in the back of the taxi taking her home on their previous night out together.

It was the first time Georgia had been kissed – properly, as she described it to the twins. She found it exciting in one way but unnerving in another, and had been unsure whether she was supposed to return the kiss or whether the man sitting with his arm round her shoulders would think her fast. 'Fast' was a word often used by the twins when they were discussing some of the young society women who came to buy flowers at their shop. They had given Georgia some advice about going out at night on a date with a man like Fedrik Anyos.

'Men can get carried away!' Rose had said.

'And they don't always stop kissing when you want them to,' Lily added.

'So you just have to be firm and say "stop!"'

'And if they don't stop, then you rap on the window and tell the taxi driver to stop and let you out.'

A gentleman would never ask for more than a kiss or two, Rose had told her, and Lily said reassuringly that although Fedrik was a foreigner, she was sure he was a gentleman. Moreover, his aunt was their grandmother's best friend so he must be trustworthy.

Thus armed with this advice, Georgia stared happily across the table at Fedrik's handsome profile as he ordered a bottle of Moët & Chandon – to celebrate her literary achievements, he said – Georgia felt a thrill of excitement.

'I am going to write an article about my ancestor and the pirate who kidnapped her.' Seeing that Fedrik looked genuinely interested in what she was saying she continued excitedly: 'It was his boat that sank with all its treasure off the island where you live. You did say that if ever I decided to go to Madeira, you would very kindly help me make some enquiries about shipwrecks off the coast in those days. Well, as soon as I can have my inheritance, I am as determined as ever to spend some of it searching for the ship and if possible, raise it. It would make a wonderful follow-up article.'

When she paused for breath, Fedrik leaned forward, his interest now serious on several counts as he said:

'That could be a very costly business, Georgia.'

'Oh, it wouldn't matter how much it cost,' Georgia said, adding: 'my father said I'd been left enough money.'

Her face suddenly clouded. 'My parents think the whole idea is stupid, and that it would be a terrible waste of money.'

'Well, I have to disagree,' Fedrik said, and taking her hand in his, he added: 'whenever you can, Georgia, come to Madeira and I promise to help you in any way I am able.'

The band was now playing one of the current popular songs, 'Night and Day', and Fedrik stood up abruptly and held out his arms.

'Let's dance!' he said. 'It's a slow foxtrot and I seem to remember you telling me that this was one of your favourite tunes.'

Georgia stood up happily and allowed him to guide her

onto the crowded dance floor. Drawing her very close against him they began to dance, Freddie so expertly that Georgia was able to follow his lead without thinking. His mouth was close to her ear as he murmured the words of the song, and suddenly he drew her even closer and pressed his cheek to hers.

For one brief moment, Georgia was unsure if she liked the intimacy of his body pressing against hers. There were, however, many other couples dancing as close, and she found herself enjoying the strange sensation she was feeling as she relaxed and melted against him. For a few blissful minutes, they moved almost as one and then the music ended. Fedrik held her for a fraction of a second longer than necessary, and before releasing her, placed a light kiss on top of her head.

When he led her back to their table, his arm tucked through hers, she became aware of a feeling of joy marred only because Fedrik had told her he was soon to return to Madeira.

Was she falling in love, she wondered? Were these feelings of excitement, euphoria what being in love meant? He reached across the table and covered her hand with his, and when she looked up, it was to see his eyes burning into hers. She wished then that they were not in this crowded room and that he could kiss her.

Fedrik, she suspected, must be feeling the same way, as after one more dance and they had finished the bottle of champagne, he suggested they should leave. 'I know you have to be at your office quite early tomorrow,' he said, 'so I mustn't be selfish and keep you up too late.'

Georgia would not have minded staying up all night if he had been willing to do so, but clearly he had other plans. When the doorman called up a taxi for them, Fedrik told the driver to take them up to Hampstead Heath. As soon as they set off, he said softly:

'I've been wanting to kiss you all evening. You are one of the sweetest girls I have ever met, Georgia!' And he drew her into his arms and kissed her, at first softly, tenderly, and then with increasing passion.

Succumbing to the wonderful feelings that were engulfing her, Georgia suddenly remembered the twins' warnings: *'If he doesn't stop kissing you when you tell him to, tell the taxi driver to stop, and get out of the cab'*. The trouble was, she hadn't the slightest wish for Fedrik to stop kissing her, and as the taxi drove slowly up the hill to the Heath, the rain-wet streets shining in the passing lamplights, she no longer doubted that she had fallen in love.

Fedrik, however, had no intention whatever of seducing the young girl in his arms, although she was both charming and unusually attractive. His consuming interest in her was that she was young, gullible and extremely rich. She was therefore a possible gateway to his freedom.

CHAPTER NINETEEN

1938

She would never spend a more miserable Christmas, Georgia told herself as she faced the fact that she must endure the whole week without seeing Fedrik. Her parents, united in their stance, had virtually refused to allow her to cut short the holiday and return to London after Boxing Day. Her father had given his permission when she had managed to get taken on by the newspaper to live in London, he said, for her to live with the twins, but it had been on the assumption that she would return home at weekends.

Georgia had desperately wanted to invite Fedrik and his aunt to spend Christmas with them, but her mother would not even consider having two strangers intruding on a day that traditionally they shared only with the Taylors. For once, Sebastian was unsympathetic when she complained to him when she joined him for a walk on the Downs on Boxing Day.

Georgia had confided in Sebastian a little about her ongoing relationship with Fedrik, omitting the hours spent up on the Heath in the car Fedrik had hired for his time in London. Sebastian's reaction when she told him that she'd been out dancing in nightclubs with Fedrik almost every night leading up to Christmas was strongly disapproving. The man was much too old for her, a 'lounge lizard', meaning a man hanging around drawing rooms hoping to attract women he could seduce!

It was, of course, nonsense, but for once, Sebastian was unwilling to listen to her defence of Fedrik, still less how exciting she found Fedrik's kisses and caresses, and how thrilling her evenings out with him had become. Stupidly, she'd expected that Sebastian would be pleased for her that her first experience of love was with someone so gentle and caring: that almost as exciting was Fedrik's declaration that if she truly wanted to send divers down for Dinez da Gama's ship, he could organise it all for her.

As their walk ended and they drove home in uneasy silence, Georgia thought – but now rejected the idea – of asking Sebastian to help her find a way to go to Madeira as soon as possible. Her problem was, she knew, her parents wouldn't permit her to travel there on her own; nor had she the money for her passage. She would not be getting her inheritance for another two and a half years, but she determined she was not going to wait that long. It was not only just the important link with her past that mattered, there was also her wish to spend more time with Fedrik. Now, with Sebastian so unreasonably prejudiced against him, she couldn't ask him for help.

Georgia was not aware that Fedrik's aunt, Mrs Reviezky, would not for one single moment have endorsed his invitation had she known how often he had been seeing Georgia and how their dinner dances always ended. Fedrik had told his aunt he spent those hours at a gaming club and she was thus unsuspicious of his growing interest in the girl. As was her custom, she reimbursed Fedrik for what he told her were his frequent losses at the baccarat tables; money that proved essential to pay for his frequent dates with Georgia. Only on one occasion had a friend of Resita's mentioned to her that she had seen Fedrik dancing with a young girl at a nightclub, but when she confronted him with this, he had smiled his charming smile and told her he had run into Georgia who had been with a party of their friends, and he'd thought it only polite to dance with her. Although Resita was surprised that a girl as young as she supposed Georgia to be had been allowed into a nightclub, she did not bother to query it.

Resita never doubted Fedrik's honesty. She was, however, finding London life a lot more tiring than usual and had no particular reason for remaining for the New Year's festivities. They would pack up and return to Madeira, she announced to Fedrik: the weather was unpleasantly cold, and she longed for the sunny comfort of Reid's Hotel. She had booked passages for them for the day before New Year's Eve.

It came as a nasty shock to Georgia when she found a letter from Fedrik waiting for her at the twins' house explaining his absence. He was as unhappy as he knew she would be at their parting, he'd written,

but please, please, my darling girl, try to arrange to come out here so we can be together again soon!

She would be his aunt's guest – they had a spare room in their suite at Reid's Hotel, and his aunt would happily chaperon her and send a formal invitation to her parents.

Also awaiting her return was a small, beautifully packed parcel. It had come from Cartier, which she knew to be one of London's most expensive jewellers. She carried it into her bedroom where, sitting on her bed, she unwrapped it and carefully opened the small leather box. Inside was a brooch featuring a tiny gold sailing ship with a note saying:

A small Christmas token to remind you to come soon to Madeira to find your pirate's cutter. Your devoted Freddie.

What had been Georgia's sincere wish to visit the island and find out if her great-great-grandmother's lover had ever existed now, with the added desire to be reunited with Fedrik, became her firm resolve.

Perhaps, she thought as she put the little ship back in its box, if she put the idea to Mr Batten that a real-life search for treasure must surely make exciting reading, he would consider paying for her ticket to go to Madeira. She'd say it

would be an exclusive: the only newspaper to carry the story.
Maybe he would even finance the whole adventure.

Not only would she need money for her fare, and a far
greater sum to pay for the boat and the divers hired to search
for the wreck, but Fedrik had assured her that speaking fluent
Portuguese he could arrange for a suitable team to be assem-
bled and a boat to be chartered.

Was there a possibility her boss might be interested in
the articles she could write, she wondered, or would he
consider them a total waste of space, especially as he and
a great many other members of staff, as well as her father,
seemed to think that war with Germany was almost a
certainty in the near future. Everyone was saying that despite
the Munich Agreement, which the Prime Minister had
orchestrated with Hitler, Germany had now occupied more
than just the Sudetenland, and was gradually occupying the
whole of Czechoslovakia. Georgia knew enough about journalism now to be well aware that the newspaper would need
every column of space it could get for details of war devel-
opments. Moreover, her parents would be even more certain
to prevent her leaving the country even though an island in
the Atlantic hundreds of miles away was highly unlikely to
be involved.

The trouble, Georgia reflected, was that her parents had
not yet recovered from her 'dangerous' – as they described it
– escape from Munich. Hannah was now safe with her aunt
in Australia, but there had been no news of *Doktor* Klein and
his wife and mother. Stories of what was happening to the
Jews in Germany worsened day by day, and one of her fellow
students still living in Munich, had written to say that everyone
now knew that *Herr* Hitler was planning to rid Germany of
all the Jews, even distant Jewish relations. There had been no
word from Inge.

Fedrik Anyos's involvement in Georgia's life was not only
on her mind but on Sebastian's too. Returning to London in
time for the New Year's Eve festivities, it occurred to him that

he wouldn't want her to do what he had been doing with Nancy, still less with a fellow like Fedrik Anyos. He tried not to feel worried as he parked his car in the mews and went up to his sitting room to listen to the news.

CHAPTER TWENTY

1939

Bob Batten regarded his eighteen-year-old employee with surreptitious interest. Georgia had requested an interview with him the day before but, not wishing to reveal his curiosity, he had sent word that he could not see her until the following day. As she was shown into his office by his secretary, her bright pretty young face revealing her excitement, he knew already that he would try to agree with whatever request she had come to make. Before Christmas, her articles on the situation in Germany had elicited an unusual number of letters from women readers. Since then, she had produced a remarkably interesting account of the effects of the flooding when the Thames had burst its banks in January. When word had reached them that Eton College had become an island as a result of the flooding, she had managed to persuade a boat owner to row her over to the building where she was able to interview several of the boys, some of whom were throwing bits of their tuck to the swans from their study windows.

Not least, she had organised one of the newspaper's photographers to take pictures of the mass of protesting unemployed men who a week ago, in an organised demonstration, were lying on the street outside the Savoy Hotel. There had been pictures, too, of others, lying down in the lounge inside the hotel, and Georgia, making use of her grandmother's title, Lady Wiscote, had herself bypassed the police guarding the entrance, and subsequently written a moving article about the plight of the unemployed and their families.

She seemed to have the ability to sense which topics would

have a direct appeal to women, at whom her articles were directed.

'Sit down! Sit down!' he barked at her. 'What's it this time? Miss Smithfield, isn't it?'

Miffed that her boss had not registered her name, she bit back her reply, which would have been to tell him he ought to know it by now if he troubled to read her articles. She was, after all, about to request a very great favour. The previous day, she had received one of Fedrik's weekly, long affectionate letters saying he had located a firm of divers who would be willing to search for Dinez da Gama's wreck.

The divers think it might be possible to raise the wrecked ship so long as you have the exact location, which I believe you possess, and it is not lying too deep.

Will your employer release you for two or three weeks?

The letter had ended with the usual endearments, repeating how much he missed her. He had, he wrote, fallen hopelessly in love with her, and please would she write back by return and say if she cared even a little bit for him.

Fedrik's declaration was not on her mind at this moment as she sat facing Bob Batten. His glasses, as usual, were on the end of his nose and he was staring at her impatiently over the rims. Georgia hastened to explain her plans.

'I would need two or three weeks' sabbatical, Mr Batten!' she ended, 'and I'll need enough to pay for my fare: my friends will pay my hotel expenses, and I should be able to write several really exciting articles for you which no other reporter could so they would be exclusive.'

Once again, her boss hid his immediate interest and sat waiting for Georgia to continue.

She now produced Dinez's letter telling how he had been blown off course and his ship sunk off the coast of Madeira. Her dark eyes alight with excitement, she said:

'It was the pirate's last letter to my great-great-grandmother who he had fallen in love with, and knowing he was dying, he wanted her to have his riches. I'm convinced he has never been able to rest in peace because his ship still lies undiscovered, and now my friend in Madeira has found a firm of divers who will search for the wreck. So I want to go out there.' She paused to catch her breath before continuing:

'Apart from my own personal interest, Mr Batten, I think this would make a fantastic story. For a start, it has everything – love, riches, suspense. Of course, I would be in touch with you instantly if the wreck was found so that one of your cameramen could take photos to accompany my articles. You would only lose three weeks of my work time, and my friend in Madeira said the divers should know the situation within that time.'

Georgia did not add that if he were to refuse, she would tell him she was going to go anyway, even though it would probably mean the loss of the job she was so much enjoying. Bob Batten, however, was no longer concealing his interest.

'Tell me exactly what articles you have in mind,' he said.

Elated by his reaction, which was far from negative, Georgia said:

'Three or possibly four articles: one, the initial decision to make the search and why; two, engaging the divers and preparations for raising the wreck. The third would be when the ship was recovered, and the fourth could be what they find in it. My friend, who lives out there, says it might also be possible to find Dinez da Gama's grave as he died out there on the island. That would be a sort of conclusion to the story of his life which had been transformed from piracy by the love he had for the girl he kidnapped.'

Despite his intention not to let his young employee imagine she could dictate what and what should not go into his paper, Bob Batten was extremely interested. It was not only her unusual ancestry and the intriguing documentation she possessed, but the articles she was proposing which excited him. This was not fiction, but ongoing fact and had all the sentiments his women readers would enjoy.

'Do your parents know about this plan of yours?' he asked, aware that, still underage, she would need their approval of the venture.

'I was waiting to see if you would approve my plans before I told them,' Georgia said, adding: 'After all, I did succeed in rescuing my Jewish friend from Germany without mishap so they should not object.'

'If your parents give their approval, I will allow you four weeks' leave from the office . . .' the editor said, '. . . and don't thank me. I shall expect you to write several outstanding accounts – and I stress outstanding – of your activities. Now don't waste any more of my time. Off you go . . . er, Georgia!'

He hid his smile as his jubilant young employee hurried out of the room.

Gerald Driffield did not give his approval for the simple reason that Georgia never asked for it. She told him casually that the paper was sending her on a secret assignment that might mean she would not be home for several weekends. She omitted to tell him she was going abroad on what her father would have called her 'dangerous shenanigans': although not forbidding it, he disliked the thought that his daughter was now working for a not-very-prestigious 'rag', as he termed such newspapers as the *Daily Chronicle*. Fortunately his thoughts were diverted by a letter from Migs announcing the date of her arrival home later that summer. Both he and Isobel were delighted by the news that she was pregnant with their second grandchild, and would be coming home for the birth. Douglas, it seemed, had managed to arrange six weeks' home leave.

Desperate now to leave for Madeira as soon as possible, Georgia knew that it would be impossible to ask her father to advance her the sizeable sum of money from her inheritance she realised she would need. Consequently, she went to Ditchling, to the one person who not only loved her deeply but who trusted her unquestioningly: her grandmother.

Clarissa Driffield welcomed Georgia with her usual, 'How

lovely to see you, darling!' and led her into her sitting room where an agreeable warmth pervaded the room. Georgia divested herself of her heavy overcoat, gave her grandmother a hug and without preamble, said:

'I need your help, Granny!' as she sat down on the tapestry stool at the foot of her grandmother's armchair by the fire. 'I couldn't ask Mummy or Daddy because . . . well, it's not the sort of thing they'd understand. But you . . . you're different and . . .'

Before she could continue, Clarissa broke in, presuming that she knew what was troubling her granddaughter who on many occasions in the past had expressed curiosity about her original parents.

'Has it something to do with your adoption, darling? You aren't still worrying about it, are you?'

'Oh, no, Granny!' Georgia said, 'I decided you were quite right to discourage me from looking for my mother. I realised that of course she couldn't have kept me if we had met, and we would be strangers, so what was the point?'

Clarissa hid her surprise. She had not thought Georgia mature enough to solve such a problem so rationally.

'I think you made exactly the right decision, darling,' she said as she got up from her chair and went through to her kitchen. When she returned a few minutes later, she carried a tray on which were a plate of buttered scones, a jar of home-made quince jelly and some gingerbread.

'Now tell me how I can help you, darling,' she said as she put the tray on the table and sat down again.

Georgia drew a deep breath before the words she had prepared came out in a disjointed rush.

'I want to go to Madeira, Granny. It's the Portuguese island where that pirate lived – the one I told you about when I showed you his letters. Well his ship sank out there and Fedrik – he's a friend of mine who lives there – he's managed to find some divers who will look for it, and Fedrik says they might be able to get inside and retrieve whatever is in it.'

Finally running out of breath, she paused for a moment before resuming in a quieter tone:

'I need some money, Gran, some of my own money, I mean, but Daddy won't let me have it until I'm twenty-one and that's ages away, and now my editor has said he'll let me go for a month as a freelance so I can write articles about raising the wreck and he'll pay me for them when I get back if they are any good, so I'm going to need money for my passage out to Madeira, as well as to pay for the divers and it could be very expensive if they don't find the wreck quickly, so I may need quite a bit.'

Running out of steam, she fell silent.

For a full minute afterwards, Clarissa did not speak. Two years ago, Georgia had shown her the letters she had found in the old house, and she could understand how important they'd been to Georgia as a link to her past, most particularly following her strained relationship with her father since he'd told her about her adoption. Clarissa now found herself questioning whether she would be exacerbating the relationship between father and daughter if she advanced Georgia some of the child's undeniably huge inheritance.

To do so, she reflected, would undermine her son's authority, but on the other hand, Georgia was hardly a child now. A very mature eighteen-year-old, there had been a considerable boost to her self-confidence when she obtained her job on the newspaper. Was she, her grandmother, now prepared to act against Gerald's likely dictum?

As if divining Clarissa's thoughts, Georgia said:

'It isn't just about the money, Granny. Daddy keeps talking about there being a war soon – and you know how he panicked when I was in Munich last year so I just know he'd stop me going abroad now!'

Absent-mindedly she took a bite of her scone and added:

'Honestly, Gran, I would be perfectly safe. I'd be a guest of Fedrik's aunt, Grandmother Wiscote's friend who lives all year round on the island at Reid's Hotel which is the best on the island and Fedrik, who's her nephew, lives with her, and he told me she is extremely rich, and I've met her twice and she's very, very nice.'

It was this last bit of information that now influenced the decision Clarissa had to make. On a recent telephone call Georgia had talked quite a bit about her new friend, Fedrik, who she was 'quite keen' on. She had apparently told him about the letters and her inheritance and it had crossed her mind that the man might have designs on the child's money. She was now reassured to learn he had such a wealthy relative, so presumably had no need to marry money.

Clarissa now decided that since Gerald had not actually forbidden Georgia to go on this extraordinary assignment sanctioned by her employer, it would not be too heavily on her conscience if she agreed to finance the enterprise. After all was said and done, she intended leaving all her money to Georgia and Migs when she died, so why should she not give the child some of it now when she needed it so urgently? Even were the boat and its treasure not found, the gift need not be repaid.

Perhaps she was splitting a few hairs, she thought as she poured out two cups of tea, but it was possible that Georgia's search for her ancestry might somehow heal the rift that was still ongoing between her and her father.

Her mind made up, Clarissa said:

'I don't suppose you know how much money you think you'll need, darling. The best thing I can do is give you travellers' cheques. They would be much safer than taking money, and you can cash them one by one as you need. I will arrange it with my bank tomorrow, but it may take a day or two before you get them. When had you thought of going?'

Georgia got up from her stool and went round her grandmother's chair to hug her.

'I'm just so very, very grateful, Gran!' she said huskily. 'I don't think in the whole of my life that I have asked for your help and you haven't given it.' She hugged Clarissa once more before returning to the stool, her eyes shining.

'I'm not planning to leave for another fortnight at least!' she said. 'I'll send Fedrik a telegram tonight to say I will be coming. Thank you so very, very much!'

They spent the next hour together happily reminiscing and then Georgia said regretfully that she must leave in order to catch the bus back to Haywards Heath from where she could get a train to London.

'I'll telephone you and let you know just as soon as Fedrik tells me when the divers will be ready to start and I can book my passage. I asked at Thomas Cook's and they told me a liner goes to Madeira via Gibraltar and takes about five days,' she said, as Clarissa helped her back into her overcoat.

'And I shall ask my bank to send the travellers' cheques direct to you in London,' her grandmother said, handing Georgia her hat and gloves. 'Good luck, darling! I do hope you find your pirate's ship. It all sounds quite exciting. If I were not as old as I am, I'd come with you! I shall have to content myself with your letters!'

Maybe I am a wicked old woman who should know better than to offer to finance this extraordinary enterprise, she told herself as she watched Georgia all but skipping down the garden path. On the other hand, she could well afford to do so, she thought as she closed the front door and went back to her warm sitting room, and it made her so happy to see the child she loved so radiant.

Journeying back to London, Georgia was elated. She had been reasonably hopeful that Granny Driffield would lend her the money. Rose and Lily would most certainly have done so, they'd told her, but they had two new leases to pay for, in Knightsbridge and Mayfair, and didn't have sufficient money to meet her needs. As for Sebastian, he never had any spare money, and in any case she rarely saw him now. He seldom went home and was absent from the mews most nights so Georgia assumed his affair with his editor was on going and she accepted that his romances were none of her business.

It came as a very agreeable surprise when three weeks after

her visit to her grandmother, having informed her boss that
Fedrik had written to say the divers were now on standby,
Georgia found a note on her desk from Mr Batten. It said she
could go to Accounts who had been instructed to add four
weeks' salary to her usual pay packet – '*to help pay for your
passage*', the note explained.

Georgia now had twenty travellers' cheques safely in her
suitcase, each of them worth five pounds. The bonus in her pay
packet would come in handy to bring back a really nice present
for her grandmother, perhaps one of the filigree embroidered
tablecloths Fedrik's aunt had told her about on their previous
meeting in London, which all the female members of a family
living in hillside villages in Madeira could spend a lifetime
making.

Back in the twins' flat that evening, Georgia did the last of
her packing. She checked that she had her passport and her
precious boat ticket to Madeira. Safe in an interior pocket of
her suitcase were the few pieces of jewellery she possessed, to
wear in the evenings. Among them was the gold brooch Fedrik
had given her and which she had not yet had an occasion to
wear since his departure. There had been a visit to the cinema
with the twins to see Laurence Olivier in *Wuthering Heights*,
and one evening when Sebastian had taken her to a cocktail
party at Monty's house. He and Monty had spent most of the
time talking to some of their friends from their schooldays so
she had spent the evening with guests she barely knew, and
had slipped away unnoticed and taken a taxicab back to the
mews.

As later that night she tried to sleep, Georgia thought how
much she missed the exciting nights out after Fedrik and his
aunt had returned to Madeira. She missed his kisses, his
embraces, and the unaccustomed thrill of his proximity when
he held her close against his body as they danced. Gradually,
as January had given way to February and now to March,
she had difficulty recalling his features; the sound of his voice
with its faintly foreign accent; the feel of his lips on hers.

Would she still find him so attractive when she saw him again, she asked herself anxiously, as she turned restlessly in bed? His letters were unquestionably love letters, which, although they delighted her, also made her feel nervous. What if she found she no longer wanted him to kiss her, caress her, put his arms round her and hold her close? If that happened, it would be difficult to avoid him when she was in Madeira. Not only was he organising everything, which meant they would be spending many hours together, but they would be living in the same hotel.

I can always go home, she told herself as sleep began to overcome her. The boat ticket was an open-ended return, and although she desperately wanted to find Dinez da Gama's ship, it was not absolutely imperative that she do so on this occasion. Conversely, her last thought before her eyelids closed was that if she did fall in love with Fedrik, she might want to remain on the island for ever.

CHAPTER TWENTY-ONE

1939

Georgia was thoroughly enjoying the new experience of her life on board ship. She had been given a two-berth cabin to share with a young naval wife called Esmé who was going to Gibraltar to join her husband. They had meals together and exchanged details of their lives. Esmé thought that so far Georgia's life had been a hundred times more exciting than her own. Her childhood had been a conventional and uneventful one.

'My father didn't want me to leave England,' Esmé confided, as with rugs over their knees, they sat side by side on deck sheltered from the wind, which was causing the lifeboats to sway from side to side, the noise drowning the sound of the ship's engines. She gave a deep sigh.

'I'm surprised your father is allowing you to go abroad, Georgia, and on your own, too! You're only eighteen aren't you?'

'My father doesn't know where I am!' Georgia confessed. 'All I told him was that I was on a four-week assignment for my newspaper.'

But by now Gerald did know his young daughter had left the country. Quite by chance there was a telephone call from Michael Taylor to say that his wife had been rushed into hospital dangerously ill with a burst appendix, and he'd wanted Sebastian to come home at once, but there had been no reply to his telephone call, so he had rung Gerald to enquire if he would contact Georgia to see if she knew where Sebastian was. Assuming Georgia to be at work, Gerald immediately telephoned Mr Batten and was told by his secretary that Georgia was on her way to Madeira, and had sailed two days ago.

Relating this extraordinary and disturbing news to Michael Taylor, Gerald was embarrassed by his friend's obvious astonishment that his daughter had actually left the country without first telling him where she was going. Eighteen-year-old girls should not be allowed to make such decisions without their parents' knowledge and approval, Michael Taylor agreed. They then considered the possibility that Sebastian had embarked with Georgia on yet another undesirable adventure.

An enquiry to the shipping agency elicited the fact that his daughter – but not Sebastian – had indeed booked a passage to Madeira, and that the liner was now well on its way. At that point, Gerald began to regret that Sebastian was not there to look after her, having guessed at once why Georgia was going to the island. As he said later that evening to Isobel, their errant daughter had never hidden the fact that she intended one day to look into the background of those precious letters of hers. As far as they were concerned, he'd never believed they had any validity, which Georgia would doubtless discover soon enough and return home. However, he did not like the idea that his daughter was almost certainly in touch with the foreign chap, Anyos, a much older man who she had been going out with when he and his aunt were in London before Christmas. Gerald was far from certain if he could be trusted and the thought added to his disquiet.

As a consequence he obtained the telephone number of Reid's Hotel in Madeira where he knew Mrs Resita Reviezky and her nephew lived, and put through a trunk call to her. When finally he was connected, she expressed surprise that he was unaware of his daughter's movements, but she reassured him that she personally would ensure that no harm came to Georgia during her stay and she would telephone him the moment Georgia had arrived.

Although now a little less concerned, Gerald was still far

from happy with the situation, even while he realised that there was nothing he could do about it.

Meanwhile, as the ship approached the island, Georgia's excitement mounted and at the same time, so did her doubts. Would she still like Fedrik as much as she had done in London? Would he still like her? Most of all, would she still want to be kissed by him – those long, breathless kisses he had bestowed on her in the back of the taxis at the end of their evenings out?

When finally the ship anchored in Funchal bay and a launch came out to meet them, her confidence returned as she saw Fedrik waiting to meet her. He looked very handsome in a cream-coloured suit and shirt with a paisley silk scarf tied at the neck. He waved his panama hat when he caught sight of her and she could see that he was quite bronzed compared to the men who had travelled out from England on the boat.

Beside her stood a fellow passenger, a smartly dressed woman in a navy blue jacket worn over a frilled shirt tucked into a white pleated skirt. She was holding a white straw hat firmly on her head in case it blew off in the sea breeze. She turned to Georgia and, pointing in Fedrik's direction, remarked *sotto voce*:

'Do look at that utterly divinely handsome man waving his hat at us! I do hope I'll run into him in the hotel.'

As there were no other men waving to them, Georgia knew it was Fedrik to whom the woman was referring. After their holiday in Madeira the twins had reported that all the guests staying at Reid's were frightfully smart and Georgia wondered anxiously if her own clothes would be adequate. Rose had lent her the dress she had worn at last summer's Henley Regatta, and Lily, the beautiful dress and hat she had worn at Ascot; but Georgia herself had nothing else for daytime other than last summer's cotton frocks and her tennis skirt, which she had worn when playing deck quoits on board. None of her few day clothes would be considered chic enough to wear at Fedrik's smart hotel, she thought anxiously, as nobody seemed to bother what she wore in the office, so there had been no necessity to equip herself with fashionable daywear.

Time seemed to fly past as the passengers were ferried by the launch to the mainland, and her concerns were forgotten as she was finally deposited on the jetty, where Fedrik's handsome face was smiling broadly as he bent to give her a quick kiss on either cheek and then, with his arm tucked through hers, he guided her through the passport office and out into the sunshine. Waiting there was an immaculate car gleaming in the sunshine, its roof down, the leather seats looking as luxurious as the car itself.

'My precious Bugatti,' Fedrik said as a porter put her suitcases into the dickey and helped her into the passenger seat. Having tipped him handsomely, he climbed in beside her, saying:

'I expect you are wondering, Georgia, why I asked you not to disembark in the Reid's Hotel launch.' He smiled at her. 'Two reasons – one to show you my car, and the other to drive you slowly back to the hotel so that I can have you all to myself before my aunt monopolises you.'

To her annoyance, Georgia felt herself blushing like a schoolgirl as he took hold of her hands and kissed each in turn.

'My aunt had the Bugatti shipped over here from France as a surprise for my birthday,' he continued, as he slipped the car into gear. 'Regrettably there are not many proper roads on the island, but I love driving whenever I can. The locals are used to the car now, but some do stop and gawp at it!'

He drove smoothly out of the harbour onto the main road leading to the hotel, skilfully avoiding a donkey pulling a cart laden with vegetables. Then he reached over and clasped one of her ungloved hands in his.

'You are just as beautiful as I remember!' he said, and before she could protest at the exaggeration, he released her hand and returned to the subject of his aunt's generosity.

'If you look down to the bay, you can just see my motorboat, which was another of my aunt's presents. It will be my pleasure to take you over to the island of Porto Santo where we could enjoy a picnic lunch and sea bathe if you wish.'

As if sensing Georgia's shyness, he went on to tell her a little of the local history: how an Englishman was supposed to have discovered the island after Moorish pirates had captured it, and later still, how the King of Portugal's army had invaded it.

With genuine interest, Georgia asked him if he had other such facts to relate as they would make lovely backing for the articles she planned to write for her newspaper. He smiled, saying:

'Many years ago there was a huge fire which burned down all the island's forests – you can see the trees that have grown up since then on the mountains over to our right. Folklore has it that the fire burned for seven years, and the island remained unoccupied until the 1400s.'

As the car climbed steadily upwards he continued:

'Then wine growers arrived and found the climate and soil perfect for their grapes. They imported slaves from Africa to work here.'

'You sound just like the history teacher at my boarding school,' Georgia said, smiling, as she relaxed.

Fedrik now took one hand off the steering wheel and covered hers.

'You cannot know, *querida*, how happy I am that you are here,' he said, his voice low and intense. 'Ever since you told me you had finally arranged your visit, each day has seemed like a year. Have you missed me a little bit, Georgia?'

Of course she had, she told Fedrik, remembering the evenings dancing with him at a nightclub, and the kisses and caresses that always followed.

'Tomorrow, *querida*,' he said, 'I shall take you back to the harbour to introduce you to the owner of the salvage company who will be searching for your pirate's sunken ship. You will be able to give him such information as you have on its whereabouts. His name is *Senhor* Gomez. He's Portuguese and needless to say speaks almost no English at all, so I shall act as interpreter for you both.'

Georgia felt a renewed rush of gratitude for the assistance this good-looking man was giving her.

'None of this could be happening without your help,' she told him with genuine warmth. His grip on her hand tightened.

'We must not raise our hopes too high,' he said gently. 'I was talking to Jose Lourenco, the man who will be in charge of the divers, and he warned me it could take them days, perhaps weeks, to find the wreck, and even if they do, they may be unable to raise it.'

Undeterred, Georgia looked at him, her eyes shining.

'I'm only just beginning to believe this is all happening. I've thought about it ever since I found Dinez da Gama's letters. I think I told you that they don't say exactly what he was carrying on his ship; only that he was taking his wealth home to Portugal to fund the building of an orphanage. He said he and the ship's three surviving crew escaped with only what they could carry, so there must be something of value still in the *Cantara*.'

'I don't want you to raise your hopes too highly, Georgia!' Fedrik repeated. 'As Jose said, other divers may already have come upon the wreck and robbed it of its booty: that innumerable sunken vessels, mostly pirates', were salvaged in the sixteenth, seventeenth and eighteenth centuries, perhaps even still more in the nineteenth century when your pirate's cutter foundered.'

'I do understand,' Georgia replied. 'And you said in your last letter that there was a limit to how deep the divers can go, but although it may sound silly I have always had this strange feeling that I was meant to find the letters so that Dinez could fulfil his wish to make good the wrongs he did before he met Chantal.'

Fedrik was saved a reply as he drove through the big iron gates into the tree-lined driveway of the hotel and drew to a halt outside the pillared entrance. Georgia had little time to do more than take in the scent and colours of all the beautiful flowers visible from the car before Fedrik and the smartly uniformed doorman ushered her indoors. Waiting in the foyer was Fedrik's Aunt Sita. Despite her age, she was looking immensely chic in a floral silk frock, her hair swept back from her face with short curls on either side.

'You must be quite exhausted after so much travelling, my dear,' she said, bestowing a kiss on each of Georgia's cheeks. 'Freddie shall show you to your room which is adjacent to our suite. As the sun is now setting, you will get a very pretty view from your window looking over the clifftop to the sea below. I hope you will be comfortable.'

'It's so good of you to invite me to stay with you, *Senhora* Reviezky, or should I say Dona Reviezky?' Georgia asked. 'I have been studying a book about Portuguese customs, but I didn't have enough time to learn the language.'

Resita smiled.

'You will find nearly every servant in the hotel understands and speaks a little English,' she said reassuringly. 'Since 1901 many famous people have stayed here; Bernard Shaw, the Duke of Windsor when he was Prince of Wales, your famous author, Sir Walter Scott. The hotel quickly became famous after it was built at the end of the last century, and two years ago it was bought by the Blandy family. Since then they have added two heated water pools which have proved immensely popular with my Freddie and other young guests who enjoy swimming.'

She tilted her face up to kiss Fedrik, and turned back to Georgia, apologising for her thoughtlessness.

'Here am I talking to you like a travel guide. You must forgive an old lady, my dear. It's just that I do so love this place, and it is my great pleasure to introduce you to our "island of flowers", as it is called.'

Georgia followed the porter who was carrying her suitcase into the luxuriously appointed bedroom. As soon as the man left, Fedrik gathered her into his arms and began kissing her. When finally he released her, he kept hold of her hands, saying:

'Forgive me, *querida*! I have been wanting to do that ever since I caught sight of you on the boat.' He bent to kiss her again, this time more gently. 'You cannot believe how greatly I have missed you, Georgia. When Tia Sita and I returned after Christmas, I realised how meaningless my life has been here without you. Do you care just a little bit for me, *querida*?'

'Oh, Freddie, of course I care!' Georgia said, uneasily aware that his aunt might come into her bedroom and see them.

Was she being priggish, she wondered? Fedrik was nearly thirty-eight years old with years of experience of life behind him, so he might well think her childish and immature if she said she wasn't sure exactly what she did feel about him. She loved his attentiveness, the care he took of her, the caressing tone of his voice and, indeed, his kisses and embraces, which left her excited and frightened at the same time, but did that mean she was in love with him?

She wished suddenly and quite fervently that Migs did not live so far away. Now she was married, her sister would have been able to enlighten her as to how you knew for certain you were in love. She could also have asked her what exactly it was that married people did. It had to be something very special since no one would explain about it. Not even Sebastian when she'd asked him when they shared a bed in France. Not least she wanted to know if what she felt about Fedrik when he kissed her had anything to do with it, which she now suspected it might.

Fedrik suddenly moved away from her towards the door.

'I shouldn't be asking you these silly questions,' he said. 'You must be longing to unpack and settle in. My aunt likes to dine at about eight o'clock, so you will have plenty of time to rest before you join us then in the foyer.' He gave her a sudden, devastatingly attractive smile that made her heart jolt. 'Tomorrow we will begin our search for your ship, my darling girl,' he added, 'and I promise I will not pester you for your kisses unless you ask me to!'

A maid came in almost as soon as he had left. She spoke only a few words of English but made Georgia aware that she was going to unpack for her. After hanging up Georgia's clothes in the wardrobe, she opened her pigskin dressing case and drew out her nightdress. The pretty smiling maid then turned down the beautiful embroidered quilt, and laid Georgia's nightdress in the charming shape of a dancer on top of the sheet. Finally, she opened the sliding glass doors to the balcony and beckoned Georgia to join her. As Dona Sita – a mode of address Fedrik had said was appropriate – had promised, the sun was setting and the sky above the tops of the subtropical trees in the garden was turning a fiery red which she now supposed the maid intended her to see. It was, indeed, a spectacular backdrop at which Georgia remained gazing for a few minutes.

While her back was turned, the girl had been busying herself in a shady corner of the balcony. When Georgia turned round, it was to see the maid holding in her arms the largest and most beautiful bouquet of flowers Georgia had ever seen, even at Rose and Lily's flower shop. She recognised the delicate white ones as orchids, and the brilliant red blooms as camellias, but could only guess at the jacaranda, agapanthus and protea that had been mentioned in her borrowed library book.

The maid disappeared into the bathroom and came out again carrying a large pottery vase into which she arranged the flowers. Only then did she extract the small card buried in the centre, and hand it to Georgia. It said:

A big welcome from your loving Freddie, and on the back:
I have given instructions for these to be put in a shady
corner of your balcony to await your arrival.

The flowers were indeed beautiful. No wonder Rose and Lily loved this island's flora, she thought as she bent over to smell their delicious scent a second time. How typical it was of Fedrik to welcome her in this as in every other way! She felt both excited and suddenly at ease. When she had bathed and changed into the prettiest of her evening dresses, she went to meet Fedrik and his aunt with none of her former shyness.

Resita was sitting in the foyer, watching but not really seeing the hotel guests making their way to the dining room. Her thoughts were entirely tied up with her darling Fedrik. She had first started to wonder when they were in London about his growing interest in Georgia. The girl was so much younger than he was, so unsophisticated, and despite her job as a journalist, so conventional. Unlike Fedrik's past interests in the opposite sex, such as his affair with the young American woman, Christobel, she suspected that this present relationship had, because of the girl's youth, so far been very circumspect.

Now, however, it was with a growing feeling of unease that Resita realised her nephew might actually have fallen in love. Since they'd left London, he had been like a boy with his first love as he waited restlessly for replies to his letters to Georgia; using her obsession about some shipwreck or other as a reason for doing so.

Resita's thoughts now jumped forward to the future. If by chance Georgia did fall in love with Fedrik, it would be every bit the disaster for her that she had begun to fear. For eighteen years he had been at her side; her companion, carer, devoted and affectionate. If he married, a new young wife would be highly unlikely to consider living in a hotel where her husband's attentions were divided between her and his aunt. It was unrealistic to suppose so. On the other hand, Fedrik was without an income, all his needs being provided by herself. If she withdrew her support, he could not afford to get married, but then he might grow to hate her if she stood in the way of his desires.

She realised suddenly that her imagination had entirely run away with her: that his interest in Georgia might simply stem from the fact that this was the first time in his life when a girl or woman had not been instantly attracted to him.

He came towards her, looking, as always, quite devastatingly handsome in his dark blue tailcoat and white double-breasted waistcoat, a white camellia in his buttonhole, and her heart filled with love for him as she reached up and touched his cheek.

'I shall, as always, feel so proud when I walk into the dining room with my hand on your arm, dear boy!' she said. 'Now where can your pretty Georgia have got to?'

Unaware of Resita's anxieties, Georgia came into the foyer. She was feeling both confident and happy. In the first instance, she was wearing a beautiful green and midnight blue silk dress with a chiffon scarf tied round her waist that Rose had lent her. It fitted her to perfection. She had a velvet band holding back her hair, and she had pinned one of Fedrik's beautiful, cyclamen-coloured camellias in the centre of the heart-shaped neckline of her dress. Her appearance, she thought happily, made her look far older and more sophisticated than she was.

Tomorrow, Fedrik had told her, he was taking her down to the harbour to arrange a date for the first attempt to be made to discover Dinez da Gama's ship. It was something she could never have organised on her own in a strange country whose language she did not understand. She felt breathless with excitement, which was heightened when she looked across the dinner table at him and saw an undisguised look of admiration on his handsome face. Her heart quickened its beat and, filled as it was with gratitude and intense happiness, she decided that without doubt, she really was falling in love.

CHAPTER TWENTY-TWO

1939

Gerald poured himself a much needed whisky and soda. His wife had not been in the easiest of moods since she had first learned of Georgia's disappearance.

'That boss of hers should never have agreed to Georgia going off like that on her own,' Isobel said as she put down the glass of sherry he had given her on the side table. 'I ask you, sending a young girl on a three-week assignment abroad when he knows perfectly well that Georgia is a minor.'

She paused only to draw breath before continuing:

'He knew all about that dangerous episode in Germany, as if that wasn't enough!'

Gerald sighed. The subject of Georgia's dangerous if admirable plans for her friend's escape had been recurring all too frequently, with Isobel's usual accusation of his being far too indulgent with Georgia and no wonder she behaved as she did.

'Have you forgotten how worried you were?' she reminded him now. 'You must speak to Mr Batten again, Gerald. She's only eighteen, for heaven's sake. She shouldn't be going anywhere without our consent. She should never have been allowed to leave home.'

She was interrupted by Polly announcing dinner was ready. During the meal Gerald refrained from pointing out to his wife that she had readily agreed to allow Georgia to stay in London with Rose and Lily as her guardians despite the fact that the twins – her nieces – were well known by both families for their independence and disregard for conventional behaviour. He knew Isobel considered them to be 'fast' with their bobbed hair, short skirts and scarlet lipstick, and supposed justifiably that they enjoyed the new dances such as the Charleston, the Black Bottom and the tango. Heavy drinking, smooching – even kissing – were de rigueur with today's young women, she complained, and their sexual morals were probably as lax.

Gerald thought better not to aggravate the situation by referring to the fact that Rose and Lily were enterprising, hard-working young women who seemed to be making a success of their business.

The following morning he made a second telephone call to Bob Batten, who confirmed his suspicion that Georgia was on her way to Madeira and that he had been led to believe she had her parents' consent.

'Well, what do you intend to do about it, Gerald?' Isobel asked when he rang her from his office with this news. 'Do you intend to go to the island and fetch her home?'

Gerald was stung to a sharp retort.

'Of course not, Isobel! Georgia has been sent out there by her newspaper. The fact that she is hoping to find a sunken ship is neither here nor there. However much her boss is paying her, I doubt he will be willing to spend a lot of money on such flimsy evidence as a dog-eared letter from a pirate! If she overstays the time her newspaper has allotted her, she will run out of money and have to come home. I suppose that man financed her since she hasn't the money to finance herself.'

Gerald's refusal yet again to find fault with Georgia revived Isobel's resentments, which had never been far below the surface. In point of fact, she was genuinely concerned to hear that Georgia was hundreds of miles away on a Portuguese island pursuing her ridiculous belief that a ship belonging to one of her ancestors' pirate lovers was recoverable from where it had sunk nearly ninety years ago. Dreadful things could happen to a young girl on a distant island among strangers who could not speak her language, or she theirs. She might well be robbed, have her passport stolen, even be assaulted, unprotected as she was. At least when they had allowed her to go on holiday to Germany, Hannah's parents had sent her a formal invitation. They had said they would be responsible for her safety, unaware at the time of the imminent danger they were in.

Putting down the telephone, Isobel sat staring uneasily out of the study window at the windswept lawn. The girls' see-saw, which Gerald had never dismantled after they'd grown out of it, had been blown onto its side. March was an unpredictable month, she thought, neither winter nor spring. What would the weather be like on the island of Madeira? It was more than possible that Georgia had not bothered to pack warm clothing. She was reminded suddenly of an occasion many years ago when they had woken up to a snow-covered garden and seen Georgia outside building a snowman in her bedroom slippers and pyjamas.

Going into the drawing room to distract herself by answering several letters for which replies were now overdue, she found herself too restless to concentrate. It suddenly struck her how bizarre it was that it should now be she, not Gerald, who was most concerned about Georgia. She could not put her daughter out of her mind. Although Georgia might have been a trial to her throughout her eighteen years, if anything awful happened to the child, she would be deeply remorseful that she'd not been a more caring mother to her. She tried to comfort herself with the thought that any wife would have been jealous of her husband's obvious preference for the company of an adopted daughter to that of the woman he had married. That close father–daughter relationship had, of course, come to an abrupt end when Gerald had told Georgia, belatedly, that she was adopted.

For the first time in her life, Isobel found herself regretting that she had not tried to establish the same loving relationship with Georgia as she'd had with Migs. Had they been as close, Georgia might have confided in her mother her plan to go adventuring abroad. Now, if by some terrible mischance Georgia's life was endangered, she would never forgive herself for the consequences, and would feel Gerald was justified in blaming her, too.

CHAPTER TWENTY-THREE

1939

The divers were now making a third attempt to find the *Cantara*. Georgia had already handed over several of her travellers' cheques, and Fedrik was anxious on her behalf that it was all costing a very large sum of money. She told him that even if the chances of finding the wreck were now thought to be slim, she was not yet willing to give up hope.

As Fedrik helped her out of his speedboat and then into the Bugatti parked on the quayside, she said:

'Please don't worry about the cost. As I told you, when I'm twenty-one, I shall be inheriting far more than I can ever spend, even if I do give some to my sister. She and her husband are living on his army pay which my mother says is not all that much.'

She sat back in her seat, confident that Fedrik could handle the big car no matter how fast he drove.

'I heard from Migs the week before I came out here,' she now told him. 'She said she can't wait to have her second baby and that her little boy, Georgie, is enchanting but becoming quite a handful, but of course, out in India they have an *ayah* to help look after him. Migs sent us some lovely photographs.'

While she was busy talking, she failed to notice that Fedrik had turned right instead of left towards the hotel.

'It's my surprise for you, *querida*,' he told her when eventually she questioned where they were going. 'I have been saving it for just such a moment when your hopes for salvaging your pirate's boat were taking a bit of a tumble.' He covered her hand with his, squeezing it gently. 'I have located the *cemiterio* where your pirate is buried. It was not easy as there are so many *cemiterios* on this island, probably because in 1856 so many people were dying of cholera.'

He paused as the road became rougher and steeper, and Georgia's cheeks flushed with excitement as she waited for him to continue.

'It's not far from Funchal,' he said. 'The grave is in the grounds of the Capela dos Milagres. I made enquiries, and discovered that the chapel was probably built on the site of an old chapel which had been built in the fifteenth century. It may be the oldest church on the island.'

Excited as Georgia was by this news, it took several minutes for her to find her voice.

'You wouldn't believe how thrilled I am to hear this,' she said breathlessly. 'My parents said I was romanticising when I told them I thought Dinez's wrecked ship might still be here. They wanted me to forget about trying to trace the past. This will prove that Dinez did exist. I'm so grateful, Freddie! I just can't wait to see the grave.'

Fedrik stole a quick look at Georgia's flushed cheeks, her excitement quite palpable, and congratulated himself on having earned this young girl's gratitude.

'You'll have to be patient, *querida*,' he told her, smiling as he drove expertly along a winding road through the dense forest of trees. 'It will take us a good half hour before we get to the *cemetario*.'

When they reached the chapel, it and the surroundings were bathed in sunlight. Georgia noticed several ancient cedars standing at intervals between the rows of old, weather-beaten headstones as Fedrik led her down a dusty path towards the north of the cemetery. The ground was covered with clumps of purple and blue agapanthus, giant yellow buttercups and saxifrage, all growing wild among the graves. Finally he stopped and pointed to a large headstone.

'See, Georgia, the name of your pirate,' he said quietly. 'No date of birth, but the date of death "15 *Juhno 1856*". The lettering DINEZ DA GAMA is unmistakeable, no doubt because we have such a mild climate here in Madeira.'

Georgia stared in silence at the faint writing on the tombstone to which Fedrik was pointing. Standing there in the bright sunshine, she could now see the indisputable proof that the pirate who had written those letters to her great-great-grandmother had truly existed and there was every hope that the *Cantara* would indeed be lying where he had thought at the bottom of the sea.

'I took some snapshots last week,' Fedrik was saying. 'You will be able to take them home to show your family.'

Georgia's face was radiant as she looked up at him.

'I'm just so grateful to you, Freddie!' she said again, her voice husky with emotion. Impulsively she stood on tiptoe to kiss him. Immediately his arms went round her, and she could feel his heart beating against her thin dress as he kissed her with barely controlled passion.

It was such an emotional moment that Georgia's body inclined towards his, and she returned his kisses. Her heart was racing, her breathing rapid as he pressed his body even closer against hers.

'You know I'm in love with you, *querida*,' he whispered. 'Tell me you do care about me? That you love me a little bit?'

Slowly Georgia drew away from him. The last thing she wanted to do was hurt his feelings, yet the same doubts as before surfaced as she questioned silently if the passion she had just been feeling was not love but gratitude? She was so deeply indebted to Fedrik for everything he had done for her, including this amazing surprise, that she wanted to give him something in return . . . something . . . but did she really want to give herself?

She looked up into his dark eyes, which were gazing intently into hers.

'Oh, Freddie!' she said weakly, 'I do care about you but I'm not sure if what I'm feeling is being in love. I want us to stay as we are, sort of loving friends. If I wanted a more serious relationship with anyone, it would be with you,' she added truthfully, 'but I don't think I am ready for that yet.'

'And the last thing I should be doing is rushing you,' Fedrik replied quickly. He wanted desperately to make love to her but managed nevertheless to keep the tone of his voice casual as he said, smiling:

'That, my sweet Georgia, is quite enough soul-searching for one day. There is still plenty of time left for you to sort out your feelings, and I am content for now to know that you do love me a little bit! Come now, bid your pirate rest in peace, and before you go home to England, we will return here and you can put flowers on his grave.'

When he says things like that, I really do love him, Georgia thought as they made their way back up the path to the car.

Before returning to the hotel, they stopped off at the harbour to see if the divers had returned from their morning's search. Knowing they would not be long doing so, Fedrik parked the car in order to put a question to Georgia that he had meant to ask when she first told him about her inheritance.

'How did it come about that you and not your sister, Migs, have inherited so large a sum of money from a relation?'

Georgia's hesitation was momentary. Normally she never spoke about her adoption, but now she felt close enough to Fedrik to explain. 'It's why I'm so happy that I can now prove to my adopted parents that there is no longer any doubt that those letters to my real ancestor were real. Do you think it's silly of me to care so much about my past?'

'No, I don't!' Fedrik said. 'You have been very fortunate, have you not, to be left so much money.' Using part of her inheritance to raise a wreck in the hope of retrieving a fortune in gold was, however, very much a gamble, he thought.

He, himself, he thought bitterly, was likely to remain penniless and entirely dependent upon his aunt for a good many years to come, unless somehow he could persuade Georgia to marry him. Even were she willing, her parents would almost certainly consider there was too big a disparity between their ages. Although he knew he did not look thirty-eight, there was no altering the fact that he was twenty years older than she was. Not least of the obstacles was that it would be over two years before she came of age and could marry him without parental consent. Yet another problem was the distance between their two countries. He doubted very much that a lovely young girl like Georgia would lack for suitors to rival him, besides which his aunt would most certainly not consent to his leaving her in order to pursue his courtship in London.

In many ways, he thought, as he drove on to the main road to the hotel, his aunt's increasing dependence upon him was becoming intolerably restrictive. She took his attentions to her for granted, although he had to admit they never went un-rewarded. She was always buying him presents, expensive gifts such as the powerboat she had given him for his thirtieth birthday. That she loved him as she would the son she had never had was not in doubt, but gradually over the years, he had grown to resent his financial dependence upon her. He knew it was highly unlikely she would want him to get married. Even though she had taken quite a fancy to Georgia, it would mean someone else coming first in his life.

While such thoughts were occupying Fedrik's mind, Georgia, too, was silent on the drive back to the hotel but as he helped her out of the car, Georgia looked at him, her eyes shining, and in a sudden rush of words thanked him again for what she called the happiest day of her life.

'Think nothing of it, *querida!*' Freddie said as he handed his car keys to the doorman who was waiting to park the Bugatti for him. He tucked his arm through Georgia's, adding: 'I think we may be a little late for lunch, and Tia Sita will not be pleased with us!'

Nor, indeed, was Resita pleased. She had been waiting over half an hour for them and now, seeing Georgia's radiant face and Freddie's adoring one, she knew that she did, indeed, have something to fear.

*   *   *

Gerald was unusually silent as he sat eating his dinner. Despite Resita's telephone conversation assuring him that his daughter was safe and well, and that she and her nephew were taking good care of her, Gerald was still concerned. He wished that he had had the opportunity to talk to the good lady's nephew. On the one occasion when Georgia had brought him down from London for a Sunday lunch, he had not been able to fault the fellow's perfect manners and friendly behaviour, but as he'd said afterwards to Isobel, he wished Georgia preferred the company of a normal, upper-class English chap like Migs's Douglas. He put down his knife and fork and said now to Isobel:

'I just hope they find this wrecked boat quickly. The sooner Georgia comes home the happier I shall be.'

Isobel looked at him across the dining table, her expression critical.

'She has always been self-willed and impetuous, and now – after the German episode – she has gone off once again without having the slightest consideration for our feelings,' she said testily. 'This may well be our own fault, Gerald, allowing her too much freedom, going on holiday to Germany by herself, nearly ending up being arrested by those Nazis!'

Gerald sighed.

'You have to admit, my dear, that it was very brave of her, and clever, to have helped that poor Jewish child to get out from under their noses.'

Isobel's mouth tightened.

'Brave or not, Gerald, it was a stupid risk to have taken and you were worried to death at the time. Why on earth can't she behave like . . . like Migs: be presented and meet some nice young boys who she could invite home for tennis and such like?'

Gerald managed to withhold a smile. However 'nice' the young men Isobel had in mind, they might not wish to play tennis or croquet! As for Douglas, although he liked him, he'd found him very conventional, and he did not doubt that Georgia, too, would quickly become bored with his ilk.

Isobel had not yet finished. She returned to a former point of dispute between them.

'As I said at the time, Gerald, do you honestly think journalism is a suitable occupation for an eighteen-year-old? Everyone knows reporters are a rough, ill-mannered bunch who push their way into people's private lives and exploit them.'

'Isobel, I don't wish to argue with everything you say but I do have to challenge your last statement. When have you ever met a reporter? Or been bothered by one? I agree it might not be our first choice of career for a girl of Georgia's background, and that it would have been preferable if she'd managed instead to get a job on one of the women's magazines you tell me are now so popular.'

Summoning a little of his remaining patience, he reminded Isobel, by no means for the first time, that Georgia was very far from stupid: that she had a good brain and was imaginative and courageous.

Isobel met his gaze defiantly.

'Even if you can't see anything wrong with the way she behaves, you cannot deny that she is now once again putting herself at serious risk. That man Fedrik Anyos – he's a good deal older than she is and who knows, he might seduce an inexperienced girl of eighteen. I doubt Georgia has the slightest idea how persuasive men can be.'

Having finished their dinner, Isobel stood up, preparing to leave the table.

Gerald, too, stood up. He gave a long sigh. He still loved his wife but she was, if anything, very much an old fashioned product of her own mother's upbringing. Attitudes to sex had become far more liberal since the last war, and although virginity before marriage was still considered important if not essential, the recent advent of birth control had lessened the fear of getting pregnant that, in the past, had kept women from taking such a risk. It was a pity Isobel had not considered giving both girls more information about the opposite sex, he told himself. A girl was much less likely to be seduced if she understood what might happen if she behaved too liberally.

Removing himself to his study, he placed his cup of coffee on his desk and, opening a drawer, drew out a snapshot of Charles in army uniform, looking immensely young, and very handsome, and thought how Georgia's resemblance to her father had become ever more marked since she had grown up.

His concern for her was not just because she was Charles's child but because he loved her. If this madcap search for something of her past was successful, would it reconcile her to her father's memory? To himself, he now wondered? If it did so, it was worth every minute of his current anxious concerns.

CHAPTER TWENTY-FOUR

1939

Unknown to Gerald, the search for the wreck was not going well. On their fourth attempt, the divers had found some iron balls that, they presumed, had come from a man-o'-war cannon, but there was no sign of the *Cantara* or its cargo. Fedrik felt obliged to suggest once more to Georgia that she should not waste her money further.

On several occasions, he had taken her out in his speedboat to watch the divers at work. She had realised then how vast the ocean was, and how easily Dinez's ship could have drifted far from the position he had noted. As Fedrik gently pointed out to her, even that position may not have been accurate seeing that the ship was sinking and a storm was raging at the time the pirate noted it.

In an attempt to lessen the gradual fading of her hopes, Fedrik decided to take Georgia to the little fish restaurant on the far side of the bay for lunch. The fish were caught on the morning they were to be eaten, and although there were only rough wooden tables and benches in one single room, it was always crammed with people and had become a favourite haunt of his, which Georgia, too, enjoyed. It also had the advantage of being far away from the hotel where they would have been expected to join his aunt for the elaborate buffet luncheon the hotel provided. Georgia was enchanted by the view overlooking the bay, the smiling waiters and the jolly atmosphere, which reminded her of the Faisan Noir.

Fedrik ordered them *espada* – the local, succulent fish flavoured with banana, which was utterly different from

anything she had eaten before. When she told him about the
Faisan Noir and how often she went there with Sebastian and
the twins, his handsome face was marred by a scowl.

'This man you talk about so often – he is important to
you?' he enquired, making no effort to hide his jealousy.

Georgia laughed.

'Of course Seb's important. I've known him ever since we
were tiny and he's my best friend.'

'But not your lover?' Fedrik persisted.

'Of course not!' Georgia retorted, not a little shocked by
the question. 'Anyway, he was my sister's boyfriend.'

Fedrik reached across the table and, taking both her hands
in his, said in a deep, husky voice:

'Then I am very happy, *querida*. It means I can try to steal
more than a small piece of your heart!'

Georgia's heart quickened. In London, she'd found his
extravagant compliments a little embarrassing as well as
exciting. Now she found his compliments entirely welcome.

'I'm so pleased I came out here, Freddie,' she said. 'You –
and your aunt, too, of course – have been so kind to me, and
it's all so beautiful and . . . well, different. I know the descrip-
tions you posted to my editor for me yesterday will interest
him. I don't suppose many – if any – of the readers know, for
instance, that "taxis' here are not cars but covered sledges:
that they have greased runners called *"carros"* and are pulled
by oxen over the cobbled streets. I've also described the men
wearing funny acorn-shaped hats, and the women and girls
in their pretty costumes, carrying baskets of beautiful flowers
on their heads, to offer to tourists like myself.'

'You would certainly not be taken for a local girl in that
charming frock!' Freddie told her, smiling. 'Some of the flower
girls are very pretty, but I've never yet seen one as pretty as
you!'

Fedrik had been watching Georgia while she was talking,
her rapt face filling him with a mixture of desire and anxiety
lest this lovely young girl might not return his interest. He

feared it was not going to be easy to continue to monopolise her. His aunt had already made it clear that she was not happy being left alone for all but a few hours when she took her siesta or on the occasions when she was otherwise occupied visiting friends. Once, on a visit to Biarritz in the yacht, she had spent a long weekend there with an old school friend and he had not been obliged to accompany her so had spent most of the time in a quayside hotel with one of the casino's female croupiers who was on her summer holiday.

It was the memory of that taste of freedom that had nagged at him ever since, and now not only would Georgia's inheritance achieve this but he was finding her a very desirable girl with whom he could easily fall in love. There had been moments when he was close to her when he suspected she, too, wanted greater intimacy. He found her innocence enchanting and thought how much he would enjoy teaching her the pleasures of love.

Georgia, meanwhile, was having difficulty sorting her feelings as they left the restaurant and began the short journey back to the hotel. So many different emotions were following one after the other. There was the ongoing tension of waiting to see if the divers were successful; there was the surge of excitement when Fedrik had shown her Dinez's grave; the overwhelming gratitude she felt towards him for all the many ways he was helping her. The thought of leaving him when she went home in another week's time was distressing. Whenever she thought about it, she believed she might really have fallen in love. When he held her hand, pressing kisses into her palm, or she caught sight of his amazingly handsome face as he approached her, her heart would miss several beats and then double its pace. One thing about which she had little doubt was that *he* loved *her* for he never missed an opportunity to tell her so! On the other hand, she would not want to marry him if that meant leaving home, her parents, her job, the twins and her best friend Sebastian. There had even been moments – not many – when she was homesick: wished she had Migs to talk to; the twins to counsel her; wished she had a simple, uncomplicated, familiar, unromantic companion like Sebastian with whom she always knew exactly where she was and what she felt.

Adult life was not proving as simple as she had imagined, Georgia realised. As a child, there had been definite conse-quences for everything, good or bad, but now she seemed constantly to be uncertain of her feelings. The only certainty there was, she reflected, was that she didn't have one single regret about coming to Madeira and seeing Dinez's grave; confirming as it did that the love letters he had written to the mysterious Chantal were real. She wished now that she could be as certain that the wreck of the *Cantara* would yet be found.

CHAPTER TWENTY-FIVE

1939

Fedrik was looking far from happy as throughout the elaborate breakfast they were having, Georgia and his aunt talked of little else other than Georgia's voyage home in two days' time. He had been counting on spending the morning alone with her down by the swimming pool, but Resita had decided to take Georgia on a shopping trip so that she could buy presents to take home with her. Fedrik would drive them up into the hills, she announced, where the beautifully embroidered tablecloths were made. The drawn thread work was so intricate, she told Georgia, it could take a whole family a lifetime to complete a single one.

Fedrik's good humour was restored however when later they returned to the hotel with their parcels, and his aunt raised no objections to his plan to take Georgia to see the Cabo Girão cliff. It rose nearly six hundred metres above the sea, he told her, and was the second highest in the world. Resita even offered to cancel the appointment she had made for Georgia at the *cabeleireiro* to have her hair cut and book it for the following morning instead so that the two of them could leave immediately after lunch. Fedrik found himself wondering uneasily if his aunt had guessed how serious he was about Georgia, and that time was running out for him to propose formally to her. He knew it was far too soon for her to consider marriage, but she might agree to an engagement, if necessary a secret one if she thought her parents would disapprove.

At last lunch was over and Georgia went to her room to

collect her sunhat and camera. Fedrik kissed his aunt dutifully on both cheeks before she retired to her room for her siesta, and waited impatiently for Georgia's return. When she returned looking surprisingly young in a simple cotton frock and sandals, he hurried towards her intending to take her arm and tell her how enchanting she looked, but before he could do so, the concierge came across to them saying that the *Senhorita* was wanted on the telephone by *Senhor* Taylor.

Georgia looked apologetically at Fedrik.

'Seb may have contacted the newspaper and found out I have overstayed the three weeks Mr Batten allowed me and he's wondering what's up. I'll be as quick as I can.'

She hurried after the concierge and went into the telephone booth.

'Took your time, slowcoach!' Sebastian greeted her. 'Trunk calls cost money, you know.'

Pleased to hear his familiar voice, Georgia enquired why he was making the telephone call if he couldn't afford to do so.

Sebastian promptly told her not to be 'such an ass'.

'I'm ringing because your father asked me to,' he said. 'I gather you haven't told him when you are coming back. What in heaven's name are you up to out there?'

'I suppose I should have told him I was staying on longer but he would only have found a way to stop me,' she explained. 'He twice told me I was living in cloud cuckoo land if I expected to find Dinez's grave, but Freddie has located it, so you can tell him Dinez's ship must have existed, too; how else would he have got from the Seychelles islands to this one?'

Pausing for breath, she heard Sebastian chuckle so clearly he might have been in the same room.

'He could easily have sailed to your precious island in someone else's boat, Dimwit,' Sebastian said, 'and before we are cut off, tell me when you are coming home? According to your papa, who is having kittens, your editor told him you are a week overdue at your desk.'

'I know,' Georgia answered, 'but Freddie spoke to the boss man of the divers, and he thought they may have been searching too far to the west. Freddie says . . .'

'What's all this Freddie business?' Sebastian interrupted. 'Freddie this, that and the next thing! You haven't got a crush on him, have you? What exactly is going on?'

Glad he could not see that she was blushing, Georgia replied: 'You might like to know that Freddie has been quite incredibly helpful.' 'He has acted as my interpreter, my guide and . . .'

'And your escort?' came the interruption from the other end of the line.

'Not that it's any of your business,' Georgia was stung to reply, 'but yes, of course he has been my escort. He drives me everywhere in his Bugatti. I could hardly walk, could I?'

She heard Sebastian's laugh.

'Calm down, Jo-Jo, or else I shall think the lady doth protest too much, as Shakespeare had Gertrude say to Hamlet.' His voice suddenly changed to a different tone. 'Look, idiot, I'm only asking because you're such a ninny! However nice your Freddie is, I understand he's years older than you are, and I can't see him dancing attendance on you without wanting some reward. Just watch your step, that's all. Now what am I to tell your anxious parent?'

'That I'm sorry I haven't been in touch but I am perfectly all right and will be leaving here the day after tomorrow. And now, Sebastian Taylor, I strongly suggest that you M.Y.O.B.'

She just had time to hear his chuckle before he rang off. As she walked back to rejoin Fedrik, she found herself wondering if she really did want Sebastian to 'mind-your-own-business', an abbreviation they had so often used in childhood. Was he right and she *was* getting out of her depth where Fedrik was concerned? The nearer the time came for her to leave the island, the more intense he was becoming. Last night he had pleaded with her – begged her not to go; begged her to stay in Madeira a little longer as he would be 'desolate' without her! She had tried to make him understand that she must go back to her job, but he had failed to see why it was so important to her; why she loved what she did and that she was working for fun, not money. Finally Fedrik had accused her of not really caring for him at all.

Of course she cared, Georgia had told him, a very great deal. She would be more than happy if he would promise to come to England and they could get to know one another better. She would, she had promised, arrange her annual holiday from work to coincide with his visit so they could spend all day as well as the evenings together.

Now, as she saw him looking so downcast, her feelings were even more confused. She hated to see him so unhappy. She herself was also far from happy when she thought about their parting when she boarded the liner that was to take her back to England far away from him. She knew she was going to miss him a very great deal; miss all his many little attentions, kindnesses, company, not to mention their wonderful evenings alone together. Not least, she would miss his passionate kisses, which were as exciting as they were disturbing, so intimate that she had been tempted to allow him greater intimacies . . . even, the previous evening, to let him 'do it', whatever that might be.

They left the hotel in silence. The sun was shining but it was not too hot, so the hood of the car was down for the hour's drive to the coastal village of *Camera de Lobos*. From there, the condition of the road deteriorated as it wound its way up and inland before finally descending a short distance towards the clifftop. Fedrik then drew to a halt and helped her out of the car. He kept a tight hold of her arm as he led the way down a rocky path to the cliff's edge. Georgia caught her breath as she looked downwards at the row upon row of small terraces descending one below the other down the whole of the cliff face. The terraces were not unlike those in Switzerland leading from her school down the mountain to Vevey, she told Fedrik. He explained that when the island had been reinhabited after the devastating fires in 1420, the local people had somehow managed to make use of the exceptionally steep slopes, planting vines, figs, avocados, oranges, in fact anything that would grow in those conditions. Small man-made waterways all over the island called *levadas* formed an irrigation system that kept the plants from drying out on the steep terrain.

But he did not bring her here to give her a history lesson, he told himself. He was here to ask a question that would alter the whole of the rest of his life. He put his arm round her as they stood looking down the frighteningly long drop to the sparkling blue-grey waters of the Atlantic nearly two thousand feet below. Seeing Georgia's rapt expression, he turned her towards him and, holding her body tightly against his own, he kissed her fiercely. Unhesitatingly, Georgia returned his kisses.

'There are so many other wonderful sights to be seen on this island, *querida*,' he murmured, his lips now touching her hair, his hands caressing her breasts, 'would you not like to live here with me in so beautiful a place? You know, don't you, my darling girl, that I'm hopelessly in love with you.'

Georgia felt her heartbeat quickening even more as Fedrik raised both her hands to his lips and kissed each one in turn. A little frightened by the intensity of his emotion, she tried to keep her own feelings steady. His suggestion that she should come to live permanently on Madeira was little short of a proposal, but she was certainly not ready to make such a serious commitment and she was still very uncertain if the huge attraction to him that she felt was love. To attempt to lighten the moment, she pretended not to take his words too seriously.

'It's too soon to make promises,' she said, in what she hoped was a level tone. 'All I do know for certain is that I absolutely hate the thought of leaving you.'

His voice was low and husky as he said urgently: 'I don't want you to go home, Georgia! Stay here with me! I will do everything in my power to make you happy. I'm desperately in love with you, *querida*!'

He pulled her down on to the dry grass and put his arms tightly round her body, twisting her close against him. Georgia could feel the thudding of his heart against her breast – or was it her own heart that was beating so furiously, she wondered? His kisses were now on her face, her throat, her mouth and his hands caressed her body slowly, sensuously, whereupon her body instantly came alive with the strange sensations his intimate touches always aroused.

As he fondled her breasts, she arched involuntarily towards him, and made no attempt to stop him as skilfully he opened the tiny pearl buttons on her dress. She caught her breath as he undid her brassiere and bent to kiss her nipples, half afraid suddenly of the intensity of Fedrik's passion and her own, as strange longings seemed to be setting her body on fire.

Could this be what falling in love was all about, she asked herself, the thought followed quickly by another – could this be the way babies were made? The twins' cautionary warnings now flashed across her mind: how ardent was too ardent?

'I love you! I want you! I want to marry you!' Fedrik was murmuring in her ear. 'I could make you so happy if you would let me. Marry me, Georgia! I beg you, say you will marry me! I am quite desperately in love with you! If you did not want to live here, I would come to London with you. I beg you not to go! Stay here with me, *querida*! I love you. I need you . . .'

Georgia tried to think calmly, logically, while all the time Fedrik was holding her and her body seemed to be on fire, yearning for something more than kisses and caresses.

She had no doubt that Fedrik loved her, needed her; but she was very far from certain if she wanted to be married to him – indeed, to anyone. At the same time, the extraordinary sensations he aroused with his lovemaking were tempting her to stay here longer. Did this feeling equate with the way Migs had felt about Douglas? Would she abandon everything and everyone she knew and go to the other side of the world in order to be with Fedrik?

Knowing then that she would never consider doing so, she drew back from Fedrik's embrace; she felt perilously close to tears as she whispered:

'I'm sorry, Freddie, really sorry! I did think I might have fallen in love with you and I do love you, but . . . but I don't want to marry you. I mean I have to go home. I've loved every minute of my time here and . . . and you have been quite wonderful . . . and I hate the thought of leaving you. I do care for you very much, but I have to go home. Please, Freddie, can't we just stay . . . well . . . friends?'

Although Georgia's reply to his proposal was not un-expected, with an effort, Fedrik curbed his feelings. There was still time to get her to change her mind, he told himself. It was a mistake to mention marriage when an engagement would have sufficed for the present.

'I should not have scared you with thoughts of marriage, *querida*,' he said, gently stroking a wisp of hair from her forehead. 'I can visit you in England where we would have more time to get to know each other better. Do not deny me any hope for the future, *querida*.'

Georgia was momentarily silenced. She had not forgotten how much she'd missed Fedrik when he had returned to Madeira after his visit to London, nor how exciting these past weeks in his company had been, how his kisses always left her craving something more, as they did now.

Seeing her hesitation, Fedrik said quickly as he helped her refasten her blouse and straighten her hair: 'Let's not worry about our parting now. We'll talk about it tomorrow. By then you will have had a little time to think . . . about us, I mean. I spoke too soon and realise I should have waited to tell you my feelings, but knowing you were leaving so soon, I felt compelled to do so.' Helping her to her feet, he continued: 'I understand completely that you are far too young to consider marriage, but an engagement, maybe. I beg you to consider a secret one if you think your parents won't agree. I need to know you do care for me.'

'But of course I do!' Georgia replied truthfully, 'but . . .' she was silenced by Fedrik putting a finger gently over her lips.

They drove back to the hotel almost in silence, their only topic of conversation the sad ending to the search for Dinez's ship. After three weeks, the divers had said with great honesty that they thought Georgia was wasting her money: that with a fierce storm raging the night the ship had gone down, it could have been swept a considerable distance away from Dinez's noted position. One thing was certain, it was not at the position Dinez had thought. The most senior diver had said that the sea was immensely deep round the coast, and more sophisticated equipment had yet to be invented which might have been able to take the exploration far enough down for he and his men to dive safely.

Disappointed as Georgia was – and it was a bitter blow when Freddie had translated the man's remarks – she had come to accept that the *Cantara* might never be found. Somehow, it no longer had the same importance as before, due almost entirely to the fact that Fedrik had located Dinez's grave. For some reason unknown to her, it was enough to know that the pirate once existed and that his love for her ancestor was not a fantasy. Any bitterness she might have felt about her adoption had vanished, as had her fear that she didn't really belong to the family who had raised her.

When she went home, she decided, she would be reconciled with her father; maybe with her mother, too. After all, she told herself, although her parents would never have consented to her coming out here to Madeira on her own, it was the way they had brought her up that had made her sufficiently self-confident to travel here alone, without coming to any harm.

Somewhat to her surprise, Fedrik made no further references that day to his feelings. He was particularly attentive to his aunt and fell in with her wishes to join her friends for bridge that evening, leaving Georgia free to finish the article for her paper. She was now able to describe the astonishing cliff at Cabo Girão and the story Dona Resita had told her of the invasion of the island in the sixteenth century by pirates. She decided on an early night and did not see Fedrik again until the following morning.

He seemed unusually silent at breakfast and remained so when, after she had finished her packing, he drove her to the Praia de Lobo. It was their third visit to the tiny cove, which was not far from the beach where the pirates had landed and attacked Funchal. It was a pretty drive along a poorly surfaced road past terraces of banana trees and colourful wild flowers growing on the verges.

When they made their way on foot to the beach, the only other people were a few local barefooted children fishing for crabs in the rock pools left by the aquamarine sea after it had ebbed. Fedrik seemed then to regain his good humour and they sat talking companionably in the sun. From time to time, he kissed Georgia lovingly but, to her surprise, not passionately. She felt herself relaxing, and it occurred to her that she felt far happier with this gentle, affectionate relationship than when he was demanding so much more. It left her somehow feeling out of her depth when he was so intense.

The afternoon seemed to pass quite quickly and not even as they drove back to the hotel did he raise the subject of their relationship. All he asked of her was her promise to spend this last evening with him regardless of his aunt's wishes for her company. Only too well aware of how much she owed him as well as his aunt, she agreed to do so although she knew Dona Resita was planning a special farewell evening for her.

Resita, however, was in an unusually happy frame of mind and she raised no objection when Fedrik told her he would be taking Georgia out for a last evening together after dinner in the hotel restaurant.

He was unaware of the reason for Resita's change of attitude – namely that after tomorrow, there would be no rival for Fedrik's time and affection to upset her. Georgia's passage home was booked on the liner anchored in the bay, and by midday, the girl would be gone. It was not, Resita told herself, that she disliked Georgia – on the contrary, she had grown quite fond of her, but Fedrik's increasing obsession, which he was unable to conceal, had concerned her deeply, so deeply that it had begun to dominate her thoughts. It had even crossed her mind that although he would know she would not dream of paying his fare to England to be with the girl, he could easily sell his gold watch, his gold antique shirt buttons, his silver cigarette case and lighter, if he needed to.

Now, from the conversation she'd had with Georgia when she visited her bedroom that morning, she was no longer worried that the girl might decide to extend her visit still further. Georgia had spoken enthusiastically of the job she clearly loved, of the twins she lived with and her friends.

Resita had accepted the fact that Fedrik was genuinely in love for the first time in his life. Accustomed as he was to getting what he wanted, even having his wishes anticipated by her, he might well intend to follow Georgia to England to pursue his courtship. Were that to happen, she knew she could not bear his prolonged absence.

Those fears were even further lessened when Georgia had told Resita that she had every hope of seeing her sister and the baby, who were returning from India in August for the birth of her second child. Not least, Georgia had that very morning received a telegram from her newspaper editor saying he was really pleased with the articles she had sent him.

No! Resita reassured herself, she had nothing to fear. Doubtless her darling Freddie would be very unhappy for a while after Georgia had left, but she didn't think he would be heartbroken. She would suggest a change of scene, a little trip over to Monte Carlo or to Biarritz perhaps. He always loved such holidays, especially if they went to a casino and with limitless backing by her, he could enjoy himself at the baccarat tables. Sometimes he was on a winning streak, and he would arrive back at the hotel with a pocket full of banknotes, which she never asked him to return. He had never asked her for money but then he had not had need to do so.

With such thoughts in mind, Resita sat contentedly at the dinner table between Fedrik and Georgia, and ordered a bottle of champagne, saying:

'We will drink to your safe return home, my dear, and to the future when happily we might see you and your parents one summer for a holiday here. Unfortunately, I don't think we shall have the pleasure of seeing you on our annual trip to London as I have planned a change of venue. Did I tell you, Freddie dear, that I have booked a suite in the Regina, that lovely hotel in Wengen?' She smiled at him as she added: 'I know you will enjoy the skiing, Freddie.'

As Georgia touched glasses with Fedrik and his aunt, she felt a small frisson of regret. If Dona Resita and Fedrik were not coming to England for Christmas, she would not see Fedrik again for a very long time. There would be no more dancing cheek to cheek held tightly in his arms; no more kisses and caresses in the back of the taxi on Hampstead Heath. At the same time, despite these regrets, she realised she could not possibly be in love when she could consider their approaching separation so equably; indeed, almost with a sense of relief.

She turned her head and found Fedrik's eyes burning into her.

'Our last evening!' Freddie said suddenly as the waiter served the second course of their elaborate meal. 'We mustn't waste it, Georgia.' He turned to his aunt. 'My plan is to take Georgia up to Pico dos Barcelos. The moon is nearly full tonight and I want to show her the wonderful view of the sea and the church spires which you so admired, Tia Sita, when I took you there last year. It's one of the sights you have not yet enjoyed, Georgia, and I'm sure Tia Sita will agree that it should not be missed.'

As his aunt nodded her agreement, Freddie felt a tightening of his nerve ends. He was banking everything on Georgia's willingness to go out with him. He'd feared that at the last minute, she might plead a headache or wish to remain in the hotel with his aunt. This, he knew, was his last chance of achieving what he now wanted more than anything in the world, but time had all but run out. Once Georgia was far away from him it was all too likely he would lose the slender physical hold he had upon her, and she would be lost to him. Other younger men of her own nationality would step into his shoes, and he would become no more than a distant memory. Tonight Georgia must tell him outright if there was any hope for him and he would find some way to follow her to England.

All too aware that his whole future lay in the balance, Fedrik had lain awake most of the night considering what he must do. Although his need for money was the catalyst in his desire to achieve the future he wanted, at first he'd thought only of seducing Georgia for his own purpose, but he had fallen in love with her. She was now the key to his freedom from his existing life of bondage and if she failed tonight to give him real hope for the future, he feared there was no other way to achieve what he wanted a great deal more than he wanted her.

CHAPTER TWENTY-SIX

1939

Having seen Fedrik and Georgia drive off in the Bugatti Resita made her way back to her suite. Without his hand beneath her elbow, quite suddenly, a wave of foreboding engulfed her. She recalled the many times during this past year when she had sensed Freddie's restlessness: his slight frown when she had asked him to take her somewhere when he had planned a different activity for himself. Then there had been his less ill-concealed anger when she had scotched his ongoing affair with the American girl. Until now, she'd managed to ignore these many warning signs that he was finding his allegiance to her tiresome.

As she walked through the door into her suite, she thought suddenly that she had probably been buying his uncomplaining devotion. If that were so, then it was now possible for Georgia to offer him as much if not more than she did. It was not just money, but something she could not give him – her youth. Now, unless she could think of a way to circumvent it, she was in serious danger of losing the former precious hold she had over him. How to do so, she could not for the moment envisage, but one shocking, disturbing fact came into her head: she would rather he died than that he voluntarily deserted her.

As they drove west towards the hills surrounding Funchal, Georgia fought off her fatigue believing that she owed Fedrik this last few hours of her time, Fedrik having given so very much of his time to her. He barely spoke as he drove them through the soft night air up to Pica dos Barcelos. As he had promised, the view of the moonlit sea and the lights of Funchal far below was breathtaking. He switched off the engine and turned to look at her. There was considerable tension in his voice as he said:

'You are quite sure, *querida*, that you will not change your mind? I shall miss you so terribly, and I cannot bear the thought of continuing my life here in the hotel without you, of waking up every morning knowing there is another predictable day to be passed. I beg you, Georgia, even if you cannot contemplate marrying me now, tell me that you think it possible you might change your mind: if we were to see more of one another you . . .'

'No, Freddie!' Georgia interrupted. 'Please don't ask me again. I don't want to get married – not to you or to anyone else. I'm sorry if I let you think I might be falling in love with you. I did wonder once or twice if what I felt was love but I've realised it can't be or I wouldn't be looking forward to leaving tomorrow – to going home; returning to my job. I'm really sorry, Freddie.'

Were it not for Dona Resita's comments when she watched her packing, it might have been harder to deny Fedrik even a modicum of hope: but she'd said that although Fedrik might believe himself to be in love with her, once she was out of sight he would quickly find another girl, just as he had when the girl, Christobel, had ended their flirtation: that he was undeniably an exceptionally handsome man, and very attractive to the opposite sex, nearly all of whom succumbed to his charm. Georgia mustn't take it to heart if once again it would be a question of 'out of sight, out of mind'.

Her words had brought Georgia an unexpected surge of relief.

'I'm sorry, Freddie,' she said again now, '. . . really sorry. You've been so very good to me and I'll always be grateful, even though we couldn't find the *Cantara*. It doesn't seem to matter now that you've found Dinez's grave.'

For one long minute Fedrik did not answer. When he did, it was to say in surprisingly calm tones:

'I wish it could have been otherwise, *querida*. I really, really do! One day you will understand how huge a difference you have made to my life. Nothing will ever be the same. I should have realised long ago how barren my life had become before I met you.'

'Oh, Freddie, please don't go on!' Georgia begged, close to tears. 'The very last thing I wanted was to upset you. In a week or two you will realise that we don't really have much in common. I couldn't spend the rest of my life living the life you do, and you would hate my life. I'm determined to have a career as a foreign correspondent and you'd soon get bored while I was away, perhaps for weeks on end. I'd hate it if I wasn't free to do as I wanted, go where I wanted.'

Although he made no move to touch her, Fedrik turned to look at her intently as she continued:

'I don't want to have a huge house and masses of servants and be smartly dressed all the time and go to cocktail parties.' She paused momentarily before saying: 'I don't really care about being rich and I plan to give a lot of my inheritance to my sister and to my cousins, Lily and Rose, for their flower business.' She broke off, aware of Fedrik's silence as he listened to her. After a few moments, he said abruptly:

'I don't understand you. To have money is to live as you choose. To give it away is madness.'

Georgia frowned.

'That's just what I mean, Freddie: we would never see life the same way. I'm just so sorry if this hurts you.'

Fedrik made no reply but drew her roughly into his arms, his fierce kisses bruising her lips. When he released her, it was to say in a strange, tight voice:

'Don't ever forget that I love you, *querida*. Whatever happens in the future, I will never stop loving you.'

There were tears in Georgia's eyes as he drew back in his seat saying abruptly:

'I had planned to take you to see the Opera House in Funchal but I don't think either of us is feeling like any more sightseeing. There is one more thing, though, that you should see before you leave tomorrow, Georgia. Will you permit me to show it to you?'

Relieved that Fedrik appeared finally to have accepted the situation, tired though she was and wanting nothing more than to be back in her own comfortable bed in the hotel, Georgia nevertheless agreed to fall in with his wishes, believing it was the least she could do.

'Of course I will!' she told him with as much enthusiasm as she could muster. 'Where are you taking me?'

Fedrik pulled the starter and the engine sprang into life.

'I'm taking you to see the interior of Tia Sita's yacht!' he said as he turned the car round towards the harbour. 'You've only seen it from the outside, but I'd like you to see inside. It's truly magnificent. When my aunt decided she wanted to keep her late husband's yacht, she had the interior rebuilt entirely to her own design. It has all the most modern equipment, the most beautiful fitments. We don't use it often enough,' he said sighing, 'but it is a wonderful experience when we do. At present, I am having some of the woodwork on deck revarnished as Tia Sita likes everything always to be in perfect condition.'

He was driving down towards the bay now, and Georgia could smell the salt of the sea in the night air. There were several lights shining on the water and she could make out one or two fishing boats way beyond the jetty. Further out lay at anchor the liner that was to take her home next day. Dona Resita's yacht was rocking gently against the far end of the jetty wall.

'What happens to the crew when you are not using the yacht?' she asked as Fedrik parked the car. With his hand holding her arm he walked towards the yacht. It was in darkness and she could see no sign of life on board.

'The crew are paid a retainer and live on shore,' Fedrik replied abruptly as they reached the gangway. Pointing to a shadowy flight of steps leading down the jetty wall, only half visible in the darkness, he said:

'You're not afraid to go down there? They may be a trifle slippery but I will hold your arm.'

Georgia looked at him in surprise.

'Of course I'm not afraid, Freddie! Why ever should I be?'

Fedrik gave a wry smile, which she could only just discern in the semi-darkness.

'Because we are quite alone here, and were I not in love with you, I might be planning to seduce you!'

Georgia laughed, although even as she did so, she felt surprised by Fedrik's comment.

'Of course I'm not afraid!' she repeated. 'I trust you!'

It was a minute or two before Fedrik spoke again, then he said:

'You should not do so, *querida*. No man is to be trusted if he is alone in the moonlight with a beautiful girl! That is . . .' he added, '. . . unless he loves her. No harm will come to you, Georgia, I promise.'

Back at the hotel, despite the lateness of the hour, Resita was not in bed. She was too disturbed to be able to fall asleep. She sat on one of the comfortable chairs on her balcony, staring out at the silvery path made by the moonlight on the surface of the sea far below. The light was bright enough to discern the movement of the palm trees waving gently in the soft evening breeze. Her thoughts were on Georgia's comment that she hoped, when and if they met again, that she and Fedrik could be friends. Somehow it left a door open a crack for Fedrik to pursue Georgia to England. Why, she asked herself, should she have this strange feeling of unease that he intended to do so?

She rang for room service and asked the waiter to bring her a small brandy, which, she thought, might help her to feel sleepy. Half an hour later, however, she was still no more able to stop her mind twisting and turning with ever-crazier thoughts. She even found herself questioning whether Freddie might take her yacht and sail away with Georgia in it! It was the stupidest of thoughts, she chided herself. Apart from anything else, the crew were on standby and it always took at the very least two days to prepare the yacht for sailing. Moreover, even if Freddie did do anything so unthinkable, what would he live on? As far as she knew he had no money and Georgia had made it clear she could not inherit until she came of age.

When midnight passed without the couple returning, Resita's reasoning gave way to fantasy. There had been a liner anchored in Funchal bay all day: Fedrik had his speedboat and could, if he wished, take Georgia out to it. The girl would have enough to pay for a passage if a berth was available. Was it possible Fedrik had booked it without Georgia knowing?

Deriding herself for being such a stupid, illogical old woman, Resita nevertheless found the spare key and went through to Fedrik's bedroom. The clothes he had been wearing that afternoon had been tidied away by the maid. His bed cover had been removed and the top sheet turned down. As was the custom, his navy blue silk pyjamas had been artistically presented on top of the pillow. She wandered over to the chest of drawers and guiltily pulled open the top one. Did he have any money hidden away? Had he been saving part of his allowance? Had any of his clothes gone?

Horrified by her behaviour, Resita closed the drawer and hurried back to her own bedroom. Slowly she undressed, washed herself, brushed her thinning grey hair and climbed stiffly into her bed. Believing she had proved to herself that she had been absurdly fanciful, she put out the light and lay back on her pillows. What, she now asked herself, could have possessed her to think these ridiculous things? During the past hour, she had built up an utterly unrealistic, impossible and uncalled-for spate of suspicions. Even, she told herself as she turned off the bedside light, even if Fedrik had wanted to elope with Georgia, he must know only too well that he hadn't the wherewithal to keep himself when he got to England, besides which Georgia had made it quite clear to her that she was not in love with him.

'I shall go to sleep now and forget all this stupid nonsense,' she said aloud as she settled into a more comfortable position, and tried to ignore the fact that her voice sounded absurdly tremulous. It was only when she was finally on the brink of falling asleep that she remembered Fedrik's words as he was leaving the hotel. They had been standing in the foyer where she was waiting to see them leave. He and Georgia were at the front door about to go out when Fedrik, who had already kissed her hand as was his custom when he was leaving or greeting her, suddenly turned and came back. Tall as he was, he'd bent down to kiss her cheek, not once, but twice.

'You've always been unbelievably good, kind and generous to me, Tia Sita,' he had said unexpectedly. 'I haven't often thanked you, have I? But I want you to know that I could never forget everything you have given me, not least the chance to have a new and wonderful life as your nephew.'

At the time, she had been very touched. It occurred to her that the reason for this statement might have been his way of thanking her for not demanding his time and spoiling this last night alone with Georgia. She might so easily have suggested that all three of them should spend a jolly evening together. Only now, as once again she turned restlessly in her bed, did the frightening thought suddenly strike her that Fedrik's un-expected declaration by the front door might have been his way of saying a permanent goodbye.

With sleep eluding her, her anxiety increased to such an intensity that she knew she must have the courage to disprove her fears. She would go once more to his room and look in the top drawer of his dressing table where she knew he kept his passport. If, as she now told herself, it was there, she could forget all her silly old woman's fear that he might be planning to join Georgia on the boat, leaving her for ever.

Slowly, silently, clad only in her nightdress, she went along the passage into Fedrik's room. Her hands trembling, she switched on the light and went over to the dressing table. Hesitating only for a few seconds, her heart pounding, her

brain telling her not to be so ridiculously fanciful, she pulled
the drawer open. Fedrik's precious passport had gone.

Resita stood perfectly still waiting for the furious beating
of her heart to subside. One thought only now consumed her:
she would not let that girl take her beloved Freddie away.

CHAPTER TWENTY-SEVEN

1939

It was nearly midnight and Georgia was standing with Fedrik in Resita's cabin. He was holding an oil lamp that he had lit before extinguishing his torch, and explaining that when the yacht was in use, a generator provided all the electricity needed. The lamps were everywhere in case it broke down. He was now holding one up as he urged her to look more closely around the cabin,

'I'm anxious for your opinion, Georgia,' he said. 'Is anything missing which an occupant might need?'

'Indeed not,' was Georgia's reply, as her glance went to the large bed facing them. It looked very luxurious with a gold satin bedspread and matching gold damask covers on the two armchairs. The dressing table and mirror, silver grey in colour, looked as if they might have been imported from France, as did the two small occasional tables placed conveniently beside each armchair. On the polished wood floor were several white woven rugs. Two pretty gold damask curtains concealed what Fedrik told her was the porthole.

'It's charming, nicer even than the hotel's bedrooms,' she said, 'and I've loved seeing it but it's getting late, and it will be a long day for me tomorrow so I really think we should go back to the hotel now.'

Ignoring her remark, Fedrik pointed to a door leading off the cabin and told her it opened into a small bathroom with all the necessary amenities. 'Further along the corridor,' he said, 'there is a spare cabin for guests, my cabin, and in the stern there is a kitchen with all the latest gadgets. The yacht also has a large lounge with a cocktail bar and a mahogany dining table and chairs.'

He was obviously very proud of the yacht's opulence and beauty, Georgia realised as he continued to describe the other amenities. Even the wooden rails and decking were currently being re-varnished. Below deck in a storeroom next to the kitchen, he informed her, were shelves stacked with tinned, bottled and dried food, and that fresh dairy products, eggs, fish and meat were brought in when they were about to sail.

Georgia was doing her best to memorise the details, which could in the future make useful background for one of her newspaper articles; but now she was really too tired. She turned to Fedrik and repeated her desire to leave and was surprised to see a strange look on his face – one she had never seen before. He was standing with his back to the closed door staring at her in such a way as to alarm her.

'What is it? What's wrong?' she asked anxiously.

Fedrik hesitated and his eyes narrowed.

'I'm sorry, Georgia,' he said. 'I'm really, really sorry, but you have left me with no alternative. I am leaving now, but I'm afraid you are staying here. You will find in a suitcase under the bed such things as you might need while you are here.' He gave a brief smile: 'I didn't think, *querida*, that you would want to remain in your evening dress both day and night for several days!'

Georgia frowned.

'Several days?' she repeated. 'What are you talking about?'

Fedrik drew a deep breath that was almost a sigh.

'Please do not concern yourself that I might have rummaged in your suitcase. Had you agreed there was a future for us, I would not have hindered your return home tomorrow in this fashion.' Glancing at his wristwatch, he added: 'Your liner is due to sail at half past three, I believe, and as it is now well past midnight, it will actually be leaving today! No, *querida*, I anticipated your rejection of my proposal, and purchased what I thought you might need in Santa Cruz where I knew I would not be recognised.'

He grimaced as he pointed towards the suitcase. 'I'm afraid these are not the kind of clothes you usually wear. I could only get what the local girls wear in Madeira, and a few toiletry necessities. You must tell me at once if there is anything further you need.'

Unable to believe what she was hearing, Georgia stared at him speechlessly. A sudden thought came into her mind: was he trying to stop her leaving the island that day, hoping, perhaps, that if he could delay her departure, it would give him time to make her change her mind? He must know that such a crazy scheme would forfeit such affection as she felt for him.

'I'm sorry, *querida*,' he said again, 'but although I hoped you might agree to an engagement, I knew it was highly unlikely, so I made contingency plans.' He sighed, adding softly:

'You see, Georgia, spending these wonderful weeks with you made me realise that luxurious though my life here on the island might be, I don't want to continue to live here with my aunt any longer.'

It was several moments before Georgia could bring herself to believe what he was saying.

'But what is the point of keeping me here?' she demanded incredulously. 'I'm not going to change my mind.'

'I no longer expect you to do so, *querida*. I have made other plans. I am going to ask your parents to pay me for your release.'

For a moment, Georgia was speechless. Then she said disbelievingly:

'You mean, you're *kidnapping* me? I don't believe it! Why? Why do you need money? I don't understand,' she repeated.

He was still standing with his back to the closed door, no longer looking at her but at the chair by Resita's bed – as if his aunt was sitting in it. In a curiously toneless voice he said:

'Perhaps I should confess that Tia Sita isn't really my aunt, although she believes so.' Seeing the look of utter astonishment on Georgia's face, a slight smile twisted a corner of his mouth. 'Only one other person in the world knows that I am not the nephew she believes me to be! But I might as well tell you,' he continued, 'because soon it won't matter any longer who knows.'

Georgia sat down heavily on the bed and watched him as he went over to stand by the porthole. He placed the lamp on the top of Resita's dressing table, and the soft light cast shadows across his face.

'It all began thirty-eight years ago when I was a baby,' he said tonelessly. 'My mother, who was a personal maid to a titled lady, was made pregnant by the son of the house who, my mother told me, refused to acknowledge his paternity. She was thrown out onto the streets by her employer, and worse still, by her family, who I never knew. They refused to have her home. In due course I was born. We were very poor and only survived because my mother was a good needlewoman and was able to take in sewing.'

Fedrik's face, as he turned to look at Georgia, was expressionless as he continued his story.

'In the early years, my mother insisted I attended school, but when I was twelve, her health began to fail and I left school to work in a restaurant in the kitchens. When she died I was fifteen years old and I found a better paid job as a waiter.'

A cynical smile twisted his handsome face, his features clearly visible in the golden glow of the lamplight.

'I trust I'm not boring you, *querida?*'

Wordlessly, Georgia shook her head.

'Stefan, the proprietor, was not an unkind man,' Fedrik continued, 'but he was avaricious and determined to improve his prospects, so I was obliged to work long hours and was only paid a pittance. One afternoon a distinguished-looking lady in a luxurious fur coat came to the restaurant and ordered a cognac. I was not allowed to serve the customers so Stefan did so. She showed him a photograph of a man she said was her late brother and she was searching for his son. All she knew about the boy's possible whereabouts had been told her by a former neighbour – simply that her nephew had left the orphanage where he'd been raised and was working as a waiter somewhere in the district.'

Fedrik paused and Georgia drew in her breath sharply as she guessed who the distinguished customer was.

'Dona Resita!' she whispered.

Fedrik nodded.

'Yes, Tia Sita. All those early years of my life, she had been living in America, but when her husband died, having no children of her own to console her, she decided to go in search of her brother. Finding that both he and his wife were dead, she assumed her nephew must be in an orphanage and decided to search for him.'

There was a curious half smile on Fedrik's face as he continued.

'You may call it Fate or, as I do, call it luck, but Stefan realised that evening when he thought about his well-to-do customer that I was about the same age as her nephew.'

'You mean you impersonated him?' Georgia whispered. Fedrik smiled.

'I see I have shocked you, *querida*, but I should say in my defence that it was Stefan's idea for me to do so, not mine!'

He was no longer looking at her as his thoughts went back to the events that had changed his life so drastically.

'In those early days of my youth,' he said quietly, 'I was ashamed of my illegitimacy and so I had changed my name to Rudi after the American film star, Rudolf Valentino! After a year as Stefan's kitchen boy, I asked him to give me a job as a waiter in place of the old waiter who had fallen ill. Stefan refused to promote me on the grounds of my extreme youth despite the fact that I had added three years to my real age when I first applied to him for work. He was not an unkind man and he knew I was anxious to better myself. Since there were kitchen boys aplenty to replace me, when he heard there was a vacancy for a waiter at his cousin's restaurant in the next street, he allowed me to apply for it. He gave me a good reference and I was given the job.'

Forgetting the reason Fedrik was telling her this story, while he paused for breath, Georgia found herself waiting impatiently for him to continue. He was staring unseeingly at the water jug on the table by Resita's bed as he said:

'I'd been working as a waiter for almost a year when my new employer told me Stefan had telephoned him asking me to call in and see him that day after I finished work. I was curious at this unusual request but did as I was asked.'

Fedrik now turned back to look directly at Georgia as he said:

'To my surprise, Stefan invited me to sit down at one of the tables and join him in a *schnapps*. Then he told me about the foreign lady's visit and her fruitless search for her nephew: how she had shown him a snapshot of her brother, the boy's father, who she called Nikolai Anyos. It was not until two days later that it had suddenly struck Stefan that I bore a likeness to the man in the photograph.'

'So you decided to impersonate Dona Resita's nephew?' Georgia said accusingly.

Fedrik shook his head.

'No, not me! It was Stefan who suggested I should do so. "You have a marked likeness to the man in the photograph," he said. "Can you even begin to understand how rich you would be if you really were the nephew that woman has been searching for? I'll wager a very tidy sum of money that she wouldn't question your identity – unless, of course, she has found her real nephew in the last two days".'

Fedrik paused once more before continuing, in a strange way relieved to be telling the truth about himself:

'I was too surprised – and excited, I suppose – to speak. Stefan knew that the woman's brother's only child was called Fedrik, and that he would be the same age as myself. As if it was Fate, Tia Sita had left with Stefan the name of the hotel where she was staying in case he had any replies to the queries he'd promised to make. "Don't you see?" Stefan pointed out to me, "she's a widow without relatives and desperate to find her nephew, so she'll want to believe you are the one she is searching for. We can tell her you grew up in an orphanage, so never knew your parents but could recall your father's name was Nicolai, and that at the orphanage you were called Fedrik."'

He paused momentarily to light a cigarette, then resumed his story.

'"All you need to know," Stefan elaborated, "is that your parents are dead, and you were too young to remember anything else about your past." Needless to say, Stefan was right,' Fedrik said now. 'He was a devious man. Once he knew I was willing to carry out his plan, he telephoned the hotel to tell Tia Sita that he *thought* he might have located her nephew, which was his way of ensuring that she had not already found him. When she told him she'd had no success, he sent me to the hotel the following evening to see her.'

Fedrik inhaled deeply on his cigarette. Then he turned back to Georgia and with an ironic smile, said:

'Stefan was right! Tia Sita did believe she had found her nephew. What also helped to convince her was that before my real mother died, she had worked as a lady's maid in the home of titled people, so she taught me how to speak and behave as a person of good birth. It helped to convince Tia Sita who said to me: "No ordinary waiter would behave as you do, Fedrik. I shall take you to live with me on a beautiful island called Madeira. I am a very wealthy woman so you will be very spoilt!"'

Georgia let go her breath.

'And so you have lived in luxury with Dona Resita ever since without a worry in the world,' she murmured.

Fedrik shook his head.

'No, not entirely free of worry. You see, there was one man

who knew the truth about my impersonation – Stefan. Although Tia Sita paid him very handsomely for the part he'd played in "finding" me, he wanted more. When I said goodbye to him, he told me that I owed my future well-being to him and he then mentioned a sum of money which I must pay him every six months. Were I to fail to do this, he would reveal the truth.'

'But that's blackmail!' Georgia whispered.

Fedrik grimaced and shrugged.

'Of course, but I dared not refuse to pay him for his silence. Fortunately Tia Sita has always been generous to a fault and provided me with an allowance from which I made regular payments to Stefan. He does not acknowledge them but I know he receives them as my cheques are always cashed a fortnight after I have posted them to him.' He paused to draw deeply on his cigarette. 'From time to time, I worry lest one of my cheques were to be lost in the postal system or not honoured for some mistaken reason. I imagine the consequences if Stefan thought I had defaulted and Tia Sita discovered the truth. However, these last few years I have had other more pressing concerns. Although Tia Sita has always provided me with every luxury – and I have not been ungrateful – I realised one day that almost without my knowing it, my life had become one of bondage.'

Georgia stared at him disbelievingly and said accusingly:

'How *could* you deceive Dona Resita in such a way? You must know how much she loves you and trusts you?'

Fedrik stubbed out his cigarette in the ashtray.

'I consider my conscience is clear, for eighteen years I have contributed immeasurably to her happiness. Besides, I am fond of her – grateful to her – and I'm not proud of the fact that I am leaving her.'

Georgia looked at him aghast.

'Leaving her? Not for ever?' she gasped.

Fedrik smiled wryly.

'Yes, for ever! I had begun to give up hope of ever starting a new life. Then I met you, *querida*, and when you spoke of your inheritance, it came to me quite suddenly that here was a way to realise my dream – an opportunity to escape that might never come again. A wonderful added bonus was that I fell in love with you.'

'So when I said I wouldn't marry you, you decided to get hold of my money some other way!' Georgia's shocked voice was tinged with bitterness.

'Not all of it, *querida*!' Fedrik said gently. 'I am only asking your family for enough to gain my freedom. From everything you have told me, you will not miss it!'

He sat down in the chair by the porthole and took another cigarette from his slim, silver case and lit it.

Georgia realised she had been holding her breath. Her voice a little unsteady, she asked:

'For how long do you intend to keep me here?'

It was a moment before Fedrik replied. Then he said in a tone that sounded genuinely regretful:

'I am truly sorry to have to hold you hostage in this way, but I will not give up my plan. I will release you as soon as your parents pay the ransom, then I shall disappear somewhere far away where Stefan can never find me.'

Georgia shook her head, a deep frown furrowing her forehead.

'Your impersonation was a very wicked thing to do even if it has made Dona Resita so happy,' she said, 'but how *can* you repay her now for everything she has done for you by deserting her? It will break her heart if you do as you say and "escape".'

Fedrik shrugged.

'Don't you see, *querida*, Tia Sita's love for me has been the exact cause of my problem? She wants me with her all the time. Her dependence on me has been – indeed is – total. I need a life of my own.'

Georgia's voice was bitter as she said accusingly:

'You wanted me to fall in love with you so you could marry me and live on my inheritance!'

Fedrik looked across at his young prisoner, his face unexpectedly sad.

'I really did fall in love with you, Georgia. I love you now,
but please try to understand, I do not have money of my own.
It would not have been possible for us to be married if you
had been as poor as I am!' He drew a deep sigh. 'I was penniless in my youth, and I vowed I would never be poor again.'
He drew on his cigarette before saying in a different tone of
voice: 'You told me your father was one of your trustees so
he should have no difficulty in borrowing the sum I will be
demanding if he does not have the money himself. I only
intend to ask for enough for me to live in reasonable comfort
far away from here. I *must* take this chance of freedom which
may never come again.'

He stood up suddenly and, reaching in his coat pocket,
withdrew two sheets of hotel writing paper and a notepad
that was covered in neat handwriting, and placed them on the
occasional table.

'It's late, and we are wasting time. Before we get on with
the matter in hand, I might as well tell you that I left in your
hotel room a rough map of the route to your pirate's grave.
When they find you missing in the morning, they will suppose
you have gone there for a last look at it.'

Georgia frowned and said disbelievingly:

'That's ridiculous! How was I supposed to get there? At
that time of night? Or was it early morning? There would be
no passing cars. Obviously I hadn't stolen the Bugatti, and I
have no doubt at all that the police will check out the taxi
drivers.'

Fedrik looked momentarily disconcerted. Then he shrugged
his shoulders dismissively.

'I shall say you are an independent adventurous English
girl quite unlike the Portuguese *senhoritas* of good family, who
would never venture out alone. I shall suggest that you went
down to the pool for a swim and may have fallen off the
rocks into the sea and drowned!'

Georgia felt the first real stirrings of fear.

'You do intend to release me, don't you?' she whispered.

Fedrik nodded his head vigorously.

'Of course you are to go free, *querida*, but not until your family pay the ransom. It will take time: time for the letter you are now going to write to your family to reach them, get the necessary money and bring it here to me.'

'Why do you want *me* to write a letter?' Georgia asked. 'I thought kidnappers wrote their own ransom note?'

'Because, I want your parents to recognise your handwriting so they will know it is a genuine demand from you for money. I have no wish to be implicated.'

Georgia's eyes narrowed. 'You've thought it all through, haven't you, Freddie?' she said bitterly. 'Suppose I refuse to write the letter?'

'Then you will have to remain my prisoner until you do so, although you might be found here so I would take you to one of many hiding places on this island with which I am familiar, places you would not find as comfortable as this.'

His voice suddenly softened. 'I don't want to distress you any more than is necessary, *querida*, so for your own sake, please write now asking your family for twenty thousand pounds.'

Georgia gasped. 'But that's a huge amount of money. You can't expect them to raise so much and . . .'

'Even so, you have a great deal more than that have you not?' Fedrik interrupted. 'So I have every confidence they will give me this.'

For a moment Georgia did not reply: then she stood up and went over to the chair, and sitting down she said quietly:

'What do you want me to say?'

'You must copy the draft I have written on this notepad, using the hotel paper. You will not say that you have been kidnapped but have run up some shockingly large gambling debts when you went with a group of new friends to the casino: that repayment is being demanded before they will allow you to leave. Quite obviously, should your letter be intercepted, I don't wish it to have any connection with me.'

He gave a sardonic smile. He reached into his breast pocket and took out a fountain pen, which he handed to her.

'You write articles so I'm certain that you can make the wording sound like your own. You should add that your need for money is both urgent and genuine if you are not going to be kept a prisoner much longer.'

Georgia's mind was now working furiously. She said in level tones:

'My father knows perfectly well that I never gamble. I have never even been inside a casino!'

Fedrik stubbed out his cigarette.

'I am well aware of that, *querida*, but there is always a first time, is there not?'

He picked up the notepad in front of her and started to read.

'I am afraid I have been very silly and that you are going to be very cross with me, but I desperately need your help. Last night, when Freddie was playing bridge with his aunt, a woman who lives on the island and her husband persuaded me to go with them to a private poker school in Funchal. I thought it would be a new experience for me to write about in one of my articles so I agreed to go on my own as Freddie said he couldn't leave the bridge game they were playing.'

He paused and glanced briefly at Georgia:
'So far quite believable, don't you think?' he commented before he continued reading:

'At first I was winning but then I lost all the money I had with me. The woman lent me some more but I lost that, too. I said I would pay it back as soon as I got home, but they knew I was going home next day and that's when they refused to take me back to the hotel, and the man said he will keep me locked up here where they live until I have paid them what I owe them.

'I know I have been very silly but we weren't playing with real money. They gave me different coloured plaques, without telling me they were worth a huge sum of money. The man won't tell me where he has hidden me or allow me to telephone you as you would then know where to find me, and he says you must bring the money here and he will meet you off the liner.

'I know how busy you are, but please, Daddy, come and get me as I am quite frightened, and Freddie and Dona Sita will be desperately worried about me. The man – I don't know his name – has promised I won't be harmed so long as you don't tell anyone what has happened.'

Freddie looked up from the pages he had been reading and added:

'You can sign it as you usually sign your letters to your parents.'

'I can't believe this is happening!' Georgia gasped. 'It's ridiculous . . .' She broke off as she realised suddenly that no matter how bizarre the situation she was in or how unlikely such a story might seem to her father, he would not ignore it. He knew nothing of the people she might have met during her weeks on the island. Moreover, he knew only too well how much she enjoyed new ventures and believed in the adage that one should try anything once. It was more than possible that he might think this episode a very useful cautionary lesson for her.

She took the notebook Fedrik was holding out to her and said:

'I will write the letter, but I can't guarantee my father will take it seriously. Perhaps I should also send one to Sebastian, who would be able to persuade him that this isn't a silly joke and I really am in trouble. Seb knows it is typical of me to be so trusting of a stranger.' Her voice hardened. 'I have indeed been an idiot to trust you, haven't I, Freddie?'

She could see by his expression that her remark had struck home. Speaking curtly, he said:

'You can write to your friend, if you think it will help,' he said quietly, 'but I shall read both letters before I post them, and the sooner they're done, the better it will be for us both. You can use your own words to add that I want your father to bring the money in person here to Madeira and that he is to wear a panama hat and carry a pair of binoculars round his neck, so I can be certain to recognise him when I meet him on his arrival.'

Seeing the look of uncertainty on Georgia's face, Fedrik added:

'Don't imagine you will be found here, *querida*. Your letters will be two among the boxful of mail collected every evening from the hotel, so our *policia*, should your father think to alert them, would not know where to look for you. There are only a limited number of police on the island, you know, as there is very little crime here.'

While he was talking, Georgia's mind had been working furiously. Fedrik wanted her to copy his letter to her father, but had made no objection to a second letter to Sebastian. There were many coded ways to let Sebastian know that she was in trouble and needed help. If anyone could find a way to set her free, it would be he.

'You have been planning this for quite a while, haven't you, Freddie?' she stated bitterly.

Fedrik flushed, his eyes angry as he all but shouted the words:

'I was in love with you! I still am! If you would only change your mind and agree to go away with me, you wouldn't spend another minute here.'

'How can you say you love me?' Georgia demanded, 'yet now demand money so you can get away from me? How can you possibly believe that I could ever love you now? You are corrupt, devious, a cheat and a liar. You have also been planning to ruin the life of the woman who rescued you, loved you, gave you everything you ever wanted. Hard though that bondage may have been for you, Freddie, for a very long time you were prepared to submit to it, taking as much as you could from the one person in the world who loved you.'

She looked at him scornfully.

'Yes, I will write your letter and . . .' she added with sudden conviction '. . . my father loves me very much and although I am only his adopted daughter, he loves me just as much as he ever loved my sister; and don't worry, I won't say anything incriminating.' She had already made up her mind exactly what she was going to say.

There was a strange look on Fedrik's face as he stood motionless, staring at her.

'When you came out to Madeira with your mad scheme to waste so much money trying to find the pirate's ship, I couldn't believe the huge costs were as nothing to you: that you were going to be so rich that, as you spelt it out to me this evening, you were going to give huge sums of money away. When I fell in love with you, it seemed the answer to all my prayers, my needs, but I would have earned my keep, Georgia. I would have made every day one of great happiness, giving you the kind of things money can't buy.'

It was a long speech, and by the end of it, he looked pale and drained. Georgia, in her turn, looked deeply shocked. The depth of Freddie's emotions was something she had never previously encountered.

'Kidnapping is a serious crime,' she repeated, 'and if you were caught, even if you were not hanged, you might face the rest of your life in prison.'

Fedrik had a strange look on his face as he said quietly:

'My life with Tia Sita has been a kind of prison – a luxurious one but a prison none the less. Please don't be frightened, *querida*. I do not expect to keep you captive here for very long.'

'People will start enquiring where I am if I don't join the boat home tomorrow,' Georgia said. 'Besides I shall shout for help and people passing by the yacht will hear me. I can lean out of that porthole and wave a towel or something, and when I escaped I would tell everyone that you kept me a prisoner.'

Fedrik regarded her pityingly.

'You can't believe me to be stupid enough not to think of such possibilities? In the first place, I have sealed the porthole so you cannot open it. In the second, the glass is thick enough for you to be unable to signal with the lamp. As for calling for help, Tia Sita's cabin is on the starboard side facing the sea and it is highly unlikely a passing fishing boat would hear you and lastly, you may remember I told you the crew were on standby, and only the man I have employed to varnish the woodwork will come to the yacht. Not only is he a mute but he is very poor and I shall bribe him not to draw attention to you. I shall tell him you are my wife and had planned to run off with a lover, so I need to keep you shut away where the lover can't find you.'

Only now did Georgia realise fully just how devious Freddie was – and how clever. He had gambled on the fact that she was likely to turn down his proposal and, knowing that she had no reason whatever to suspect his motives in asking her out on her last night on the island, had made these contingency plans. Surely he now knew that the story he had told her about his past – one of almost cruel deception – would turn her against him? If, as it seemed, he intended to let her go free after a few days, a week, he must realise she would tell everyone that he had kept her a prisoner?

'I shall only keep you here as long as is necessary,' he said. 'It could be as long as ten days, perhaps two weeks, but I don't expect it to be much longer before your family meet my demands. Meanwhile, you will be perfectly safe here. My man, Tomé, will start up the generator before dawn and bring you food, fresh milk and water while it is still dark and he will not be seen. I shall come and visit you whenever I can escape from Tia Sita. In the cupboard you will find a few books, a pack of cards, a jigsaw puzzle, to occupy you, and you have only to ask me if there is anything else you need, and I shall buy it for you.'

'Freddie, for your own sake, let me go now,' Georgia demanded. 'I give you my word I'll never tell anyone what you were planning. If you were caught . . .'

'But I don't intend to be caught, *querida*,' he interrupted. 'There is no turning back now and I shall go through with my plan.' His handsome face was now distorted by a grim look of determination. 'Let us waste no more time. Please write those letters, Georgia. The sooner your father receives my demand, the sooner you will be free . . .'

He made no further comment while Georgia began the task. Half an hour later when Fedrik had read and approved them, his only comment was that she had been sensible making her letter to Sebastian sound so normal. Putting them in his pocket he turned to leave the cabin.

Only then did Georgia speak, her voice harsh with bitterness as she said: 'Don't ever again think of saying you love me. You have made it amply clear to me that you only love yourself.'

Fedrik turned quickly away and, without looking at her, he went out through the cabin door and she heard the unmistakable noise of a bolt being drawn and a key turning in the lock. Then she heard the faint sound of Fedrik's footsteps on the deck above her, after which there was no sound at all.

CHAPTER TWENTY-EIGHT

1939

Bob Batten's voice was sharp as he barked down the telephone connecting him to the newsroom:

'I thought I said I wanted the Driffield girl to report to me? Tell her I don't like being kept waiting.'

As it happened, he had only been waiting ten minutes but he was an impatient man.

'Sorry, sir, but no one seems to have seen her this morning.'

'Then get on the blower to her home, for goodness' sake, and find out why she isn't here. I want a reply in ten minutes.'

It wasn't really all that important, he admitted to himself with a chuckle, but he liked to keep his staff on tiptoe. He wanted to go through the last article Georgia had sent him describing the grave where her pet pirate had been buried. Together with the detail about the cholera epidemic that had wiped out thousands on the island, her article also included interesting facts about the pirates who had plundered the island in the sixteenth century.

Exactly nine minutes later, his telephone rang.

'I'm very sorry, Mr Batten, but no one seems to know exactly where Georgia is. I spoke to her mother who said her daughter was due home yesterday on the *SS Alexandra*. I checked the passenger list and her name was on it, so presumably she missed the boat. Mrs Driffield said she would telephone the hotel in Madeira, and ask the lady she was staying with if she knew what Georgia was up to. She promised to ring me back if she received word of Georgia's movements.'

Bob Batten was about to comment when his outside telephone rang.

'Is that Mr Batten? It's Isobel Driffield here. I asked your operator to put me straight through to you because I have just spoken to the lady Georgia has been staying with in Madeira, she tells me that my daughter is missing. Nobody seems to know where she is, and no one in the hotel has seen her since last Saturday night. I can't think why Mrs Reviezky never informed us. My husband is going to be horrified, as indeed am I. The only thing that I can think is being a foreigner with no children of her own she may not be as worried as we are.'

Her voice broke, but before Bob Batten could speak, she continued:

'I know it's not the first time our daughter has failed to tell us what she is up to, but she has never disappeared before. I'm about to telephone my husband to ask what is the best thing to do. I'm so afraid something terrible has happened to her.'

Bob Batten was effectively silenced. He had become fond of his new young reporter in a fatherly way, and the last thing he wanted was for her to have come to harm.

'I'm sure she will turn up soon, Mrs Driffield,' he said with a conviction he was not altogether feeling. 'People cannot simply disappear.'

'There's just one other thing,' Isobel said, her voice sounding on the edge of hysteria. 'Apparently the police found a map in her room – a rough drawing of the route to a place called Machico, which I believe is where the pirate's grave she was so anxious to find has been located, but Mrs Reviezky says Georgia would not have tried to find her way there alone in the middle of the night.'

Bob Batten pricked up his ears; with a familiar tingling of his nerve ends, he foresaw a fascinating embellishment for the story he had planned for Georgia's sojourn in Madeira. He now did his best to make reassuring noises to her mother.

Encouraged by Bob Batten, Isobel now elaborated.

'Mrs Reviezky said that her nephew, Fedrik Anyos, and Georgia had become very good friends in the three weeks Georgia has been staying with them, and that they had been out for a farewell evening together, returning to the hotel very late. She said she knew it was late because her nephew had come into her bedroom to ask if she had some aspirin as Georgia had a headache. Mrs Reviezky had looked at her bedside clock, which indicated it was after two. Her nephew was distraught when it was discovered next morning that Georgia was not in her room or anywhere else. He even drove up to Machico just to make sure Georgia hadn't found some way there for a last visit to the pirate's grave.'

By now, Bob Batten was in little doubt that here indeed was a story. If the Portuguese press had not yet been alerted, it had all the makings of a scoop. Usefully, he now had instant access to Georgia's mother who promised to keep him up to date.

As he put the telephone down, words came rushing into his head.

Missing. Our own young reporter, Georgia Driffield, aged eighteen, whose articles you have been enjoying since her return from Nazi Germany with a Jewish school friend, is now missing on the island of Madeira in the Atlantic Ocean. Georgia, who should have been returning home after a working trip to the island in search of a pirate ancestor's grave, has not been seen since last Saturday night when she returned to the famous Reid's Hotel after a farewell evening out. We hope you will soon be back with us safe and well, Georgia.

He was not, however, going to print the story just yet as he thought it more than probable that the adventurous young girl was off on some private escapade and would turn up in a day or two, hopefully with an even better story than the one he proposed writing. It would be all the more exciting were Georgia's disappearance to continue for a little longer.

Gerald, however, had a sleepless night having received the worrying news from Isobel. First thing the following morning he took an earlier train than usual to London and then a taxi to Prince's Gate Mews where, as he'd hoped, he found Sebastian at home. Refusing the offer of a cup of coffee or a glass of sherry, he sat down on the somewhat dilapidated sofa and relayed to him such few facts as he had, only dimly aware of the untidy heap of scrunched-up balls of discarded type-written pages and piles of reference books scattered around Sebastian's desk.

'Her mother thinks Georgia is hiding somewhere in order to miss the boat home so she can stay out there. What doesn't make sense is that Georgia said nothing of her intentions to her hostess. Frankly, I find that a very serious breach of good manners.'

'It doesn't add up, does it?' Sebastian said frowning. 'In Georgia's last letter to me, she said she had accepted the fact that the wreck was not going to be recovered.'

Gerald got to his feet and went to stand by the window. It was a beautiful spring morning and the cobbled street below was glistening with last night's rain. Sebastian's M.G. was parked down below outside what had at the turn of the century been the stables housing the carriage horses.

'I half hoped she might have said something to you, old chap!' Gerald said, adding with a hint of a smile: 'You were always her accomplice, weren't you? Or should I say she was yours?!' His worried expression returned as he looked at the young man who he knew had supplanted him in his daughter's affections. He said gruffly:

'Facts don't seem to be adding up, do they? What my wife was told was that Georgia had been out enjoying herself with that foreign chap, Anyos, the aunt's nephew, on the night she went missing. When the fellow was interviewed by the police, he told them that Georgia had spoken obliquely about a tremendously exciting story she'd been researching "under cover" for an article for her newspaper.'

'That does sound a bit like Jo-Jo talking!' Sebastian said, but then Gerald elaborated.

'Yes, I agree, but Isobel had a second telephone call yesterday afternoon from Mrs Reviezky who told her that her nephew was now taking his boat round the coast in case she'd got lost and had found her way on to one of the beaches. Frankly, I don't like the sound of that one little bit.'

Hearing the anxiety in Gerald's voice, which now mirrored his own, Sebastian said quickly:

'That seems unlikely, Sir. Jo-Jo is far too level-headed to go wandering off without knowing where she was going. In my opinion the most likely explanation is that she is grabbing an extra week out there as she's onto a story and needs to be incognito. I'm sure she's simply in hiding, and that she will soon be found. Madeira is a pretty small island, isn't it, sir?'

Gerald's face looked a little less strained as he replied:

'I agree that's a possibility, Sebastian, but I can't imagine what on earth could have necessitated her going off somewhere in the middle of the night. She could be in trouble of some sort. I suppose we'll just have to wait and see, although if Georgia doesn't turn up, I intend to go out there. It takes five days by sea so I thought if you could find out if there is an airfield or landing strip on the island, I could if necessary get a flight out there much more quickly.'

He got no further before Sebastian, now equally concerned, broke in saying:

'If there is no scheduled flight, maybe I could fly you there, sir. It would be quite possible in the Moth so long as there is somewhere I can refuel.' He smiled momentarily, adding: 'I don't mind flying over land if the petrol gauge is showing nearly empty, but not over water!'

Gerald was looking doubtful.

'Don't mind my asking, Sebastian, but are you qualified to . . . er . . .' he broke off, obviously embarrassed by his suggestion that the young pilot was without the necessary experience to fly so long a distance.

'I've got a fair few flying hours under my belt, sir,' Sebastian said reassuringly. 'Try not to worry too much. You'll probably hear at any moment that someone has found Georgia; or, knowing her, that she has suddenly popped up with some sort of an explanation as to where she has been. Personally if I were around then, I'd give her a major telling-off for scaring us all so inconsiderately. However, my bet is that we have no need to be so concerned.'

But he was very far from believing it. People did not just vanish into thin air, and his misgivings doubled when, two hours later, Gerald rang him from his office to say that according to Mrs Reviezky's latest telephone call, the Portuguese police were suggesting Georgia might have gone down to the hotel swimming pool for a moonlight swim, fallen off the rocks and been swept out to sea.

Sebastian immediately vetoed such a macabre idea, saying he thought it highly unlikely: that she was an excellent swimmer.

Despite this reassurance to Georgia's worried father, Sebastian was now as concerned as he was. He kept telling himself that of course Georgia would be all right: that if he and her father did fly to Madeira, she would be there to greet them with a laugh, telling them how silly they were to have panicked.

Nevertheless, his hand was shaking a little as he lit a cigarette. He realised that if they did not soon hear from Georgia, he would have to call Shoreham for the information they would need if it proved necessary for them to fly out to the island to find her.

CHAPTER TWENTY-NINE

1939

The next two days of Georgia's imprisonment crawled by as, more and more uneasy, she tried to think of a way out of the extraordinary situation she was in. There was no lack of creature comforts. The moronic peasant, Tomé, who Fedrik had employed to revarnish the yacht and at the same time to look after her, came twice a day. She would have to outwit her jailer in order to attempt to escape. At present he only opened the door wide enough to push a box through the gap, leaving her with no chance to get away. He brought her goat's milk, fresh bread, fruit and cold meats and, on the second day of her imprisonment, he brought her a cooked lobster.

A large part of each day, Georgia spent wondering how it might be possible to overpower the man; but he never opened the cabin door any further than necessary to push the box of food into the room. He waited only long enough for her to push the previous day's empty box towards him before vanishing again. Once or twice she had heard him moving about on the deck above where, she presumed, he was doing his varnishing.

There was no sign of Fedrik.

On the evening of the third day of her incarceration, as Georgia yet again mulled over everything Fedrik had said before he'd left her locked in the cabin, she now began to feel increasingly frightened and angry. She even questioned whether he was entirely sane. For a man who, by his own account, had once been a penniless waiter, now to give up the incredibly privileged lifestyle he had been enjoying for the past eighteen years was at very least bizarre. He was doted upon by the woman he called his adoring aunt, given a beautiful speedboat, fashionable clothes, jewellery and as much money as he needed. For him to leave Dona Resita was surely little short of madness: yet he had sounded quite calm when he'd told her to write to her father demanding a ransom for her release – money to secure his future and what he'd called his 'freedom'. He had been clever, she reflected, in choosing the yacht on which to hide her with an illiterate peasant to act as her jailer.

To take her mind off her predicament, Georgia had spent the third day reading and writing a description of her situation on some paper she'd found in a drawer of the dressing table. Her intention was to present it to Bob Batten when she got home. She did not allow herself to think that she might never go home: that if Fedrik did not get the ransom money he wanted, he might have to kill her. It occurred to her how stupid she had been ever to have told him about her inheritance.

Later that evening Georgia was about to go to bed when she heard the sound of the door being unlocked and Fedrik let himself into the cabin. Although he glanced briefly at her, he did not approach her. He looked tired as he stood with his back to the door, and said:

'I'm really sorry I have not been able to visit you before, *querida*, but things have not been easy for me. The police have questioned me so many times about our evening out and the last time I'd seen you.'

Georgia was silent. He walked across the room and sat down in the armchair next to the seat by the porthole where she was sitting. The light from the oil lamp cast shadows on his face and deepened the furrows on his forehead so that he looked suddenly much older.

'I trust Tomé has continued to ensure you have such provisions as you need?' he enquired.

Seeing Fedrik's look of concern, Georgia asked herself

whether this whole episode was simply a bad dream. It was not as if he wanted her any more; he simply wanted his freedom – but at a price.

'I have everything I need,' she answered shortly, 'but what I have not got – and would very much like to have, Freddie – is a better understanding of how in heaven's name you expect to get away with this crazy scheme.'

There was the hint of a smile on Fedrik's face as he replied:

'I pride myself in believing my plans are quite foolproof. Would you like to hear about them?'

Without waiting for Georgia's reply, he calmly drew out his cigarette case and lighter from his jacket pocket and lit one of the Gitanes he smoked in place of the Turkish cigarettes his aunt kept for her guests.

'After leaving you here, I returned to the hotel. I knew I could count on Giuseppe, the night porter, following his usual custom to have a doze in his inner sanctum when there was no one about. I called out to him and before he could reach the front desk, I called out to you as if you were on your way to our suite: "*Don't wait for me, querida!*" I said. "*I'll only be a few minutes!*" Then when Giuseppe came to the desk I slipped him the usual tip and told him to park my car for me.'

There was now a look of self gratification on Fedrik's face as he said:

'I suppose it was a bit risky but it worked! When Giuseppe was questioned next day by the police, he swore we had both returned to the hotel at half past one, and that he knew the exact time as he had glanced at his watch when I called out to him. I made sure he'd remember the time because I apologised for disturbing him so late.'

No longer surprised by such deviousness, but astonished that Fedrik should have taken such a huge risk, Georgia questioned:

'So are you telling me the police actually took the porter's word that I returned to the hotel with you?'

Fedrik smiled.

'I'm not stupid, *querida*! I made sure they would by arranging for his statement to be corroborated by Tia Sita. You see, I went straight to her room to ask for an aspirin for you, saying that you were complaining of a bad headache but had no medication of your own to remedy it. I stayed for a moment or two, blaming myself for keeping you out as late as two o'clock in the morning; that I should not have encouraged you to help me finish a second bottle of champagne. As I expected, Tia Sita was quite cross, and reproached me for not taking better care of you. I was in no doubt that she would remember the time, as indeed she did.'

As if eager to boast of his perspicacity, Fedrik did not wait for Georgia's comments but continued:

'When I was being questioned by the police next day, I told them that I had fallen in love with you and that we had stayed out so late because we were discussing how soon we might meet again; and whether your parents would agree to us becoming affianced.'

Georgia drew a deep breath.

'I'm finding this harder and harder to believe!' she said. 'I suppose you have always known how to tell lies, Freddie. After all, you have lived a lie ever since you let Dona Resita believe you were her brother's son. I certainly won't believe anything you say to me from now on.'

Fedrik shrugged his shoulders and grimaced.

'I am saddened that you should have such a poor opinion of me, *querida*.' He stubbed out his cigarette before adding: 'I shall have to leave you now. I told Tia Sita I was coming down to Funchal to play poker so I must put in an appearance at my friends' house in case the police should enquire why I am not in the hotel as usual. I will try to come and see you tomorrow.'

Without a further word, he left the cabin, locking and bolting the door securely behind him. Suddenly, as the sound of his footsteps on the deck above her ceased, Georgia was consumed with anger, not so much with Fedrik as with herself. How could she have meekly allowed this to happen to her without putting up any resistance? That she had been taken completely by surprise was no excuse. Looking back on the past evening of her abduction, it was easy to see that she should not have allowed Fedrik to persuade her to go with him to Dona Resita's yacht. Retrospectively, it was an absurd thing for him to have suggested since she had seen it before, admittedly not below deck but many times from the jetty when she had been with Fedrik to meet and talk to the divers.

Why had she been so gullible, she questioned herself, and why had she simply accepted her incarceration with no more than a verbal objection?

She paced the cabin, her face set in determined lines as yet again she pondered the possibility of escape. A quick inspection of the room and adjoining bathroom proffered no sharp instrument with which she might prise open the porthole or the lock on the door. Frustrated, she stood staring at it for several minutes before the look of despondency on her face gave way to one of excitement.

Twice a day, in the early mornings and evenings, Tomé came to the cabin with food. If she were to stand by the door when she heard his approaching footsteps, she could hit him over the head as he bent forward to pick up the previous day's empty box, which he took away with him. She could then be free.

The plan seemed an excellent one so long as she could hit him hard enough. He would not be expecting violence from her since until now, she had politely thanked him, *obrigado* being one of the few Portuguese words she knew. The man always gave her a toothless smile when he departed, locking the door behind him. In one way, she thought now, she would not want to hurt him as he seemed to be a trifle simple as well as mute; but on the other hand, she had no alternative but to knock him more or less unconscious if she were to get away.

She turned from the door to stare round the room searching for a suitable weapon. There was nothing immediately to be seen. Then her eye lighted on the table lamp standing on a white painted cabinet beside the big bed. Beneath the delicate ivory-coloured chiffon shade, she could see a heavy bronze base curving upward in the shape of a dolphin. She had thought it very beautiful when she'd first seen it, but now her one thought was that if she removed the shade and the bulb, she would have the perfect weapon.

She moved around behind the door until she was satisfied she had found the ideal position from which she would not immediately be seen as Tomé opened it. Her plan was that as he leant forward to put the box inside the room, she could bring the bronze dolphin down on the back of his head. She practised striking the upholstered arm of the chair several times before glancing at her wristwatch. It was twenty minutes to midnight – another seven hours to go before the man would arrive with the box containing her breakfast and lunch. So far he had been exactly on the hour but she would have to be in position five minutes before, she realised, in case he arrived earlier than usual.

The ensuing seven hours seemed interminable to Georgia, whose nerves were so taut that she dozed only fitfully. By five minutes to seven, she was dressed and ready waiting by the door for the sound of Tomé's heavy footsteps. Her heart thumped in her chest as, in her highly charged imagination, she saw him lying on the floor, his red blood staining the immaculate white carpet as he bled – hopefully not to death! She had been practising the previous night the blows she might deliver, wishing she need not risk causing the poor fellow too much harm while rendering him unconscious.

Her reluctance to hurt the man too severely was her undoing. As he put his head and shoulders round the door to deposit the box of food on the floor in his customary way, the blow she struck was insufficiently heavy to render him unconscious. As she tried to step over his prostrate body, he reached out an arm and grabbed her ankle so that she fell heavily on top of him.

Her heart beating furiously, Georgia attempted to get to her feet. She was close enough to him for her to see the grey stubble on his chin and to smell the unpleasant odour of garlic on his breath. He was breathing heavily as his rough, calloused hand grasped her arm. He was making strange guttural noises as he scrambled to his feet. The contents of the now open box of food lay spread around them on the floor; a bowl of fish, prawns and squid mixed with rice in a runny sauce had tipped all over the carpet, and a bread roll had fallen on top of a bunch of grapes. Her jailer, now on his feet, pulled her up and pushed her backwards into the armchair that she had used when practising her blows, and replacing his fallen woollen barrettes back on his head, he hurried out of the cabin and she heard him locking and bolting the door.

An hour later, Fedrik came into the cabin. He stood staring at her where she sat on the bed nursing a badly bruised shoulder. His tone lacked the usual tenderness as he said:

'Tomé tells me you tried to escape. I underestimated you, didn't I, *querida*? Well, put any other ideas of escape out of your mind.'

He moved across the room and sat down beside the porthole.

'You've cost me quite a lot of money, you know. Just now after you had attacked Tomé, I had to bribe him quite heavily to continue his visits with your meals. Of course, being a mute, he could not tell me in detail what had happened, but he demonstrated quite adequately you hitting him. I do hope you have not damaged Tia Sita's lamp! She is particularly fond of it,' he added ironically.

His expression hardened.

'You won't have another opportunity to escape, Georgia. I have purchased a safety chain and Tomé is going to fix it when he arrives with your next meal. In future, he will put each item you require through the door by hand so it will not be necessary to open it so widely. You won't be able to hit him again.'

He drew a long sigh.

'Surely you realise that I cannot possibly risk letting you free until I have the money that I need to escape? Were I to do so, within minutes you would be free to reveal my identity and my one chance of a new life would be gone for ever.'

CHAPTER THIRTY

1939

Sebastian tried not to be worried about Georgia as he waited for the telephone call her father had promised to make the moment he received any news, however insignificant it might prove to be.

He realised suddenly that after half an hour at his desk, he had not written one word for the current chapter of his book: that he'd been staring out of the window at the leaves of the lime tree on the opposite side of the mews, wondering at its ability to flourish when its roots were buried beneath the cobbled street. Spring had well and truly arrived, he reflected, with all its promise of new life, but what if Georgia's father was right, and she might have suffered a fatal accident?

The sudden ring of the telephone at that moment compounded his anxiety. Putting the receiver to his ear, he heard Mr Driffield's voice:

'I have managed to speak to the Assistant Consul in Madeira, and he assured me he is overseeing the search for Georgia. I think I should go out there as soon as possible,' Gerald said, 'but between you and me, Sebastian, there's a bit of a flap on here at the office – the ramifications of the Anglo-French agreement between Chamberlain and Lebrun is coming to a head. They're hoping it will call a halt to that wretched fellow, Adolf Hitler marching into Poland. So I should not really be away.'

At once Sebastian volunteered to go out to Madeira in his place, but Gerald suggested they wait another twenty-four hours.

'You know as well as I do what that daughter of mine is like,' he said. 'It's more than possible she'll turn up bright as a button having been off on one of her madcap adventures. I'll ring at once when I hear they've found her.'

Far from reassured, Sebastian reflected uneasily that Mr Driffield's comments were made to bolster his own fears. As he wound a fresh sheet of paper into his typewriter, he tried to settle down once more to work, but the truth of the situation kept returning to his mind. Not even Jo-Jo would go off secretly on a so-called adventure in the early hours of the morning, he told himself, let alone with only a few hours before the liner taking her home was due to sail. Besides, she had no means of transport other than a taxi, *if* the island sported such a thing.

That evening, he went round to see Rose and Lily who showed as deep a concern as his.

'Maybe she went off on her own to take a last look at that pirate's grave!' Lily suggested. 'You know how thrilled she was to have found it!'

'And her letter had far more to say about it than about the wrecked ship,' Rose added. 'Maybe she got lost in the woods on her way to the cemetery!'

Sebastian considered such a possibility highly unlikely. For one thing, the Anyos fellow would surely have driven her there if she'd asked him to do so, albeit not in the middle of the night.

Nevertheless the recurring thought of Georgia alone, on a mountain in a foreign country, lost in a forest, kept Sebastian feeling uneasy for the remainder of the day. When Gerald had still not rung him the following day, he telephoned Isobel who, usually such a calm emotionless person, now sounded close to tears.

'It's so worrying, Sebastian!' she said tremulously, 'and Gerald is so tied up at the War Office, he had to stay in London last night, and when he rang me, he said he has to be on hand all the time to answer any questions the Prime Minister might raise over this pact with the French. He's worried stiff about Georgia, and so am I. Do you realise it's now eight days since she went missing?'

Sebastian tried to be as reassuring as he could, but once again he slept very badly that night, disturbed by a dream in which Georgia fell off a rock into a stormy sea, and he was poised hundreds of feet above on a clifftop, and he could do nothing to save her.

It was both a shock and a relief when the telephone bell woke him next morning. He sprang out of bed and hurried to answer it. As he hoped, it was Georgia's father.

'Something very strange has happened,' Gerald said. 'The post has brought an airmail letter from Georgia. The postmark is a week old – that means she must have written it the day she was first reported missing.'

'So she's alive!' Sebastian said joyfully. 'Where is she, sir? What happened to her? She isn't hurt, is she?'

Gerald broke in before Sebastian could ask any more questions:

'You're on your own, I take it? What I'm going to tell you is as confidential as it comes.' His voice deepened as he added: 'Georgia's life may depend on it.'

Sebastian felt his nerves tighten in apprehension as he listened to the voice on the telephone.

'I'll read you the letter, Sebastian. Maybe you can make more sense of it than I can. It's written on Reid's Hotel notepaper:

'Darling Daddy,

This may come as a bit of a shock, but do you think you could possibly bring me £20,000?

If you don't have it, can you get the bank manager to bring you some of my money? I am unable to talk to you on the telephone which is a pity as this is very urgent. I may be in big trouble if you can't get it for me.

Let me know if you can and how soon so I can meet your boat. The person who lent me the money says he must have it soon as he needs it himself, and he won't let me leave his house until he gets it.

I know I have been very silly betting money but some people at the hotel persuaded me to go with them to a poker school at the house where they were staying. I didn't tell Freddie or Dona Resita where I was going as I thought they might stop me going there with strangers.

Tell Bes I hope she hasn't broken the butterfly brooch I gave her for her birthday and it can still be used – at least I think it's a butterfly and not some other insect like a moth! Love to Mummy.

Your loving daughter, Jo-Jo.

P.S. Please come as quickly as you can, Daddy, as I hate being where I am.

P.P.S. I am at present very well but anxious to see you. When you come please will you wear your new panama hat, and bring your binoculars.

P.P.P.S. Did Sebastian get my letter?

P.P.P.P.S. Please don't tell anyone except Seb about my gambling.'

Telling Gerald to hold on, Sebastian raced downstairs where he found an airmail envelope on the doormat. He opened it as he took the stairs two at a time, and picking up the telephone, he read the contents to Gerald.

'Dear Seb,

Has Daddy told you about my betting? I know he will be very angry with me for losing so much money. When you took me to the casino in London and we played roulette, you didn't let me bet more than £1, but a foreign man in

the hotel told me if I went with him and his wife to a
friend's house, I could play poker which was much more
fun than roulette.

I know you'll say it was very silly of me to trust him
but each time I lost, the man insisted on lending me some
more to win it back. Now he wants me to pay him what
I owe him before I leave here and he won't let me go back
to the hotel until I do so. So please tell Daddy I really do
need the money quickly. The man wants Daddy to bring it
as he says it wouldn't be safe to send it to the bank out
here as he'd have to let me free in order to collect it. He
is to come on his own.

I know you've always said gambling was a mug's game.
Please ask Daddy to forgive me and to bring me the money
as quickly as he can.

Jo-Jo.'

For a moment, neither of the men spoke, then Sebastian said:
'This isn't some silly joke, Mr Driffield. She is in some sort
of trouble.'

'But what on earth is she talking about, Sebastian?' Gerald
asked gruffly. 'I just don't believe she has gambled thousands
of pounds away in a casino. That's quite ridiculous! And who
on earth is this Bes she talks about in her letter to me?
Moreover £20,000 is a ludicrous amount of money. If it's so
urgent, why could she not telephone me? A telephone call
would have been much quicker . . .'

Sebastian interrupted him.

'The fellow to whom she owes money is undoubtedly
holding her hostage, so she might not be free to telephone
you, sir. As to that bit about the butterfly brooch, it's a secret
message for me. In the old days when we were kids, one of
our codes was spelling names backwards. "Bes" is "Seb":
Jo-Jo's way of doing her best to inform me she's in trouble.
The butterfly brooch is obviously a reference to my Gipsy
Moth, and she wishes it – i.e. I – was out there!'

'I think you're right and this loan repayment thing is really a ransom demand: that she has been kidnapped,' Gerald said, his voice husky with anxiety. 'But if I'm right, why hasn't the scoundrel who has kidnapped her written a confounded ransom note himself?'

Gerald pursued his theory:

'Georgia could not possibly want such a huge sum of money,' he said. 'She has never been a gambler and even if this was a one-off, she would never have borrowed such a huge sum. She says whoever has her i.o.u. won't release her until she has handed the money to him, which explains her disappearance. I'll raise it somehow. I can give the bank the deeds of my house as security and I have one or two investments I can cash in; but that wouldn't be nearly enough.'

'Sir, it isn't for me to say this,' Sebastian broke in, 'but Georgia has often told me that she could never spend all the money she is to receive when she comes of age. You wouldn't be robbing her if you could get the bank to give you some of it now, whereas if you don't . . .'

It was Gerald's turn to break in.

'You're right. John Saunders, the bank manager, and I are her trustees. We've been friends for years; partner each other in the occasional golf tournament, that sort of thing. He won't question me when I show him Georgia's letter and I explain I think it might be professional kidnappers who are holding her to ransom. I have no doubt he will fix things for me and won't betray any confidences. The last thing I want is for the police or the press to get hold of the story. The fellow who is keeping her prisoner has no reason to harm her so long as he believes he will get what he wants.'

Sebastian's mind was working furiously.

'You said her letter was written on the hotel notepaper. I will reply to her there, not referring to our suspicions but making it clear you will be coming out with the money. The man must have some way of accessing her mail or she wouldn't have told you to write there.' After a moment of silence Sebastian added reassuringly: 'We can be fairly certain that whoever has abducted her won't harm her unless he believes he won't get the money.'

'Splendid idea,' Gerald said approvingly, 'just so long as you are careful of the wording. Simply let Georgia know that I'll be coming to Madeira with the money she needs.'

'Just one thing, sir,' Sebastian said before Gerald could ring off, 'I think I should go with you – just in case you need help if things were to get tricky. I'll go down to Shoreham as soon as I have written the letter, then I'll have the Moth ready to fly you out there the moment you are ready to leave.'

'Bless you, my boy!' Gerald muttered before he rang off. Sebastian posted the promised letter by airmail before leaving for the airfield.

'Dear Jo-Jo

Thanks for your letter. Your father telephoned me this morning and asked me to tell you he hasn't time to write himself but that he hopes to be with you before the end of next week. He's extremely busy right now trying to get hold of the money you asked for. He is none too pleased, to put it very mildly, to hear you have been gambling so wildly. He says it is "totally irresponsible", and frankly, Jo-Jo, I agree. He is going to insist on you returning home with him and put an end to what he calls "this outrageous escap-ade" which he wants you to know will not go unpunished.

Bes said to tell you the brooch sounds just fine. She can't wait to wear it and if you intend to prolong your holiday in Madeira, she will come out and get it! Ha! Ha!

Everyone sends best wishes to Mrs Reviezky and her nephew and all the best from me.

Love Sebastian.

P.S. Why are you staying out there? You said you were only going for three weeks. Are you onto a good story for your newspaper? RSVP.'

Reading it through, he was happy that it sounded as if her father would be going on his own.

He was not in touch with Gerald again until late that afternoon, during which he had spent a frustrating few hours at Shoreham airport. After several unsuccessful attempts, he was finally put through to Gerald's office and was able to convey the bad news that there was no chance whatever of his being able to fly him to Madeira in the Moth. In the first place, he explained, there was no landing strip and even if he could find a field where he could touch down, the nearest place to the island where he could have refuelled on the way was Lisbon, a distance far too great for a small aeroplane to fly without another fuel stop.

'The chap I've been talking to here says he thinks there is a mail service by flying boat and if so, Thomas Cook will almost certainly know about it,' he added. 'He told me that a few days ago, a friend of his was saying the mail service sometimes took passengers, so it would be possible for us, sir, to make the trip in a day.'

Without hesitation, Gerald said:

'I'm pretty sure I can pull a few strings and get a passage quickly. Were you told which port the flying boats depart from?'

'I gathered it was almost certainly Plymouth. You can take a train direct there from London.'

'Top hole!' Gerald replied without hesitation. 'I shall try to get seats for some time tomorrow! I shall not tell my wife where I will be going or why. She's quite worried enough already. "Called away for a few days on urgent business," I shall say. I'm most grateful for your support, Sebastian. Two heads better than one, eh? Bless you, m'boy. You've been a great help.'

It was, however, a further five days before Gerald
could get the money he needed and the Empire flying boat
carrying mail and its two passengers left England to fly to
Madeira.

CHAPTER THIRTY-ONE

1939

Georgia was becoming increasingly impatient with her imprisonment. Added to her dislike of forced inactivity was her growing concern about her father's reactions to Fedrik's demands that perhaps he was unable to raise so large an amount of money immediately. She had even begun to wonder, in the early hours of the morning when sleep eluded her, what Fedrik would do if he thought her father had involved the police. He would have no alternative but to kill her and dispose of her body before she could be found and denounce him.

Her vivid imagination envisaged Fedrik driving out to sea in his speedboat and dumping her body in the Atlantic so that no blame for her disappearance could be traced to him.

With no one to talk to the days seemed interminable and she was not far from tears, mostly of frustration, when nearing midnight late on the ninth day of her incarceration, Fedrik appeared. Hiding her relief that he had not abandoned her for some unknown reason, she ignored his apology and the bouquet of flowers he was holding out to her, and picking up the book she had been reading, she pretended to continue doing so.

'I would have come sooner had I not feared my frequent visits to the yacht would look somewhat suspicious to anyone watching my movements,' he said. 'As you can imagine, the police are everywhere and some of your former divers are searching the coastline in boats.'

Fedrik, immaculate as always in his dinner jacket, took a letter from his pocket. When Georgia did not speak, he said:

'I am aware that you are angry with me, *querida*, but I think you will be happy that it's from England.'

He had intercepted it, he told her, when he collected his aunt's mail from the hotel reception. He had opened it, read it and was elated that Georgia's father was coming out to Madeira to hand over the vast sum of money without alerting the police. He had counted on the fact that the very conventional Englishman would not want his daughter's gambling habits questioned and her reputation tarnished. Nor, it seemed, had Mr Driffield informed his aunt of the situation, which he had feared the man might do.

The police had interviewed him on several more occasions, and were still questioning anyone in the hotel who might have seen Georgia the night she went missing. They had now extended their search to the opposite side of the island, and a party of police and volunteers had been exploring the dense forests that covered the mountains. His aunt, he now told Georgia, had only once been questioned as a formality; that her being a responsible resident on the island for nearly twenty years, they did not think a seventy-year-old lady likely to harm a cat let alone a young girl.

Georgia took Sebastian's letter from Fedrik but ignored the bouquet of flowers he was holding out to her. She struggled hard not to show her soaring elation as she read the letter. Sebastian had understood her innuendos, and was aware that she needed help.

'I see you have read my letter,' she said in a cold tone of voice. 'In my country, we are not so ill-mannered.' For a brief moment he looked distressed by her criticism but then resumed his attempts to please her.

'Please, *querida*, please take the flowers!' he said. 'They are to celebrate the probability that now you and I will both soon be free!' When once again Georgia ignored the bouquet Fedrik was holding out to her, he added: 'I know you don't believe I love you, but please don't hate me. If there were another way of freeing myself, I would not be doing this. If you had agreed to marry me . . .' He broke off as he saw the look on Georgia's face.

Putting the untouched flowers on a chair, he walked over to the porthole and, drawing back the heavy curtain, stared out into the darkness. He did not need to see her expression to know that even if he were crazy enough to release her, she would never forgive him or let him close to her again.

'I have written a telegram from you to your friend,' he said shortly. 'I shall give it to Tomé to take to the post office as I cannot afford to be recognised communicating with your country.'

He handed her a telegram form on which was written in capital letters:

SO GLAD DADDY CAN VISIT ME STOP TELL HIM THAT HE MUST NOT FORGET TO BRING HIS BINOCULARS STOP SO HE CAN BE SAFELY MET ON HIS ARRIVAL STOP JOE.

'That's your pet name I recall,' he said.

Realising quickly that this mistaken abbreviation of her name would at once alert Sebastian that the message in the telegram had in all probability been dictated by her abductor, she added Sebastian's surname TAYLOR and his address on the telegraph form, and handed it back to Fedrik.

Fedrik, she noted, looked tired. No doubt the tension was keeping him awake at nights, she thought as he turned to leave. Before doing so, he tried to put his arms round her and kiss her. When she quickly turned her face away and struggled free, he looked unutterably sad.

'Try not to hate me, *querida*!' he said huskily. 'You may not believe me but *eu te amo*,' and he went out of the room and locked the cabin door securely behind him. Georgia was once more alone, and although greatly cheered and relieved by Sebastian's letter, at the same time, the uncertainty remained as to whether her father had raised enough money to meet

Fedrik's huge demand and was not just trying for him to be apprehended.

With an effort, she put such speculations out of her mind and concentrated on coping with her continued isolation, with only Fedrik's occasional short visits and those of her jailer who, since she had hit him over the head, no longer smiled at her. On one occasion she tried to bribe him. She took off the little gold wristwatch her father had given her on her eighteenth birthday, and held it out to him. For the briefest moment of time, his rheumy eyes had widened as his hand came through the gap in the door. But when Georgia pointed to the chain securing it, he shook his head and hurriedly closed and locked the door again.

Were it not for Sebastian's letter, Georgia thought, as she awoke to the twelfth day of her lonely imprisonment, she would be feeling desperate. As it was, she did now have a very real hope of being rescued despite knowing how devious Fedrik was. He had spoken of escaping with the money in his speedboat in which, she'd told him, he would never be able to reach the mainland at least three hundred miles away.

'There are other means of escape!' Fedrik had replied when she'd put the question to him on one of his visits. 'I am not an *idiota, querida*!'

Georgia was unaware that many years previously he had found a passport belonging to an inebriate tourist who happened to have the same Latin colouring and similarity of features as himself. He had kept it in case Stefan one day betrayed him and he might have need to use it. Just such an occasion had now presented itself and having gone in his speedboat to hide on Porto Santo, he would be able to board a passing liner under an assumed name. His only concern was that Georgia's father might, as a precaution, come armed. He himself had purchased a handgun small enough to conceal in his blazer pocket. It pleased him to realise that he, not Georgia's father, held all the trump cards – the knowledge of his daughter's whereabouts, the location of the yacht and the key to the cabin. Only when he had possession of the money would he hand over the key to the cabin, after which he knew exactly how he was going to execute the final part of his plan.

It was a beautiful bright sunny April day when Gerald, carrying a large attaché case, wearing his cream-coloured linen summer suit and his panama hat, boarded the *Claudia* with Sebastian. For once he, too, was tidily dressed in grey flannels and a belted jacket. The shining silver flying boat was waiting in Plymouth harbour to take them first to Oporto, from thence south to Lisbon and finally to Funchal.

Despite the very serious reason for, and the possibly dangerous consequences of, the journey they were about to make, Sebastian could not be otherwise than interested in the workings of the seaplane. With a crew of five, over four thousand pounds of cargo, most of it mail, the flying boat was large enough to carry in addition seventeen passengers whose destination, other than their own, was Lisbon.

He and Gerald were given comfortable seats on the starboard side of the cabin just aft one of the great wings. In front of them was a smoking compartment where Sebastian guessed Gerald would soon be lighting the pipe which was never far from his hand. The cabin quickly filled up with other passengers, and then the seaplane took off, at first taxiing, then with ever-increasing speed skimming across the water on its floats. As the rush of displaced water swept past the cabin windows, Sebastian felt a thrill of excitement. The thought crossed his mind that however wonderful it was to be up in the sky flying his Gipsy Moth, to be piloting this huge seaplane across the ocean at what was at least three hundred miles an hour must be many times more exciting.

He and Gerald had embarked at the early hour of six a.m. and it was eight o'clock when one of the stewards placed a mouth-watering breakfast on the table in front of them. Gerald ate very little but Sebastian could not resist eating a large meal.

After breakfast had been cleared away by the attentive steward, the skipper handed over the controls to the second pilot and came into the cabin to talk briefly to the occupants. When Sebastian informed him that he, too, was a pilot, albeit of a very small aeroplane, the captain invited him into the cockpit to see the controls.

The morning, therefore, passed pleasantly for Sebastian, but on returning to his seat, he noticed Gerald reach beneath his seat three times in succession to touch the attaché case with its large sum of money.

Gerald had refused to allow the steward to put it away with the other hand luggage. He was trying hard not to allow himself to consider that rather than risk her discovery, her abductor had already killed her. The memory of the horrible outcome of the kidnapping seven years previously of the Lindbergh baby was still fresh in his mind, for the beautiful toddler had been killed by his abductors despite the full payment of the ransom.

Hearing Gerald's long-drawn-out sigh, Sebastian said: 'You love Jo-Jo very much, don't you, sir?'

Gerald nodded.

'As much as a father can love his daughter!' he replied. He was silent for a moment as if he were lost in thought. A man's emotions were private, he told himself, but somehow he felt he owed it to Sebastian to share his concerns.

'You know, don't you, Sebastian, that Georgia is an adopted child!' he said. His hands were closed tightly together as if he were having difficulty controlling his emotions. 'Her real father was a very dear friend who begged me to take care of his child when he knew he was dying.' He paused before adding: 'It made no difference, I grew to love Georgia every bit as much as I love Migs.'

He smiled briefly as he said: 'At one time, their mother and I thought you had fallen in love with Migs.'

Sebastian's smile reflected Gerald's.

'I thought so, too, sir. I believed my heart was broken when

Migs got engaged to that army fellow. That's why I rushed off to Spain, not caring whether I lived or died.' He chuckled. 'I certainly cared about preserving my life when I got out there and found myself in serious danger of being killed! But go on, sir. I can understand why you love Jo-Jo. I've always loved her, too, but in a different way to how I felt about Migs. I suppose with a chap's typical selfishness, I loved Jo-Jo because as you know she was my unquestioning, willing slave, and I could boss her about to my heart's content! I think I was pretty rotten to her a large part of the time, especially on those days when one of my chums came to stay and we excluded her from our games!'

Looking a lot more relaxed, Gerald now said:

'I made a huge mistake, Sebastian. Because I loved Georgia so much and it meant so much to me that she loved me, for years I never told her that she was adopted; was not my real daughter. When I had to tell her after the lawyers insisted on her signature to the papers concerning her inheritance, she . . .' his voice was now husky with emotion, '. . . she accused me of lying to her: of letting her believe the lie that she was my child as much as was Migs. For months she rarely spoke to me. My mother, her grandmother, who was always very close to her, said I should give Georgia time, but although eventually we became on speaking terms once more, she has never allowed me close to her again. To tell you the truth, Sebastian, I don't think I have had a truly happy day since then.'

Sebastian felt intensely sorry for the man beside him. It even occurred to him that even if hearts did not break, they could be terribly badly bruised. When Georgia was home again, safe and sound, he must knock some sense into her, he told himself. If she were only a little less passionate about everything, maybe she would see that however mistakenly her father had behaved, he had done so out of his love for her.

Quite suddenly, it struck Sebastian with an uneasy jolt that there might be more than one man meeting Gerald and he might be attacked before being told Georgia's whereabouts or was able to call for his help.

His reflections were interrupted by the steward, who announced they would soon be coming into Lisbon's harbour. It was only then that Sebastian realised they would be in Madeira in only a few more hours' time and would discover the difficulties that might be awaiting them. He did not allow himself to consider the possibility that Georgia might already be dead.

CHAPTER THIRTY-TWO

1939

When Isobel went down to breakfast on Saturday morning, Gerald's place at the dining room table was vacant. Polly put a cup of tea and a plate of kedgeree in front of her, and then handed her a folded piece of paper.

'The Master said to give you this, Madam,' the girl said. 'He told me to tell you as how he'd been called to go to London for an emergency and he was catching the milk train.'

Isobel attempted to hide her surprise and, indeed, her anxiety. For several years now, Gerald had been sleeping in his dressing room having said he thought they would both get a better night's rest if he did so. She had not been unduly worried about it as he still came to her bed, and their love-making had continued very nearly as before. It had become less frequent in the past few years, which she put down to the fact that they were both growing older. It was not that she needed or particularly welcomed it, but it was practically the only time these days they were in complete accord. She had told Joan, her only confidante, that Gerald's continuing concerns about his alienation from Georgia were responsible for this as they so often argued about their daughter, and when she had recounted some new irritation, Gerald had 'switched off', refusing to be drawn into a discussion about the child.

Not that Georgia was a child any longer, Isobel thought, as she opened Gerald's note.

May be away for several days, it said. Sorry not to warn
you sooner. Only just been advised I was needed. Will keep
in touch. Gerald.

Isobel caught her breath. Gerald had never once in all their
married life, left the house without telling her where he was
going and when he expected to be home. What could have
happened to make him rush off in such a way? He must have
been exceptionally quiet getting up as she had not heard a
sound. As far as she knew, he'd only had one telephone call
the previous night after she had gone to bed, but she had not
bothered to enquire, when he'd come into her room to say
his customary goodnight, who it was ringing him so late.

   She pushed the plate of food away, her normal good appetite
now vanished as a memory of something Michael had once
said when they'd been discussing the increasing number of
divorces, joking that there might well be a great deal more if
wives knew what went on behind their backs; that even,
sometimes, if they were happy enough in their marriages, they
needed something more.

   It now crossed Isobel's mind that for all she knew, she might
be one of those unfortunate wives who went happily about
their day-to-day lives without any idea of the mischief their
husbands were up to. The more she thought about it, the more
possible this seemed. These past few weeks, Gerald had been
late home from work with little to say when he did return.
His goodnight kiss had been no more than a desultory peck
on the cheek. He'd taken several telephone calls in his study
without telling her who had been ringing him or why. She
knew that he had been busy over some panic at the War Office,
but wondered now if it had more to do with Georgia's disappearance. After all, she told herself, she, too, was worried.

   'I'm afraid I wasn't very hungry, Polly,' she told the maid
as she came in with a fresh rack of toast and saw the untouched
plate of kedgeree. 'Tell Cook it looked as delicious as always
but I am suffering from a slight indisposition.'

When Polly had departed, she picked up Gerald's note and read it a second time, her anxiety deepening. If the War Office had wanted him for some hush-hush assignment, he could have said so in his note. He had been away on these assignments before – sometimes for as long as a week; sometimes he had needed his passport for a meeting abroad. Remembering Michael Taylor's remark that lots of married men had mistresses, Gerald's so-called business trips without her might well have been meetings with some woman who was more interesting in bed than she was.

Such horrible suspicions magnified when she looked in his desk and found his passport missing. She decided to go next door to Joan, her only close confidante, hopefully to be told such fears were quite ridiculous.

Joan was in the kitchen instructing her new cook how to make a charlotte russe the way she liked to serve it. She was being very patient with her new servant, domestic help being so hard to come by these days, when even fourteen-year-old girls leaving school could get a job in a shop or a factory where they were far better paid and enjoyed far shorter working hours than as skivvies in domestic service.

When her maid announced Isobel's arrival, her friend's unexpected visit at such an early hour came as a considerable surprise as she joined Isobel in the drawing room. Had there been some disaster out in India? she wondered, as she could think of nothing else which would have brought her closest friend hurrying round so soon after breakfast – and looking so flustered. She was even more bewildered when Isobel sat down heavily in one of the armchairs and announced:

'Gerald left the house this morning leaving only a note saying he didn't know when he would be back, and . . . he's been so distracted, so silent this past week, and last night he looked . . . well, almost guilty. I wondered if . . . well if he might be . . .' she broke off, her voice trailing into silence.

Joan regarded Isobel, usually so calm, so in command of herself, in disbelief.

'I simply don't believe Gerald is capable of doing anything to hurt you,' she said firmly, adding as a sudden afterthought: 'You didn't have a row or anything?'

Isobel shook her head.

'No, we don't have rows – arguments sometimes, but never rows.'

Joan hesitated before saying gently, 'Well, you did once say, dear, you had rows about Georgia – you know, how she had come between you two. I mean, you did tell me once that there were times when you felt a little jealous of Gerald's devotion to Georgia. I mean I know they weren't rows but I think you have to admit that you *have* had tiffs quite often with Gerald about the child.'

Isobel was about to protest but she saw at once that Joan may well have found an explanation. Only two days ago she had told him it was his own fault when Georgia went missing, once again causing them such worries; that he'd nobody to blame but himself if she came to harm. Had he now gone to another woman who was less critical . . . less cruel than she'd been? Quite suddenly, she burst into tears.

She dabbed at her eyes with a handkerchief and said tremulously:

'I'm sorry, Joan dear. I don't know what came over me. It's so stupid of me to imagine – well, the worst – just because of a silly note. I'm afraid my nerves have been on edge ever since Gerald heard that Georgia was missing.'

For a moment, Isobel did not speak. Then, her voice shaking, she said: 'You don't think, Joan . . . you don't think that Gerald has gone off to Madeira to look for Georgia – without telling me, I mean? Surely . . .' She broke off as Joan reached over and put a comforting hand over hers.

'Yes, I do think that's possible,' she said thoughtfully. 'It does explain Gerald's unusual behaviour which you described, doesn't it? In fact the more I think about it, the more certain I am that he and that son of mine have gone off to Madeira together. You see, Sebastian cancelled the lunch date we had for next

Sunday despite knowing how much I was looking forward to it. He wouldn't say why: only that he would tell me when he next saw me.'

She patted Isobel's arm, her voice gaining conviction as she continued:

'At the time, I assumed he probably wanted to meet up with a new girlfriend, but my guess is he and your Gerald have gone together.'

Isobel caught her breath.

'But why . . . why, if you're right, didn't Gerald tell me that's where they were going?'

'Well, my dear, Seb as you know never tells me anything,' Joan replied. Then her voice became hesitant. 'Perhaps Gerald was afraid you would try to stop him going?'

Close once more to tears, Isobel said: 'If Georgia really is in trouble . . . well I couldn't bear it if anything awful happened to her.'

'But perhaps Gerald doesn't know that's how you would feel . . . I mean, I know you have always done your very best for Georgia and you've been the best mother you could, but . . .'

Isobel drew a shaky sigh and nodded her head.

'I suppose you're right, Joan, but it hasn't always been easy. I mean she was a self-willed child and . . . well Gerald doted on her – always took her side – not that she knew it. But Joan . . .' Isobel's voice thickened once more with threatening tears, '. . . I do care very much about her. When we learned from the woman she has been staying with that she couldn't be found, I lay awake imagining all sorts of awful things – a car accident, a fall down some rocks, getting lost in a forest. I wanted her safely home. I wanted to tell her that . . . that I do love her – and I know now that I do. Oh, Joan, I do so, so hope you are right and that Gerald has gone out there to bring her safely home.'

Once again, Joan patted Isobel's hand reassuringly.

'Of course that's where he and Seb have gone. I'm sure you needn't be worried.'

Isobel's expression, which had become hopeful, now became anxious again.

'You may well be right, but if . . . if anything awful has happened . . . to Georgia, I mean, it will break Gerald's heart, and I . . .' she broke off too choked to say any more.

Joan, looking at her friend's stricken face, thought suddenly that Isobel seemed suddenly to have aged at least ten years. Although she, herself, was somewhat concerned about Sebastian's safety, she knew he was well able to take care of himself as he had proved a number of times in his brief twenty-one years!

It had never occurred to Isobel before that Joan might have thought badly of her for the way she'd treated Georgia. She now felt a need to justify herself. Her voice shaking slightly, she said:

'You have always known, Joan, that I blamed Gerald for foisting Georgia on me and you agreed with me that he should not have assumed that I either could, or would want someone else's child in our family. In spite of his going against my wishes in so serious a matter, I did endeavour to give Georgia the same advantages, presents, treats that I gave Migs, and which all too frequently, she didn't want! It did so irritate me that she wanted boys' toys and clothes – to be like your Sebastian! She often left me feeling inadequate in some way, and Gerald maintained I failed to get the kind of gratitude I expected because I gave the child the things I wanted her to have and not what she wanted; nor – and he stressed this – what she most needed, which was a mother's love.'

She broke off, appalled by what she heard herself saying.

Joan now said impulsively:

'It shouldn't have been a case of one more than another, Isobel. Michael always said that a man's love for his wife is quite different from a man's love for his children.'

'I know! I know!' Isobel blurted out, 'but I thought if Gerald really loved me, he would put me first. I admit it, Joan, I *was* jealous, jealous.'

She broke off, her face momentarily hidden by her handkerchief as she blew her nose. Her eyes closed as if to shut out the pain of her confession. Joan was both shocked and fascinated by these intimate revelations from a woman she had always thought so self-confident; who had always avoided any kind of personal intimacy.

'You mustn't upset yourself, Isobel!' she said now, not liking to reach out a comforting hand again which she feared Isobel, being very far from a tactile person, might not like. 'Why, all of us feel a bit miffed at times. I was always put out when Michael used to take Seb to rugger or cricket matches and never once asked me to go with them.'

It was not entirely true that she had minded, as she did not like watching those sorts of games and would not have wanted to go with them had she been invited.

Her thoughts were interrupted by Isobel's tortured voice:

'I don't have to tell you, Joan, how close Gerald and Georgia became in those early years. Gerald wouldn't allow me to tell her that he was not her real father, saying it would be time enough when her inheritance was finalised. That time came three years ago when he was forced to tell her the truth, and she has never forgiven him for letting her think he was her father, Migs her real sister, and said she would never trust him again. For a while, she wouldn't even speak to him, and she has never let him close to her since then. She's civil to him but no more. I've never seen Gerald so unhappy – and now this . . . The rift has not been healed, and if anything dreadful has happened to Georgia, I don't think he will ever be happy again.'

Isobel was no longer crying as she turned to her friend, saying:

'It has taken this to make me realise what a selfish, childish, jealous person I've been, Joan. I can see now how for years I have taken my anger with Gerald out on Georgia. None of it was her fault, and she probably would have been as loving to me as to Gerald if I'd let myself love her.'

Her voice breaking once more, she whispered:

'Although I go to church every Sunday, I'm not really a very religious person, but I am going to pray to God to keep Georgia safe. I want to tell her I'm sorry. She probably won't understand what I'm apologising for, but I can tell her truthfully that I love her very much and want her to be happy.'

Looking at Joan, her eyes brimming with tears, she asked:

'Do you hate me now that you know what a horrible person I've been all this time?'

Although Joan was younger than Isobel, she was now feeling ten years older as she said warmly:

'How can you even think I might hate you? I think you've been enormously brave just talking about the past. Lots of women would have felt as you did, Isobel: been unprepared to have a baby forced upon them as Gerald forced poor little Georgia on you.'

She patted Isobel's hand, her voice as reassuring as she could make it as she added: 'I really think we should try not to worry. You know how many times your daughter and my son have "diced with death", as they say. Remember the time we saw them jumping off the garage roof, our precious opera cloaks flapping from their arms as they played, so they said, at being aeroplanes? Georgia twisted her ankle and Sebastian was in bed with concussion for five days. And that awful winter when they sneaked off to skate on the village pond and the ice had thawed so much they both fell in? Seb got out and dragged Georgia to safety on that occasion, and I've absolutely no doubt now that if she is in trouble, he and your Gerald will bring her safely home. So please stop crying, Isobel, or you'll have me in tears, too.'

She wanted Isobel to stay and have lunch with her rather than return home alone, but Isobel refused.

'Gerald may telephone or telegraph me,' she said. 'If he does, I'll come and tell you, Joan, the moment I have any news. And you'll tell me if you hear from Sebastian, won't you?'

'Of course I will!' Joan said as she stood up and, linking her arm through Isobel's, she led her to the door. 'You know, dear,' she added, 'your Georgia is such a dear girl. I can't think who might harm her.'

'One thing's for sure,' Isobel said as they reached the front door. 'Georgia won't be crying.'

'Nor will she!' Joan agreed smiling. 'My Seb has always said she's the bravest girl he knows!'

As Isobel opened her own front door a few minutes later and went inside, she found herself praying that on this occasion, Georgia did not have anything horrible to cry about.

CHAPTER THIRTY-THREE

1939

It was shortly before noon when the *Claudia* began to lose height and glided down on to the calm waters of Lisbon harbour. Gerald and Sebastian joined the other passengers in the launch, from which they disembarked to wait in a nearby hotel while the seaplane was refuelled. By one o'clock, they were once more back in their seats. As the seaplane gained speed, skimming ever more swiftly across the dazzling surface of the water, the wash obscured the view from the cabin windows until finally the big silver bird, glinting in the bright sunlight, rose up into the air.

'Funchal next stop!' Gerald said as the steward arrived with lunch and a pleasing bottle of wine to accompany the meal. He was impatient for the next three hours to pass before they arrived in Madeira. Sebastian remained silent, thinking that had there been a different reason for the journey, he would be revelling in the thrill of his first flight in a seaplane. The *Claudia* was now flying far faster than he had ever flown in his Moth, and was high above the few wisps of cloud beneath them. He had thoroughly enjoyed his visit to the cockpit after breakfast, when he'd spent half an hour being instructed by the captain about the management of the controls and the necessary skills needed to land so smoothly on the floats that no damage was done to the struts.

Never far from his mind, however, was the trouble Georgia might be in.

'It has just occurred to me, sir!' he said to the older man when their lunch had been cleared away, 'that letter I received from Georgia, why didn't the kidnapper simply telephone or write his demands in the usual way?'

Gerald nodded.

'I've wondered about that, too, and I imagine it is because the police can make checks on outgoing telephone calls, telegrams and so on.' He drew a deep breath before adding: 'In my opinion, this is no common or garden fraudster. This chap is clever. He needed to be in order to kidnap and conceal a girl like Georgia living at a prestigious hotel like Reid's, and on a small island like Madeira.'

'I can't understand why, if it's so small, the police haven't been able to find her,' Sebastian remarked. 'There can't be all that many places to hide her. Of course the police don't know that she has been kidnapped – only that she is missing.'

'When I telephoned Mrs Reviezky yesterday telling her the time of my arrival she said that her nephew knew every aspect of the island and was out every day in the car searching for her,' Gerald said, 'but in that first article Georgia wrote for her newspaper, she said there were vast areas of uninhabited woodland up in the hills, and dozens of tiny villages dotted round the coastline. If my memory serves me right, I recall her saying that the island covers over three hundred square miles and there are mountains which can be as much as six thousand feet high, so there must be a vast number of places she could be hidden. My Baedeker says there are off-shore islands, too, the smaller of which aren't inhabited, which might explain why she has not yet been found. The truth is, Sebastian, Georgia could be absolutely anywhere. We can do no more than hope that the kidnappers, if such they are, will lead us to her once they see I have brought the money. You know . . .' he added shakily, '. . . we don't even know for certain whether it's one man or several of them.'

'I asked myself that, too,' Sebastian said. 'We are, of course, assuming that she has been kidnapped and not, as her letter said, that she really does owe someone money.'

'It makes little difference!' Gerald said sharply. 'In your

reply to Georgia you told her I would bring an adequate sum to pay her gambling debts – if such they are. I can tell you this much, my boy, I shall insist the blackguard shows Georgia to me alive and well, before I will hand it over to him.'

He looked so distressed, Sebastian said quickly:

'Let's run through our plan once more, sir. We get to the harbour at Funchal. As requested, you are wearing your panama hat and have your binoculars round your neck so that you can be recognised. You are carrying the attaché case which the fellows can't snatch from you because it is chained to your wrist. He or they will not be aware that I have come with you, as I am dressed like any other visiting tourist carrying my camera and appearing to be busy taking snapshots of the scenery.'

'So far so good,' Gerald replied. 'As we have agreed, you, of course, will remain out of sight.' He gave a worried sigh before adding: 'There is one thing we haven't taken into account – suppose they have a car? They could drag me into their car and drive off to some hidden destination. They'd have no difficulty forcing the lock and chain of the attaché case and . . .'

He broke off as Sebastian interrupted. 'I did think about that!' Sebastian said. 'You told me Mrs Reviezky has instructed the hotel car to meet us, so I get in it and tell the driver to wait. If I see you getting into another car, I'll make my driver follow you.' He gave Gerald a reassuring smile. 'Jo-Jo did say in her earlier letters that there are few proper roads for cars, so even if the chaps made a quick getaway, they wouldn't get far without being noticed.'

Somewhat reassured, and with a renewed sense of gratitude to Sebastian for his support, Gerald said:

'That's about as far as we can go, isn't it? A lot will depend where Georgia has been hidden.'

The steward's arrival with an English afternoon tea brought their speculations to an end, after which Sebastian pointed out a possible situation they had so far overlooked.

'What if nobody approaches you when we land,' he asked Gerald, 'where do we go from there?'

Gerald hesitated.

'To the hotel, I suppose,' he said uneasily. He glanced down at the attaché case by his feet, and after a short pause, he added in worried tones: 'We don't actually know for a fact that Georgia has been kidnapped, do we? Suppose . . .'

'Sir, we've been through all this a dozen times,' Sebastian broke in gently. 'Point one, we know Georgia wrote the letter. Point two, we know she would never in a hundred years borrow such a vast sum of money: and not least, point three, if she'd had an accident or was lost somewhere in the mountains, she couldn't have written the letter, could she? Lastly, why would she ask what she called "a friend" to meet you when, if she were free to do so, she could meet you herself?'

Gerald looked a little less anxious as he replied:

'You're right, of course, my boy! As I said before, however unorthodox my darling girl might be, she would know very well that I would never give or lend her that amount of money for any other reason than for her safety.'

Any further conversation was brought to a halt as the steward came over to their table to remove the tea trays, and told them they would be landing in Funchal harbour in the next ten minutes. They were aware the seaplane was losing height and Sebastian, who was seated near the window, could now see the sea far below and the group of islands, the largest of which was Madeira.

His heart was thudding with a mixture of tension and excitement as he realised that within the next hour or so, Georgia's father might know where she was. Knowing her as well as he did, he feared she would not have taken her incarceration quietly and might have antagonised her captors. Sebastian dreaded to think what might have befallen the defenceless girl of whom he was so fond. There had been cases where even when the ransom money had been paid, the kidnappers' victim had been found dead.

His thoughts were now diverted as water hissed past the window until finally the seaplane slowed and the hull touched down on the surface of the sea. It skimmed gently across the water until it came to a halt not far from land. The captain turned off the engines and the passengers were helped into the small boat to be taken to the dockside. The luggage and mailbags were unloaded into another boat, while the passengers climbed the steep steps up to the jetty.

As they all made their way towards the customs shed, Sebastian stared about him in the bright sunlight, and saw police as well as customs officials and several porters on the quayside, but no single individual who might be one of the kidnappers. Gerald walked some distance ahead of him, the requisite panama hat and binoculars in place, the attaché case firmly secured to his left wrist, his passport in his right hand. He moved purposefully apart from the other passengers while Sebastian hurried off to search for the hotel taxi that should be waiting for them.

From where he stood waiting, Gerald could see no sign of the hotel taxi nor the expected kidnapper. He was certain he would not approach from the far end of the jetty, which was not wide enough for vehicles, and was only occupied by a few seagulls and a lone fisherman. To his surprise a man suddenly appeared from behind the customs shed. The stranger was a dark-haired gentleman, smartly dressed in a navy blue, gold-buttoned blazer over well-cut white flannel trousers and a yachting cap. He was smiling as he greeted Gerald.

'Perhaps you do not recognise me, Mr Driffield,' he said, adding: 'Fedrik Anyos. We met once several years ago when your daughter invited me to your house for luncheon. I have sported a moustache this past year which my aunt tells me entirely alters my appearance.'

'So you are Mrs Reviezky's nephew?' Gerald said, adding quickly: 'It is very kind of you to meet me, Mr Anyos, but actually I am being met by a friend and he . . . er . . . he might be confused if he sees I am not alone. If you . . .'

He got no further before Fedrik broke in:

'Forgive me for interrupting you, sir, but I am this person you are expecting.' He glanced briefly at the attaché case in Gerald's left hand and added: 'I see you have honoured your side of our bargain. I will now be happy to honour mine!'

Making no attempt to take the attaché case from Gerald, he turned and started to walk along the jetty towards the sea.

CHAPTER THIRTY-FOUR

1939

The seagulls were circling and screeching above their heads as, too dumbfounded to speak, Gerald followed Fedrik. He was finding it difficult to believe that it was to this presentable young man, Mrs Reviezky's nephew, that Georgia owed so much money; still less that he would be holding her to ransom to get the debt paid.

Seeing Gerald's hesitancy, Fedrik paused and, looking directly at Gerald's anxious face, he said:

'I do assure you, Mr Driffield, that whatever you may be thinking, I am a man of my word. Once you have shown me you have all the money I want, I will release Georgia into your care.'

Gerald was even further confused. Anyos was very believable. Was he, in fact, the kidnapper and not the person who had encouraged Georgia to gamble, merely keeping her from leaving the island until she repaid what she owed?

His speculations got no further before Fedrik reached out without warning as if to take the attaché case from his grasp. Relieved that he had strapped it to his wrist, Gerald stopped in his tracks, saying sharply:

'I suggest you leave that alone!'

Fedrik shrugged; there was an ironic smile on his face as he said:

'I was not so silly as to imagine you might hand the money to me without my first releasing your daughter. She is in good health and quite safe, by the way.'

No longer in doubt that unbelievable though it might be,

this was indeed the man he had come to meet, Gerald's heart missed a beat.

'Show me where my daughter is!' he demanded. 'If as you say, she is safe and well, then I will give you your money.'

Fedrik's face showed little emotion as he repeated:

'Georgia is quite unharmed, I assure you.'

'Then take me to her,' Gerald said once more. 'You won't get your money until I know she's alive and safe.'

'I didn't imagine you would meet my demands without such reassurance,' Fedrik replied. 'Georgia is in a locked cabin in that yacht. There is no one else on board. We will go there together and you can talk to her. She will reassure you that she is unharmed and perfectly well at which point you will hand over the money for me to check. If it is all there as you say, I will lock you in together to give me a chance to get away and then I will give the key to the man who has been working for me and ask him to unlock the door in two hours' time. I shall now take you to her, at which point we can effect the exchange to our mutual satisfaction.' Before Gerald could voice a reply, he added: 'Perhaps you would care to accompany me?'

He began walking further along the quay, making no further attempt to wrest the case from Gerald's grasp. Gerald's glance now went to the many boats anchored in the bay; he found it hard to believe that the fellow had hidden Georgia without being seen. One thing he had no doubt about was that his daughter would not have been taken anywhere without putting up a fight. How was it possible no one had seen her struggling to get free? Or had she been drugged?

Fedrik finally stopped at the end of the jetty where a large yacht, its brass fittings glinting in the afternoon sunshine, was rocking gently against the stone wall. As far as Gerald could see, there was no crew on board; in fact, it looked so devoid of life that he said harshly:

'If you have hurt my daughter, Anyos, I will kill you, even if I hang for your murder.'

Fedrik's face remained impassive, his tone of voice unconcerned as he replied:

'I can but assure you again, sir, that Georgia is unharmed. You see, I happen to care far too much for her to hurt her.' Now the sardonic look returned to his handsome face as he said: 'You may be loath to part with your money, sir, but no more so than I am to part with Georgia. Believe it or not, I fell in love with her. I would have married her had she returned my feelings. Right up to our last evening together, I hoped she would change her mind. I really love her, you see; but she left me with no alternative other than to take her prisoner as a means to acquiring enough money to start my life elsewhere again. I am entirely financially dependent upon my aunt and as a consequence, I am unable to enjoy a life of my own.'

Good God! Gerald thought, the man was a kidnapper and actually admitting that if he couldn't have Georgia, he wanted her money. His anger intensified when Fedrik produced a small handgun from the pocket of his blazer. Curiously, he had no fear that the fellow would shoot him: murder was a more serious crime than that of kidnapping. Moreover, he gauged correctly, the last thing Anyos would want at this moment was to draw attention to himself by the noise of a shot.

'How exactly do you plan to proceed?' he asked stiffly. 'You must know I will not hand over the money until I see for myself that you have been speaking the truth.'

To his surprise, Fedrik smiled.

'Which fact I have taken into account,' he said calmly. 'Please follow me and I will take you to her.'

Although elated that Georgia's captor would take him to her so readily, Gerald hesitated to follow him lest it was a trap of some kind. Seeing Gerald's reluctance, Fedrik said:

'I have no intention of harming you, Mr Driffield, and I trust that you have no such intention of harming me. I fully intend to permit you to join your daughter, and reassure yourself that she is perfectly well.'

Gerald hesitated. Provided Georgia was indeed unharmed,

he would give her captor the money. But – and it was a big but – he was no longer sure that his and Sebastian's plan to overpower the kidnapper and retrieve the money was still possible. When he had last seen him, Sebastian had been looking in exactly the opposite direction to that of the quay. He was clearly looking for the hotel car, which, it seemed, had not appeared. He had most probably not seen him walking seaward with Anyos, and even now, was probably wondering what had become of him.

Anyos interrupted such thoughts, saying:

'Unfortunately, I shall be obliged to lock you in with Georgia for the rest of the day so you cannot raise an alarm while I effect my disappearance. At seven o'clock, Tomé, the labourer I employ, will be bringing Georgia's evening meal. He, of course, has the key to the cabin and he will have instructions to release you both. If we proceed as I have planned, there will be no danger for any of us.'

For a moment, Gerald did not speak. Then he said:

'You must know that as soon as we are free, I shall tell the police and they will begin searching for you.'

Fedrik smiled.

'Of course I realise it, but I have my speedboat, and I shall be perfectly safe from discovery where I intend to go.' His smile was enigmatic as he added: 'I learned a long time ago that provided one has enough money, anything is possible, and thanks to what you will presently be giving me, I shall not lack for adequate funds to ensure my safety.'

Gerald was effectively silenced. Feeling a little more confident that he would find his daughter unharmed, he followed Anyos up the gangway and onto the deck. His heart beating furiously, he then followed him down a flight of thickly carpeted stairs and past several closed cabin doors. He was far too preoccupied with anxiety to notice the opulence of his surroundings. Only one thing was now on his mind – that Georgia was imprisoned somewhere here and he was, pray to God, about to see her.

Anyos paused outside one of the brightly polished cabin doors, which Gerald noticed was secured with a bolt and chain, and said:

'I anticipated we would arrive at this juncture of our negotiations, and now I will explain the second part which will satisfy us both. After you have ascertained Georgia has come to no harm, you will then free the attaché case from your wrist and open it. If you fail to do so, I shall shoot you. After I have verified the contents, I shall depart, leaving you two in the cabin. I will of course lock the door behind me.'

He glanced at Gerald's face and shrugged.

'I promise you, you will be a prisoner for only a few hours, a necessity, as I shall need time to get away. Moreover, it will be a lot more difficult for the *policia* to search for me if you cannot denounce me until after dark. You will find food, some excellent wines in the cabin and, of course, you will have your daughter for company, so may I assume you have no objection to this very civilised way to complete the exchange?'

His plan had an element of risk for himself, Fedrik knew. If there was a brick instead of banknotes in the attaché case, he would have to keep both Georgia and her father prisoner for a great deal longer than he planned while he tried to obtain the money he must now have from another member of the family. He was fairly certain that there was no danger of his aunt deciding on the spur of the moment, that she wanted to ready the yacht to sail to the Canary Islands or Portugal or Morocco; places she had several times recently spoken of visiting on what she called one of their 'little holidays'.

Although when he first formed his plan, he knew that Georgia was not Driffield's own flesh and blood, she had frequently mentioned her father's devotion, so he'd no real doubt that he would raise the money somehow, even if he'd had to make inroads into Georgia's vast inheritance.

While he and Georgia's father had been talking in the gangway outside the cabin, Georgia must have heard their voices. She was now calling to him.

'Is that you, Freddie? Please open the door! Is that Tomé with you? Who are you talking to? I want . . .'

She got no further before Gerald turned to Fedrik, saying hoarsely:

'Well, open it, damn you! Georgia? It's me, Daddy!'

Silently, Fedrik unlocked the door. Gerald had barely put a foot inside the cabin before Georgia flung herself into his arms, a look of intense joy and relief on her face.

'I knew you would come,' she said breathlessly, and turned suddenly to look at Fedrik who was watching them silently. Now holding out one hand, he pointed to the attaché case and demanded:

'Unlock the case from your wrist and hand it to me please, Mr Driffield.'

Albeit reluctantly, Gerald did so.

Georgia stood looking from one to the other, an expression of disbelief on her face. Surely, she thought, her father was not going to hand over such a fortune as if it was a ten-pound note?

Shoving the case towards the waiting man, Gerald said hoarsely to Fedrik:

'Take it! It's all there! And get out! One day you will regret this, Anyos, I promise.'

Ignoring him, Fedrik calmly checked the bundles of notes before turning to look at Georgia. His voice unsteady, he said quietly: 'I wish you could have loved me, *querida*: I feel a little like your pirate – finding a farewell almost impossible. I shall never forget you! One day, I hope, you will remember the good times we shared and think of me more kindly than you do now.'

Closing the attaché case, he left the room pulling the door shut behind him. As the key turned in the lock, Gerald heard him saying:

'You have my word, *querida*, Tomé will let you out this evening. I'm sorry, really sorry. I shall never forget you! *Adeus!*' and the two prisoners heard the sound of his footsteps fading away.

Georgia was close to tears as Gerald's arm tightened round her.

'The money . . . you let him have it!' she said stupidly. 'Oh, Daddy, I'm so sorry. I'm very, very sorry!' The words began to pour from her. 'I shouldn't have trusted him. He said he loved me, wanted to marry me. How could he have done this? Dona Resita gave him everything . . . everything he wanted. He can never go back to her now. This will break her heart.' She paused only to draw breath before in a voice close to a whisper, she said: 'The money, Daddy: I never gambled and owed it to him. I'd been silly enough to let him know about my inheritance and he saw a way of getting enough to leave poor Dona Resita and start life on his own. You warned me never to talk about it. Is it all gone?'

She sounded so like a little girl enquiring if she had lost her precious dolly that Gerald drew her to him once more, holding her close.

'No, darling! The bank manager allowed me to borrow a large amount against the security of the house. He was arranging a mortgage: and I had quite a bit of money in savings and investments. Besides . . .' he broke off, adding after a moment: 'I don't think you have any need to worry: you aren't going to be penniless.'

Georgia was now staring up at him, her eyes full of tears.

'He wanted such a lot, Daddy,' she repeated, 'and now you've had to mortgage the house, sell your shares and things . . .' Her voice trailed away as the tears started to fall.

'I would have paid it all had I been able,' Gerald said fiercely. 'You are my daughter, darling. What father would not beggar himself if necessary for the life of his own child?'

It was on the very tip of Georgia's tongue to say: 'But I'm not your child. I'm only adopted!' But the words died in her throat. Her father had always fiercely denied that he loved her any less than he loved Migs; that if anything, he loved her more. How could she ever again doubt him? As she reached up to hug him, she said huskily:

'I don't care any more about being kidnapped, or being adopted,' she added in a shaky voice. 'I love you, Daddy!'

Somewhat embarrassed by so much emotion, Gerald drew her down beside him on the bed with his arm round her.

'I love you, too, darling. Now all we can do is wait here and hope it won't be too long before we are released.'

'But Freddie said it wouldn't be until Tomé comes this evening and . . .'

Gerald drew a long, anxious sigh.

I hope we won't have to wait for Tomé, darling. If our plan succeeds, it will be our very good friend, Sebastian, who lets us out. We planned that he should keep sight of me so he will have seen where Anyos was leading me!'

Georgia broke away, a look of incredulity mixed with excitement lighting up her face as the questions poured from her.

'Seb's here? In Madeira? He came with you? Where is he? Why isn't he here with you now?'

Gerald smiled.

'Answer one, yes, Sebastian is here. Answer two, yes in Madeira. Answer three, yes he came with me. He plans to catch your kidnapper and get back the money.'

'So that's why you let Freddie take it so easily!' Georgia said, her eyes shining. 'But how will Seb do it?'

'Let's wait and see what happens,' Gerald suggested. 'Right now, all we can do is pray he will succeed.'

CHAPTER THIRTY-FIVE

1939

With growing anxiety, Sebastian stood by the side of the hotel taxi that had finally arrived, searching the crowds for a sight of Gerald's tall figure. He had disappeared five long minutes ago. From inside the large hotel courtesy car, the driver leant out of the window to say apologetically to Sebastian that he would have to return to the hotel as he was supposed to be taking one of the guests to the old part of Funchal to visit the cathedral. As the car disappeared, Sebastian looked anxiously around him wondering if the kidnapper had been late arriving and had parked in a less obvious place; but at present there was only a deserted bullock cart loaded with fish to be seen.

The crowd of people who had surrounded the seaplane's passengers had now dispersed and his gaze was drawn to two men who were walking along the jetty towards the sea. For a brief moment, a bright flash of sunlight reflected off something the taller of the two men was carrying.

Sebastian's heart missed a beat as he recognised the somewhat ostentatious attaché case Gerald had purchased to contain the ransom money. Its four corners and lock were silver – the whole singularly ornate, which, Gerald had explained, was in order to ensure the kidnapper would easily spot him among the disembarking passengers.

For a moment Sebastian did not move, but seeing that the two men were striding purposefully along the jetty, he decided that they must indeed be Gerald and the man who was to have met him. The fact that they were on foot explained the absence of the kidnapper's car.

Following them as quickly as he could, he realised with a sigh of relief that he had not been mistaken. The taller of the two was unmistakably Gerald. The shorter was wearing a yachting cap, white trousers and a navy blue blazer and did not in the very least resemble his idea of a kidnapper, if such he was. He seemed to be leading the way towards a strikingly beautiful yacht moored at the end of the jetty.

With growing excitement Sebastian saw the two men disappearing up the gangplank onto the yacht. His instinct was to follow them but he had given Gerald his word that he would not take any action until Georgia was free.

The ensuing fifteen minutes seemed more like fifteen years. When he did finally see signs of movement on the yacht, it was with a deep sense of foreboding as only the stranger appeared, and there was no sign of Gerald or, indeed, of Georgia.

Quickly, he lifted his camera up in front of his face in order to look like any ordinary tourist taking photographs of his surroundings. The man seemed unhurried, but as he drew closer, Sebastian could see quite clearly that he was carrying Gerald's attaché case in his right hand. He neared Sebastian, glanced at him briefly and then, without warning, he began to run.

As he did so, Sebastian stuck out his foot, sending the fellow sprawling. Although he fought violently to release himself, Sebastian had played rugger in his schooldays, and with youth on his side, was a great deal stronger than his quarry. Within a few minutes, he had the man on his knees, his arms fastened securely behind his back with his belt.

Reaching out to kick aside the attaché case, which had fallen a few feet away, he said: 'I see you were planning to take that with you. Well you won't be going anywhere now but to the nearest police station, so I'll take care of it, if you don't mind!'

Retaining an iron grip on the stranger's arm, he pulled him to his feet.

When Fedrik regained his breath, although physically unhurt, he was consumed with anger at himself for not having suspected that Georgia's father might well have brought someone with him, and that had he done so, such a person would not have made himself obvious.

Immediately following upon his anger for such stupidity came the almost unbearable realisation that in the past two minutes, his plans for his future had been demolished. Never once since the moment he had locked Georgia safely in the cabin had he seriously considered failure. Now, without the ransom money, he had no future. Although the small handgun was still in his pocket, he could see no chance of using it. Of a certainty, he would now be arrested, tried, convicted, sentenced, and when eventually he did get out of prison, there was no hope that his aunt would ever take him back when she learned his true identity and that he had intended to leave her.

Sebastian's grip on his arm had tightened and Fedrik's brief hope that he might break free gave way to a sickening sense of despair.

'I didn't know Mr Driffield was bringing you with him,' he muttered stupidly. 'Unbelievably careless of me! Haven't had much experience of this kind of thing!' he added with a twisted smile.

Sebastian was not smiling as he pulled his captive back towards the yacht from which the fellow had disembarked.

'If you've hurt one single hair of Georgia's head, I'll bloody well kill you!' he swore violently.

Fedrik's voice was now quite calm as he replied:

'Of course I haven't hurt her or her father. I have locked him into the cabin with Georgia and had you not disrupted my plan, they would have been released this evening by the man I paid to guard her!'

His temper now cooling slightly, Sebastian said more quietly:

'So what did you think you would do when they were released? You must have known Mr Driffield would tell the police you were Georgia's abductor. However well you hid yourself, it would be only a matter of time before you were apprehended on an island as small as this.'

Fedrik now drew a deep sigh.

'You must think me very stupid to have ignored such a possibility when I made my plan,' he replied. 'I was not intending to be caught. I have my own speedboat close by. I also have another passport, which belonged to a visitor who left it behind in the hotel. I kept it in case at some time in my life it came in handy.'

'You'd have been caught long before you could make use of it,' Sebastian said dryly. 'You didn't stand a chance of getting away with this.'

Fedrik shook his head.

'On the contrary, I had intended taking my boat over to one of the many surrounding islands, and hiding up until the next liner calls in on its way to Gibraltar.'

Fedrik's expression was suddenly akin to despair as Sebastian said dryly: 'Well, you won't be going anywhere now, will you?'

Suddenly, as he peered at the man's face, he had the strange feeling that he had come across him before. The fellow's yachting cap had come off in the scuffle, and Sebastian was now seeing the sleek black hair, dark almond-shaped eyes, thick, arched eyebrows and slightly angular tanned face of his prisoner. His features struck a chord in his memory that he could not immediately identify. Without knowing where or how he might have done so, he was convinced he had seen that face before.

Surely, he thought, his captive could not be the man Georgia had described in her recent letter to him – the nephew of the hospitable foreign lady whose guest she was? The nephew whose aunt had said was out day and night searching for Georgia? Moreover, in one of her letters, Georgia had said that she thought he seemed to be getting rather keen on her, and that she wished Sebastian was there to advise her how to deal with the situation.

The man made no attempt to break free when Sebastian said accusingly:

'So you knew all the time where Georgia was because you were the one who had hidden her!' Fedrik was not listening. He was now staring intently at Sebastian's face.

'If my memory serves me right,' he said, 'you are the desperate young man who was infatuated with Georgia's sister.'

Certain now that they had actually met before, Sebastian nodded. The memory of the evening of Migs's coming-out ball, which now seemed so long ago, resurfaced.

Fedrik's mind was also working at top speed, but not on the past.

'Look there!' he said, nodding his head in the direction of the attaché case still lying on the jetty. 'You've got the money back, and I have told my man to release Georgia and her father when he pays his customary visit to the cabin this evening.' The look he now gave Sebastian was strangely composed as he continued matter-of-factly: 'No doubt it is your intention to have me arrested but it would serve no purpose, since I am not a serial kidnapper, or even a criminal. Even if I wanted to, I won't ever have the opportunity to do such a thing as this again. After all,' he added wryly, 'one is unlikely to fall in love twice in a lifetime with a lovely young heiress who one wanted to marry.'

He paused momentarily and then said forcibly:

'Let me go! All I ask is that you give me time to get away. I know you won't believe this but I do care about my so-called aunt, and she has been incredibly generous to me – but at the price of my freedom.' He paused, drawing a long sigh before saying: 'Of course, I knew if my plan had succeeded, she would be devastated when I left her. As things now stand, she will be mortified, indeed horrified, if I am now arrested, charged with a dreadful crime, sentenced to spend the best part of my life in prison. If you let me go, she may find ways in her heart to forgive me for leaving her, and be the happier for it.' His voice deepening with urgency, he said: 'You may not believe me but I mean it when I say it is for her sake as much as mine that I am asking you to let me go.'

It was on the tip of Sebastian's tongue to tell Georgia's abductor that his aunt's feelings were not his concern and that there wasn't a hope in hell that he would do as the fellow asked; although, on reflection, the chap was at least showing some compassion for his doting relative. The thought now came into his head that if it was his own mother, he knew without doubt she would rather he disappeared than be locked up for life in prison. Nor would Georgia have to be the major witness at the man's trial, and her parents would abhor the publicity.

Such considerations should not alter his need for justice, he argued with himself. Despite the fact that the fellow was clearly not a practised criminal, he needed to be punished for the anxiety he had put them all through, and most of all for the fear and horror Georgia must have suffered.

Would Georgia want the fellow imprisoned for what must be a very large part of his life? Somehow, he doubted it as her letters had praised the man's extreme kindness to her throughout her stay. On the other hand, he doubted very much if Mr Driffield would for one moment be willing to make such an irregular and, indeed, unlawful decision.

It suddenly struck Sebastian that as yet, he had only the fellow's word that Georgia was unharmed.

As if divining Sebastian's train of thought, Fedrik said quickly:

'You don't imagine I would ever have harmed Georgia, do you? In spite of what you may think, I genuinely love her – in fact, she is the only girl I have ever truly loved. It wasn't simply her money that attracted me to her, although I admit that at first, it was her inheritance which intrigued me, and that was the reason I persuaded her to come out here. Then . . . well, I discovered that she was far more important to me than money. She made me realise even more than before how empty my life was – a kept man dancing attendance upon a rich elderly woman. I realised how empty life was without the kind of love a man and woman share, and Georgia . . . well, her inheritance would have made that possible.'

He paused briefly before adding:

'I know my aunt loves me; has given everything to me she could which I wanted, but it lacked the only really important thing – love, and I fell in love with Georgia.'

Noticing the doubtful expression on Sebastian's face and aware that he was all but fighting for his life, he said forcefully:

'That sounds like someone speaking in one of my aunt's romantic novels, doesn't it? But I assure you I am telling you the truth. Georgia's inheritance mattered because it would enable me to leave my aunt, take Georgia away with me and for us to live in some degree of comfort.'

Sebastian's face darkened as he looked at his captive.

'If it is true you loved Georgia, why didn't you allow her to go home when you knew she didn't return your feelings?' he demanded. 'Why not simply return to that luxurious life you say you had with your aunt? Why this . . . this drastic – and dangerous – plot to kidnap her?'

For a fleeting moment, Fedrik's voice held a hint of the desperation he was feeling, aware as he was that at any moment, Sebastian might decide to march him off to the police station.

'I don't expect you to understand,' he now pleaded, 'but I can only liken my situation to that of a man who has been imprisoned all his life – not in discomfort, but always caged; then suddenly the door opens and he sees outside the flowers and trees and feels the warmth of the sunshine, and he realises that if he can find the courage, he could walk free.' Seeing the expression on Sebastian's face becoming fractionally less determined, he continued quickly: 'Of course, I was not so silly that I failed to realise that if my plan did not succeed,

I would – and indeed now will – be without all the wealth and comforts I'm accustomed to. Believe me, it took courage to risk the horror I would face if, as has happened, my gamble failed.'

Sebastian was effectively silenced. It was hard to believe, he told himself, that he was standing here in the evening sunshine holding Georgia's kidnapper with a sudden feeling of pity tending to override common sense.

As if divining Sebastian's train of thought, Fedrik said:

'If you let me go free now, I wouldn't be escaping without punishment. As I told you, I am virtually penniless and I cannot go back to my aunt; so even if you release me, what kind of life will I have without the ransom money there in that attaché case? My life will be one of extreme poverty,' he repeated.

His tone suddenly hardened. 'Believe me, I know what poverty is because I suffered many years of it in my childhood, and it will be far, far harder to endure now that I have become accustomed to the luxuries life offers the rich. If you let me go free it will be a kind of hell for me after years of having everything I wanted – everything but my freedom, that is.'

He was watching Sebastian's face as he spoke and saw that the hatred that had been in it had given way to uncertainty. As Sebastian's grip on him slackened, he pleaded further:

'Your future is full of promise, is it not? Georgia told me you were becoming a successful author. She is very proud of you. You can marry, have a wife and children. Those possibilities are lost to me now. Let me go! No one will blame you. You can say I got away in the scuffle we had.'

There was a hint of hesitation now in Sebastian's expression. He stared into Fedrik's face, saying:

'You have sworn to me that you have not harmed one hair of Georgia's head, but for all I know, you might have killed both her and her father.' His tone of voice hardened again. 'If I discover you have lied to me, I will happily kill you. You wouldn't be the first man I've killed,' he added, thinking of his enemies in the Spanish Civil War. 'Do you understand?'

Holding Sebastian's gaze, Fedrik said calmly:

'You can take me down to the cabin and speak to them both.' A faint smile came to his face as he played his last card:

'That night – how many years ago? – the night when you and I met when Georgia's sister had her coming-out ball,' he said quietly. 'Do you remember? You were in disguise and your moustache slipped. Do you remember how mortified you were?'

The episode came quickly back to Sebastian's mind; how crazily in love he had then been with Migs – a calf love that now seemed a little ridiculous although it had hurt terribly at the time. He remembered, too, Georgia's and Monty's help getting him invited to the dance only to find Migs's dance card fully booked, and his horror when he realised his disguise was about to be discovered; that he would be a laughing stock.

'I see you do remember,' Fedrik said quietly. 'Do you also recall what you said to me when I helped you out of the house?' Fedrik continued. 'You said: "I can't thank you enough. If ever I can do you a good turn, you have my word I'll do it." Then you said: "I owe you one, and that's a promise!"'

Yes, Sebastian remembered the words just as he recalled how sincerely he had meant them at the time: how sincere was his gratitude to the stranger who had saved him from what, in those youthful days, he'd believed would be an embarrassment and disgrace not only in his parents' eyes, but in Migs's, too.

Sensing Sebastian's uncertainty, Fedrik continued persuasively:

'Let me take you to the cabin so you can be reassured that Georgia and her father are unharmed.'

For a moment, Sebastian neither spoke nor moved as he

tried to come to terms with the fact that this man who had put not only himself and Gerald through such considerable anxiety, but Georgia, too; that the man his mother would have considered a perfect gentleman, was in fact a villain, a kidnapper, a blackmailer. Somehow he was having difficulty thinking of Anyos as a common criminal. Nor could he disregard the fact that he *had* indeed given his word all those years ago – however juvenile he'd been at the time. Scout's honour! he thought with a sense of unreality. Yet it *had* been a promise . . .

Was he being stupidly gullible trusting this man, he asked himself? Granted he had but to pick up the attaché case to retrieve the ransom money, but there was still no certainty that Georgia and her father were safe and unharmed.

Fedrik was watching Sebastian's expression, his heart racing as he faced the fact that freedom for the rest of his life lay in this young man's hands. His tone of voice as level as he could make it, he said:

'If you feel in my jacket right-hand pocket, you will find a small handgun. Take it! It is loaded. If I tried to get away, you could use it. Meanwhile, once it is in your possession,' he added with a laconic smile, 'you can let go of me. All I am asking for is my freedom in exchange for Georgia's!'

Still Sebastian did not entirely trust his captive, but Fedrik made no move to pull away as Sebastian withdrew the gun from his pocket, and instructed him tersely to lead the way to the place where Georgia and her father were incarcerated.

As he followed Fedrik on to the yacht, the gun pressing into his captive's back, his mind was working furiously, his emotions see-sawing in a totally unaccustomed way. Georgia had written glowing reports of Anyos's care and attentions to her. Would she want him imprisoned for goodness knew how long? Once he saw for himself that both she and her father were unharmed, should he seriously consider letting Anyos go free? Even if he were not recaptured, as was highly likely on so small an island, he would be a wanted man – a fugitive

– for the rest of his life. Was he really bound to honour a promise made on the spur of the moment in his youth? It was a chance he had no alternative but to take.

A few minutes later, the two men were standing outside Resita's cabin door. At Fedrik's request, Sebastian released his hands from behind his back so that he could draw back the bolt and undo the door-chain, before reaching to take the key from the ledge above the door. Without speaking, he handed it to Sebastian. Sebastian could now hear the faint murmur of Georgia's and her father's voices. So relieved was he to know that both were alive, he turned away from Fedrik and fumbled for the lock. Impeded by the strap holding the attaché case still round his wrist, his gun was no longer pointing at his prisoner.

Realisation flashed into Fedrik's mind that this might be his only chance to get away. Sebastian had given him no promise of freedom, and even if he intended to let him go, Georgia's father might all too probably prevent it. Now, if he moved quickly enough, he might reach the staircase before Sebastian turned and saw him.

He felt only a brief instant of regret, regret that if he took this chance to escape, it left no hope of retrieving the ransom money from the attaché case. It was too big a risk to delay and he dared not let the opportunity, quite probably the only one, go by.

He went so quickly and quietly that Sebastian turned only in time to see his captive's back as he was clambering up the narrow stairway. He raised the gun but could not bring himself to pull the trigger. He recalled the highly undesirable future the fellow had foreseen for himself. To be born into poverty was one thing, but to be forced back into it after years of matchless luxury and wealth would be a very real kind of punishment for what he had tried, but failed, to do. Judging by the cheerful tone of Georgia's voice as she spoke to her father, she sounded unharmed and in excellent spirits. His mind made up, he lowered the gun and unlocked the door.

He had barely put one foot inside the cabin before Georgia came rushing across the floor and flung herself into his arms. Her eyes were shining as she covered his face with kisses.

'I just knew you'd come!' she said. 'Daddy told me your plan to follow him and take Fedrik by surprise!' She paused, her eyes narrowing as she asked: 'Where is he, Seb? You haven't killed him, have you?'

'Good thing if he had killed the blighter!' Gerald muttered from the far side of the room. His eyes went to the attaché case in Sebastian's hand. 'Good chap! See you got that back, although I would have let it go had there been no other way of ensuring this madcap daughter of mine had come to no harm.'

Georgia's eyes shone suddenly with tears as she crossed the room to her father's side. Grasping his hand and clinging to it as she'd done so many times before the rift in their relationship, she reached up and kissed his cheek. For both of them, it was as if she was his devoted little girl again. She turned back to look at Sebastian.

'So where is Freddie?' she asked, a frown replacing the glow of happiness that had lit up her face.

Sebastian handed the attaché case to Gerald and, looking from one to the other, he said quietly:

'I'm afraid he got away. I . . . I was bothered about holding on to the money and should have kept a better hold on him. He . . . he just disappeared. Don't suppose he'll get far though, if we report him to the police as soon as we can.'

'Then the sooner we do so the better,' Gerald said gruffly. 'Hope they string him up!'

Georgia regarded him thoughtfully:

'Daddy, I was speaking the truth when I told you, Freddie never once hurt me. He just wouldn't! He did his best to make me comfortable and . . . and he . . . he even brought me flowers. He wasn't a cruel man. For goodness knows how many years he took care of Dona Resita, did everything possible to make her happy. He just needed so badly to get

away . . . get a life of his own before he grew too old to do
so. I know what he did was terribly wrong but . . .'

'But poppycock!' Gerald interrupted. 'If you choose to disregard what he did to you, what about that aunt of his? How
is she going to feel? And far more importantly, just what do
you think the fellow would have done to you if I hadn't arrived
with the money? Once I let him know I wasn't going to give
it to him, do you think he would have released you? Stood
by and let you report him to the police? Of course not! He
would have had to kill you or face a lifetime prison sentence
. . . maybe even the death penalty. I don't imagine the
Portuguese are particularly lenient.'

For a moment, Georgia did not speak. Then she said:

'But I would have given Freddie my word I wouldn't tell
anyone – that I'd tell the police I got lost, or something.'

'And you think he would have risked you breaking that
promise?' Sebastian broke in. 'He may not have *wanted* to
hurt you, but he'd have had no alternative. Your father is
right, Jo-Jo, so just be glad he has got away, although heaven
alone knows what kind of life he'll be going to.'

Fedrik meanwhile was climbing into his motorboat, and as
he started the engine, he, too, was thinking about – and
dreading – his future. The euphoria that had sustained him
since he had got away from Sebastian unharmed was replaced
now with something close to despair. He was having to face
the fact that he had lost everything, everything but his freedom,
and even that would be in jeopardy for the rest of his life. He
needed to get away to the other side of the world where he
couldn't be found, he told himself, as he steered the boat out
of the bay, but he barely had enough money in his pocket to
buy the necessary passage to Gibraltar. There was, too, the
added fear of what Stefan might do when his regular cheque
ceased to arrive. If Stefan ever found him, he was more than
capable of killing him.

As Fedrik headed towards the island of Porto Santo, the
look of elation that had lit up his handsome face gave way

to one very close to despair, and when he glanced back at the beautiful yacht rocking gently against the harbour wall, he thought of Georgia, her innocence and sweetness, and he could no longer see the white lines of his boat's wave for the tears that had filled his eyes.

CHAPTER THIRTY-SIX

1939

It was after five o'clock when Gerald finally succeeded in getting the hotel taxi to take the three of them to the police station. Despite Georgia's protests, he insisted upon a search for his daughter's kidnapper being made at once. There appeared to be only one policeman on duty until later that afternoon and he was unwilling to leave his post on the whim of a strange English gentleman telling an improbable story about an escaping kidnapper. He would come himself to the hotel at five-thirty, he said, where the *gerente do hotel* could translate the facts from English to Portuguese, and Gerald could then make a formal statement.

When the taxi finally deposited its three untidy passengers at the hotel, the *gerente do hotel* came hurrying out of his office towards them, a huge smile lighting up his somewhat swarthy face as he recognised Georgia.

'*Senhorita Driffield!*' he exclaimed, 'you are no more lost, *O Born Deus*. He look for you so you not harm.' He turned to Gerald, no longer smiling as he said he must use his telephone at once to inform the *Senhora* Reviezky.

'So worry, the poor lady! She tell me her *sobrinho* is leaving hotel after the luncheon to go to Funchal to meet you, *Senhor*: you are the *Senhorita's* father, no? who come on the *avião*, but *Senhor* Anyos he not find you, *Senhor*? *Senhora* Reviezky ask we send the waiter, Giuseppe, to see for him, but Giuseppe say *avião* is safe arrived but no *Senhor* Driffield, and he not see *Senhor* Anyos. *Senhora* Reviezky ask me make the telephone to *policia* look also for him, but I say maybe you are coming very soon, so we wait. Poor *Senhora*, she very unhappy. Now she happy *Senhorita* again and . . .'

Georgia halted the flow of words, saying to Gerald:

'Will you go and tell Dona Resita what has happened, Daddy? I don't think she will want to hear about Freddie from me. In a sort of way, I am responsible for his leaving her, aren't I? I mean if I hadn't told him about my inheritance . . .'

She broke off, close to tears at the thought of the terrible shock Dona Resita was about to receive. It would seem so unbelievable that her beloved nephew could actually resort to kidnapping her in order to start a new life away from her.

'Will you, Daddy?' she repeated, 'but please, don't say dreadful things to her about Freddie. She doted on him and I don't think she will ever, ever get over his leaving her. Please, please don't make him sound as . . . well, as wicked as I know you think he is.'

It crossed her mind, as she pleaded with Gerald, that she was never going to tell Resita how Freddie had impersonated her real nephew all those years ago. Far better that she should believe this was a single moment of need to lead his own life; that he was not also an imposter who had cheated her these past eighteen years.

'Very well, darling!' Gerald said. He had handed the precious attaché case to the *gerente do hotel,* asking him to put it in the hotel safe, and then turned to Sebastian. 'You can check us into our rooms, and by the look of you both, you must be wanting a wash and change of clothes. I'll join you later.' He drew a deep sigh. 'Can't say I'm looking forward to this. I just hope this is not going to prove too much for the good lady if, as you told me, the fellow meant so much to her.'

Sebastian put his arm round Georgia's shoulders. 'It's time you got out of those awful clothes you're wearing. Even the porter looked astonished to see such a tramp come into this hotel. I suppose you speak the lingo by now, so off you go and tell him to collect your father's and my suitcases from the

customs house where we left them.' He gave her shoulder a
gentle squeeze, adding with a smile: 'Jump to it, Slave!'

Sebastian's reversal to their childhood, his obvious affection
for her, brought unexpected tears to Georgia's eyes. Until this
moment, she had been keyed up with all the emotions that
had followed her father's arrival – relief, joy, even surprise at
the sudden awareness of his love for her. She'd known the
moment he'd stepped into the cabin and put his arms round
her that she had been wrong ever to deny her childish trust
and adoration of him. Now, suddenly, her thoughts turned
once more to poor Dona Resita whose happiness was about
to be destroyed just as her own was paramount.

With the beaming hotel manager fussing around them, she
and Sebastian watched as Gerald disappeared down the
corridor in the direction she had given him to Resita's room.

It was at that moment the *Chefe de Polícia* arrived to take
the details of Fedrik's disappearance. With the hotel manager's
assistance, they sat once more in his office, Sebastian following
Georgia's wishes for Fedrik not to be too vilified despite the
fact – as he had told her in the cabin – Fedrik might well
have had to kill her if her father had not paid the ransom.

To her relief, Sebastian stressed the indubitable fact that
without the ransom money, Fedrik would in effect be a pauper
even if he managed to get away. The *Chefe de Policia* clearly
did not regard the villain's actions to be suitably punished by
poverty.

'He is *un homem perverso!*' he declared stubbornly. 'It is
my duty to apprehend so evil a man.' He noticed Georgia's
expression and added kindly: 'Do not distress yourself,
Senhorita. In this country we do not shoot *raptadors*. We make
only prisoner for long time. Your ordeal will be avenged.'

When he had completed writing his notes and Georgia and
Sebastian were free to go to their rooms, Sebastian once more
put an arm round Georgia's shoulders.

'For goodness' sake, Aigroeg, don't start blubbing!' he said
gently as he walked with her down the corridor. Hearing his

fond, teasing voice, Georgia was once more able to smile through her tears.

It was nearly seven o'clock when she and Sebastian, both now respectably attired, sat on the terrace with a bottle of Madeira as they waited for Gerald. Unusually for them when they were alone together, they had not spoken for quite some time, each lost in their own thoughts. Then Sebastian said suddenly:

'That's the last time you go off on one of your silly ideas without me!'

Georgia smiled.

'It wasn't a silly idea. Even if the divers couldn't raise the *Cantara*, Freddie found Dinez's grave, and now I know those letters were real . . . that Chantal was real and Dinez really, really loved her.'

For a moment, Sebastian did not speak. Then he said again.

'I mean it, Jo-Jo, you aren't going off gallivanting again without at least telling me.'

Georgia drew a long breath before saying:

'I'm not exactly a child any more, Seb. I don't need your permission to go where I want. Anyway, you went off to Spain without telling me!'

Suddenly, Sebastian smiled.

'That's quite different. I never promised to obey you. I suppose you've forgotten your Declaration of Obedience.'

'My what?' Georgia asked, frowning.

'Look!' Sebastian said. 'I've got it in my wallet. I found it in the back of my desk when I was hunting for my passport. I wanted to show it to you. Listen . . .' He took out a dog-eared piece of his parents' headed notepaper, and read:

'Dekalrashun Of Obeadence. I promis orlways to obay what
Seb says for ever and ever until I die in the name of the
holly gost Amen.

Spelt wrong, of course. Then . . .' he smiled: 'then it's signed in blood – see that brown blob there – Aigerog, also spelt wrong.'

Georgia was now grinning broadly.

'I do remember that. You cut my finger with your penknife so I could sign in blood but there wasn't enough blood so you had to cut your finger as you said it wasn't fair to do mine twice! Fancy you keeping that!'

'Well, I intended to keep my slave's promise!' he said. 'At least until I was about twelve. Then I forgot I had it.'

'Well, we aren't children any more, Sebastian Taylor!' Georgia said firmly, but to her surprise, Sebastian was no longer smiling as he replied:

'I know that, Jo-Jo. But you swore "for ever and ever until you died", and I'm forbidding you to do anything dangerous ever again without me.'

'So I consider that silly promise I made when I was about six is no longer valid!'

Sebastian suddenly leant forward and took hold of her hand. When he did so, the smile left Georgia's face as the strangest sensation coursed through her body. Sebastian, too, was no longer smiling as he said:

'Then I'm going to have to find another way to ensure you love, honour and obey me, aren't I? I really don't intend to lose my Slave a second time. You know, Jo-Jo . . .'

But she never knew what he had been about to say as she saw her father coming towards them across the terrace. His expression was far from happy as, looking now immaculate in his dinner jacket, he seated himself beside them.

'I'm afraid the poor lady was horribly shocked,' he told them as Sebastian waved to a passing waiter to bring another glass. 'At first, she refused to believe what I was telling her, but then . . . she went very white and I feared she was going to faint so I suggested I ask the hotel doctor to come. She would not hear of it.' He turned to take Georgia's hand. 'She wants to see you, my darling, but will understand if you don't wish to speak to her "*after the ordeal my nephew put her through*" to use her own words.'

Georgia was instantly on her feet.

'Of course I don't blame her!' she declared. 'I'm just so terribly sad for her.'

She hurried indoors and down the familiar corridor to Resita's suite. The door was unlocked, and when she entered the sitting room, it was to find the old lady sitting stiffly upright in a chair by the French windows. Georgia had half expected to find her weeping, her hair and clothes dishevelled, but Resita was immaculately dressed and only the extreme pallor of her cheeks and the noticeably ageing lines on her face betrayed the shock she had received. Her voice trembled only slightly as she greeted Georgia and indicated the chair opposite her. It was barely audible when she said as if to a stranger:

'Freddie is my nephew, you know, my own darling boy! The only family I have!'

She seemed unable to accept his perfidy – the ugly truth that he had kidnapped Georgia, and held her to ransom. All she seemed able to realise was the fact that he had left her, not just for a little while, but for ever.

It was beyond Georgia's ability to tell Resita of Fedrik's confession – that he was not really her nephew at all but an imposter. It did cross her mind that if his aunt knew of all the lies Fedrik had told her about his past, Resita might now be a little less unhappy at his loss; but somehow Georgia could not bring herself to add to her distress by delivering this second blow. Instead, she told her how Sebastian had given Fedrik time to escape.

Seeing the instant look of relief on Dona Resita's face – or was it hope? – she added that Fedrik possessed a foreign passport lost by a former hotel guest; that he'd indicated he might take his speedboat over to Porto Santo while he waited for a boat to arrive that would enable him to escape to the mainland.

It was a moment or two before Resita spoke. Then, her hands clasped tightly together, her face whiter than ever, she looked directly into Georgia's eyes and said:

'You are very kind! Kinder to me than I deserve. No, child, let me speak. These past weeks, I hated you – yes, I even wished you were dead! And don't look so disbelieving. It is true what I am telling you. I could see that Freddie was falling in love with you and I thought you were encouraging him. Girls, women, have always fallen for his charm, his good looks, and you . . . well, you were not only very pretty but you had an inheritance that would allow him to live in the same luxury with which I have always surrounded him.'

She drew a long, trembling sigh.

'When I lay awake at night, listening for the sound of you opening your bedroom door, imagining you with Freddie . . . planning . . . planning to take him away from me . . .' Her voice broke but before Georgia could speak, she regained control of it. 'I spent those hours imagining ways I could get rid of you . . . crazy schemes . . . pushing you off the rocks into the sea; coming to your room while you slept and putting a pillow over your mouth and nose so you couldn't breathe; giving you something to eat which I knew was poisonous . . . and don't look so disbelieving, Georgia. I have been a very selfish, wicked woman.'

The look of tension suddenly left her face as she added:

'I realise now that it is I, and I alone, who am responsible for my darling Freddie's behaviour. I loved him so much: I wanted him with me all the time. Before you came we were invited always as a couple. We went on holiday together . . .' Her voice suddenly broke and it was several minutes before she could continue.

'Don't you see, my dear, if I had not been so possessive, he would not have needed to find a new life. Now I have lost him for ever!'

Tears rolled down her cheeks as she said huskily to Georgia:

'Forgive me! I have been thinking only of myself. Your father told me what an ordeal this must have been for you, although I know you said Freddie had treated you well. I am so sorry – so very sorry!'

Georgia was too choked to speak, standing up she went over and clasped the old lady's hands, holding them tightly as she whispered:

'Freddie did love you – he told me so, and how grateful he was to you for the way you had indulged him.'

For the first time, Resita's voice hardened.

'They mustn't catch him!' she said. 'It would kill him to be shut away, imprisoned for years to come. Nor could I bear it. Is it very wrong of me to say I am glad . . . yes, glad he managed to get away!'

'I, too!' Georgia admitted. 'We must hope he stays free, Dona Resita.'

Dona Resita smiled wryly.

'You know, Georgia, my dear, you may think this an extra-ordinary statement I am about to make, but if . . . if my Freddie had perforce married anyone, I don't think I would have minded so very much if it had been you!'

Georgia smiled and released Resita's hands as she said:

'My father will be worried about me so I should leave you now. I suppose it is too much to hope that you will join us for dinner? I know both Daddy and my friend, Sebastian, would be so happy if you would, but . . .'

'But you will understand if I say I cannot do so!' Resita broke in. 'Run along now, child. I shall be all right, I promise. And . . .' she smiled unexpectedly, '. . . and I'm so glad you were not drowned as the *Chefe de Policia* supposed.'

As Georgia left the room she found herself asking: did real love bring both grief as well as joy? Was it this depth of love, which her father had felt for his friend, Charles, that had compelled him to fulfil his last wish and adopt her?

When she rejoined Sebastian and her father, he stood up and put his arm round her.

'Try not to be sad, darling,' he said solicitously. 'Mrs Reviezky struck me as being an indomitable old lady. It is you who has been through such a frightening ordeal.'

Georgia's look of anxiety returned.

'I hated leaving her all alone in her room,' she said, but her father shook his head.

'No, darling! However stalwart she might be, she has had a terrible shock and the last thing she would want was to be sociable.'

It was not until half an hour later, as they were about to go to the restaurant for dinner, that the bellboy came hurrying towards them and handed Gerald a note. It was from Resita saying she would be dining with them after all and would like them to be her guests.

'There you are, you silly goose!' Sebastian said. 'She's feeling better already!' and was relieved to see the glimmer of a smile return to Georgia's face.

For the first time in eighteen years, Resita was now without Freddie as she prepared to join Georgia, Mr Driffield and the young man he had brought with him, for dinner. She had been trying to come to terms with her grief, her irreparable loss, and, despite his betrayal, her fear for Fedrik's safety.

Looking far older than her seventy-two years, her lined face white except for the two dabs of rouge she had rubbed into her cheeks, she'd nevertheless taken the usual meticulous care to look as elegant as she could. In the past she hadn't wanted her Freddie ever to be anything but proud to be her escort. This evening, she had put on her diamond and emerald necklace with the matching drop earrings, her star-shaped diamond brooch, the gold slave bracelet that Freddie had bought for her at Asprey's on their last visit to London, and the emerald ring given to her by her husband many years ago. Her jewellery flashed against her black silk evening gown.

Before leaving the room, she went out on to her balcony. The sun had set and the cotton wool clouds were drifting gently across the darkening sky still tinged with pink. The sea was mirror-glass calm, dotted here and there with the little black shapes of the fishing boats making their way home.

It all looked so pretty in the soft evening light – like a

picture postcard, she thought. Her eyes turned to the eastern end of the bay, and her heart suddenly missed a beat as she saw a tiny speedboat heading towards Porto Santo.

It could have been – perhaps was – Freddie's boat, she thought, hot tears suddenly stinging her eyes. With a determined effort, she did not allow them to fall. Turning to go back indoors, she paused, remembering Freddie's voice at this time of the evening when he would tuck his arm through hers, saying: 'It's about time we finished our drinks and went along to dinner, Tia Sita!'

Maybe, she thought as she picked up her evening bag and wiped the insistent tears from her eyes, maybe just for this one night, she would pretend she could hear him now, saying as he so often did:

'How lovely you look in that gown, Tia Sita! I shall be so proud of you!'

As she left the room and started to walk along the passage towards the foyer, she could almost believe that he had placed his warm supporting hand beneath her arm.

CHAPTER THIRTY-SEVEN

June, 1939

Sebastian was sitting beside Georgia in the shade of the mulberry tree at the bottom of the Driffields' garden. With them were Migs, Douglas and their little son, George, 'named for you, Jo-Jo,' Migs had said. The sunshine was living up to its name 'flaming June', and Isobel came out of the house carrying a fresh jug of home-made lemonade. Gerald, who was in London at work, had promised to come home early so he could see his little grandson before the toddler went to bed.

At Migs's request, Georgia was recounting once more her ordeal at the hands of the kidnapper and how Sebastian and her father had rescued her. As she came to the end of the story, Douglas asked incredulously:

'Do you mean the man still hasn't been caught? I thought you said it was only a small island, Georgia.'

'I know, but Freddie was very lucky,' she said. 'When we left Madeira, we saw a cruise ship which Daddy thought was American, approaching the bay. Freddie must have hidden on Porto Santo until it docked and he could get on board.'

No one spoke for a few moments, then Douglas said:

'What I don't understand is how the fellow got away in the first place.'

Sebastian had agreed with a reluctant Gerald not to reveal that Fedrik had been more or less allowed to escape, and he took up the story with a vague half truth, saying that he'd left Fedrik unguarded in his excitement at finding Georgia in the cabin with her father alive and well. He then fell silent thinking how even after all these weeks, he was still uncertain whether he'd been an irresponsible idiot to give the fellow time to get away – and for no better reason than to honour a stupid remark he'd made when he was too young to know better!

'I really don't understand,' Migs said to Georgia when she fell silent, 'why on earth this Fedrik fellow took such a dreadful risk kidnapping you like that.' She was wearing a loose, flower-patterned smock that hid her pregnancy – a second child due that autumn. She had put on weight since little Georgie's birth but somehow still managed to look dainty. 'Surely he already had nearly everything he could ever want from the wealthy aunt?'

'For some people, "nearly" is never enough!' Sebastian said, stretching his long legs out in front of him as he leant back against the trunk of the tree.

'No!' Georgia interjected, her eyes thoughtful. 'No, Migs, it wasn't because he wanted more than Dona Resita gave him. It was that she couldn't give him what he really wanted – his freedom. She was lonely and monopolised him.'

'Why couldn't a chap like him have left her and got himself a job like anyone else?' Douglas intervened.

It was a moment or two before Georgia replied. Then she said slowly:

'I've never told anyone other than Seb about Freddie's past because when Daddy brought me home, I just wanted to forget all about those awful days and . . . well, what a stupid idiot I'd been ever to think I might fall in love with someone like him: but he could be very charming,' she added. 'One evening when I was in the cabin, he confessed he wasn't Dona Sita's nephew; that he had tricked her into believing he was her brother's son who she'd been searching for. He was a sixteen-year-old waiter in an Austrian restaurant at the time.'

She paused, briefly finding it strangely difficult to relate the story Fedrik had told her, how Dona Resita suddenly appeared in his life and, like a fairy godmother, offered to transform his drab existence.

Claire Lorrimer

'I suppose she was pretty gullible, wanting so much to believe it was true!' Georgia concluded.

'What a shocking trick to have played on a lonely old lady!' Migs murmured. Georgia drew a deep sigh.

'I know, but it didn't turn out to be as cruel as you may be thinking. Freddie was genuinely fond of her, and he took enormous care of her. Of course, he was more than well rewarded but . . .' She broke off, feeling strangely close to tears.

'She must have been heartbroken when you told her the truth about him,' Isobel said.

Georgia turned to face her mother.

'I didn't tell her, Mummy. I didn't tell anyone. I simply couldn't bring myself to. She loved him so much that even after she'd learned what he had done she made excuses for him. She referred to him as "my poor boy!" and to herself as "a selfish old fool!" But when she joined us for dinner that night, she somehow managed to behave as if everything was perfectly normal although she knew as well as we did that the police were searching for Freddie. The only time Dona Resita looked close to tears was when she kissed me goodbye and made me promise to go back to visit her sometime in the future. I was her last link to Freddie, she said.'

Several minutes went by then Isobel said:

'Suppose one day the police do find him and the truth about his subterfuge is discovered? Or he gets in touch with his aunt begging her to take him back? I think you've just got to write and tell her he's an imposter, darling, however much it hurts her.' She looked at her daughter, adding gently: 'Remember how you felt when you found out you'd spent the previous fifteen years of your life believing you were someone else? You were unforgiving of Daddy for keeping the truth from you.'

'But that was different, Mummy!' Georgia said quickly. 'I don't see why Dona Resita has to know. Freddie may never be found, and if she is happier believing he was really her nephew, she might never find out he'd deceived her.'

'Oh, Georgia, darling!' Migs broke in. 'Mummy's absolutely right. Don't you remember how you kept saying that Daddy should have told you about your adoption and not let you go on believing a lie?'

'But that was when I was still a child!' Georgia protested. 'I don't even think about it now.' She turned to look at her mother who, to her immense surprise, had tears in her eyes.

'Mrs Reviezky might come to terms with the truth, just as you have done, Jo-Jo,' Sebastian broke in. 'Far better you tell her, you silly goose, than that some bumbling policeman did so. Don't be such a coward!'

'I'm not a coward and you know perfectly well that . . .' She broke off, realising that Sebastian had decided to lighten the mood with one of his old, teasing remarks. The tension left her face and she said: 'So maybe I will tell her if I go out to see her next spring. You would find time to come with me if I wanted to go, wouldn't you, Seb?'

He nodded, not trusting himself to put another cloud over the happy gathering that beautiful summer afternoon. He would keep his fears to himself a little longer, he decided, only too aware of the gas masks heaped at the back of the tree; the front page of a newspaper nearby showing pictures of sandbags at the entrances to buildings in London streets; the picture of a young boy helping his father to build an Anderson shelter at the bottom of their garden.

Like most of the population, he had no doubt that it was only a matter of time – very little time – before the country went to war with Germany. Only the previous day, he had helped his mother hang the obligatory blackout curtains in all their windows so that the lights at night would not reveal the buildings to enemy aircraft. Gerald had told him that Germany had now signed a non-aggression pact with Russia, and warned him of the inevitable consequences. Preparations were even now being made for London's vast numbers of children to be evacuated to the safety of the country if the expected bombing became a reality.

Let them all keep on pretending that all was well for a little while longer, he thought as he looked round the family group – Isobel, so pleased to have Migs and the baby home and another grandchild soon to be born; Jo-Jo loving every minute of the unexpected holiday Bob Batten had awarded her on her return from Madeira as a bonus for the exciting articles she had written. Only Migs's husband, Douglas, whose occasional loving glances at his little family, showed a glimmer of the fear of approaching war that was gripping the nation.

While Sebastian's thoughts were thus occupied, Migs, when she wasn't bouncing the little boy on her knees, was asking Georgia how, after all Fedrik had put her through, she seemed not to think of him as evil.

'He didn't want to harm me,' Georgia said quietly. 'It was just that he wasn't getting any younger and so he saw me as his only means of escape.'

Sebastian's voice was tinged with anger as he said:

'Migs is right, Jo-Jo. You should despise the fellow. "Unscrupulous devil": that's what your father called him, and I think he hit the nail on the head. In heaven's name, Jo-Jo, what do you think he would have done to you if he didn't get the money? Killed you, and don't shake your head, he'd have had no alternative. The way you go on, Georgia, you seem to think the scoundrel was completely justified in behaving as he did!'

'No, that's not true,' Georgia argued. 'I'm only saying that his nature wasn't cruel or evil. He never harmed me and he was immensely kind to Dona Resita. I had a letter from her yesterday saying that despite everything, she still loved him and hoped that one day she would see him again.'

'Huh!' Sebastian grunted. 'You women are all the same – gullible, sentimental, and foolhardy!'

Douglas was smiling and shaking his head as he put an arm affectionately round his wife's shoulders.

'Gullible, maybe; sentimental, I will allow; but not necessarily foolhardy. At least, I wouldn't want you to think my darling Migs was foolhardy, rushing off and marrying me the way she did!'

Migs looked up at him adoringly, and then turned to look at her mother, saying:

'That must have been the only time in my life, Mummy, that I really shocked you!'

'And how right you were to do so, my darling!' Isobel said lovingly.

Douglas now turned to Georgia.

'Did you ever hear what happened to your friend Hannah's family?' he asked. 'Migs told me that in one of your letters you said they were in great danger.'

It was Isobel, not Georgia who answered him.

'Didn't Georgia tell you what happened?' she said. 'It was all quite dramatic! Georgia was in London so my husband and I were on our own here when, quite late one evening, we were listening to the nine o'clock news. Polly came in to say that a strange couple were at the front door asking to see us, but wouldn't give their names.'

Isobel paused briefly to smile at Georgia.

'They were Hannah's parents, *Doktor* and *Frau* Klein. Perhaps *you* should tell them their story, darling!'

'Yes, it was quite a miracle in its way!' Georgia took up the tale. 'They had just arrived by the evening ferry from France. You see, the old grandmother had died suddenly, leaving them free to escape if they could find a way to do so. *Doktor* Klein contacted a cardiologist he knew who had become a prominent member of the Party. He'd been shocked by the Party's increasingly bad attitude to the Jews and did what he could to help those he knew, including the Kleins. He proceeded to organise a private ambulance to take two hypothetically dangerously ill patients into Switzerland, the only country who could, he informed the authorities, supposedly treat the couple and possibly save their lives!'

'Indeed a brave man!' Douglas remarked as Georgia paused. 'From everything I have read and you have told us, Georgia, the man might well have been killed if his deception had been discovered.'

'So what happened next?' Migs asked, hoping for the happy outcome she suspected was coming.

Isobel now continued the story.

'*Doktor* Klein's saviour had only been able to give the couple enough money to get to England. He'd been afraid to give them more in case, if they had been arrested before they reached the border, the banknotes were traced back to him. So you see, that is why Hannah's parents came here – to ask your father to give them the money to buy tickets to Australia where they would join Hannah. *Frau* Klein had several of her mother-in-law's valuable rings which she had sewn into the lining of her coat, and they wanted to give these to us in exchange.'

'Did Daddy take them?' Migs asked, intrigued by the story.

Isobel nodded.

'*Doktor* Klein insisted he do so, and your father agreed to a compromise – that he would sell the rings and if, as he expected, they fetched far more than the cost of the Kleins' passages to Australia, he would send them the surplus. We both felt so sorry for them. I don't think either of us had really taken in what dreadful things were happening in Germany.'

To lighten the sombre mood that had now fallen, Sebastian turned to Migs, asking:

'Did Jo-Jo tell you the extraordinary news about the twins? They are in America at the invitation of a complete stranger who ordered flowers from them when he was visiting London. He invited them to visit him in New York.'

Migs's eyes widened.

'A complete stranger?' she questioned in astonishment.

Georgia smiled as she replied:

'You are never going to believe this, Migs, but the day they arrived, they were having drinks with their host and his wife before dinner, when who should walk into the room but his two sons – and just like Rose and Lily they were identical twins! He had planned it all, of course, because the young men were not exactly handsome and had never married, but they were really charming, and adventurous and were planning to take their car over to Kenya and explore Africa. After only two weeks in each other's company, they invited Rose and Lily to go with them – she paused before adding dramatically, 'AFTER THE TWINS HAD AGREED TO MARRY THEM!'

Migs's face was now a picture of incredulity as Georgia elaborated.

'The wedding is next month in London, at St Margaret's Westminster, and Rose and Lily are insisting they should do the flowers themselves.'

'Silly girls!' Isobel commented suddenly. 'As if they will have time when they return to England, buying their trousseaux and such like.'

Migs was now laughing.

'It's wonderful news and I'm so pleased for the twins. I think they had resigned themselves to spinsterhood! I trust Douglas and I will get invitations now we are in England.'

'But of course you will, silly!' Georgia said, hugging her sister. 'Rose wrote and said I was to be chief bridesmaid and she and Lily want you to be matron of honour, Migs.' Seeing that Isobel was busy playing with little Georgie on the lawn, she added with a conspiratorial smile:

'Mummy and Daddy won't be going though because the wedding coincides with the week Daddy has arranged for them to go to the South of France to celebrate their twenty-first wedding anniversary. Honestly, Migs, you'd think they were going on their honeymoon what with Mummy fussing about her clothes as if it was her trousseaux, and Daddy making endless telephone calls to the French hotel threatening to cancel the booking if they didn't guarantee the particular room he wanted. Fancy them getting all romantic at their age!'

Before Migs could comment, her little boy came running

towards them. The child reached the tea tray before his grand-mother could carry out her intention to gather up the tea things. He quickly snatched the last of the sponge fingers, which he could see Sebastian was about to take, and stuffed as much as would go into his small mouth.

'You rascal!' Sebastian said, laughing as the child ran off with the remains of his prize. 'He really is a charmer, Migs!' Pointing to the toddler, he turned to Georgia, saying matter-of-factly: 'You know, Jo-Jo, you and I ought to get married and have one of those. He's great fun, isn't he?'

'George is hardly a puppy you can go out and buy.' Isobel spoke with mock severity as Douglas stood up to take the tea tray from her. '"Have one of those", indeed!' she echoed.

Everyone but Georgia laughed. Sebastian's words had evoked the strangest feelings. She realised that he had only been joking when he'd suggested they should get married, but suppose he *had* meant it? How would she feel?

Her heart pounding, she looked across at him. His hair was tousled, his eyes were very blue in his tanned face. His body, now stretched out on the grass with his arms behind his head, was that of an athlete. He was staring at her in the strangest way. Frantically, she tried to harness the rush of emotions she was feeling. Yes, she thought, yes, yes, she would want to marry him – not to have children right away because they both had careers, but . . .

Sebastian now stood up.

'Time we were on our way, Jo-Jo!' he said pulling her to her feet and tucking his arm through hers. 'There's bound to be quite a bit of traffic on the way back to London and you've got that article to write before you return to work tomorrow.'

When goodbyes had been said, and a promise given by Douglas and Migs to visit them in town, Sebastian planted a dutiful kiss on Isobel's cheek before taking Georgia round to the front of the house where he had parked his car. Stopping only to pop next door to say a brief goodbye to his mother, they were on their way.

Georgia was the first to break the silence – a silence that was most unusual when they were together.

'What did you mean about the need to get back to town?' she asked finally. 'I never said I had an article to write or . . .'

'Calm down!' Sebastian broke in cheerfully. 'It was just a fib as I thought it was about time I had you to myself. For a start, you haven't answered my question yet.'

'What question?' Georgia asked. 'You haven't asked me a question.'

'Whether we should get married, be happy like Migs and Douglas,' Sebastian said as he edged the car past a farm cart.

Georgia's heart quickened its beat: 'I don't think they are much of a reason for us to get married. We aren't a bit like them.'

'Well how about if I join the air force and get sent abroad like Douglas? You could come with me. Or I've got a good idea. Suppose we do something different and elope!'

The remark was said lightly but Sebastian's thoughts were momentarily on the approaching threat of war. 'I think it would be a really good idea if we got married now . . . before it's too late,' he added.

Sebastian's 'good ideas' – a reminder of their childhood – had not then required her approval, but as she hesitated, he repeated it. 'We really should get married,' he said.

'Why?' she asked again as he slowed down through a small village.

'Because I suddenly realised when you went missing in Madeira, that I might have lost my Agent Aigroeg for ever,' he said, his tone of voice deepening, 'and how I'd feel if that happened. Come on, Jo-Jo; say you think it's a good idea. You always do what I tell you, so say "yes".'

Georgia swallowed the lump in her throat.

'Is that a proposal?' she asked huskily.

Sebastian swerved into the side of the road and turned off the engine.

'Of course it is, Stupid!' he replied, putting his arms round her. 'I've thought a lot about it and how we like doing the same things like flying and . . . and playing cricket, not that you were ever much good as a batsman but you could bowl quite well. Come on, Jo-Jo, stop being silly and say yes. You're my best friend as well as my slave.'

His face was very close to hers now.

'You haven't said you love me!' she murmured, conscious of the fact that her heart was now beating three times as fast as usual.

'Well you haven't said *you* love *me*!' he retaliated. 'Bags you say it first, Jo-Jo.'

He was laughing now, a happy carefree, loving laugh.

'No, you always insisted upon being first,' she said huskily. 'Do you love me?'

'Idiot!' Sebastian said tenderly as he bent his head to kiss her. 'Of course I do. I always have.'

Love. Passion. War.
Family. Secrets. History.

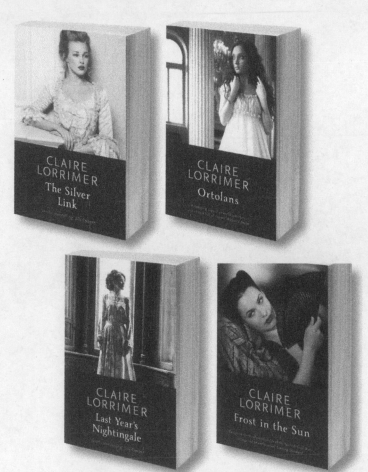

Stunning timeless classics from the bestselling
novelist Claire Lorrimer.

Available in paperback and ebook.